TRUSTED WITH HER HEART

"My name is Martin. And I know your name is Katherine," he said. "You need to be still a few minutes longer. As far as anyone knows, you are my woman, and you are to be my wife as soon as possible. Don't fight me, Katherine," he said against her protesting lips. "You'll be in great danger if you don't cooperate. You can trust me."

He took her hand and placed it on the worn black leather Bible, then put his roughened hand atop hers.

"Martin," she spoke softly, "I have no choice but to trust you. . . ."

THE BLACK PEARL

FRANCINE CRAFT

PINNACLE BOOKS
KENSINGTON PUBLISHING CORP.

PINNACLE BOOKS are published by

Kensington Publishing Corp.
850 Third Avenue
New York, NY 10022

Pinnacle and the P logo Reg. U.S. Pat. & TM Off.

First Printing: January, 1996

Printed in the United States of America

Acknowledgments

I wish to express appreciation to the volunteers who staff the Costume and Transportation Departments of the Smithsonian Institution for the information they so helpfully provided.

Many thanks to friends in New Orleans—then and now—who were and are very kind.

To Myles, who knows how to be a very good friend.

And to the memory of my grandfather, Frank Craft,
who was always there for me,
and who always wanted me to write.

Part One

Abducted From
the Bayou Country—1869

Prologue

Folks said the moon didn't rise boldly on the leaf doctor's house as it did on the rest of the houses on what, before the Civil War, had been called Keyes Plantation. Instead, the moon's shadows crept in shyly, close to the chimney, scattering moonbeams onto the roof and gently illuminating the window-panes.

Early on a sweltering June night, that moonlight caressed Katherine Keyes's slender, rounded, twenty-year-old body, highlighting her nutmeg-colored, satiny skin as she tossed in a quick nap. Lying on a pallet on the side porch just outside her grandfather's sickroom, she was bone tired. Still, it felt good to know that, thanks to her devoted nursing, Papa Frank was slowly recovering from the yellow fever that had recently taken forty-three people in their bayou countryside.

Katherine smiled as she slipped into the dream that had haunted her for almost a year. Warm mist, fragrant with honeysuckle and cape jasmine, wafted through the brightly moonlit night of her dream. As she walked alone on a deserted path, a tall stranger stepped from the woods near the bay that lay a short distance from their house. At first he waited for her to come to him. Then, as her heart beat too fast, he impatiently came to her.

Oh, he was handsome! Tall, with thick, charcoal-black rough hair and facial features that combined his black-Indian-white heritage well. Set deep under thick, black, silken brows in a long, olive face, his hazel eyes devoured her. Reaching her side, her prince held out his hand, her knees going weak as he drew her close.

"You are safe with me, my love," he said softly, stroking her hair, soothing her soft, brown trembling body, making her spirits soar.

The dream ended as despair overcame her. Katherine awoke with the voices of her friends echoing in her head. Gossip said she must marry Louis Duplessis, the widow Duplessis's stepson. Katherine liked the widow well enough and deeply appreciated her help in caring for Papa Frank. She was in sympathy, too, with the widow's desire to make Papa Frank her second husband. But she loathed the widow's slick stepson, who watched Katherine with greedy possessiveness, already calling her "my woman."

Perhaps her friends were wrong, she told herself. But she knew they were not. Papa Frank looked at her sorrowfully these days, too smitten with love for his granddaughter to tell her the truth.

How well she knew her grandfather. When she was seventeen, he had urged her to marry Albert, a slight, attractive brown youth also formerly a slave on Keyes Plantation. "You are smart and lively, and blessed with a passion for living," he had told her. "Use that passion wisely and it will help to make you happy. You and Albert are both young. You can grow together. . . ." Resigned, but far from being in love, they married.

Happy to be free, Katherine and Albert made plans that were cruelly cut short two years later when he had apparently gotten cramps and drowned in the Gulf of Mexico waters where he often swam. Born with a *caul over her face,* which was the growth of membrane over the face, Katherine had simply "known" some misfortune would befall her young husband and had begged him not to go swimming. But he had laughed at her fear, gone ahead, and drowned.

Widowed at nineteen and childless, she was even more grateful that the slaves had been freed, for she would have been forced by her former master to marry again to try to produce more slaves. She had miscarried her first pregnancy shortly before Albert's death, and the double loss was hard to endure.

After having granted them freedom, Theodore Keyes asked his slaves to stay on for fairly decent wages and work to farm Keyes Community together. Many had agreed, Papa Frank among them.

"I am an old man," he'd told Katherine. "My own roots, and the roots and herbs of the forests I know best, are here. Still, I may leave one day if I live and nothing happens. But I love the land, and these woods yield more of their secrets to me than to any white man."

Their former master had also been considered an "enlightened" slaveowner who whipped no more than he considered absolutely necessary. To the derisive disapproval of some of his fellow plantation owners, the mistress taught the slaves to read and write. They predicted an "educated darky" uprising that would leave them all destroyed. A few others felt as Keyes did.

Keyes had laughed at the prophecy. "I would trust a literate Negro a hundred times over an illiterate one," he'd declared. In the end, he'd proved to be wise. His was one of the most prosperous plantations in the area. His home had escaped burning during the war, and after the war, more of his former slaves had remained. He'd been especially fond of Papa Frank, granting young Katherine full use of the big library in his house before and after freedom. Of course, there was little time for reading, but the master said she had a head for learning.

Katherine's job was to help with the housework and take care of the women's clothes. The mistress and her two daughters had often shown Katherine sketches of dazzling garments sent to them from Paris and New Orleans. Happy to parade before her when the finished garments arrived or were brought back from shopping trips, they would preen and ask what she thought of them. She behaved graciously as she had been taught, and took care of the clothing, trying to stifle the dream that one day *she* might own such gowns and wear such jewels.

The fine white-columned Keyes mansion was enhanced by slave-quarter houses that were painted, not whitewashed, and Theodore Keyes encouraged each slave family to work a vegetable and flower garden. Still, it had been slavery and Papa Frank had chafed under that yoke, although he was freer than most. His skills as an herbalist—what bayou people called a "leaf doctor"—had made him a beloved legend in their community. Katherine took great pride in being her grandfather's valued right hand.

She stroked the old but pretty blue wedding-ring quilt that had belonged to her mother. Katherine sorely missed the merry woman, who had trained her well in midwifery and had loved her greatly.

Now with the growing chaos, women—especially young black ones—needed to marry for their own protection from those same Union soldiers who had once protected them, as well as from the ex-Confederate soldiers, who were too angry or too dispirited to walk a civil path.

Morosely, Katherine realized that the threat of plundering soldiers was preferable to being Louis Duplessis's wife. Her "second sight" had frightened her as a child, but now she felt comfortable with her "visions." She could tell that something strange would happen—and soon.

Ruff, Papa Frank's old dark red hound, barked loudly nearby. Katherine sighed and stretched. It was going to be a long night.

Martin Dominguez stood alone on the deck of *The Robber Baron,* named for a former pirate ship and now used as a freighter to carry silks and fine clothes, jewels, and occasional contraband from the port of New Orleans. Returning, it was loaded with the huge cantaloupes, figs, watermelons, strawberries, and a variety of vegetables for which the bayou country was famous. Now the ship lay freshly anchored in the inlet less than a mile from Keyes Community and Katherine's house.

A tall, lithe man, with weathered olive skin and rough, soot-black hair, Martin watched the full moon and thought about the girl.

Accompanied by two other dark-skinned crew members, he and Jules had walked along the beach on a brief work respite that past February, mindful of possible encounters with hostile white men. They had passed in front of a clump of trees and bramble that grew near the edge of the beach, happening upon three girls and an old man gathering herbs about twenty feet away from them.

Martin had felt his heart lurch as his eyes met those of the girl he had heard called Katherine. He saw then that she was beautiful, and he could not prevent a stab of pain. Martin had been badly hurt by such beauty, and the hurt still festered.

For a long moment they had breathlessly looked at one another, drawn beyond the telling, strangers yet not strangers. Hostage to past betrayal, he'd lifted his cap, said a simple "Good evening"—from the southern custom of calling the afternoon the evening—and moved on. The powerful surges in his body had shaken him, much to the amusement of his shipmates.

Calling himself a fool, he'd still intended to find out more about her, but they had returned to port faster than expected. Nevertheless, Martin had seen then that Katherine comported herself like a young queen.

Lord, she was lovely! Nutmeg-colored skin stretched with flawless luminescence over high cheekbones. Her nose was pert, her lips carved, full, and luscious. She was a portrait in spice brown. He'd bet her almond-shaped eyes were brown as well.

Her blue gingham head covering slipped off, revealing hair the rough texture of his own, but earth-brown and smoother. She quickly bent to retrieve it, her movement attracting him.

He watched her rounded, graceful body bend and sway as

she studied the plants and talked with her friends. Her skirts obscured what he thought was surely worthy of the lush Botticelli nudes he'd seen at the Prado in Madrid. But no clothing could hide the curve of those full breasts.

Jules had watched his friend, smiling at him, as Martin watched the girl.

"She is beautiful," Martin remarked simply.

And Jules grinned. It had been so long since he'd seen that look of keen and eager interest on his friend's face. For a moment, it had replaced the edge of pain that had begun with Celié's betrayal and worsened with the death of his mother, Annalise, and his older brother, Raoul, in one of several uprisings that persisted on Santo Domingo when new would-be masters sought to affix an old yoke of slavery.

Now, looking down at the dark blue, rippling waves of the Gulf of Mexico as they slapped against the hull of the ship, Martin ached to see that lissome body, but she had been well shielded by her simple, full-skirted blue gingham cotton dress. No matter, he would settle for simply holding her close.

Again and again after he'd seen her, he could hear his own hoarsely eager voice saying "Good evening," followed by the response from the old man and the three girls. Her lilting voice had stood out above the others and he'd remembered it well.

He touched the small black leather Bible he always carried with him and began to quote from "The Song of Songs."

"I am black, but comely, O ye daughters of Jerusalem."

He had read the moving passages thousands of times. Now he mentally changed that phrase to: "I am black *and* comely, O ye daughters of Jerusalem."

It often angered Martin that the pain cut when he least expected it. He had loved a woman once, too deeply for his years, his friends said. He'd been eighteen then and Celié seventeen.

The fires between them had kindled rapidly. Inexperienced, they taught each other, and he had worshiped her. Celié had wanted to marry him, but as much as he loved her, he wanted to wait one year until he finished his apprenticeship in Spain. But she had refused to wait, had married his brother Raoul, and had begun the spin of lies and horror. Hell, he wasn't going to think about Celié.

Four months ago Paul DeBeau had asked him to help make the run to the bayou country until his son could better heal from a lingering illness no doctor had been able to diagnose.

Being on board this ship always reminded Martin of his early teen years sailing with his father in Santo Domingo. Pablo Dominguez had been both a sea captain and a wealthy landowner—handsome, brilliant, and arrogant.

"Life is not for the timid, my boy," he used to tell Martin and Raoul when they sailed with him. "You will take by whatever means necessary what you want in this world, or you will not get it. A dream realized is worth *any* sacrifice."

As much as he loved him, Martin, not blind to his father's flaws, could never quite believe what this ruthless man said. His brother Raoul became his father's alter ego, while Martin remained closer to his mother.

Pablo Dominguez was the scion and renegade of an old Castilian family, and he had taken Annalise, a beautiful sixteen-year-old girl of black and Indian descent, to be his mistress. It was a circumstance common to the island.

Martin's father's wife, Bianca, was beautiful, too, and her parentage was higher than Pablo's. Bianca hated Annalise and her two "bastard" sons. Her own son with Pablo was somewhat sickly, not so much from nature as from being caught in a crushing bind between his adoring mother, whom he in turn adored, and a father who plainly hurt her.

Even now, Martin could recall the joy he had experienced when his father showed him how to hoist a sail, read a compass, or keep a ship's log as they sailed the Atlantic Ocean from Santo Domingo to the Gulf of Mexico to New Orleans and other ports.

But Martin had his own dreams and plans. He was artistic in a rough and tumble way, and from a young age he'd enjoyed working with iron and steel. At seventeen his father sent him to Spain to be apprenticed to a *forgeron,* a molder of exquisite iron structures. After his apprenticeship was finished, Martin had studied art and literature at the university. He already spoke English, but because the *forgeron* who'd trained him in Spain had been English-born, Martin came to speak the language almost as well as his native Spanish. He'd become an excellent *forgeron,* a master fashioner of the iron grillwork so prevalent on the estates of wealthy and not-so-wealthy New Orleanians. His companions knew he possessed a keenly analytical, incisive mind, yet he was quietly assured and helpful. He was liked and well trusted by employers, so he had become quite successful.

Now at thirty, he had lived for ten years in Louisiana, migrating as a free man. Slavery had ended on Santo Domingo twenty-five years before it ended in America. He had constantly negotiated his life and his livelihood as a free artisan in a slave society. DeBeau, a ship's captain, son of a pirate and a pirate himself in his youth, had been a bosom buddy of Martin's father. Having migrated years before and become wealthy and respected, he had helped Martin avoid trouble in a city filled with different races and cultures and fraught with myriad dangers.

Martin had gone back to visit Santo Domingo and . . . He stopped thinking for a moment and shielded his eyes, as if that would stop the pain. His adored mother and beloved brother had had their lives ruthlessly ended while he was visiting there, and Martin had needed to flee the country of his birth—with Celié.

His heart felt heavy with his past anguish, yet full of hope. It seemed to him the moon cheered him on as a shadow fell across him.

"You're dreaming again. You're always miles away from me these days," his friend, Jules Macklin, teased him. "You have not spoken of the beauty we saw here in February. But somehow, I don't think you've forgotten her."

Martin turned, smiling at his good-looking, stocky, jet-hued childhood friend, who often proclaimed that he'd never met an ugly woman.

"I must find some way to meet her," Martin said now, an urgency in his voice that Jules had not heard for some time. "I know it could be dangerous, but let us make plans to go before dark and ask questions. We saw a settlement beyond that forest."

Amused, Jules listened to his friend and clapped him on the shoulder.

"Nothing could make me happier," he said.

"No. I've not forgotten her, and damn the haste that made DeBeau need to leave both times I would have sought her out. She makes me dream, my friend." Martin was silent for a while. "She makes me think that perhaps I *can* begin to truly live again instead of just existing. Jules"—he struck the railing with his palm—"I tell you this woman has set my heart on fire."

Jules was thirty-four to Martin's thirty years. He had helped him pick up the pieces of his life after the terrible crimes against his family. He knew about his fevered affair with Celié and his pain when she had married his brother.

"We will find this woman," he said, "and if she has no husband, no suitor to drive us both away, then do not wait. Make her yours as soon as you can. This is wild, virgin country, my friend. Here, women are like rare treasures. Some knave will surely steal her if you wait."

One

As Katherine came into Papa Frank's sickroom, her heart felt like lead in her high young bosom. She and the widow Duplessis had pulled him back from the brink of death. Thinking that her grandfather slept, she silently walked to the bed and gently placed a slender hand on his long, gnarled fingers. His parchment-colored skin was so dry, she thought sadly. Thin now, although his tall frame had once held over two hundred forty pounds, he looked all of his seventy years.

The old man's crisp salt-and-pepper hair seemed the only healthy thing about him now. Katherine sat down on the bed beside him, reflecting on how the love he had always showered on her had sustained her in the long year since Delpha, her mother, had died this past July. Papa Frank had always done what was best for her.

The widow Duplessis—Miss Ada—dozed peacefully in a cane-backed rocking chair by the bed, exhausted from her weeklong vigil.

"Kate, my grand girl," Papa Frank exclaimed, opening pale watery gray eyes dimmed by the just-ended fever. His voice was gravelly, his breathing still labored. He glanced over at the widow, then closed his eyes, but not before Katherine had seen his tears. He swallowed hard.

"Miss Ada's sleeping, maybe," he said, glancing fondly at the widow again. "But if she's not, no matter, since she already knows. While you were in the woods for a while today, Miss Ada and me talked about you, baby, about how since the war's ended and we're free, a whole lot of things haven't been the way we'd hoped. More and more loose and marauding men've come to the bayou country, looking to plunder. I've been thinking about this a long time. You need a husband for your own protection, and the best one available right now is Miss Ada's stepson, Louis."

Bile rose in Katherine's throat, until she thought she'd choke. Papa Frank hadn't raised her to be a coward, but she held her tongue as he continued to speak.

"You know I nearly died, granddaughter," he went on. "You and Miss Ada saved me, but I'm seventy. You're a wonderful-looking young woman, and you're kind and good, like your mama and your grandma and Miss Ada. You shouldn't be alone in these times. . . ."

He closed his eyes as Katherine sadly nodded and looked about the room. Mosquitoes buzzed around, seeking to draw fresh blood. Smoke from the slow-burning pots outside the house came through the open window to help drive out the mosquitoes; white netting had been drawn back and knotted over his bed. Even at seven-thirty in the evening it was still miserably hot, but a welcome breeze stirred. As in the dream, the fragrance of cape jasmine, honeysuckle, and roses mingled in the air. She looked at Miss Ada. The plump, molasses-brown, middle-aged, attractive woman slept on—or pretended to.

Papa Frank opened his eyes again and smiled at her.

"Life's been pretty good to us," he said. "I've protected you as much as I could . . . taught you how to protect yourself." He chuckled. "You can shoot about as well as I can. We were slaves all right, but the old used-to-be master brags even now that he never separated a family. We got married same as they did. Lord, it could have been so much worse. . . . Still, it *was* slavery, and folks was meant to be *free*. You make the best of your freedom, Kate."

Plainly weakening physically, Papa Frank began to cough, alarming Katherine.

"Don't try to speak," she pleaded. "I'll do whatever I have to do. Don't you know it's been like heaven living here with you . . . and with Mama, before she died? Oh, Papa, please don't keep worrying about me."

He raised a gnarled hand, then let it fall back limply on the snow-white covers. "No, let me talk while I can. Louis is not the man I want for you. He'll never appreciate a woman like you, but I want *you* to always know and appreciate your own self. Believe in yourself, Katie, every second of every day. Then I reckon that while it surely matters who you marry, a less-than-good choice's not goin' to ruin your life."

Katherine nodded, announcing, "I'm going to sponge you down again." She noted the peeling and flaking of his skin from the recent fever, comparing its wrinkled, parchment texture to her own satiny young brown skin and the widow's slightly darker, still-smooth complexion. Black people, she had always thought, were a beautiful bouquet.

Papa Frank grinned crookedly. "You don't need to wash me off again right now. Let Miss Ada do it. Go out and get some fresh air, but don't go too far. It's not real safe around here anymore."

When Katherine rose from the bed to go outside, his words pulled her back. "Like I said, Katie, Louis is not a bad man, just an unknowing one. He's so caught up in what's outside of him, he's got no time for what's inside. I don't guess he'll *ever* realize what he's got in you, but I'll warn him never to beat or mistreat you in any way. And if God don't see fit to let me stay here, Miss Ada'll keep him in line."

Miss Ada came alive. "You believe me, chile, between us, ain't nothing Louis is going to start that's not right. Yes, ma'am, I'll keep that stepson of mine in line and teach you how to do the same."

The widow Duplessis didn't mind the lie, knowing she had little influence over Louis. Although she had loved Louis's father, she had, in truth, never cared much for his spoiled-rotten only son. They *tolerated* each other. But she truly liked Katherine and sought her help in landing the major fish of her turbulent life—Papa Frank. She thought his granddaughter deserved a lot better than her stepson, but all the same she was happy that their paths had crossed. And Katherine seemed to be coming to like her a lot as well.

"People have been suggesting your wedding ought to be soon," Papa Frank said, "but I thought with my sickness and all, we ought to wait until after your birthday. That make you a little happier?"

Katherine nodded quickly, trying to smile, her chest less constricted. She would be twenty-one in early September—just three months away. It was a reprieve, but not a long-enough one. Papa Frank coughed again, and when Katherine saw the pain in his eyes, she felt it as her own.

"Papa, sleep," she begged. "Or at least try to relax. You raised me to be the woman my mother was, and that's a lot to be proud of and live up to. I told you, don't worry so much about me. I got you well, didn't I . . . with Miss Ada's help? Didn't I handle mixing that lobelia about as well as you could? And you know lobelia can be dangerous."

Papa Frank nodded, his eyes shining now with pride.

"Yes. Yes, you did. You walk with God, Katie, the way your mother and I taught you. You'll be able to tame devils, and mayhap with the times we're getting into, you'll need everything we could give you."

Katherine bent and kissed him, smoothing his beetling white brows. "I'm going out a bit," she said to Miss Ada, who upon looking at her realized that giving this girl in marriage to Louis was like throwing pearls to swine.

Now that what she had hoped to escape would soon become real, Katherine felt she had to be alone. It didn't matter that it wasn't safe, that for years it hadn't, in fact, been safe for women to wander around the plantation at night or early evening. She decided she would only walk down to the bottom of the hill and the magnolia tree. It was dusk and would be turning dark quickly, so she lit one of the freshly filled kerosene lanterns and put it over her arm. She would stay only a few minutes.

The one chance encounter, and the dreams of the past year of the stranger who promised her safety in his arms, seemed more vivid than ever, yet farther away. Her days of security were numbered. Her young friend, Singing Bird, of the Cherokee mother and Negro-slave father, seemed to like Louis.

There was no way she could ever forget the day that past February when she, Singing Bird, Zell, and Papa Frank had gathered herbs in the woods, later in the afternoon than usual. Foxglove grew in abundance near a clearing, the warm climate forcing it to early white and lavender bloom. Not quite of her own volition, Katherine had suddenly stood up. She saw no one at first, then noticed that several men walked along the beach nearby. One was tall, black-haired, and surely the most handsome man she had ever seen.

Their eyes had met and a feeling of warmth had suffused her for a moment. He had paused and smiled faintly. Had she returned his smile? She couldn't remember. They had exchanged "Good evenings," and Papa Frank had looked at her strangely. Katherine had been widowed for over a year and, like him, strongly felt the stirrings of the blood.

Mildly, Papa had said, "Perhaps, my girl, there will be someone else for you after all. Then you can know what your grandmother and I knew together, and your mother, sadly, never did."

He spoke of the fact that her own father had come from a neighboring plantation, had courted Delpha, her mother, then been sold away.

That night Katherine had begun to dream of the stranger, and it occurred to her that she had *continued* to dream, because she had dreamed of him even before she met him. But she had not seen him again.

Now, in fantasy, she wrote a hateful *Katherine Duplessis*. Likewise in fantasy, she completely blotted out the "Duplessis" with pokeberry ink. But fantasies didn't matter. Reality did. So much for the chance encounter and the dreams of the tall, handsome stranger. His presence and words of love and comfort were just that—wonderful, never-to-come-true *dreams*.

As Martin started toward the cabin he shared with Jules, Captain Paul DeBeau stopped him. A grizzled, swarthy man of medium height with a powerful build, DeBeau's countenance often belied his actions. He was gentle with those he liked; with enemies, he was ruthless. He had known Martin's family a long time in Santo Domingo, had been his father's best friend; he and Martin had been able to greatly help each other.

"I'd thought we'd have started back before now, lad," De-Beau said, "but there is something I must do not to my liking. I'd thought not to speak of it to you, knowing your sensitivity." He smiled wryly, pausing a long while before he continued. "I guess you'll just have to trust me, Martin. Have I ever been false with you?"

Martin answered slowly, wondering what the old seadog was leading up to. "I don't believe so. You saved my life. I can't forget that."

"As you saved mine. And I never will betray you—*if* I can help it. A bit later I will explain everything, because I value your good opinion of me. God knows there are those who think I should be hanged."

Martin could not dispute this. From what he knew, DeBeau had far more enemies than friends.

"Captain?"

"Yes, Martin."

"Will we anchor here much longer?"

DeBeau hesitated. "We wait for this occurrence I spoke of. I believe we can carry out our plans within no more than a couple of days. Why do you ask?"

Martin took a deep breath. "I'll need more time away from the ship than usual. . . ."

DeBeau could be generous. Seadogs were usually merciless with each other where women were concerned, none more so than whites when women of other races were involved. DeBeau said only, "Then go! And remember *my* giving in here when *you* want my old carcass flayed for what I *must* do later."

DeBeau's words disturbed Martin, but his heart leapt at the chance of spending time inland tomorrow to seek out Katherine.

"I am black and comely . . ."

As soon as he had gotten to the cabin and begun to strip off his clothes in preparation for bed, Martin decided he was too excited to sleep. He'd take a walk along the sandy strip and perhaps go even farther. Last February, she had been less than twenty feet away in the clearing near the woods when he'd seen her with the old man and two other girls.

Katherine. He said it gently, rolling the *r* over his tongue like savored honey. Hastily throwing his clothes back on, he woke Jules and they made plans to lower a boat from the side of the ship and row the distance beside the sandy strip, then walk through the woods. That would save time. It was eight o'clock. At that hour of the clear, moonlit night, there was no chance that he'd catch a glimpse of her. But there *was* a chance he'd come across some of the men who lived on the plantation and adroitly question them about her. "Let us hope," Jules said, "that no night riders sight our hides and decide to make us pay for being free. Lord, what a man will do for friendship."

Pleased about going to find at least solid information about Katherine, Martin didn't answer. What if she were married? He thought about the fact that a lot of black men had been killed in the recent war. Was she a widow at such a young age? He wanted her free of encumbrances, available for his suit.

What if she were another man's *intended* wife? His loins tightened. He swore he'd get around that—somehow.

DeBeau met them a few feet from their cabin door.

"You're not going ashore tonight, are you?" he asked.

"Yes," Martin answered shortly, annoyed.

DeBeau looked down. "I meant to tell you," he said. "We must be up long before daybreak, so we need to turn in early. I'm sorry to spring this on you so late, Martin, but I've got something hellishly important to do tomorrow. We'll all need to be up and roaring."

"Very well, Captain," Martin replied tightly. He and Jules looked at each other. Along with a keen sense of disappointment, he felt a less-than-honest wave of vibrations from De-Beau's averted eyes and the hunch of his shoulders. DeBeau cleared his throat. "I'm worried about my son, Martin. I've got to get back to him as soon as I can. A bit of luck, and we *could* ship out tomorrow."

Martin clenched his fist, his disappointment evident as De-Beau left the room. Should he press Jules to go anyway? After all, they were not DeBeau's crew members by necessity, but to repay favors he'd done Martin as his father's friend.

"Don't let it rile you, man," Jules cautioned. "We can come back here on our own, find your Katherine—if she's free."

Martin looked at his friend, a scowl deepening on his face. He considered going ashore anyway, without involving Jules, but what could he find out about her? And this bayou country had not taken as kindly to the freeing of its slaves as had New Orleans, and God knew New Orleans was bad enough.

"Am I being a fool, Jules?" he asked slowly. "Isn't once in a lifetime enough for a man to risk getting his heart ripped out by a woman—even a beautiful one?"

Jules shook his head. "I'm four years older than you. Thirty-four. And I've had my share of hurting from women. I'm still looking. Still *hoping*. You're not a fool. At heart, you're a lover."

"A hell of a lot of good it's done me."

"Go to bed. We'll come back on our own, I tell you."

Martin undressed, doused the lantern, and lay on the top

bunk. His talk with DeBeau bothered him. Why was the old salt suddenly devious in a way Martin had never known him to be? Before he drifted off to sleep, scenarios of Katherine and him played and replayed themselves in his mind. He put his arms behind his head and imagined her here with him. And his body tingled as a rush of pleasure assaulted him, just thinking of the slender, laughing, spicebrown girl.

Two

Once outside, Katherine walked with quick steps to the huge magnolia tree about one hundred yards from the house. Greatly agitated, she set the lantern on the ground and paced back and forth when she got to the tree. Reaching up, she removed two large, white waxy blossoms from a low-growing branch, slipping one into the pocket of her full-skirted, blue gingham dress. She favored this dress because her mother had made it for her, had told her how pretty she looked in it.

She took the other blossom and began to alternately crush and shred it.

Married? she thought. To a fool like Louis? Katherine had always tried to be tender, kind, compassionate. Was Louis to be her reward? Albert, her young deceased husband, had been sweet, their time together pleasurable if not exciting. She sighed deeply, blinking back angry, acid tears of disappointment, refusing to even think of her dreams of the loving stranger or their fleeting encounter.

She was leaning against the rough bark of the tree, inhaling the fragrance of the wood and blossoms, when she felt his hot breath on her neck. Louis had come up on her as stealthily as a wolf.

"You *wanted* me to ketch up with you, wanderin' around out here this late, lookin' for me. That's why you come out here."

Louis's voice was sly, faintly cruel. Oddly enough, he would have been attractive had he not been so domineering. Gingerskinned and healthily husky, he had caught the eye of many of the plantation women and he knew it. He worked a small crop of first-class vegetables and fruits that sold well in neighboring town. Louis could marry a different woman every day for a couple of weeks if he wanted. But he wanted Katherine.

He laughed now. "I watched you goin' back and forth like you think you own the world. When we get hitched, you won't be so hincty then. I'm gonna have lotsa' fun with you bein' my woman . . . my *wife*."

His rough hands clutched the back of her neck, bringing her head forward, forcing her mouth to his. The fumes from corn whiskey were nearly overwhelming to Katherine.

Fury boiled in her. Perhaps she would have no choice later, but for now . . .

Savagely, she kicked him in the shin, grateful for the clod boots she had worn into the woods. Her elbows jabbed into his belly as the liquor on his breath continued to make her dizzy. But thank heavens for his drunkenness. He held on until she took part of the crushed magnolia blossom still in her hand and rubbed it into his eyes. Immediately, Louis lurched away from her, grating, "Damn it, girl!" as he tried to rub the sting of the crushed blossom from his eyes.

Sensing trouble, Ruff, Papa Frank's old red hound dog, came running over from where he'd been lying under an oak. But the dog knew Louis and he just stood there, anxiously whining, switching his tail, until Muffin, his younger, brown-spotted mate, joined him.

Unable to whistle, Katherine called, "Here, Ruff! Here, Muffin!" in a strong voice, turned sharply, and began to run. She had been as much a fool as Louis, walking in the dark even a short distance from the house. With his well-known temper, he might have struck her. Well, no matter, she had gotten away.

Katherine had been running for a couple of minutes when she realized she had meant to go toward the plantation mansion. An ill Papa Frank couldn't protect her now. There would be people at the mansion who would help her. Damn it, she thought, in her haste to leave the house, she'd forgotten to bring Papa's pistol. Ruff and Muffin followed hard on her heels, yelping.

When her senses had cleared a little, she realized she had run toward the inlet and the sandy strip that opened farther up onto the Gulf of Mexico. A shaft of fear struck her then, but she was still too angry and too relieved to have gotten away from Louis.

"Katherine! Wait!"

Two out-of-breath young girls, Zell and Singing Bird, caught up with her, panting.

"Katherine," Zell called, "Louis has slunk back to his cabin. Stinking like white lightning mash. Stop running, I tell you!"

When the drumming in her ears had calmed, Katherine could distinguish the voices of her friends. She slowed and sank to the ground, winded, as they reached her. They threw themselves on the ground with her, as if they would protect her. Zell was her own age of twenty, with a husband she'd married at fifteen who had died in the recent war. Singing Bird was fifteen and hadn't spoken since she was eight. Both girls had also been told that they must marry. Only Zell looked forward to it.

Zell hugged her close, her thin body shaking with sympathetic anger for her friend.

"We saw you from my porch when you started to run, and we came after you. I stuck out my foot and tripped Louis when he went by," she said. "He fell on that rotten stump. I thought maybe it stuck in his evil heart. . . . But no such luck," Zell giggled, continuing. "I looked back and he was limping along, back home, after he fell."

Mute and waiting, Singing Bird said nothing, merely squeezing Katherine's hand tightly.

Katherine thought about how she and Zell were both twenty, both young widows who'd lost husbands. Zell had been far more in love and had grieved more deeply. Unlike them, Singing Bird, who was fifteen, had been born on Keyes Plantation to a male slave and a Cherokee Indian woman whom he'd loved in chance meetings by a creek where the field hands went for water. She'd come to the plantation as his slave wife, with their child, Sing. The overseer had taken a fancy to Gray Eagle, Singing Bird's mother, and in drunken lust had raped her.

Like the African warrior he had once been, Singing Bird's father, Luster, had dared to fight the overseer, who had killed him. Gray Eagle had died of malaria and a broken heart a month later.

At Zell's voice, Katherine stopped musing.

"What are you going to do, Katie? What are *we* going to do? You can't marry Louis. He's just too rough for someone like you," Zell wailed. Zell, always in moments of anxiety, rattled on. "Well, he *does* work real hard. He's said to be smart enough, when he's not drinking. He makes a pretty good living. And Sing writes that he's not as rough as he seems. He sure likes to feel the women up, though. Oh, Katherine, why don't we *all* run away? No one will miss us."

But they knew very well that running away posed its own special dangers. Katherine reached out and petted Muffin's coarsely bristled fur as the dog flattened her forepaws on the ground. She loved both Ruff and Muffin nearly as much as did Papa Frank. Moving over to Singing Bird, Katherine stroked the younger girl's back. After Singing Bird's mother died, she had lived with Zell's family. They called her Sing and helped her to recover from the shock of her mother's death. Things had gone well for Sing until she was eleven, with a rounding body and quite lovely. She had come back from the woods one day, where she had been sent to gather berries, scratched and bleeding.

She had not spoken since, but made it plain that she listened and understood. She began then to write whatever she wished to say, refusing to be forced to write that which she did not wish to express.

And it was Katherine to whom she first wrote that Louis was better than he seemed.

He is not for you, Katherine, but he is not a drunken devil like you all think. He saved me. I could have died.

But no amount of coaxing would get her to write more, as she healed as best she could in silence.

Lord, Katherine thought, she was so fortunate to have such good friends as Zell and Singing Bird. Her life had been pleasant enough since freedom had come four years ago. Was it wrong of her to dream of an even better life . . . with the black prince of her dreams?

Ruff growled low and deep in his throat.

"Look out!" Zell screamed, starting up.

Three large white men clumped brutishly through the underbrush. Before the screaming girls could get up, two of the men threw nets over Singing Bird and Zell, who sat on either side of Katherine. Singing Bird tried to cling to Katherine, but one man wrenched her arms away roughly.

Katherine willed herself to be calm as a big blond man, evidently the leader of the outlaws, snatched her to her feet.

"This one here's the one named Katherine," he snickered. "Captain's had me watching her. She's the only one he really wants. He told me to be real careful. Said she's *special,* and he'd have my head if I let her get hurt, 'magine that."

Growling and ignored, Ruff finally sprang into action, trying to sink his old fangs into the bulky blond man's leg, who snarled to his companions, "One o' you can hold both these wenches. Hit these damned hounds and knock 'em out, but don't kill them. Cap'n said to be careful . . . and knowing him he damned well meant it."

"Well," one of the other men said, after knocking Ruff and Muffin out, "I ain't heard you say the cap'n said nothin' about the other wenches here. Why d'we need 'em, anyhow?" He nudged his fellow sailor. "I say we show all these wenches a good time and send the other two home."

The blond man shook his head, narrowing his eyes in the lantern's light.

"Cap'n said we take whoever's wit' this filly. We can't leave the other two to alarm the place."

"How come you know her name 'n everything, you sly ol' dog?" one of the smaller men guffawed as he asked the question.

"Cap'ns had me watchin' the woods ev'ry day. Now, I can't tell you ev'rythin', but there's a lot o' sense to this—if we get away with it. Slavery may not be legal no more, but it's still a gosh-damned *fact* in a whole lot more countries than this'n. . . ."

"You ain't plannin' on sellin' 'em f' *slaves?*"

The blond man shrugged as Katherine's heart plummeted with fear, then rose swiftly with fury.

"How the hell do I know what the old rascal has in mind for them? Mayhaps he's jus' collectin' good-lookin' women."

The most brutal-looking of the three men flicked a glance over at the terrified girls.

"Aw, forgit it. Cap'n DeBeau's a patsy f' lookin' out f' women. His ma musta loved him a whole lot."

"Yeah."

The tall, heavy blond man took Katherine's arm in a viselike grip.

"Please! Just a moment, sir," she said sweetly, looking deeply into the man's eyes. Until Louis had begun to pursue her, she had felt she could disarm the devil himself with love and tenderness. The moment the outlaw's grip slackened, Katherine was off in a flash, fear fueling her feet.

But he caught her before she had gone fifty yards, as the men ahead of them stood looking back. In the moonlight she could clearly see that this man had more rage in him than perhaps even *he* knew.

"You try that again, you little bitch," he snarled, "and I'll just pr'tend to th' cap'n you got hurt real bad tryin' to get away. You hear me? *He* might love women, but I sure as hell got no cause to."

Katherine nodded. "Yes, sir."

How could *two* incidents like this happen in one night? Wouldn't it be better to die than go to a certain hell with Louis—or these beasts?

This time as she agilely moved to escape again, he caught her, pressed his thumbs expertly into her throat, then there was only blackness.

Captain Paul DeBeau stood near the porthole in his cabin, his large, rough hands clenching and unclenching behind his back. Should he have told Martin his plan? He laughed shortly. Hell, no! Slow to anger, the lad had a pretty hot temper when aroused. Damned good with his fists, too. As young men on Santo Domingo, DeBeau and Pablo Dominguez, Martin's father, had been good friends, fellow carousers, and reluctant family men.

Breathing deeply, the captain walked to his bar and poured himself a stiff shot of dark Betancourt rum, a Haitian import he favored. He glanced at the clock. Eight-fifteen. He'd best be getting back on deck to talk with Martin. Those three damned fools he'd sent for the old leaf doctor's granddaughter were not the ones he'd have wanted to send, but any other crewmen would have only been worse.

"Why in hell couldn't the old leaf doctor have stayed well?" he asked aloud. Then this damned foolishness, the kidnapping, wouldn't have been necessary. It was a nasty business. But his son was dying. Was the girl knowledgeable enough to help his son? Something akin to fear began to lodge itself in DeBeau's chest. If he were a praying man, he'd have begged that Guy's life be saved. He set the heavy glass down with a thud. No use turning into a weakling now. He'd done what he had to do.

"Now Martin had best remember," he grumbled to himself as he walked across his cabin, "it was as much as anything at *my* behest that my friend Pablo acted as well as he did toward Annalise, Martin, and his older brother Raoul. Aye, it was a hellish time for Pablo and *me* when Pablo took up with that black Indian-blooded beauty, Annalise, although Lord knows, that kind of thing had happened before, *was* happening then, and happened afterwards with other masters and their desirable slave women."

DeBeau left his cabin reluctantly, feeling a need to quickly warn Martin about the women being brought aboard. He had known the young man from childhood, had admired his intelligence, his steadiness. It had been DeBeau, as well as his father, who had taught Martin to sail, who had seen his artistic leanings and recommended that he study in Spain to be a *forgeron,* crafting the beautiful iron grillwork that graced buildings.

He chuckled drily. Pablo had taught both his sons fencing, though, incurring the wrath of his Castilian wife. "You cannot make your two bastard black rascals *white,"* she'd screamed at Pablo in DeBeau's presence. "Would to God you loved poor Ricardo, your *real* son, the way you do them."

Pablo had looked at DeBeau in abject guilt. The sick pallor and the whining of Ricardo completely disgusted him. His two sons by Annalise were healthy, strong, and handsome—like him. Debeau was jerked back to the present.

"What in the hell is the meaning of this, Captain?" As DeBeau reached the deck, Martin faced him. "Pace says *you* ordered these young women brought aboard!" His voice shook with anger, and DeBeau groaned inwardly. He hadn't come up quickly enough.

DeBeau placed a hand on Martin's arm as the big blond man called Pace held an obviously unconscious Katherine in his arms. Zell and Singing Bird cowered together, out of their nets, wanting to be close to their friend, yet wanting to be as far away from the hateful Pace and the others as possible.

Acting from his furious gut, Martin demanded, "Give her to me. She's hurt. I'll take her to my cabin."

Pace roared with laughter, followed by the raucous laughter of his two accomplices. "Better tell your smart nigra here that he ain't been free long enough to question what I or any other white man does."

Pace pressed Katherine's limp body closer to him, his face going to her thick and fragrant earth-brown hair.

His smaller, swarthier sidekick snickered to Martin, "I'd reckon the captain in his wisdom knows sailors gets lonesome, so he got us three right sharp wenches for company. . . ."

"That's enough, Fitch!" DeBeau bellowed. "Dominguez has *always* been free! Now I'll have no more damned foolishness out of any man on board, white *or* black. We've got a job to do." He turned to Martin. "We'll talk in a minute, but I'll say this now, lad. I'm truly sorry, but I meant to ask the old leaf doctor to go with me to treat Guy. My son could be dying. He's been your friend, as *I* have been your friend all your life. Surely you won't hold this against me. What choice did I have? She surely would not have come willingly."

"You might at least have *asked* her, Captain. She might have come. What if that fool has really hurt her?" Martin asked, concern for Katherine etched on his face.

"No. He'd damned well better not have. Had I asked and she refused me, what then?"

Martin looked at him a long moment. "What if taking her is useless? What if she refuses to help you?"

DeBeau's eyes blazed with fury for one second. "She wouldn't dare. . . ." He stopped himself. His early years of pirate plundering had come back, almost erasing his recent life as a respected merchant and citizen.

Here they were talking, Martin thought heatedly to himself, while Katherine was unconscious. And he was not a "lad" but a *man*, and DeBeau had best know it. Levelheaded by nature, Martin felt it would do no good to challenge Pace, the man who held Katherine. Pace enjoyed a good brawl and he was with two other fools like himself. No, fighting at this moment would only serve to further hurt Katherine. Martin could best help her by letting the men do as DeBeau had told them. But his old friend had better realize that over this woman their friendship could end. For reasons he didn't quite understand himself, Martin felt he would kill for her. And DeBeau felt Martin's fury keenly and began planning how to ameliorate it.

"That woman you brought on board like a slave is my intended *wife*, Captain."

The lie came so effortlessly, surprising him no end.

DeBeau's eyes said he knew Martin lied and he wondered why. "Pace, take the girl into Martin's and Jules's cabin and lay her down. And don't tamper with her in any way. Hell, I'll go with you and see that you don't."

DeBeau turned to Zell, who trembled with fear and anger. Singing Bird alone seemed calmer; she was no stranger to terror.

As Pace, with Katherine in his arms, went below deck, followed by DeBeau and the two girls, Martin hit the sturdy steel wall with his fist, feeling the pain in his hand as anodyne for the torment of his helplessness. This was the girl he'd seen and wanted on his walk up the beach in February. Damn DeBeau! The captain knew him well enough to talk with him about this. But, Martin asked himself scathingly, does *any* black man know *any* white man well enough to trust him? Yet DeBeau *had* proved trustworthy again and again, each having saved the other's life.

"I stood away from you, but at your back, my friend," Jules said quietly when Debeau left.

Martin couldn't answer for the anger seething in his belly, but he felt grateful for Jules's presence, and he knew his friend was aware of it.

Unable to control his glee, the ruffianly Fitch pulled away from the slender, sandy-haired man, the third member of the kidnapper trio who had carried out his orders as gleefully as the other two.

"Aw, let it go, Fitch," he said now. "Ain't you had enough excitement for one night?"

"Man," Fitch chortled, "you think I'm lettin' these two darkies have all the fun? There's three of them women, ain't there? And me, *I* favor the sassy, pretty wench, the one named—"

Martin's fists were swift and punishing, hitting his old friend DeBeau in absentia as well through the brutal Fitch. Trained to box, trained to fence, trained to *fight*, Martin wanted to teach this man that Katherine was not for a defiling fiend like him. She deserved the tenderness, the charm that she offered.

Fitch was tough. At first he came back with as good as Martin had given him, but Martin was younger, tougher, stronger. Fitch got just one telling punch to Martin's midsection, nearly knocking the wind out of him. And he never really felt the blow from Martin's fists that proved his waterloo for that night.

Martin stood over him a moment, then sat down, winded, wiping the sweat and blood from his face with the handkerchief that Jules handed him.

"You got some pretty bad cuts, my friend," Jules said, bending to his side and clapping him on the shoulder. "That was one hell of a beating you gave that bastard. We'll have to watch our backs for the rest of the trip." He paused as Martin nodded in agreement. "Look, I think together we can guard the women. And we can probably get Yokey and Smith to help." The men he named were two black crewmen.

The thin, sandy-haired man ministered to Fitch, sloshing water over him. He did not revive.

"What the hell is going on here?"

The captain bellowed his question as he came back on deck with Pace. He glanced at Fitch, whom he basically disliked, and grinned inwardly. No doubt his damned foul tongue had gotten him in trouble again.

Martin stood up. He wasn't going to apologize.

"What the hell's happened here now?"

No one answered him. Fitch was coming around, groaning loudly, holding his head. He sat up. The captain walked over to him and looked down, showing no emotion. "One warning, Fitch. You've sailed with me a long time and I've done you favors above and beyond the call of duty. Plan on taking this like the man I know you can sometimes be. If you try to strike back at Dominguez or at me, you'll never know what hit you. Do you understand?"

Fitch nodded glumly. He was a bully and a coward, but not a fool.

Three

Katherine heard the soft lapping of the waves against the ship's hull as she slowly regained consciousness. Her head throbbed steadily. Briefly, she opened her eyes against the brightness of lanterns and lamps, then closed them again, wincing. In that one moment she saw someone who caused her to open her eyes wider, no matter how much her head hurt.

She blinked rapidly, trying to focus on the man sitting on the bed beside her, who looked like the stranger in her dreams.

"You—you said I'd be safe with you. You said . . ." She began to babble. Hazily remembering the rough, cruel kidnappers, Katherine was half hysterical with terror, yet part of her remained steady. Her love was here, so it was all right. She must still be dreaming, but what had happened?

The young man knelt beside the bunk bed, stroking Katherine's brow, his face tense with concern.

"Yes, I'm here," he said kindly. "I know you're hurt, but I want you to listen carefully to me. Can you hear me? Are you *able* to listen?"

Katherine nodded yes.

He spoke slowly. "My name is Martin—Martin Dominguez. And I know your name is Katherine."

Her eyes widened, remembering fully now the three brutal men on the woodland path, her friends . . . Where were Zell and Singing Bird? She tried to sit up. Gently, the man pressed her back.

"You need to be still a few minutes longer," he insisted, placing his finger on her lips.

"As far as anyone knows, you are my woman, and you are to be my wife as soon as possible. For God's sake, Katherine, don't fight me," he said. "You'll be in great danger if you don't cooperate with me. You can trust me. I promise you on this."

He took her hand and placed it on the worn black leather Bible, then put his roughened hand atop hers, squeezing it gently. Even as her throbbing head made her wince again, Katherine felt dizzy at his touch. The salty, invigorating ocean breezes swept in from the Gulf, clearing her head a bit. When he had called her "his woman," it had been a verbal caress, light years away from Louis's clutching words.

"Martin," she repeated softly, needing to say his name, "I have no choice but to trust you."

"Good," he replied, both pleased and relieved. "I will explain everything to you as soon as I can. You are in grave danger here alone, as are your friends, and marriage is the only way I can help you. Do you understand?" He paused, looking at her closely. "No, you cannot possibly understand."

"I don't understand," she said, "but I know I must trust you for now, Martin. It's as if I've known you a very long time."

"And I you," he told her, wanting more than anything to savor that tender mouth, to bury his face in her soft, fragrant hair and bosom.

Katherine started as the door swung open to admit Captain DeBeau and her two friends, who looked frightened out of their wits.

"Go on in, girls," DeBeau said to them. "You need not fear me. Embrace your friend. I know you've been worried about her and she about you."

Zell and Singing Bird came to her narrow bunk and kneeled, hugging her in turn. Singing Bird sat on the bed and cried as Katherine held her.

Martin watched the scene grimly, his mind returning to an

earlier time tonight. He and the captain looked at each other, and in a new part of him, Martin felt DeBeau a stranger. De-Beau looked at the younger man somberly. Aye, it was fitting that a beautiful woman had driven a wedge between him and Martin, even as Annalise had drawn Pablo's allegiance.

"Captain . . ." Martin drew a deep breath. "The woman you have here is the reason I've spent time on shore during our other visits here. Her father has given her hand to me."

DeBeau raised his eyebrows and looked at Martin. Was he lying? If he was, fate had dealt DeBeau quite a hand this time. He knew now that he should have taken Martin more fully into his confidence before tonight, but would the younger man have agreed to his plan? Hell, no! Martin would *not* have gone along with this. He didn't need to ponder that. And he, De-Beau, needed this woman.

"You know your men, Captain, as Jules and I know these men where women are concerned. They respect no woman, not even their own. And you cannot stay awake and on guard until we get back to New Orleans." He shook his head. "I have to do what I can to protect them."

Very dryly, DeBeau said, "Especially Katherine."

Martin looked at him levelly. "Yes, Captain, *especially* Katherine."

"Yes. Yes, of course, Martin, I'll marry you to Katherine" the captain declared glumly. What else could he do? Besides, this way, the girl would probably be *willing* to help him. "I'll perform the ceremony as soon as we get back to New Orleans."

"I ask that you marry us *now,* sir," Martin said shortly. "You have that power as a ship's captain."

"And when do you want me to do this?" DeBeau asked with an edge to his voice.

"I would like you to marry us in an hour, if that is possible."

The captain laughed aloud, then realized the seriousness of his friend. For a long time, DeBeau stared at Martin, then he turned to study Katherine, who still lay on the bottom bunk.

"Yes," he muttered to himself. "I think I can pull this off to my satisfaction—*and* yours."

Once DeBeau left the room to get his book of ceremonies, Martin went to Katherine and sat down again on the edge of the bed.

"This is the only way I can protect you," he said. "Later, I will bring you back if you want to leave me. Now there is just too much danger for you and your two friends to be alone on this ship."

Tears misted Katherine's eyes. She blinked them back, not wanting him to see her cry. He was unquestionably the man whose eyes had sought and met hers as she and the others had gathered herbs in the woodland in February. Lord, he *was* as handsome as she'd remembered him, even more so than in her dreams of him, which puzzled her because those dreams had begun *before* she ever saw him. Months before. He seemed nice, yes, but if he were, then why was he with this band of ruffians and kidnappers? Yes, he surely attracted her greatly— but bodies were known to betray.

His voice was warm with concern for her; she didn't feel she was mistaken about that. She closed her eyes as he whispered "Katherine." Or was it her imagination?

Zell and Singing Bird huddled by Katherine's bed, their fear still bordering on panic. Katherine lay still, her daze lessening. Martin tried as best he could to soothe all three women. "It's a terrible situation for you," he said as gently as he could. "Can you focus on what I'm saying, Katherine?"

"Yes," she softly assured him.

"Captain DeBeau—the man who was here a minute ago— his son is very ill, perhaps dying. He wanted to try to persuade your grandfather to go with him to heal his son, since his son is far too ill to come here. The best doctors in New Orleans have not been able to do anything. But then your grandfather himself is very ill . . ."

"He is healing," Katherine said quickly.

"I'm glad, especially since it's probably largely due to you.

I despise what Captain DeBeau has done by treating you this way, and I've told him so. He said he was desperate. Still . . ."

Katherine waited silently. The eyes of all three women were fixed on his face. Sharp vibrations of fear from the women permeated the room.

"It was *you* who walked with the other men near the woods last February, wasn't it?" Katherine asked, remembering again, her skin flushing.

"Yes. So we have at least glimpsed each other. And I saw you twice more at a distance, but we were rushing to move on to Mobile and to get back to New Orleans. I fully intended to meet you . . . if you were not married, or betrothed. . . ."

Martin waited for her to speak, more anxious than he realized.

"I am a widow," she responded gently. "But I *was* to marry a man I did not want to marry."

"Which pleases me," he stated simply.

Zell spoke up, liking this tall, handsome man who seemed so kind. "Those white men are monsters. They would have . . ." She stopped, shuddering. Singing Bird's eyes were somber.

Martin nodded. "Listen, I want you all to be very careful. Go nowhere without me or Jules, who will be here shortly. Should you, God forbid, get cornered by one of the men, scream and don't stop screaming."

They agreed to do as he said. Was Martin, too, an evil man? Katherine wondered. Beneath that handsome exterior that appeared so tender, was he actually very different? Somehow she didn't think so. Intuition she had been taught to respect and in part live by guided her through this present emotional mine field, giving her courage. And if this man were other than he seemed, he would not find her an easy dupe.

The door swung open as a jet-hued man of medium height entered. He approached the bed and Martin introduced him to the women as Jules Macklin. He bowed.

"You three add so much grace and loveliness to our poor

ship. I'm sure Martin has told you how we hate the circumstances that brought you here, but we *will* protect you."

Katherine nodded slightly, liking this charming friend of Martin's, then said to herself, yes, you both will protect us *as best you can.* Pray God that best is enough. She knew that she, Zell, and Singing Bird would fight to protect themselves.

Sitting on the edge of the bed, Martin took Katherine's hand. This woman stirred his blood, heating it in a way he hadn't felt in years. It came to him with a pang of wariness that she also touched his heart in a way he hadn't felt in years. And he surely didn't welcome that hurt again.

"If I could," Martin said to Katherine, "I would at least get magnolias and wild roses from the forest to ease your sadness at our wedding, but you understand that Jules cannot go into the forest alone, and I must stay here to see that you all are safe."

Katherine thought about the incredible evening this had been, beginning with dreams of this man before her and happiness at Papa Frank's beginning recovery, then ending with this nightmare. Yet looking at Martin brought a small edge of excitement along with the fear.

"Shall we begin?" DeBeau asked gruffly as he came into the room.

Martin knew very well that he didn't fool DeBeau. A usually guarded man who played what romantic cards he held close to his vest, he had not *looked* the part of a lover lately. DeBeau's voice was dry, raspy with rum and tension.

"Do you take this woman to be your lawfully wedded wife?"

The worn black leather-bound book he held contained the words he read. DeBeau sat in a chair by Katherine's bunk as Martin, Jules, and the girls knelt. And when he reached that all-important question, he looked at Martin keenly.

"I do." Martin's voice was steady. Strong. His big hands covered hers.

"Do you take this man to be your lawfully wedded husband?"

"I do." Her voice trembled so.

Although the ceremony was short, it seemed to Katherine to take an interminable length of time. But DeBeau was finally at the end, intoning the words.

"I now pronounce you man and wife! You may kiss the bride!"

DeBeau looked at Martin sharply, his eyes narrowed. As Martin leaned forward and kissed her gently on the lips, Katherine felt a sense of melting, of flowing out to him, so that he lingered longer than he had intended.

DeBeau leaned over and patted Katherine's shoulder, speaking gruffly, "Katherine, had there been any other way, I would have taken it. Believe me."

It was his way of saying he was sorry. Now he added, "I would have seen to it that you returned home safely once we knew if you *could* help my son. But it is my luck that you and Martin know each other and are betrothed. I surely regret the way you were brought on board. You were not fiddled with . . . ?"

"No," she answered evenly, catching his meaning, thinking angrily that not only might she damned well have been fiddled with, but also killed from the pressure on her throat that had caused her blackout.

DeBeau wet his lips. "I congratulate you both." He shook Martin's hand, patted Katherine's shoulder, then left.

Kaleidoscopic visions of her broomstick wedding and life with her first husband, Albert, flashed through Katherine's mind. He had been safe, their life gentle and unassuming. She blocked the thought that it had also been dull. When Martin had looked at her a moment ago, as well as that time on the beach, his eyes had been rife with passion, awakening fires she had only known faintly existed before.

The usually effervescent Zell was quiet now as she spoke. "I would serenade you, *ma chère,* but I am still too shaken.

But I will *say* the words. Standing up, she began to intone, without smiling:

> *"Ma chère,* on this your wedding day,
>   I wish you love!
> *Mon cher,* on this your wedding day,
>   I wish you joy!
> For him, the first nine months,
>   a dimpled baby girl!
> For her, the second year,
>   a bouncing baby boy!"

As crowded as the cabin was with the three added women, the ship provided no other available quarters. Martin knew that if he and Jules left the women alone, one of the fools on board might take the risk of breaking in and trying to rape the women. Oddly enough, Pace and Fitch would not be the most likely ones. They valued their jobs and would do nothing to antagonize the captain. But this run had been too hastily planned; there were several seamen aboard who would not be there but for that reason.

Martin thought wryly that he had wondered about that haste but had said nothing, because he was glad for the chance to return to the bayou country to try to meet this woman, whose tender, exquisitely brown face and body haunted him. He'd gone back even though his heart had asked if it were worth the pain again.

Jules rigged a makeshift curtain from rope stretched across part of the room and coarse cotton sheets. Quietly, he tried to reassure Zell and Singing Bird.

Martin sat on the bunk and took Katherine's hand.

"Lord, how scared you must be," he said.

"Yes. But I am less afraid with you than with the others. You and Jules."

Martin smiled sadly. "I'm glad for that, because I surely would not hurt you. Nor would Jules. Katherine," he began more urgently, "somehow I couldn't bear the thought of your being in danger from a couple of these scoundrels. No, not the two who captured you, but a couple of others they would use to get back at me for daring to hit Fitch, a *white* man." He fairly spat the words.

Katherine placed a soft hand on his. "I'm sorry to cause you all this trouble."

"The trouble you cause me I welcome. . . ." He paused. "Do you speak Spanish?"

"No," she said. "A little French, but our plantation had English owners. Why?"

"Because I want to call you *corazón,* which is Spanish for 'heart.' "

No matter the fear, the pain, the knowledge that he could be anything, no matter what her foolish heart said, she was strangely drawn to him. But no, some part of her insisted, of course I will not be a fool about this, but I will trust him—within reason.

Damn it, Katherine thought, why couldn't she have felt for Albert, her *safe* husband, what she felt for this possibly dangerous stranger?

"I am your *novio,* I will take care of you," he declared. "I own a *forgeron* business where I design and construct ornamental iron. We will live in the outer part of New Orleans, where I own a farm."

Rising a little from the bed, pain lancing her shoulder where she had hit it when she'd fallen, Katherine quietly said to him, "You're a good man, Martin. I can feel it."

"I want you to trust me, but you've little reason to do so. You don't know me, Katherine, but I will prove myself to you. I'm taking you into a strange world, an often dangerous world, as you must sense from the way you were brought on board."

"Yes," Katherine spoke quickly, "the captain of this ship and the others . . . *they* are dangerous, but not you and not, I don't believe, your friend Jules." Looking shyly at him as she lay back, she whispered, "I have dreamed of you so many times."

He looked at her steadily. "And I want to hear all about those dreams—everything—but there is something else I must talk with you about."

Glumly, she thought that she was right. He had married her only to save her. What other reason could there be? He was an accomplished *forgeron,* a man the captain of this ship treated with no little respect. Even the largely ruffian crew didn't crowd him; they respected no one, save that they had to pay their dues to their captain. No, she liked and thought well enough of herself, but she was a freed slave. This black prince had come from a distant land.

"Katherine?"

"Yes, Martin."

He drew a deep breath. "Captain DeBeau told you it was not you he intended to capture, but your grandfather."

"Yes," she said. "But why? He is a gentle man who would harm no one. He has spent his life healing others."

Martin nodded. "It is for his power to heal that he is needed. The captain's son has an illness now that no doctor can diagnose. Papa Frank, from what the captain tells me, is known throughout the state."

She nodded. "Yes. People come from a very long way for his help."

"The captain says he would have begged your grandfather to go to New Orleans with him for the time needed to heal his son. But when he learned that he was ill, *you* became his only hope. It is said that you are nearly as accomplished as he is."

Katherine cast her eyes downward. "Perhaps. He has taught me a lot, but no one is as good as Papa Frank. Taking me might have been a mistake. Were you ever a part of this . . . plot?" Her voice caught in her throat. "Did you know how we would be treated?"

"Dear God, no! I would never have willingly gone along

with it. DeBeau swears he was coming to tell me, but Pace and Fitch came back earlier than he'd expected." Martin paused a moment before he continued. "I did the only thing I could think of to protect you. They are rough men, most of them, and value women little, even their own. However, Captain De-Beau is a better man than he seems, or so I've thought. He and I are both from Santo Domingo, and we have known each other a long time."

"I see," she lied. Her heart said to trust him; her head said perhaps she was being a fool to do so. "How long will I be kept in New Orleans?"

"A couple of months. The son is very ill. I would see that you return to visit your grandfather if he continues to survive this terrible fever."

"He has turned the corner," she said proudly. "He is old, but he will survive."

Martin looked at her with admiration. "No doubt you cured him." Then he could not help asking, "So you had been promised to someone else . . . in marriage?"

Katherine shuddered. Her voice was very low when she spoke. "I loathe him. At least I am happy to escape him." Her mind was again filled with thoughts of Louis Duplessis pawing her body.

Martin's heart jumped with delight at her words. He had been jealous. "We will talk in a few minutes," he told her.

She looked at him, her voice steady now. "It's just that the times are hard, and we women seem not to be thought safe anymore without men."

Having spoken thusly, Katherine paused a moment, as that was the reason she had married a stranger. "I am not an unduly fearful woman. Still, I suppose I would have married, if only to bear children. Only now . . ."

She stopped, looking down, as he caught her hands and brought them to his mouth, kissing them.

At the delicious phrase "bear children," Martin imagined

many love scenes all wrapped up in one, the softly swelling belly of Katherine blossoming with the child of *his* seed. Looking at him, Katherine felt she saw something special in his eyes that spoke of a deeper passion, but it was gone so quickly, she thought she must be wrong.

Jules knocked and entered, carrying a bottle of red wine, a tin pitcher of water, and some food. Zell and Singing Bird stood in the doorway, waving, blowing her kisses, but they didn't come in. Quickly, Jules placed the large tray on a table near the bed, saluted them, and left.

Martin brought the food, heaped on one plate, and the water to the bed. Rough slabs of boiled beef, French bread, sliced tomatoes, and boiled new potatoes comprised the meal. The food was well seasoned, but it was nearly cold since supper had been served a couple of hours before. Nevertheless, Katherine thought it all fairly good. Dessert was a rich bread pudding, filled with juicy raisins and coconut, soaked in lemon and rum sauce. They both ate little, stealing glances at each other. Fear still chilled her, but she relaxed a bit with him so near.

"Jules has done well as usual, with little to work with," Martin told her.

"He is the ship's cook?"

"Yes. We call a ship's cook a 'ship's doctor.' He is many other very good things as well."

When they had finished eating, Martin took the platter and utensils and placed them on the table, then popped the cork on the bottle of red wine, poured two glasses half full, and brought them to the bed. The bouquet of the wine was light and heady.

"Wait," he said, raising his glass. Looking deep into her eyes, he toasted her: "May the minutes of the days of your life be as beautiful, as desirable, as you are."

Katherine was momentarily taken aback, but she could not check her response.

"Your tongue, *novio,* is as silver as you are handsome."

He raised her left hand to his lips and kissed it, then turned the palm upward and moved his lips over it for the briefest of moments. Even with all her misgivings, it still seemed to Katherine as if they would devour and savor each other at once.

"Katherine," he said simply, and nothing else.

His bronzed skin, together with the rippling muscles of his arms and shoulders under his white shirt, stirred her, but not half as much as the tender, warm look in his eyes. Katherine thought she wanted this man as she had never wanted anyone, and she hurt with the wanting. The intensity of it frightened her. Martin read that fear and held his own desire in check. He went to the porthole and drew back the coarse burlap curtains. A full moon reigned over the star-studded sky. Martin went back to the bed and stood over her, embracing her with his eyes.

"My dear Katherine," he began, "I am your husband, and I want to be that in every way. But until I can prove myself to you, I will *not* physically possess you. When you are ready, I will welcome you, but it must be of your own free will that you come to me."

He left her then. The *Robber Baron* had set out for New Orleans and he was needed topside for a few minutes.

Part Two

New Orleans—Desire, Happiness,
and Strife—1869–1870

Four

Katherine gazed in awe upon the fabled city of New Orleans as the hackney-for-hire carried them along the red cobbled streets. Much gossiped about in the bayou country, the Crescent City was extolled as being next door to paradise and damned as one big den of iniquity. For one thing, Katherine mused, it certainly seemed a fascinating city. Under different circumstances, she would have loved it. Still, she absorbed its varied beauty and let it serve to comfort the unease in her bosom over being brought here. Martin looked on as Zell chattered half hysterically. Singing Bird and DeBeau were quietly preoccupied.

Men and women of every race and socioeconomic class could be seen on the narrow streets. And the people of color! Every hue was represented—from the coal-hued newly arrived African, to the mahogany of Jules, to the *passe pour blancs* like her grandfather. Katherine noted the pride in their carriage, the sense of purpose on their faces, the rich silk and lace and fine cotton garments and dainty parasols of the women, and the excellent cut of the men's summer attire. Her former slave mistress and her daughters had talked endlessly of fashion as they pored over drawings sent by New Orleans modistes and Paris couturier houses. Katherine had listened and learned well.

No less than the people did Katherine study the magnificent buildings. There were superb examples of English-, French-, American-, and Spanish-inspired architecture. The mansions of the bayou country were often beautiful, but very few were like these. She saw that buildings had also been burned down or gutted, and in some areas there was extensive rebuilding and newly finished houses. In several instances the owners had perished along with their fortunes and their homes. These houses would wait for new blood to rebuild or restore them.

Martin pointed out some of the city's landmarks, although DeBeau had tersely instructed the hackney driver to hurry. New Orleans abounded in statues set in lovely squares, fronting memorable buildings. Jackson Square was closest to the riverfront. They passed St. Louis Cathedral, standing tall, white, and majestic; the museum, the Cabildo; the French Opera House; Congo Square; and Market Square as they neared the French Quarter.

Martin was happy that Katherine found so much of this section entrancing. DeBeau grumbled that if she couldn't help his son, he would quit this damnable wicked, gossiping city, where he had long been rich and powerful. But he well knew that there was nowhere else he could live.

St. Louis Cemetery number one fascinated Katherine. The spiked iron fence and huge moss-hung oak, which she would later discover was called the dueling oak, as well as the stacked crypts, were part and parcel of that huge land of the dead. Only in New Orleans would it exist in that form.

Katherine rode with Martin, Zell, Singing Bird, Jules, and DeBeau. It was some time before they stopped in front of a large, handsome red brick dwelling nestled back from the street and surrounded by black wrought iron fences and gates.

When a black man dressed in a dark blue, gold-trimmed uniform opened the gates, DeBeau held up his hand, pointing to the startling, elaborate fluid pattern of thick-growing "iron cornstalks." "This, my dear, is the work of your bridegroom, a master *forgeron.*"

"Oh, this is beautiful, Martin," Katherine told him, her voice formal. "You must be very proud."

Martin caught her hand. "Thank you. I am proud of my work and of those who work with me."

Once inside, DeBeau lost no time in taking Katherine to his son's sickroom. Twenty-two-year-old Guy DeBeau lay on a large canopied bed covered with immaculate white bed linen and a heavy white linen quilted counterpane. He was wan, his dark blue eyes sunken. Yellow fever had taken its toll of New Orleanians in bygone times, but it had not been one of the most recent devastations. Newspapers reported that *only* one hundred nine had died this time. The city had learned from the really bad former sieges, and had cleaned up its sewer systems and been more stringent with its quarantines.

Katherine had to admit that an illness of this severity would frighten anyone who cared. Still, it was *she* who had been kidnapped. And she would be a long time forgiving him for that.

A slender brown woman in a white turban bathed Guy's face. Paul DeBeau stood at the foot of his son's bed, his eyes pleading with Katherine. "Can you help him?" he asked, no longer the former pirate or the rich merchant, but simply a helpless man who loved his son.

Katherine examined Guy cursorily. This was not yellow fever, not yet, but should it strike, it would take him within the hour. She did not think his pale skin had become unhealthy all at once. From Papa Frank's teaching and her own careful observations, she had come to assess the heart, the mind, and the emotions even before the body. This frail body housed a *spirit* at least as frail. Although since childhood she had worked closely with Papa Frank on worse cases than this, Katherine still wished for his guidance.

Turning to Paul DeBeau, she asked bluntly, "Has there been recent trouble in your son's life, sir? Has he perhaps suffered a severe disappointment? A separation? A death?"

DeBeau's shoulders rose in fear and in anger. How dare this young filly ask such painful questions?

"Yes," he answered simply as Katherine stood waiting. "He

loved a girl I . . . felt was unsuitable. He lost her in the recent yellow fever epidemic. Oh, my God, like the doctors, are you, too, saying that there is no hope? . . ."

Unsmiling, Katherine told him, "My grandfather and I both feel that while there is life, there is hope, sir."

How comforting her words were to DeBeau. Martin looked at his new wife with ever-deepening respect.

Approaching the bed, Katherine sat down beside Guy, took his hand, and squeezed it gently.

"Can you talk to me at all, sir?" she asked. "Do you even *wish* to talk to me?"

The young man looked at her. As sick as he was, his eyes appeared amused and pleasant.

"To you," he began before he coughed harshly. She took a handkerchief from her pocket and held it to his mouth until he had finished coughing.

"I will talk to you," he said with effort, but he seemed to *want* to talk. "I'm glad you came. But you're not an old, white-haired man."

Another fit of coughing interrupted his speech. Katherine was surprised at the fairly strong timbre of his voice. There was *life* in that voice, humor, and, yes, she thought, bitterness as potent as gall. She felt a sense of relief.

"No," she said, "I'm not a white-haired old man. My grandfather is the leaf doctor you wanted. I am Katherine, his assistant. I have helped him to heal many people, and I pulled him through a bad siege of yellow fever when everyone expected us to lose him. Perhaps I can help you . . . if you'll let me."

The young man smiled weakly. "My father says I'm a fool for a pretty woman. God knows you're that. Yes, if you don't make it too hard for me, I'll try to cooperate."

Very briefly, Katherine thought about DeBeau and his son. Far from vain, she nonetheless noted the young white man's calling her "pretty." Master Keyes and his friends would never have been so complimentary to a black woman. And the degree of ease between DeBeau and Martin, although certainly re-

flecting the difference in their ages, was not something she
had witnessed in the bayou country.

Still, *she* had been one of the ones most often chosen to
serve when the master had entertained important guests. Katherine had heard from others that lighter skin color played no
small role in the selection of house slaves on many plantations.
That had *not* been the case on Keyes Plantation, where the
satiny, nutmeg-skinned Katherine had liked her own beautiful,
lustrous, pearly darkness and had been the object of much
admiration from others.

The young man on the bed had closed his eyes as her
thoughts roamed free. Katherine quickly pulled together a temporary plan of healing for him. Lord, she exclaimed to herself,
he really was skin and bones.

DeBeau's house was a luxurious French Quarter home that
a pirate-cum-importer-exporter could well afford. Katherine
briefly admired the interior, but her thoughts were with the
sick man on the bed. Her thoughts were also very much with
the handsome man who had married her. She hoped for at
least some joy from this union, but didn't dare believe that it
would be without pain and disappointment.

After dozing a few minutes, Guy woke up again.

"You can't hold down much food, can you?" Katherine
asked.

"I haven't really tried," he began, "but no, I can't. At first,
I wanted nothing to eat. I *drank* my meals in bourbon and
brandy. Now . . . no, nothing stays in my stomach."

Another fit of coughing overtook him. Katherine touched
his brow and found it hot. Along with the other woman, she
stripped Guy and gave him a salt-glow bath with rough sea
salt she found on hand. Then they bathed him with yarrow tea
left behind from a previous yellow fever epidemic.

Katherine spoke with Martin and DeBeau about the herbs
and medicines she'd need, commenting to the latter, "Had you
told me what you wanted, I surely would have brought the
proper medicines."

DeBeau looked sheepish, Martin surprised. His bride sure had spunk, Martin thought. As a woman of color, she seemed fairly unmindful of her "place," a trait he greatly admired. Would she have come with them willingly if DeBeau had explained the need? Martin didn't think so.

"Celié will know where to find what is needed," Martin told DeBeau. "I will send someone to her."

Even Celié's *name* stuck in Martin's throat. He had seen his dead brother's wife as little as he could since asking her to leave his house two and a half years ago. She said she had forgiven him long ago, but he had not forgiven himself. Yet she was the only one he could think of who'd know where to locate each herb, each medicine, immediately.

Katherine looked at him. There had been something cool yet angry when he'd spoken the name Celié. Who was she?

Martin informed Katherine that they would stay in a comfortable room next to Guy's, and then took her to look at it. Zell and Singing Bird would go on to Martin's house with Jules.

"I can help Captain DeBeau's son," she told Martin, "but it will take at least several days. After that, it will be up to him to continue what I can only begin."

Martin closed the door to their room. As she looked out on the flagstone courtyard, planted with evergreens, frangipani, and other exotic blooms, he came up behind her and put his arms around her. "Please don't be so frightened," he said, wishing fervently he could have saved her these past few days of uncertainty and pain. Katherine leaned back against him, fitting comfortably into the curve of his arms, the top of her head reaching his eyes. She felt his heavily muscled body with pleasurable warmth. He wouldn't press her, he reminded himself; he had promised her this much. But he couldn't help thrilling to her softness, and he couldn't wait to get her home where *she* would be mistress.

As he had done since first seeing her up close, Martin marveled at Katherine's flesh, its texture like a luscious, fragrant nutmeg-colored peach he wanted to savor and stroke.

Sighing, he told himself that in due time they would unite in hoped-for ecstasy. Even after such a short time together, he didn't want to let her go back to the bayou country. He intended to woo her slowly and tenderly—until she came to him of her own volition, pressed by her own desire.

It didn't take long for someone to bring Katherine the commonly used herbs she had requested, but they also brought a few Oriental herbs she hadn't been sure they would be able to locate. With the assistance of the cook's helper, she set about, in the massive kitchen, brewing the delicious teas of red clover, nettle, and hyssop. Having separately steeped, strained, and put those teas aside in glass jars, she then prepared the far stronger brews, the decoctions. The yarrow and lobelia teas were especially good for fever. And the sick man could probably hold down the slippery elm tea and slippery elm gruel when he couldn't keep down anything else. Yarrow tea had been known to break the severest fever in a few hours. There were other teas that worked as well.

Papa Frank considered lobelia teas far superior to all others for breaking fevers, but he had taught her that the herb should be understood and expertly prepared and used. It could be dangerous if used unwisely.

Katherine had also asked for very ripe strawberries, apricots, and cherries, most of which would have come from her bayou country. Not only would they be a treat, but they would also be solid food for Guy to eat.

"He's eaten more today than he has eaten in a week or two," his father informed them. To Martin he said, "It seems to me, young man, you've found yourself a jewel. See that you treasure her."

By nightfall, full of slippery elm gruel, slippery elm tea, ripe fresh fruits, and orange juice, Guy slept, this time relaxed and quietly.

"Well," DeBeau asked now, "will you be able to work the same miracles I've heard your grandfather works?"

Katherine shook her head. "You don't need a miracle," she said. "Your son is ill from lack of care for himself, because he suffers from some wound of the spirit. Set him free," she stated bluntly. "Let him live his own life."

She stood there, breathless now at her own daring. Martin smiled as DeBeau frowned.

"I have already lost my oldest son. Guy is the only son I have left," he said. "Martin understands that."

"All the more reason why you *must* let him go," Katherine told him.

Katherine understood from the anguish on the older man's face that he took her words seriously, believed them, and would at least try to loosen the chains in which he had enslaved his son.

With Guy sleeping, Katherine went to Martin, who stood looking out on the courtyard.

"It is so beautiful here," she observed. "I thought the plantation house where I grew up was beautiful, but this is even lovelier."

"You are beautiful," he told her gravely, as she wondered at the sudden anguish in his eyes.

He took her hand. "Please believe that I will never *willingly* cause you pain. . . ."

He hesitated then, and she asked him quietly, "Are you in love with someone else?"

Chiding herself that she had no right to ask, since he had married her only to protect her, Katherine nevertheless waited for his answer.

Martin looked at her, his eyes unfathomable at first, then he smiled. "You mean someone other than *you?"*

She blushed hotly as he touched her face. "No," he replied,

"there is no other woman in my life that I *want* there, except you."

He had said *that I want there,* she quickly noted.

"We're so new to each other. Of course you don't believe me when I speak of love, and perhaps it *is* too soon. But the attraction I feel to you is certainly real enough."

"I know it's what I feel, too, although I'd not be telling the truth if I said I'm not bitterly angry at being taken away from Papa Frank and my home." And away from a life with Louis? a small voice chided.

"I'll make it up to you," Martin promised. "And I *am* sorry." But that was partly a lie. He wasn't sorry. Even this soon, he felt that he wanted her always by his side.

By the end of the fourth day of Katherine's care, Guy De-Beau had rallied far beyond her expectations.

His doctor, François St. Cyr, one of the best in New Orleans, was astonished—and impressed. Martin had done the ironwork on his new house.

"You're quite young to be so wise," he said to Katherine. Turning to Martin, he went on, "I hope you will permit her to teach me at least a few of the bayou herbal secrets."

Martin turned to her, and Katherine acquiesced, pleased.

Her nightmarish journey here had begun to seem more bearable. They had been guarded by Martin, Jules, or one of two other black sailors on board the ship. DeBeau had at least readily agreed to that.

And Guy as Katherine prepared to leave, promised to continue his treatment.

"You have made a friend for life," he told her. "Whatever else, I repay my debts—always."

"And I," the older DeBeau declared fervently, "will search for ways to reward you both."

"For me, you already did when you helped Celié and me

escape from Santo Domingo," Martin announced quietly. "It is Katherine you owe."

DeBeau sighed. "A debt I will repay." He shrugged, then continued. "I will say little more, but as for Santo Domingo, it may well be that you and I *both* will find that that escape was less desirable than we thought."

As time passed, Katherine would often wonder about that conversation.

Martin turned to Katherine as they left DeBeau's house. "You're surely too tired to cook, but don't worry. I have a hunch Jules and the girls will have made something special."

She *was* too tired to cook, Katherine realized, but she was pleased to find herself really hungry for the first time since she'd been taken from the bayou country.

DeBeau's coachmen took them to Martin's house on the outer fringes of the city going toward Lake Pontchartrain, in the Gentilly section. It was a ten-acre farm in a neighborhood of wealthier artisan people of color, natives, and those who had come to Louisiana as free people valued for their mastery in building, much of it gained in apprenticeship in Spain and in France. As with many New Orleans neighborhoods, there were also whites, mostly foreign, and one Chinese merchant family.

Martin's house was a fairly large, well-built cream-colored brick with spacious grounds, surrounded by iron grillwork, the front section fashioned into a lily pattern.

It was all so much lovelier than she had expected. Katherine paused in admiration, inquiring, "This is your work?"

"Yes," he answered. "Do you like this pattern?"

"It's unbelievably lovely," she said, "as is Captain DeBeau's incredible cornstalk fence. New Orleans is an . . . *interesting* city . . . what little I've seen of it."

His eyes were nearly closed as he told her, "My island, Santo Domingo, is beautiful, too. I think you would enjoy it."

As Zell, Singing Bird, and Jules were not there, to her surprise, Martin lifted and carried her over the threshold. He carried her down the hallway and through wide glass-paned double doors. He stood with her in his arms in the middle of the polished floors of the large living room, with its Oriental rugs and plain but lovely marble-topped Victorian furniture. It was a palace compared to Katherine's house on the plantation, but she had been happy there.

Holding her in his arms, Martin rocked her softly against his own hard body. Hesitantly, she put her arms around his neck, drawing him close. She felt her heart expand with desire for this man she had seen only once before they married but had dreamed about many times. Yes, he could have reasons for marrying her that were not in her best interests. But Katherine could only hope that her trust in her own intuition did not betray her.

"Welcome home, Martin!"

Just as Martin set Katherine down, a husky, silken voice came from the archway between the living and the dining room.

Katherine turned to face a fairly tall, sylphlike woman in her late twenties, strikingly clad in a pale blue handkerchief linen dress with lace inserts. Her pale bosom was exposed and beautiful. Who was she? Katherine wondered.

Plainly surprised, Martin stiffened, then spoke. "I don't know why you're here, Celié, but as long as you are, I'd like you to meet my *wife* . . . Katherine. Katherine, Celié, my sister-in-law, the wife of my brother Raoul, now deceased."

The blood drained from the woman's face as she looked first at Martin, then at Katherine. Martin's eyes narrowed. Gossip would have made it impossible for her not to have heard about Katherine and him.

"I'm glad to meet you," Katherine said cordially, holding out her hand.

Celié ignored the proffered hand, ignored Katherine, and spoke only to Martin.

"I had heard that you have a new woman, although you were not gentleman enough to tell me. I came by because there have been heavy rains since you left. . . ."

"How did you get in? And where is Jules?" Martin asked her.

"I believe they've gone to the French Market. . . . How easily you forget," Celié reprimanded. "You once gave me a key, and since you never asked for it back, I kept it."

The woman looked at Martin with an even mixture of love and hate, before she said, "I hope the herbs I sent worked well. I will talk with you tomorrow, Martin, and I would very much appreciate it if you would come to me as soon as possible."

She walked with exquisitely arrogant grace across the room and let herself out. They heard the iron gates clang behind her, traces of her expensive perfume lingering mockingly in Katherine's nostrils as Martin looked at her, imploring her to understand, promising to explain to Katherine what seemed unexplainable.

Damn her, Martin thought with anger. He would never have sent to Celié for the herbs had there been *anyone* else. He knew she had a hot temper, but he hadn't thought she'd be *that* uncivil to Katherine.

Five

The room was hushed after Celié left, as if she had cast a spell over them. Then after a moment, Martin caught Katherine close and held her to him. His own heart beating raggedly against hers, he pressed her to him in a short embrace, before he gripped her shoulders, saying, "I am sorrier than I can tell you. Celié is a strange woman."

Katherine shuddered in memory. The woman had looked both at and *through* Katherine. It was eerie.

"She was so *angry*, Martin" was all she said. But in the intensity of Celié's eyes, Katherine had seen something beyond mere anger, something she could not quite comprehend.

Jules, Zell, and Singing Bird came in, their arms laden with groceries. "We went all the way over to the French Market. We needed more supplies. What's wrong, Martin?"

"Celié was here," Martin said shortly. "She apparently let herself in after you three left."

"And of course she performed as only Celié can," Jules stated dryly.

Martin shrugged. "For *her*, she was quite restrained. I will talk with her some time very soon, put this madness behind me once and for all. . . ."

He broke off abruptly, then, his face shadowed in raw pain. Katherine took his hand in hers and he smiled sadly. "What a wretched homecoming for you," he said.

"Nothing and no one is going to spoil your first night as mistress of this house," Jules announced staunchly. "Zell and

Singing Bird and me . . . we've got a feast prepared to welcome you."

"I thank you," Katherine told him, her throat dry, tears threatening to spill forth. How could she possibly eat?

Martin hadn't taken his eyes off her since Celié had left. Now he asked Jules, "Can you give us a little while alone? I need to talk with my bride."

Katherine looked at him, appreciation mingling with fear and anxiety.

"Take all the time you need," Jules answered, begging her silently to make the best of what seemed a bad situation. "Indeed, the girls and I will put dinner back on the warmer."

They both smiled at Jules gratefully. Zell and Singing Bird had retreated to the kitchen. Martin took Katherine's arm and led her through the dining room and into the hall, then up to their spacious front bedroom.

"Please sit here, and I'll join you shortly," he told her as he led her into the room and to the bed.

Katherine sank down on the large canopied, deep-feathered bed. It was a lovely room with pale green walls and cream paneling halfway up those walls. She was still taken by the ambience of the house but was too heartsick now to appreciate its beauty. Instead, she willed her mind to blankness and waited.

Martin had walked out onto a side balcony. He stood there, gripping the tall black iron posts, angry at the hurt Katherine was plainly feeling.

What was he going to do about Celié? Before he died, Raoul had asked Martin to look after Celié if anything happened to him. The memory of his mother's and Raoul's deaths on Santo Domingo in a revolutionary uprising three years earlier, *years* after the slaves were freed, still felt like acid in his brain.

Martin knew the deeper reasons he didn't rein in his sister-in-law had to do with *him* and their love affair, and with a hellish accident on Santo Domingo when he was a young man.

Slowly he turned, mopping his brow with a handkerchief,

and went back to Katherine. He had gone away from her to collect his thoughts, only to find them more tormented. What could he say to her?

When Martin entered the house, he went directly to a nearby walk-in closet. Katherine heard the clank of heavy metal and glanced up at his tall form, which she could see from where she sat. He returned to her side with a dark blue velvet ring box and a black leather box. Placing both in her lap, he dropped to his knees beside her.

"I don't expect you to smile," he said, "but I think you will find pleasure in these. I give them to you as my wife."

He took the ring box from her lap and snapped it open, his touch and his nearness warming her. On a blue velvet bed, the single diamond, a pear-shaped stone set in antique gold, sparkled, sending fire into the candle-lit shadows. Behind it lay a plain heavy gold wedding band. Katherine's breath caught in her throat as he took her hand, kissed it, and slipped the rings, which were a little too large, onto the third finger of her left hand.

"Oh, Martin," she whispered, admiring the rings before he took her hand again, assuring her that a jeweler could fit them.

"And do they bring you pleasure?" he asked earnestly.

Despite her anger about Celié and her displeasure at her abduction—except that it had saved her from Louis—Katherine told him gently, "*You* bring me pleasure, Martin. Can't you feel that already?"

"I feel so much with you. I want you to open the other box."

Martin watched as her fingers at first fumbled with the well-crafted black leather box, then opened it. He saw tears fall into her lap. He waited patiently, wanting to hold her close and stop the tears, but feeling she needed to cry all the same.

He held his breath as she reached into the box and removed the old, rare gem, holding it up, her reaction the same one his mother had had when first shown the jewel. Overwhelmed, she could say nothing.

The black pearl necklace that was to figure so prominently in her life was large and glowed with dark gray shadings, meshing and reflecting each other. Set in rich gold, it was surrounded by several perfect diamonds. The diamond ring and the gold wedding band were unquestionably beautiful, but the lustrous black pearl was mesmerizing in its opulence.

"You see," he said, "I have thought of *you* as the black pearl since I first saw you. *My* black pearl, for some reasons I don't yet fully realize, far more precious to me than the one you hold."

Katherine still couldn't speak. She fought to keep herself from reaching out completely to him. It was a strange new relationship she and this man had entered, and while her common sense told her she should hold back, her heart firmly opened to him in welcome.

"This was my mother's diamond ring and my mother's pearl," he told her. "I purchased the wedding band for you. What I bought could never match the old ring. I will tell you their history of love and of heartache." Rising, he took the necklace, opened the clasp, and fastened it around her neck.

Her silken brown skin was a perfect foil for the black pearl, Martin thought. He had no qualms about the expensive wedding band he had purchased since he'd been back from the bayou country. But he had pondered giving Katherine the superlative black pearl and the diamond.

He knew very well that he had never desired another woman as he desired this one, not even Celié, whose beauty had sent him nearly out of control for a short while in Santo Domingo. Already with Katherine the fires in his blood were steadier, providing a strong, lasting energy. Celié had consumed him. He and Katherine, it seemed to Martin, nourished each other.

Yes, he thought now, he wanted to give her the jewels, even if their passion dimmed and ended. He was growing wealthier with the rebuilding of a war-torn New Orleans; he could afford jewels now. But these were the jewels of his heritage. Martin smiled a bit grimly to himself. After the devastation Celié had worked on him, here he was, about to trust his *heart* again, but his *head* was leading him to Katherine as well.

No, he had not given her the jewels just to lessen his guilt about Celié or just to assuage Katherine's obvious pain. It was simply that he *wanted* her to have them.

Katherine could not help smiling. To break the intensity of what she felt, she spoke of less volatile things. "Even on this plain calico dress that Captain DeBeau's maid gave me, it looks wonderful. I like beautiful things, but I haven't much craved them. Martin, these are not just jewels; they're treasures."

"Yes, treasure of *my* heart," he said softly. He glanced at the clock on the fireplace mantel. "Jules and the girls must be starving. We should go out."

Katherine sat on the bed after Martin left her side, thinking. Celié. His sister-in-law. But it was plain to her that this woman wanted much more. And what did Martin want?

"Katherine?"

"Yes."

"Would you believe me when I say I *wanted* to marry you, even if it did seem a foolhardy thing to do, since we don't *know* each other. But I feel that we can think we *know* others for a lifetime and not really know them at all."

"Yes." What else could she say?

She was so quiet on the outside, when inside she was exploding with hurt and anger.

They both smiled as they heard Zell, Singing Bird, and Jules talking and rattling dishes in the dining room.

He stood up and took Katherine's hand, attempting to draw her to her feet, but she resisted him, her heart heavy with what had to be said.

"Martin, what is this woman to you?"

He had been kind, she thought. He could have joined in DeBeau's scheme to bring her here. He could possibly have given her some small, uncertain protection by simply announcing that she was his woman. He didn't have to *marry* her. Then why had he? Especially in light of the lovely creature who had surely come here tonight to lay claim to him.

Looking at her tear-stained, almond-shaped eyes under black silken brows, the nutmeg satin sheen on her face, throat, and upper bosom, her classic bone structure, Martin hurt because he couldn't yet tell her what she needed to know.

He pulled her to her feet, close to him, and attempted to explain. "I cannot talk to you about Celié just now, my love. But I promise you that you will soon know the whole sorry story."

Katherine closed her eyes, not moving. Gripping her shoulders lightly, he turned her face to his, saying simply, "Celié is a part of my past, *querida mia. You* are my present, and I hope you will be my future."

His words couldn't altogether dispel her hurt, but they certainly lifted her spirits.

Martin stood there thinking that he'd seen her three times, once fairly close, then twice more from a distance, until that fateful night he'd married her to keep her safe. But *had* that been the only reason?

Back in the living room, Katherine now noticed the dark blue circular velour sofa and the Victorian furniture, sleek and rounded, with the cream marble-topped tables. The large mahogany grandfather clock stood near the front windows and now struck eight. As they headed for the kitchen, Martin led her to another room.

"But this is wonderful," Katherine exclaimed, "the way the whole house is wonderful."

They had entered a big bathroom with cream tiled lower walls, cream wallpapered upper walls and ceiling, and a dark blue and white tiled floor. A large porcelain tub and lavatory occupied one room. In a much smaller room stood a very large iron, tin-lined tub, of the type used back in the bayou country, and a water closet. Martin flushed the clean water closet, demonstrating proudly, then took her back into the larger room, running the water in the lavatory, then the tub.

Katherine smiled now. She'd wash up for dinner. The towels were sky-blue plush, bath and hand. How Papa Frank and Miss Ada would love this.

"I'll leave you here for a short while," he said, pleased that she seemed happier.

As he began to close the door, Katherine told him, "Martin, it *will* be all right."

"Yes," he answered, sounding grim. "I'm going to *see* that it is." For the generosity of her response regarding Celié, coupled with her sturdy loveliness, might very well prove that what could be called his foolhardiness in marrying her was in truth the wisest thing he'd ever done.

Candelabra and kerosene lamps gave the arched living room and adjoining dining room a bright glow. They sat around the large polished mahogany dining table, festively covered with white damask over padding. China and crystal graced the table. Cape jasmine from the backyard floated in crystal bowls, and silver gleamed.

Katherine couldn't help but wonder: Had Celié once lived here with Martin as more than his sister-in-law? This house definitely had a woman's touch.

Martin seated Katherine at the table as the busy threesome bustled back and forth between the kitchen and the dining room, the girls having guarded fun at the door that swung freely between the two rooms. As they placed the food and before they sat down, Martin threw back the white silk shawl DeBeau's maid had given her and exposed the black pearl necklace on Katherine's bosom. Katherine twisted the diamond ring and the wedding band from the palm side to the top of her finger.

"Oh, Lord!" Zell shrieked, running around the table to hug Katherine. "It's the moon and the stars in the heavens!"

Singing Bird admired the jewels, her eyes sparkling for the first time since they'd begun this journey. Later, she would write Katherine a note. Jules, of course, knew all about the jewels; aware, too, of their happy and sad history.

Of the three women, Zell alone had no qualms about leaving the bayou country. Her family had been one of those wiped out by yellow fever. She was greatly impressed by Martin, by this house, and by New Orleans. Except for the hateful Celié and the brutal white sailors, she had found the trip bearable. Turning mischievously to Martin, Zell flirted. "But you must have a couple of brothers or cousins, Martin?"

Martin froze for a moment, as Zell licked her lips. "I said something wrong, didn't I? I'm sorry."

Martin smiled at her. "You couldn't know. My brother was killed in Santo Domingo some time ago."

Zell looked crestfallen.

"It's no matter," Martin reassured her.

When Zell still didn't smile, Jules went to her and hugged her gently from the side.

"I'm not his brother," he told her, "but I'm his best friend. I'm a pretty good fellow, you'll find. A little old for you . . . but sometimes that's the best match."

Zell looked at Jules as if really seeing him for the first time, then blushed, pink tingeing her yellow-rose face, and ran from the room.

"Now, did I say something wrong?" Jules asked, perplexed.

Katherine shook her head. Zell was excitable, but she was pleased. From the beginning, she had confided that she liked Jules.

"No," Katherine replied, smiling first at him, then at Martin. "I'd say you said something very right."

Katherine, Martin, Jules, and Singing Bird sat down to a done-to-a-turn meal of creamy crayfish bisque and crab-stuffed oysters, with a second course of salad vegetables from the backyard garden, fresh corn on the cob, golden fried catfish, baked white potatoes split open, then topped with chopped chives and grated cheese, green peas, and candied yams, glistening with butter and sugar-cinnamon glaze. Corn pone, rich with eggs and laced with cracklings, made Jules groan with gustatory anticipation.

They were halfway through the meal when a quiet but radiant Zell returned. Throughout the meal she looked primly at the table and never at Jules, who exchanged pleased glances with Martin.

Katherine ate with a voracious appetite. Had food ever tasted so good to her? She blushed thinking of their rough, yet oddly satisfying wedding supper on the ship.

Jules was a ravenous eater, and he mopped up his victuals with gusto, praising the cooks—Zell, Singing Bird, and himself. The girls ate heartily, too, despite having sampled the fare beforehand.

Warmth and camaraderie was palpable at the table as they sipped small glasses of homemade muscadine wine.

"Martin's special touch," Jules told them.

"This is very good," Katherine said. "You're a man of many talents." She had almost added the phrase *my husband,* but looking around at the room that Celié might have furnished, did she really have the right?

Smiling boldly, feeling absolutely among friends, Martin gave her a wicked look. "My little wife," he announced, "in the not so distant future, I'll show you talents beyond your wildest dreams."

Katherine blushed more vividly than had Zell and sputtered into her wine, sending bubbles up her nose. Martin got up quickly and patted her back to make sure she didn't choke.

"I'm fine," she said, "but thank you."

She looked up at him, then, smiling with a radiance beyond any he'd ever seen. He hadn't intended to kiss Katherine so lustfully at that moment, on her full, ripe lips, his tongue gently buzzing hers so that she hesitated for a moment, taken by surprise, then kissed him back, as the three conspirators clapped and cheered.

Martin returned to his chair as Jules and the girls cleared the table and set out dessert—fresh peach cobbler, the crust flaky with sweet cream butter and sprinkled cinnamon, butter-brandy sauce spooned all over, with gobs of fresh whipped vanilla cream.

The three chefs each finished a large helping of their cobbler and took a bit more. Martin and Katherine both dug into theirs with relish, but ate less than half the rich dessert.

Pushing aside the dessert bowls, Jules poured from the jeroboam of vintage champagne into the exquisite, wide-bowled crystal glasses.

It was all anyone could have asked, Katherine thought. She admired and cared about what she had seen and intuited in this man, no matter what happened now. But she also missed Papa Frank and Miss Ada. She was not a prisoner, though, so she would ask Martin to check up on them.

At that moment, Martin would have given her the moon and all the stars he could gather.

"Let us stand in united wedding joy!" Jules thundered, a little tipsy now.

As they all stood up, Jules walked around to Zell and stood looking down at her as she refused to look at him.

"On this, your *real* wedding feast . . ." Jules began.

Martin raised a hand. "Not yet, my friend," he said, his eyes merry. "The real wedding and the real wedding feast are yet to come. What a celebration that will be!"

Katherine looked at him. What had he planned?

They stood drinking champagne, and Martin thought that perhaps in his wisdom God had led him to this woman. Was it true, as Santo Domingans said, that one minute of joy like this paid for years of pain and suffering?

"I am black and comely . . ."

It was incredible, Martin thought, that after such a short time, more and more often he felt that Katherine was as rare as the black pearl that had been his mother's legacy to him.

"Joy, and peace, and love, and passion.
May these be the riches that fill your life."

Jules toasted them, then repeated the words a few at a time
so that Zell and Singing Bird—in mime—could accompany him.
Then all three merrily swarmed around the couple, quietly
singing, with Singing Bird miming the old bayou country song
they had only spoken after the ship ceremony:

> *Ma chère,* On this your wedding day,
>   I wish you love!
> *Mon cher,* On this your wedding day,
>   I wish you joy!
> For him, the first nine months,
>   a dimpled baby girl!
> For her, the second year,
>   a bouncing baby boy!"

This time, they sang it again and again—teasing, laughing,
nudging them on—affirming life itself, as the champagne
flowed in their veins, bringing blessed forgetfulness of pain
and sorrow and their fearful trip here, bringing rich dreams of
what their lives could be.

"Dance! Dance!" the three cried in unison.

And Katherine and Martin danced, gliding on the polished
floors and Persian rugs, the candlelight flickering and the ceiling fans whirring. They danced by the open screened doors
and windows, an impending rain misting the air and drifting
in through the screens.

They danced as one. Katherine felt soft and voluptuous in
his arms, yielding fragrance and yearning. To her he felt solid,
aggressively virile, and wonderfully demanding. Martin
opened the screen door and they danced out onto the screened-
in side porch, then out into the yard by the banked cape jasmine that reminded her of home.

Martin pulled her close and began to kiss her deeply as the

mist swirled around them, his tongue discovering her face, then her tongue, then the satiny brown hollows of her throat.

Dear Lord, if he could take her now, Martin thought, then drew away. She was his wife, and, yes, he had the *right* to possess her, but she couldn't possibly trust him yet. She *would* yield, but he wanted her in the abandoned passion his heart told him she was capable of knowing. And first he had Celié to deal with, and Martin couldn't wait to get started.

He wanted Katherine as he hadn't wanted a woman in a long time. For moments, desire was molten in his blood. But he had sworn to her that first night that he would not press her, and Martin intended to keep that promise.

Katherine couldn't quite fight down the hurt and anxiety that still welled inside her. She had known no man since Albert had died nearly two years ago. True, Martin had said he wouldn't press her, but what if *she* wanted him?

"Let us go in," he urged gently.

"Yes," she agreed. "Let us go in."

The house was silent. Jules and the girls must have turned in for the night, Katherine thought. They had worked so hard for the happiness of their friend and to dim the anxiety of their own uprooting. If need be at any time, she would work as hard for them. Martin went about dousing all but one hall light, then took her hand and walked with her back up the hall. At the door to their bedroom, Katherine paused.

"Will you give me a little while alone before you come in?"

As Martin looked at her lovely face, his eyes became sad. "There is one more aspect I need to tell you, but I must sort it out first. I hope I can finish the whole sorry story tomorrow."

"About you . . . and Celié?"

He caught her hand and squeezed it tightly. "Yes. And I beg your understanding."

"You *have* my understanding, Martin, when you wish to tell

me, but I still ask that you leave me alone for a bit . . . for perhaps fifteen minutes."

Martin's eyes nearly closed. What did she have in mind? He thought he knew and damned himself for not being able to take advantage of this joy.

"Katherine . . ." he began, seeking to dissuade her if she had the passion in mind that sparkled so newly in her eyes.

She placed her slender, soft fingers across his mouth.

"Please, my husband."

He took and kissed her fingers, then her hand.

"Very well," he said, then left.

Katherine went into the bedroom and to the bed, turning over the piece of notepaper and reading as she smiled:

Katherine,
    Remember to pray that Martin stays with us always.
                                                    Sing

Hurriedly, Katherine removed her clothes. The tan and yellow flowered calico dress that DeBeau's maidservant had given her fit well, but it seemed drab now. At DeBeau's house, where she'd been so busy that she hadn't given it a second thought. And even here tonight. The wide canopied bed, covered in shades of pale green, posed a challenge. This room had known a gracious woman's hand. She stood with hunched shoulders against unexpected jealousy.

At the marble-topped table, Katherine quickly sponged her naked body with water from the large white china vessel set out for light baths. Was she beautiful as Papa Frank and others had told her she was? For the first time in her life, she fervently hoped so.

Tingling with excitement, Katherine went to the chest of drawers and opened the same drawer she had looked in earlier when Martin had left her alone, inviting her to explore *her* house. Yes, it was still there. Although she had expected Martin to mention it, he hadn't. Now she'd surprise him with the gown she removed from the drawer and held against her body for the second time.

She had seen few garments as exquisite. The nightgown was of pale green silk. Appliquéd onto the paler silk was a slightly darker green motif—unmistakably flames—encircling the skirt bottom and the bodice. Holding the gown, she raised her hands above her head for a moment, looking into the full-length mirror. Her body was taut, yet flowed in softly pearlized brown curves, her breasts high and lovely. She slipped on the gown, then she opened the door to Martin's light knock.

Seeing her, he stood as still and as outraged as Celié had stood a few hours ago. Katherine saw plainly from his stricken face that something was wrong.

"Where did you get that gown?" he asked softly.

"Why . . . in the bureau drawer," she told him. "I . . . I thought you left it there for me. Didn't you? Oh, Martin, what have I done?"

He took her in his arms as she began to tremble.

"You've done nothing wrong, *querida mia*. But this nightgown belongs to Celié. She must have left it here today." His mouth went grim as he muttered, "So that's why she came here."

"How would *you* know it belongs to Celié?" Katherine demanded.

"Please, sweetheart, put on something else and I will tell you."

Shaken, Katherine picked up her flounced cotton petticoat and a chemise and went behind the mahogany screen. She emerged a little later, chastened. Martin patted the bed beside him, and she sat down.

He laughed mirthlessly. "How do *I* know it's Celié's gown, Katherine? I know because I ordered it made for her—at my brother Raoul's request when I was studying in Madrid. Raoul, you see, was as unfaithful as Celié is provocative. They had quarreled bitterly over his latest infidelity, and for once he was contrite. He sent me a rough sketch of a gown he wanted made up for her, sparing no cost. I did as he asked and sent it to him by ship. Of course, the modiste insisted on showing me her work in detail. . . ."

"It is a beautiful gown, Martin. I'm happy that you told me what you did. It eases my heart."

"Katherine," he spoke softly, "know always that I'd never intentionally hurt you, but it seems now that there'll be times when you *will* be hurt, and I can do little to stop it. I cannot tell you how sorry I am."

"I believe you," Katherine said heavily.

Martin laughed. "I could protect you from DeBeau's roughneck thugs but not from my own wretched affair with Celié."

Katherine stiffened but asked, as gently as she could, "Can you talk about it at all?" And she thought about how she had felt such confidence with Guy DeBeau. Now, with this man who drew her so, whose presence filled her with desire and whose love she now wanted, she felt very nearly helpless.

He stood up and began to pace slowly. After a few minutes Martin stood before her, plainly full of anguish. She looked at him, daring to lend what support she could.

"I want to begin with Santo Domingo," he said. "My beautiful green island with the mountains and beaches I grew up loving . . ."

He stopped pacing and paused a long time, remembering, as he stood before her.

"My father was a rich landowner and a sea captain, but at an early age he grew tired of constantly sailing. He and DeBeau were old friends, although DeBeau was a pirate then. He had a proper wife, plain but as wealthy and privileged as he was. He was also a notorious womanizer, and although I loved him, I swore never to be like him in that way.

"My mother became his mistress and was said to be the most beautiful woman of color on the island. I will show you her picture when I can bear to look at it again. And I cannot talk about the death of my mother, who was named Annalise, or my brother, Raoul."

Martin sat beside her on the bed and took her hand in his.

"So, we were the bastard sons of Pablo Dominguez, who freely gave us material wealth, earning him the hatred of his wife."

Bothered by Martin's troubled face, Katherine placed her hand on his knee and spoke quietly. "You don't have to tell me any of this until you want to. You are no bastard, but simply the son of two unmarried people who—*did* they love each other?"

Martin answered immediately. *"She* certainly loved *him.* . . ." He broke off, then said after a moment, "Lord, it is difficult to begin to talk about Celié and me. . . ."

A sense of unaccustomed ruthlessness filled her where this woman was concerned. Some powerful intuition told her that danger lay here.

"Do you still love her?" Katherine asked bluntly. It certainly seemed plain to her that he once had.

"No." His answer seemed forthright. "Once I loved her as I thought I could never love anyone else. She was seventeen and I was eighteen, and home on vacation from my apprenticeship in Madrid. It was summer"—he paused and smiled sadly—"as it is summer now." He looked at Katherine as she gently encouraged him to continue.

"We knew each other but only became lovers that summer. She wanted to get married. I wanted to go back to finish my apprenticeship.

"As much as I loved her, I could see how much she and my brother were attracted to each other and I was jealous. I truthfully told her I would marry her if she would wait until I finished my apprenticeship in a year. I reluctantly intended to give up my plans to stay in Spain to also study art and literature at the university. She refused to wait. She said she hated me and would find someone else. I returned to Spain, and in September of that same year, she married Raoul."

"You must have been terribly hurt."

Martin shook his head. "No. By that time and being away

from her, I could better see her shallowness, her selfishness. . . . But no, I forget, for truthfully for several years after that, she was like a *drug* to me.

"From the beginning, she and Raoul had a stormy marriage. As I told you, Raoul was our father's son."

He paused. "I'm not altogether sure why it is, but I'm grateful that I found you. You asked if my father loved my mother and I told you a bit about them. All the big island landowners—the whites and, after freedom, a few people of color—were wealthy. My mother should have had the world. What she got was a good deal of money to support us and two jewels said to be incomparable—the black pearl from India, and the diamond ring. He *did* take care of us financially, but there was still his wife . . . and other women. My mother loved him and she often cried, while my heart would nearly break. Raoul looked like him . . . *was* like our father. She adored Raoul, of course."

"Was your mother jealous, then, of Celié as Raoul's wife?"

He laughed shortly. "An *understatement*. My mother *hated* Celié, even when I courted her." He paused a long time. "Then Raoul took over Celié's heart. She worshiped him at first as my mother worshiped him."

That had been then, Katherine thought. "But now, this woman wants you for herself. You know that, don't you?"

Very slowly, he answered. "I'm no longer certain what it is Celié wants. Long ago I realized that Celié's heart did not match the beauty of her face."

"Yes, she is beautiful."

"You are beautiful."

Katherine blushed, pleased that he found her so.

"But I do not possess that kind of beauty," she protested.

"Katherine," he told her, cupping her face in his hands, "I find the language of the Bible wondrous, and so I read it for the language as much as for the comfort and wisdom I find there. Solomon's 'Song of Songs' is one of my favorites. You're the only woman ever to bring to my mind 'I am black but comely.' I changed that to 'I am black *and* comely' the first time I saw you . . . gathering herbs with your friends and your grandfather. Does my telling you that mean anything to you?"

She had read the "Song of Songs" often, reveling, too, in its lyrical evocation of love. Katherine sat silent, close to him, looking into his eyes that seemed to hold nothing back.

"Yes," she said simply, "it tells me a lot."

Martin stroked her forearm. "Then I'm glad." He sighed. "I'll sleep in another room, because I want to make love to you in a way that drives me crazy. . . ." He broke off, then continued. "But I also want no shadows between us. Give me a little time. . . . I'll leave you now. I'll be in the room next to this one if you need me.

"Oh, yes, think about it and tell me the soonest day you could marry me in a formal ceremony. I frequently attend services near here, and the minister will perform the ceremony. But the church is too small to hold all the guests. Are you too tired to talk about a wedding . . . ours?"

Katherine ran her tongue over her bottom lip as if tasting honey.

"I have dreamed," she began slowly, "of weddings at sunrise. I used to dream of such a ceremony after I'd dreamed of you. Martin, how could I have dreamed of you before I even knew you?"

"I don't know," he said, "but I'm glad you did. A sunrise wedding is what we'll have if you want it. The minister is very busy on weekends saving souls and taking care of rural churches. What day of the week would you prefer?"

"Monday, I think. I was born on a Monday. Would that be all right with you?"

"It will be on a Monday as you wish." Then he teased, *"Next* Monday?" which was only four days away.

"We could do that."

But suddenly Martin looked somber. "Three weeks," he declared, "should give me time to at least *begin* putting my life in the order a woman like you deserves to come into."

She did not want him to leave her. The champagne and the nearness of his smoothly muscled bronzed body stirred her senses. His tenderness moved her even more. "Take all the time you need," she told him. "I can wait. But I think I trust you enough not to need to wait for . . . consummation."

Katherine blushed furiously and felt overcome with shyness at her attempts to reassure him. After all, he was her husband, and wasn't that her wifely duty? She didn't need to think of duty where he was concerned. She mocked her modesty. Her heart expanded, firmly tamping down caution, swaying on the verge of some glorious adventure of the mind and the spirit, not to mention her soft, tremulous body.

"Woman, don't press me," he said, moaning in his throat. "I *want* to wait, and I will wait until I at least set out the terms for coming to you unfettered by what lay between Celié and me. It is only five days, but please don't ask me to take you back home when Guy is well as I promised you I would on the ship that first night."

Unsmiling, she told him, "But this *is* my home, as you *are* my husband."

"And you are my wife."

He crushed her to him, feeling her heart pound against his, realizing the desire he had felt with Celié was a young man's yearning. The fires that lay banked between him and this woman were far deeper.

Something in each of them drew the other in a way that had fascinated him from the beginning. It was too soon, he thought, for either of them to know heart or mind. But he found that it filled him with pleasure to be with her.

"Good night," he said, bending to kiss her. And with that, Martin left swiftly, closing the door gently.

Katherine lay awake for a long time, the scent of cape jasmine from the yard reminding her of dreams of Martin. For the moment, she did not miss Papa Frank or the bayou country. She blocked Celié's presence, too. She was *with* the man of her dreams, but he was hers, in name anyway. As sleep closed in, Katherine vowed to make him love her.

In bed that night Martin tossed, unable to sleep. He had rushed in again, he told himself, proposing a lavish wedding. Well, why not? He regarded the simple ship ceremony as binding, but Katherine deserved far better than that.

It hovered around the corners of his mind that he simply had not been this interested in a woman . . . since Celié. And he had been a young man then, unseasoned. Had any part of him warned him about Celié, he would not have listened.

Now he thought he knew his own mind. Even if the mutual attraction didn't deepen into genuine love, they somehow fit each other. Martin knew now that he wanted to be married, to be settled, as much as he wanted Katherine.

He'd give it his best shot, and if it didn't develop richly or didn't last . . . well, what in his life had lasted long except for the faith in himself that his mother, Annalise, had engendered?

Six

By the time Martin took them through the three-acre back-yard of their house, bordered by evergreens and blooming vari-colored azaleas, Katherine felt far more relaxed. Land was at a premium close in, but out here there were many small farms with vegetable gardens and patches of sweet corn.

Near the back of the house was a magnolia forest, with fifty or more trees in full bloom. Bramblebushes and square-wire fencing covered with roses ringed the sides and the back of the property. Across the front was one of Martin's tall lily-patterned iron fences that matched the pattern of the gates and the iron paneling at the front of the house.

Near the magnolia forest was a good-sized pond, with pink, orange, and yellow water lilies growing in the clear water. A pair of ducks parented their new brood through each season, and a range of poinsettia bushes, which Martin had brought back from Santo Domingo, grew nearby.

Toward the right of the magnolia forest stood the stables that sheltered Helio and Patchette, their sleek carriage horses, a pair of Cleveland bays. The carriage house held a two-horse, four-seater carriage with black horsehair-covered seats. There was also a buggy for ordinary runs about the city, and a buck-board that Martin used to go about the countryside and to work.

Rain misted still, with heavier rain forecast for the rest of the day. Katherine had slept soundly through the night, al-though she had longed to lie close to Martin's body. Up early, the chef-threesome had cooked again, and after breakfast they'd all gone to the large greenhouse in the left-hand corner of the backyard.

Entering, Katherine immediately noticed the fragrant plantings of arnica, mint, and dark opal basil. All three herbs would be useful. She would also plant bay, cloves, lavender, and lemon balm for bathing and sachets. Tonic herbs. Soothing herbs. Stimulating herbs. She'd plant them all as she had in the bayou country.

"You seem happier," Martin told her. "Am I the cause of this?"

Katherine nodded. "You are." Mindful of the way she desired to be in his arms, she chose a safe subject. "But I'm also admiring your herbs and thinking of the ones I'll plant for us. Soon the arnica and the basil will bloom. Did you plant them?"

"Yes. I think I told you my mother was fond of herbs, grew them, and knew a lot about them. That's one thing you'll like about New Orleans. Herbs are very popular here. I think nearly everybody on this block has a little garden of herbs. And today, I'll take you to Madame Le Blanc's salon to choose a wardrobe for yourself."

There were three long tables set up, with wooden benches flanking the sides of each one. Katherine asked about them.

"Jules and I tutor others who want to learn to read and write," Martin said. "We are a much *maligned* race, as you know, but then I've found that all people are maligned by someone who finds it to their own advantage. Since we have the appointed legislature, so many would try to see that that right is taken away. Our people need to *know* the laws in order to be protected by them."

Katherine looked quickly at his earnest face. "I'll help you," she promised. "Zell and Singing Bird and I have all had the advantage of some training that not every person of color has. At the plantation big house, I haunted the library every chance I got, much to the young mistresses' annoyance. But I *learned.*

Singing Bird writes well. . . . Oh, Martin, I would not have believed that all this could happen to me . . . that *you* could happen to me."

Martin teased her. "But you told me you dreamed of my coming even before we saw each other . . . and you are angry at our taking you away."

"Yes, I am angry at being kidnapped, but please don't laugh at me. I *did* dream of you."

"I'd never laugh at you, Katherine. Don't you know that? I laugh only with the pleasure you bring me. One day I hope you'll be less angry . . . that you'll forgive me."

"It was hardly your fault," Katherine said. "You *saved* me, and for that I'm grateful. I would be lying if I said I'm not angry at DeBeau, but he brought us together, Martin. What we have is far from perfect, but perhaps it can work."

The pressure of his hand holding hers was strong. "We'll *make* it work," he told her.

Zell, Singing Bird, and Jules came up from the back of the greenhouse to say they were going to the far side of the yard to examine the azaleas. The girls were bareheaded as they went out in the mist.

Katherine turned to Martin. "I will need to check on Guy DeBeau tomorrow or the next day. Can you imagine how it makes me feel to be able to help him? But I'm always afraid that some new yellow fever siege will begin before I can build him up properly."

"I'm as happy as you are about Guy," Martin declared. "It's cooler this summer, so perhaps the black bile won't hit us. Cleaning the sewers has helped prevent this plague more than anybody thought it would."

"Papa Frank has such strong beliefs on preventing, as well as treating, yellow fever and stopping what he calls 'that useless murder we invite.' He talks of the yellow fever epidemics that destroy us again and again. He has always said that we must study the ones who *live*. Learn their secret. Please help me do this."

Martin nodded. "Gladly."

Tears misted her eyes as she thought of Papa Frank. "I wonder if I'll ever see him again," Katherine murmured.

"I'll see that you do," he assured her, then smiled. "But only if you promise to stay with me."

Impulsively, she flung her soft, warm arms around him and hugged him tightly as he held her without pressing her body to his. With the shadow of Celié hanging over them, Martin felt he shouldn't try to claim her body.

Perhaps he still loved Celié and didn't know it. Unlike Martin, Katherine had not known the pain of betrayal, but she was no stranger to the terrible pain of loss. Grandmama. Albert. Her miscarriage. And her mother.

"Try to get rid of me," she told him. "You'll find I may not let *you* go."

Katherine found the trip from their house on Gentilly Way, on the outskirts of town, into the French Quarter fascinating. This time, she could enjoy it without fear, unlike her initial journey to DeBeau's house. In the light rain, they passed a section of unpainted shanties; other sections of both beautiful, gutted, and freshly rebuilt mansions; cottages in similar condition; and closer to the French Quarter, a remembered mix of architecture.

A relatively short distance from the French Quarter small bands of ragged children—white, people of color, and Indian—huddled in doorways. Their little faces registered helplessness, hopelessness, and the despair that was at least their temporary lot.

Katherine cried out, "Martin, who are these children? Where do they come from?" She had not seen their likes in the bayou country.

Martin sighed deeply. "Some call them *guttersnipes*. Among others, they are considered the city's expendables. Jules and I and others are doing what we can to help more of them. We have managed to help some."

"Shouldn't we stop and give them something . . . a few coins? Don't you have a few? Of course, I don't."

Martin shook his head. "Even at this hour, it wouldn't be wise. This area is little guarded or cared about by police. These children must live by their wits, and they would not hesitate to rob you if they took a notion. We stop and help them, give them money and food when in groups of men. Now that the state legislature is nearly half black and we have seven state senators, we can change much that we couldn't change before."

One small boy darted near the carriage, in pursuit of another small boy, yelling, "I'm gonna get you, yes."

Martin smiled but felt his heart constrict as it did every time he saw this miserable band of humanity. Public schools were to be open now in New Orleans, thanks to McDonogh's generous will, but these children had slipped through cracks that would not close to protect their descent.

Zell and Singing Bird cried unashamedly in the buggy's driver's seat with Jules, who drove. Grimly, Jules told them, "It will get better, little ladies, and you both can help us help them."

They passed DeBeau's house, set far back from the street. Both Katherine and Martin glanced at it but said nothing. They would go there tomorrow. Katherine suspected that if Guy didn't continue to improve, they'd hear his father bellowing all the way over to their house.

It was Katherine's fourth day in New Orleans, and she realized that while she missed Papa Frank terribly, she hardly missed the bayou country at all.

Madame Lillian Le Blanc's dressmaker salon was nestled snugly on the ground floor of newly constructed apartments. She greeted them effusively, evidently having awaited their arrival. Opening the door, she chirped, "Oh, Martin, my dear, your wife is beautiful!"

Martin swept the plump, white-haired woman off her feet, hugged her tightly, then presented her to Katherine, who offered her hand. She admired Madame's still-slender waist and her corseted hourglass hips. She liked this older, sparkling woman with the fresh clove-hued skin and effervescent manner.

Madame Lillian would have no formality. She clasped Katherine to her ample bosom and hugged her tightly, then stepped back to look at her more closely. "Ah, you will turn even more heads when I am finished," she predicted. Releasing Katherine, as she patted her arm, she turned to Jules and the girls.

"You are quiet today, my friend. And why don't you and Martin introduce me to these two charming girls?"

Jules grinned, introducing Zell and Singing Bird. Zell curtsied to the older woman, who seemed charmed and laughed. Singing Bird smiled warily as Katherine selected her words carefully. "She does not . . . choose . . . to talk at this time."

Madame Le Blanc was silent for a moment before she appeared to understand. "Of course," she declared evenly. "Of course." She gazed at the girl for a long moment, then touched Singing Bird's face softly. "At whatever time you wish, my dear . . ." Full of compassion, her voice trailed off.

Looking around as Madame seated them, Katherine responded to the salon that was done in mauve, rose, and wine, with heavily draped windows for privacy.

"When you sent word that you wanted garments for the three ladies, I arranged to close my shop to others when you came," she said. "So please relax and enjoy yourself as my guests. Fortunately, I have many already-finished clothes, and not one of these ladies is a difficult size. I will need measurements. Many measurements."

Madame pulled up a small, plush mauve footstool and sat opposite Katherine, studying her intently. Somehow Katherine felt comfortable beneath her scrutiny. Finally, Madame leaned back and, with her eyes half closed, spoke to Martin.

"Of course, I could not possibly do what you wish until I saw your young queen. . . ." Glancing at the other two girls, she continued. "I do not leave you out, my dears, since I regard each woman as a queen in her own right. But you will forgive me for saying that here I have an axe to grind, as they say. Martin, what joy you bring me with Katherine's coming. Her very presence will settle old scores I had despaired of settling."

Martin smiled a bit, his eyes resting proudly on his wife, but he spoke seriously. "It is not your way to reach for revenge, Madame. You are too grand a woman. I'm sure it's Celié you speak of. There is an old Santo Domingan proverb: *Live well and drive your enemies to distraction.*"

Madame nodded. "This is true, but then you are not an old woman who is often reminded by a bitter rival that her time is past." Madame sighed. "Now *she* designs and sews for the *governor's wife*, no less, and there is no containing her. She floats above ground, never walking. And what a pity the way she treats her helpers, who she works like her slaves." Madame pursed her lips, retaining her air of goodwill and gaiety. "Yet, she has the good sense to pay them very well. Otherwise, they'd leave."

They all listened quietly to Madame's lovely voice, which was surprisingly youthful and lyrical.

"I wonder," she mused, "if the governor's wife feels in need of the magic Celié is said to be so adept at invoking through her cohort, Dahomey Sinclair?" She looked at Katherine, Zell, and Singing Bird. "Forgive me, as I've said before, but I must indulge my passion for *petit* gossip; nothing *grande*, which would be a sin. But *mon Dieu*, that *woman* . . . They say here in the French Quarter, even the whites: 'Do you need to inflict a wasp's sting to punish or a viper's fang to do worse, then send for Madame Dominguez . . . who will send for Dahomey Sinclair. . . . What is it, my dear? Do I frighten you? Fiddle! As far as I'm concerned, Celié is without special power, except with the governor's wife. . . . But then I suppose that's quite a bit nowadays."

Katherine straightened, a chill going up her spine. "You make her sound so . . . ominous," she said. "Threatening." In truth, Madame's word had reawakened the fear she'd felt last night at Celié's open wrath. And yes, she and Celié were *both* Mrs. Dominguez.

Madame took her hand. "I am betting on you, Katherine. Whatever Celié believes her power to be, I feel that yours will be stronger."

"Well put, Madame," Martin acknowledged, his face solemn. "My wife has the strength of honor and honesty. Whatever wretched powers Celié now feels she wields through Dahomey Sinclair and others will not give her what she hopes for." Then he added, almost to himself, "And who knows what she hopes for?"

"Well, she is *passe pour blanc,*" Madame said. Katherine was familiar with the term, also used in the bayou country for a person of color who could pass for white.

"Were Celié a young, unmarried woman, she would have her fortune made as the mistress of some Creole. Although I don't think that is what she has in mind."

Brightening, Madame spoke in a dreamy voice. "Oh, Martin, the gown I wish to create for your bride is coming to me clearly. Yes, it is truly beautiful." Her small, plump hands described patterns, shapes, motifs. "I will take the measurements today and begin to sketch. . . ."

"Madame, you wish me to bring refreshments now, no?"

A young and well-spoken girl of about twelve, saffron-skinned and brown-haired, pushed a cart upon which sat a silver coffee service and small china plates surrounded by petit fours, small sandwiches, cut fresh vegetables, and a large chocolate cake.

Jules groaned. "You know how I love your food, Madame, but we're not too long from breakfast."

Happily getting up to serve the victuals, Madame said, "You may be hungry enough by the time you leave. There is much to be done. Monique, please say hello to my friends."

The young girl who had brought in the food looked up like a frightened rabbit and her lips trembled. Poised under certain circumstances, she crumbled at interaction with strangers like these ladies. Madame Le Blanc bent and hugged her. "It is all right, *ma chère*. They will not hurt you."

The young girl curtsied and retreated swiftly. Watching the child go, Madame asked the two men, "Will she get over the nightmares she has endured? I don't know. I only thank God that you brought her here, Martin. Really, she is fairly well most of the time, and so helpful to me. She knows you both and thanks you both—but she *says* it only to me." Madame looked thoughtful. "She has a brother, Pierre, who fared no better. Pierre!" she called.

Martin turned to Katherine, explaining, "Monique and Pierre, a year ago, were two of the children we passed on the way here. She was being torn away from the group and beaten by a man who meant to take her with him. Her little friends told us that she was weak from illness and couldn't defend herself. We gave the man a thrashing and brought her here. She told us about her brother, and Madame took him under her wing."

"Yes, Madame. You called me, no?"

"Yes, my dear. These people are my guests." Turning to them, she announced, "And this is Pierre."

She introduced each guest and Pierre shook their hands, lingering longest over Katherine's. Katherine looked at the black cap of rough curls and the coffee-brown eight-year-old face, the eyes that had seen too much sorrow far too early. He seemed to have forgotten how to laugh.

"Pierre. Monique," Katherine said. "Those are such charming names."

The boy's face relaxed a little. Swallowing, he looked at Madame.

"Yes, love, you may go if you wish, and please see that Monique eats a good lunch, even if you *are* the younger."

"I'm glad no further harm came to Monique and that you

could help Pierre," Katherine noted. "She is a pretty child. Pierre seems so sturdy and self-reliant."

"A joy to my life, both of them," Madame declared.

They sampled the food, focusing on small slices of the chocolate-raspberry jam cake with its luscious butter-rich frosting. Still glancing around the shop, Katherine was pleased to see pots of herbs growing in the windows and remarked about it.

"Why, yes, they're a good part of my trade," Madame informed her. "A woman far out from town grows them for me to sell. I package them for bathing, for relaxation, for teas. I know little about herbs other than that, and I can depend on you to teach me, no?"

Katherine smiled. She found the French-speaking custom of asking yes or no at the end of a sentence, very like their bayou country neighbors' patois.

"Those look very healthy. My grandfather and my mother taught me a great deal about herbs. I would be happy to tell you whatever you wish to know about them . . . that *I* know, of course."

Madame laughed. "Apparently, you know a great deal about herbs, my girl. I've heard a lot about how you brought Captain DeBeau's son Guy back from the river's edge."

She laughed at Katherine's surprise. "This is the *petit* gossip that we swear by," she said. "The captain has many friends in very high places. *Big bugs,* we call them. His doctor is also the governor's doctor, and a better man than most. I would say, my dear, that you have made an outstanding beginning. That, and your genuine beauty, may take you further than I suspect you wish to go."

Warmth suffused Katherine at Madame's words. Indeed, she wished to go little, if any, farther than she was now.

"Ah, yes, treat Madame Rattlesnake with care, and your life should be a really good one," Madame said now.

Martin frowned. "I would never underestimate Celié's malevolence," he cautioned, "but it was she who so quickly got us the herbs that Katherine needed to bring Guy, as you put it, back from the river's edge. She *has* done and she can do good things as well."

Was he defending Celié, Katherine wondered, or merely being fair?

"Ah, yes, you can be kind since you've given her the mitten. . . ." Katherine smiled, referring to Martin's rejection of Celié.

At a knock on the side door, Madame Le Blanc got up and looked out the window. In a lowered voice, she told them, "When one speaks of the devil . . . it is the poor wretch who works for Celié."

She flung the door open, and a wizened, pale brown man with the haughty bearing of Celié walked in. Without pausing, he went straight to Martin, ignoring the others as Celié had done the previous night.

"Mr. Martin," he began, "Miss Celié see you pass and she say she *must* see you right now."

Not moving, Martin gave him a long and level look, as did Jules. The old man felt in mild panic, except that the eyes of this new woman were compassionate, as if she knew about and sympathized with his discomfort.

Clearing his throat, he sputtered, "She say . . . she say if you don't come to her, she'll come to you . . . right here!"

With this the old man turned and fled, closing the door softly behind him.

Martin looked at Katherine, unwilling to ask her forbearance any further. How much could he hope for her to understand? Katherine met his eyes squarely and placed her slender hand over his, squeezing it.

"Celié and I are linked in ways I wish we weren't," he explained.

"Go to her, of course, love. We will wait for you here."

"Thank you, *corazón,*" he whispered. Rising slowly, he pulled her to her feet and kissed her long and thoroughly.

Then he turned to the others. "Of course, I embarrass you with this public display of affection. Please forgive me."

Impishly, Madame Le Blanc winked and applauded. "Return very soon, Martin, and give us more of this performance. I am an old lover of love, and I am too long a widow."

Without skipping a beat, after Martin departed Madame informed the three women that she would begin taking their measurements. Jules said he would walk around the French Quarter, perhaps amble over to Celié's modiste establishment. Madame nodded.

"Bring your tea along and whatever else you wish. *Mon Dieu,* isn't this cake sinfully delicious? Each ounce I eat falls in love with me and refuses to leave." She patted her ample hips.

"Don't worry, *ma chère,*" she told Katherine after she'd had them take off their dresses, seating Zell and Singing Bird as she began to take Katherine's measurements. *"M'sieu* Dominguez is a wise man beyond his years, even as you are wise beyond yours. He will somehow dissuade Celié from her madness. To give credit where it is due, she is so beautiful she could have her pick of men. She is not as young as you, but she is far from old. She runs a successful business and has enviable political connections now that she fits the governor's wife. But she is impassioned by *one* star. . . ."

"Martin," Katherine said firmly.

"Yes. Well, I must have at least six weeks to bring the dream in my head to life. *Mon Dieu,* it will be a wedding gown that all New Orleans will talk about. Lace and gossamer satin. Heavy satin and seed pearls." She spoke aloud, but it was mostly to herself that she spoke.

And in spite of Celié, Katherine held to her happiness, dreaming along with Madame, this delightful woman. But six weeks? She'd hoped they could be married in a shorter time.

Laying her measurement book aside, Madame led them to the drawers of underwear, where they selected cotton, fine linen, and silk petticoats, chemises, camisoles, and bloomers.

Zell wanted a crinoline. Katherine said she didn't care for them. Horrible stories were being circulated about the huge, stiff underskirts getting caught in coach and wagon wheels. Singing Bird wrote that she didn't like them, either.

The women found Madame Le Blanc's dresses beautiful. From the homely cotton calico to linen to pongee and other silks, they were finely made, the colors ravishing. There were bonnets and shoes and shawls and parasols. Each woman chose, selectively and sparingly, what she thought best suited her.

"He will bring you back for more," Madame predicted, "but you are right to begin in a small way. Martin is generous. You have a man you are wise enough to treasure, as he must treasure you. That is the essence of happiness."

Madame almost skipped about the shop now, her movements belying her age. "And, oh yes, I have exquisite silk organdy bags of herbs and roots for bathing. Scented oils. Cinnamon. Sandalwood. Lavender. I, myself, do not like the mixtures very much. Each scent is so special in itself. You probably know about them all, Katherine."

"Yes," Katherine answered, "many of them." She was glad to discuss her beloved herbs.

Martin paused at the side door of Celié's salon, which was the entrance to both the shop and the apartment she owned. Celié met him there.

"You were wise to come," she greeted him openly, then locked the door behind him. "I have left the shop with my assistant, so we have time. Shall we go into the living room?"

Angry at having had his shopping expedition with Katherine and the others interrupted, Martin answered her sharply. "The living room is as good a place as any. I have little time."

Celié's apartment was lavishly decorated in pale green, and in her own emerald garments she had outdone herself to be alluring.

"Please sit down. I'll get you coffee. I have sent my maid to help my assistant with the shop," she informed him with a coquettish glance.

"What is it you find so necessary to discuss that you would disturb a shopping trip with my wife and friends?"

"You did not come this morning as I requested of you last night," she began.

"Don't be absurd, Celié. I don't answer your commands."

Her anger flared. "How dare you bring this ignorant former slave baggage of a woman into our lives?" she flung at him.

Martin held up his hand in warning. "No more of this damnable nonsense, Celié. My wife Katherine is beautiful, as even *you* can plainly see. And she is more intelligent and learned than you could imagine. And yes, she has a beautiful heart *and* soul as well. Far more than I can say for you, my sister-in-law."

Martin had no real wish to hurt Celié, but he intended to keep her from hurting Katherine's feelings and he wanted her out of his life. Still, a part of him remembered every outline of her slim body against his own. You don't forget the fire that burned you.

But Celié was not to be discouraged. "I was once much more to you than a sister-in-law, Martin," she said slyly. "You were my first love, as I was yours."

Martin looked at her steadily. "I'll never deny that I loved you, but you chose Raoul, my brother."

She moved closer to him, wetting her lips. "You once cared for me, Martin—a great deal. *We* came *before* Raoul and me. You've become a man of substance. When you brought me here, I said nothing because I knew I had hurt you, and you needed time to get over it. But I've worked hard to be worthy of you. I am now the modiste for the governor's wife, and she is fond of me. Martin, I waited for you in this country—first in your house, then here. As you know, I own this property and will soon own a house in the country. Now I must speak of *us.*"

In honeyed cadence, she begged, "Put this country woman aside. As a man of color, this will be easy for you to do. Marry me. Think of the riches, the power we could know together. The passion we once knew and can know again. My business is thriving. . . . I should not have waited so long to talk of this."

Martin looked at her levelly. "You did *not* wait for me on Santo Domingo. What I have now with Katherine is based on *trust* and caring that you wouldn't understand."

He saw from her expression that she would never comprehend the way she had hurt him.

"You are still jealous that I married Raoul," she cried, "but you are wrong. Even married to him, I longed for you, and there were many women for him. For me, it was always you."

"That is a lie, Celié. Even when we were lovers, you and Raoul flirted and sought each other out. You bragged to me about his prowess as a lover. . . ."

"I was a fool and I'm sorry," she sobbed.

She threw her arms around his neck, but Martin disengaged her embrace none too gently. Even though it had lessened somewhat, her power to stir him was still there. And it angered him. She rubbed her wrists as she spoke. "I have been in this country now for three years. I knew how hurt you were at your mother and Raoul's death, so I have waited patiently for you to heal."

"That is not only in the past, Celié. I am *still* hurt by that carnage."

"I would have given my life to prevent it."

Martin looked at her coldly. "I have always wondered about that," he said.

Alarmed, she asked him, "What do you mean?"

"I think you know what I mean. We might have married, but it had to be at *your* bidding, in *your* time. You came into my family through marriage to my brother, and by custom I honor that, as I promised Raoul I would. But what happened in Santo Domingo with my family's death concerned Captain

DeBeau, too. His oldest son died there along with Raoul and my mother. I think you well know that DeBeau can be an adversary the devil himself would consider twice before betraying. Think about it, my *brother's wife*—and carefully."

"Oh, Martin, have I lost you?" she wailed.

"After you married Raoul, I was never again yours to lose, Celié."

"You married this Katherine to hurt me, as I hurt you."

Was what she said true? he wondered suddenly, frowning. Katherine's presence came between them, the French lavender scent of her skin and hair, her yielding softness.

"Martin . . ." Celié said fretfully.

What had she wanted with him? He swore to himself he'd sort this out more carefully, and come back *very* soon and end this impossible situation.

"I will return to my wife, Jules, and our friends," he announced, turning to go.

"Jules, yes, is your friend. But the others? What on earth possesses you? I am more friend to you, more love to you than even Jules . . . than anyone else can be."

"What you say was once true enough," he affirmed. "But my love for you ended when you married Raoul." Saying it, he knew it was less than true. His love for her had *haunted* him for so many years.

He waited for Celié to accuse him of the *accident* that summer. His guilt over that was worse than her betrayal. He held himself tautly, but she didn't speak of it.

Instead, Celié wet her lips again before she spoke. "And what about the black pearl, Martin?" she asked. "By rights you know that as the firstborn's, Raoul's, wife, I should have inherited it, along with the ring."

Martin couldn't believe the audacity of this woman. "My mother left verbal and written statements that under no condition were you to have the black pearl or the ring. And no law would help you to get it.

"The black pearl is Katherine's," he stated firmly, barely

containing his anger. "I knew that when I first saw her. They enhance the beauty of each other. Celié, be careful that you do not manage to harm only yourself in the end."

When she was silent, her expression unreadable, he broached another subject. "You seemed shocked when I introduced you to Katherine. You must have known about her, that she was my wife. How could you not know in this city?"

Quite sadly, Celié replied, "Yes, I knew. The man who brought the herbs to DeBeau's house told me on his return. He learned about your . . . about it from the cook. I was surprised, though, and I—I cannot say why."

But Celié knew very well why she had looked shocked and stricken. Expecting a country bumpkin rival she could easily best, she had instead faced Katherine, who radiated love and soft confidence, which added to her natural beauty, and Celié had known that winning Martin again would be no easy task.

Relieved to have spoken his mind, Martin turned and left. As he walked along the street in the muggy, warm air, a brisk breeze came in from the Mississippi River. Steamboats whistled hoarsely, pulling into and away from the docks that were only twelve blocks away. He smiled at the thought of rejoining Katherine and the others. Madame Le Blanc would have made good use of his brief time away.

Celié stood at the window watching Martin's tall, lithe body walk up the street and back to Katherine. She and Martin still belonged together even if he didn't yet realize it. She should have spoken her love to him sooner, but she had been busy gathering her dowry, letting him forget the past. Now she schemed on ways to insure what was merely a *return* to her arms.

"Oh, my dear," she said to herself. "You would never know what a wonderful lover you were then and will be for me again. I promise you."

His brother, Raoul, had sought her, and she had pressed him

when Martin wanted to wait to finish his apprenticeship before they married.

Celié had had the good sense to withhold her treasures from Raoul until he begged her to marry him. Annalise, his mother, had been furious.

"At least," Annalise had said scathingly, "you and Raoul will not hurt each other too badly. I was afraid for Martin, my son who is tender and strong the way men should be, but seldom are. You and Raoul will destroy each other—if your marriage lasts that long."

And Celié and Raoul *had* savaged each other emotionally, but both were far too selfish, too resilient, to cave in.

Celié smiled, malice touching the corners of her mouth. She had deliberately refrained from mentioning the *accident* when she and Martin had quarreled today. But sensitive as he was, he would think of it always. He had been driving the cabriolet, and she'd taunted him about the passion between Raoul and her. Men were so *vain* about their sexual prowess. Was that her fault? He would be back, she told herself. She'd seen a spark of the old flames that had lain between them. She should have *waited* for Martin, and Celié swore now that this time she would not give him up.

In her bedroom, Celié thoughtfully penned a note on her distinctive green linen stationery, slipped it into a matching envelope, and simply put the initials D.S. on its face. Calling Mims, the old man who worked for her, she gave him the envelope.

"Take this to Dahomey Sinclair . . . and quickly. Find him if you have to scour the city, and tell him I must talk with him as soon as possible. And do not waste my time in doing this."

Everyone she had ever been able to get to help her in this city had proved unreliable. Martin had brought her here after the slaves were freed. During slavery, a few wealthy people of color had owned slaves and she had wished for that, feeling she needed at least one. She had spoken to Martin about this and had thought he'd strike her. She'd never mentioned it again. Celié smiled bitterly. Raoul would have seen it as she did.

Going to the window again, she watched the old man who worked for her shuffle up the street. He would first go to Congo Square, which was by day unprepossessing, by night throbbing with magic and drums, magic and spells. Desperately, she hoped that the short journey on which she had sent the old man would serve to bring a willing Martin back to her arms.

In the early afternoon, Martin brought the group back home. In spite of Celié, the trip had left them all in a happy mood, with many packages beyond their first choosing. Martin had insisted on additional purchases.

"Madame Le Blanc," he had explained on the way home, "is one of the social powers for people of color. She truly loves people and does everything she can to help others. She loves parties and balls and is, I think, on some committee for them all." To Katherine, he said, "She's quite smitten with you, you know."

"The feeling," Katherine told him, "is mutual. Her wonderful spirit lifts everything around her. Martin, in terms of color, what are we?" She blushed. "What am *I*?"

"What are we *called*?" he asked her.

"Yes. Madame talked about Celié's being *passe pour blanc*, as Papa Frank is."

Martin laughed. "We're all *gens de couleur*," he said.

"But I was a slave . . . Not a part of this—your—world," Katherine said sadly.

"Here, with me, your past means nothing. Your beauty and your talent will tell the world who you are."

By the tenth of the coolest July that Martin could remember in New Orleans, he and Katherine had settled in. She was livelier, happier, and Martin breathed easier.

Twice weekly she had visited Guy DeBeau for two weeks. He was well enough now to be completely cared for by the woman attending him Katherine's first day in New Orleans and a male nurse.

"You're a lovely woman, Katherine," Guy had told her when she said she wouldn't be back. "I won't say goodbye. I'm too grateful. I wanted to *die*. You knew that?"

"I suspected it."

He grinned. "Well, I'm going out there to live the hell out of every day—with my father's blessings—thanks to you. I want to find me another woman like the one I lost. . . ." He paused a few moments before he continued. "Now, if Martin ever changes and mistreats you, come to me and I'll set him straight."

"But it was for *your* sake that I was captured, injured, and brought here. Don't you remember?"

Guy blushed scarlet. "I'm sorrier about that than you'll ever know. But you got old Martin, didn't you? You're quite a woman, Katherine. Quite a woman."

Looking around DeBeau's house, Katherine thought that while it was luxurious, she preferred her own lovely home. Away from her house, she filled her mind with thoughts of it—and her new life. She had posted a letter to Papa Frank, and Katherine eagerly looked forward to his reply.

"Katherine," Guy had said at the door as she was leaving, "like my father, I find talking difficult, especially to women . . . even pretty ones. But I'll tell you every day of my life that I'm sorry for what you must have suffered in fright and humiliation. My father was a pirate as a young man, you know. He's in the middle of politics and the social life of New Orleans now. We're accepted since we and the Lafittes helped save New Orleans from the English Navy. But we once lived in Barataria. It's a beautiful island not far from here, but it was . . . it *is* . . . the Sodom and Gomorrah of this century."

"You have a reason for telling me this, Guy."

"I do. I owe my life to you. My father knows that. Give

him time. I know him, and one day he will apologize to you for what he did to you. My father and I repay our debts."

She nodded. How much he had changed. He was gaining a bit of weight, and his color was much improved. He little resembled the profligate, broken young man she had been forced here to minister to.

Seven

On the second Saturday in July, Katherine rode with Martin to visit his *forgeron* works. It was spread across three acres and was completely fenced in and locked at night, with a watchman to guard it. Katherine marveled that she had never in her life seen so much iron.

It was stacked under deep sheds, on concrete pillars, imported from Europe, and mined in the States. Martin took care to purchase the finest pig iron, blast furnaces, and built and used the most intricate molds. He also hired the best craftsmen. From the beginning, he had quickly become the most sought-after *forgeron*.

Martin had twenty employees and two supervisors, one of whom was Jules. Always pleasantly surprised at how well he'd prospered in this new country, he was happy to show it all off to Katherine.

"Antoine," he said to one of his supervisors, "I'd like you to meet my wife."

The ebony-skinned, short and muscular Antoine Smith removed his cap and took the hand Katherine offered.

"Pleased to meet you, ma'am," he told her. "Mighty pretty lady you got y'self, boss man." He covertly watched Martin's wife, whom the men at his business so admired as they'd seen her ride with Martin. The man's inflections were familiar, as was the lilt of his speech.

"Aren't you from the bayou country?" she asked him.

He grinned, pleased. "Same as you, ma'am," he said, then excused himself to return to his men.

In the mid-morning sunlight Martin looked at Katherine's silken skin, partially covered by the rose and gray checked gingham she wore. It struck him at the oddest times that they'd never made love in the not quite three weeks they'd been married. He'd been caught in an onslaught of orders for grillwork for apartments being built by DeBeau and some of his new business and political friends. At night, he'd been so tired that he'd fallen into bed right after a late dinner. But it was Celié and the accident that still haunted him.

"Martin, you're so quiet," Katherine remarked. "I keep looking at your ironworks and wondering what I could say to let you know how I feel. I'm so proud of you." As he turned to her, she whispered, "But I'd be proud of you if you had *nothing* other than yourself."

Her last words caught her by surprise as much as it did him. He pulled her to him swiftly, filled with emotions he couldn't sort out at the moment. She meant what she said, and it moved him greatly. Tonight, if *she* still wanted *him,* he meant to take her. Smiling, Martin squeezed her hand.

They had walked to the gates of the ironworks yard and gone into the small white office structure, where Martin kept some of the books with the help of a bookkeeper, who was off today, although his employees normally worked a half-day on Saturdays. A considerate boss, Martin gave his workers a half-day where most worked whole Saturdays.

Katherine found the old, battered desks, the messiness of the whole office, typical of males.

From the window, they saw a fine carriage pull up. A tall, light-skinned man, sporting a beige summer dress coat, trousers, and a large straw hat, alighted and entered the office while his coachman waited.

"And who is dressed in such finery on a Saturday?" Martin began. "Well, it's Mr. Drumm, Katherine—Wilson Drumm, the lieutenant governor."

He opened the office door and called out, "We're in here, sir. And welcome."

When Martin introduced Wilson Drumm to Katherine, the lieutenant governor half closed his eyes. Her gentleness reminded him of his own wife, Inez. A housepainter by trade, Drumm was far smarter than he was given credit for, both by his own race and by whites. But his wife knew, and thank God, the governor saw his acerbity and quickly set out to make use of it.

"At the risk of repeating what you must hear from our old and young rascals in New Orleans," Wilson Drumm declared, "I'll just say we welcome charm, beauty, and femininity. All women have one of these attributes. But ma'am, it is rare to find all three so wonderfully combined."

Katherine felt humbled by his gallantry.

"Thank you, sir, for your kindness, but you flatter me."

Martin smiled from ear to ear.

"Your husband can tell you that I don't."

Martin nodded. "Please sit down." He pulled up a more comfortable armchair, pushing aside the long-backed straight chairs. "We brought lemonade with us, and sandwiches. Could we offer you some?"

Katherine waited for his answer. "Why, yes, I could certainly use a glass of lemonade, but I'll pass on the sandwiches, although I'll bet they're delicious. My wife, who I want your charming wife to meet—and soon—is having a bid whist party and she's ordered me back for lunch."

Katherine got the tall, heavy glasses they kept there and some paper napkins. Martin removed the gallon jug of lemonade from the ice compartment of the large white icebox, with its melting block of ice. Taking a wooden handled icepick, he broke off chunks and slivers of ice and put them into three glasses. Filling three quarters of a glass, he asked Drumm, "Shall I now pour the best part?"

Wilson Drumm laughed, exposing big, yellowed teeth. Katherine thought him a rather handsome man. "Why, man, need you *ask?* It's nearly eleven in the morning and I haven't had a drop. I'd much prefer gin, if you've got some."

Martin nodded. "Gin. Bourbon. Rum." He found a bottle of gin, opened it, and poured the liquid into the glass. Lieutenant Governor Drumm took three lumps of sugar from the dish Katherine offered him.

"Sweets from the sweet," he murmured. "What lovely hands you have, ma'am. Now, I'd better stop at that. Mr. Dominguez here is a gentleman, but St. Peter himself would be jealous of a woman like yourself."

Katherine thanked him again, noting how his face flushed when he laughed. She took no liquor in her lemonade, although she'd noticed that the women here drank far more than did those in the bayou country—what little she'd seen of them.

Katherine turned to Martin. "I could go outside and sit under that tall oak, since I'm sure you two have a lot to talk about."

Drumm raised a curiously long, faintly gnarled hand. "Now, don't you even consider it, little lady. Such business as I have with your husband you're welcome to hear, I assure you. Please stay."

"Yes, Katherine, please do," Martin insisted. So she chose a straight-backed chair near the window and sat there, a bit away from them in case they were merely being kind.

"How are things going with you and Governor Montrose?" Martin asked.

"Matters could not be better," Drumm replied. "The man's a prince. Twenty-nine, and he's got more horse sense than men twice his age. But Lord, how some of the whites hate him. He'd be in trouble if not for General Rousseau and his iron fist. Damn it, Martin, can't they see that *we* deserve a part in this democracy?"

Martin nodded. "I suppose we'd best be grateful that men like General Rousseau see it and enforce it. Reconstruction's worked better in New Orleans than anywhere else in the country." He broke off, nodding to Katherine.

"We've been too busy since you've been here to talk much about politics, but we have *seven* senators of color and *half* the House of Representatives is comprised of us."

"Incredible," Katherine remarked softly, "and wonderful." She hadn't known there were that many.

Grimly, Drumm informed them, "We paid a price for it. Two hundred people killed in '66 going to *vote,* something black soldiers died for as well as white. *Two hundred* slaughtered. And who were they fighting? The police and other whites." When he looked at Katherine, his eyes were sad. "I don't need to tell you, ma'am, that of that two hundred, not many were either police or white. But that devil's plan got them General Sheridan on their damned backs, and General Hancock and now General Rousseau, who's even tougher. Not to mention Governor Montrose."

He stood up slowly. "Listen, I said I can't stay. The governor could well send for me today, and I want to be home if he does. Martin, I just want to know if you can handle several extra grillwork projects for large new estates going up. *Our* side of the fence as well as theirs. Man, the *Picayune* is screaming corruption, but this city has always had plenty of that. *We're* getting some of the gravy now; that's the difference. You've hired how many new men in the past year?"

Martin thought a moment. "I believe ten," he answered. "I've never seen anything like it. Yes, I can handle more projects."

"I'm pleased about that. It'll get even better." Drumm's mouth set in a grim line. "Unless they take Grant out the way they did Lincoln."

Martin thought for a moment before he spoke. "Well, we can sure as hell *hope* not."

As effusive in departing as in arriving, Wilson Drumm left, after taking Katherine's hand and telling Martin, "Now, you bring this lovely lady to meet Inez, you hear? And soon. I'm inviting you to dinner whenever you get the time to come. And you'll be getting some visitors about that grillwork."

After he'd left, Katherine said, "Martin, he's a charming man."

"Not usually *that* charming," Martin commented with mock jealousy. "He likes you. Mr. Drumm's not usually that talkative. He's got a nice wife, but she's not in your class."

Katherine laughed. "Santo Domingan men have silken tongues. Like Jules. And certainly you. New Orleans men are quite charming. But you *all* flatter me. Just think, Martin, four years ago I was a slave. Think of that. We all called Theodore Keyes *Master* Keyes. A few still do. I'll wager you Celié knows I was a slave once. . . ."

"As Celié would have been had slavery not ended the year she was born. We were not slaves only because my father freed us. Katherine . . ." he began as he came around to her chair and knelt there, the warmth of his hand on her thigh comforting her, "I believe slavery is of the spirit as much as the body. Yes, I'm sure Celié is capable of mocking you, deriding you in every way. I see in you everything I ever thought I wanted in a woman, although it is too soon for us to really know each other."

He smiled a bit, then took her hand and kissed it, murmuring, "I am black and comely."

She lifted his hand from her thigh, bent, and pressed it to her cheek, whispering, "How romantic you are."

Martin looked at the old ship's clock on the desk. DeBeau had given it to him; it had belonged to his father when he sailed. Noon. They should go home now. The men would be leaving soon. Jules would take the girls to visit with him. He and Katherine would be alone. Martin's loins surged with anticipation.

"I think I'll get the sandwiches and put them out," Katherine announced, ambling toward the icebox.

"You go ahead," he said heartily. "I'm not hungry. I've got a lot on my mind. . . ."

* * *

As they pulled up in front of their house, Katherine noted with surprise that DeBeau's doctor, garbed in the habitual black that physicians wore, sat on their front porch, waiting.

Dr. St. Cyr approached them as Martin hitched Helio to the post.

"Martin," he began, "I will understand if you require a bit more time to prepare yourself, but I need Katherine's help with . . . someone who's having a difficult pregnancy." He frowned, then continued wryly. "This time I think her basic diagnosis of Guy DeBeau fits well. There is time to talk with this patient . . . start her on a path to healing herself so that she delivers a healthy child. Will you let Katherine come with me? Of course, I will see that she returns safely."

Martin glanced at Katherine, who nodded her assent. It always exhilarated her to try to bring health to an aching body or a sick spirit.

"If you don't mind, husband," she said.

Dr. St. Cyr continued. "It's the governor's wife. She's due in three months and she is not doing as well as I'd like. Katherine, you've talked about your midwifery, and I'd much appreciate your taking a look at her . . . talking with her."

Katherine agreed. Martin walked with her to the doctor's coach and helped her in.

"Don't be afraid," he whispered.

But Katherine *was* afraid. As rich and as influential as De-Beau was, he was not a governor, nor was Guy a governor's wife.

After Katherine left with Dr. St. Cyr, Martin worked in the backyard flower beds, weeding the lavender and white impatiens, which were glorious this year. It was a good way to burn off some of the energy he'd built up from being around Katherine this morning.

Putting aside his trowel after about an hour, Martin stood up and went into the house to get some water. But he found himself stopping at the stairwell door that led to the attic. Opening it and climbing the creaky old stairs, he ascended slowly, as if some danger lurked there.

The closed beige shades still let the sunlight through. On an old table near the door he saw the cardboard box in which Katherine had told him she'd put Celié's nightgown. He raised the lid and looked at the gown, his face impassive, then closed the box again.

And standing there, it was as if he'd gone back in time, not the three years since the carnage on Santo Domingo that had taken the lives of his mother and his brother and DeBeau's son, but back the twelve years to Celié, now married to his brother, Raoul, and to himself at nineteen.

A country road in the late afternoon. Raoul had asked him to pick up Celié from the house of a friend she was visiting. Winking, Raoul had said he had other plans.

"But you have not been married a year, Raoul," Martin had protested. "Surely one woman is enough for the *first* year."

Laughing, Raoul had slapped him on the back. "Ah Martin, for you, one woman, yes. For you, perhaps one woman for a lifetime. You love like that. But me, I am my father's progeny. His blood. I have not met the woman who can chain me. And I never will."

"Then, man, why marry at all?" Martin had asked.

Raoul had shrugged. "Because Celié demanded marriage. When she couldn't rope *you* in, she turned her sights on me. And I was willing. She is beautiful, satisfying in so many ways. But I did not promise to be faithful, my brother, *ever.*"

Martin had picked up Celié at her friend's house. He was home from Spain to comfort his mother, for his father, Pablo Caesar Antonio Dominguez, had died. His widow had buried him as quickly as possible, having sent word that no one of his bastard family was to attend his funeral. But the cemetery gates were not locked. Martin had gone to his father's grave and had stood there, feeling an outpouring of love he had not felt in Pablo's lifetime, and he had grieved. Raoul had not *seemed* to grieve at all, but Martin knew how his brother camouflaged grief by drinking and forced gaiety—and in some woman's hotly passionate embrace.

Annalise had truly seemed serene.

"He is at peace now," she'd said. "He was a tormented man, my son. He loved us, you know, in his way."

Martin remembered his father's visits to their small, rose-pink stucco house on certain nights. Martin and Raoul would lie in their bed, listening to the drunken or perhaps not drunken laughter of their father and his loud sounds of pleasure. They never heard those sounds of pleasure from their mother as she lay with him. By morning, he'd be gone. Annalise was always so happy on the days he was to come, sad when he left.

It was like an ugly secret between Raoul and Martin, which they never spoke about.

On this particular visit, Annalise had asked Martin more about his studies and his *forgeron* training than she had in the past. She had looked at him anxiously, as if he would go away before he was scheduled to depart the following week.

He'd caught her to him. "Give me time, Mama, and I will take you away from Santo Domingo. From all this misery. You cannot have been happy. I will build you a nicer house. *Forgerons* make excellent money. . . ."

Annalise had smiled and placed a long, slender hand on his. "My son," she'd said quietly, "I want for nothing. Listen, he left us land, which we may never receive, given his widow's rage. But he left us gold coins, many gold coins, Martin. And of course, it is not the money, but the thought behind it. And there is something else. . . ."

She got up and went to her room, returning in a short while with a finely tooled black leather jewel box and a blue velvet ring box. She opened the ring box first, and Martin saw for the first time the brilliant, perfect pear-shaped diamond and a slender wedding band of excellent gold.

"He slipped both rings on my finger," she recounted, "and said he was sorry for all the pain he'd caused me and you and

Raoul. 'But they are my sons and I love them,' he told me. 'DeBeau, my friend, will look after their interests, as you, a woman, could not do, so I have left money with him.' Oh, Martin, I know you hate him, but he is your *father*. . . ."

Martin had shaken his head. "No, Mama. When I was small, I may have hated him, but I long ago realized the futility of hatred. I have put my anger in my work. I have turned what I thought ugly into something beautiful—my work with iron."

Then she'd shown him the black pearl necklace, and he'd looked at its perfection with astonishment. Annalise had nodded.

"You are touched, I see. It is beautiful. He said he loved me when he gave me this. Perhaps our being together was wrong, but it is the way of the island and I loved him so much. . . ."

They had hugged then, both with tears in their eyes. He thought she had never seemed so beautiful.

"Do you blame me because I did not marry my own kind?"

Gently, he'd answered, "And what *is* your own kind, Mama? We are *all* only terribly fallible men."

It was then that she'd told him, as she'd told DeBeau, that she wanted Martin to have the diamond ring and the black pearl necklace. No matter that Raoul was the firstborn and normally would inherit. They were all outside the law as freed people of color.

"But I wish to be buried with my wedding ring on," she'd directed.

After a moment, her expression changed.

"You are fortunate that Celié married your brother, not you," she'd said then. "She is a woman with the face and body of a goddess and the heart of a poisonous serpent. How lucky that you escaped. Have you even begun to get over her?"

"I think so," he'd answered, sounding unconvincing even to himself.

"God will help you," she continued, "as He helps us to

overcome any wickedness. And He will need to help Raoul, who I fear loves her more than he himself realizes."

Now Martin glanced again at the box containing the nightgown. He was going to take the nightgown to Celié this afternoon, while Katherine was at the governor's mansion, and he was going to see that once and for all Celié got out of their lives and stayed out. The accident while he was driving the cabriolet on that country road flashed across his mind again. That was the reason he had allowed Celié to take over his life: guilt.

He could not focus on that accident clearly. When he lived in Spain, a priest had absolved him, had told him to go on with his life, and that was what he intended to do.

Pushing the nightmare accident to the back of his mind, Martin bent to open a foot locker and found Annalise's daguerreotyped face staring up at him. In sepia tones, the oval-faced brown woman with the high cheekbones and wide-set obsidian eyes, the straight, silken eyebrows, the large, straight nose and narrow lips, was one deeply etched in his memory. Of black and Indian heritage, Annalise had been of medium height and seemed frail, but she'd toiled unceasingly on their few acres, where she'd raised vegetables and melons for white landowning families. Katherine's earth-brown, full-bodied hair with its slight crinkle was like Annalise's charcoal-black locks, which had reached her waist.

Martin put the pictures in a stack and closed the trunk. There was also an old daguerreotype of his father, with his black, curly hair and aristocratic face, and one of him and Raoul, who looked like their father, at an early age. He had brought the photos with him when he moved to Louisiana. And there was one of Celié as well.

Martin sat down heavily on a chair by the closed trunk. Try as he might, he still could not bring himself to focus on the horror of those deaths on Santo Domingo, and he felt he needed to if he were ever to live his life in peace.

He found, though, that his mind spun evenly with scenes of

Celié and him and his visit from Spain after his father had died. Martin could now plainly see how his mind had always begun to relive, then flee, his memories of that painful time with Celié.

He had gone, as he'd finally agreed, and picked up Celié at her friend's house. On the winding country road, she'd turned to him. "For God's sake, Martin, *talk* to me. You've avoided me since you've been here."

It had been nearing twilight and he'd meant to be back before dark. The road was treacherous, gullied some by recent rains. "What is there to say?" he'd asked.

"I was wrong to marry Raoul," she'd answered softly. "I know that now." She'd moved closer to him, as alluring, as heady as ever. "I should have waited for you. Raoul and I don't love each other, Martin, but he is a *passionate* lover."

Angry that she seemed to assume she could facilely switch from one to the other of them, he'd lashed out. "We have to live with our mistakes, Celié . . . if your marriage *was* a mistake." Her remark about his brother had stung him, envious of Raoul as he was.

"Martin, please!" she'd cried. But he'd known that cry was just as likely to be from manipulation as it was from hurt.

She'd moved close to his side as he drove the buggy, attempting to press her slim, lush body close to his. Roughly, he'd disengaged her arms and pushed her away. And the none-too-tame young horse had felt the overtightening of the reins and lightly reared up. They'd gone with the turned-over buggy into a ditch, and Celié had struck her pelvic region and her stomach across a large, exposed tree root.

He'd rescued her and stayed a week longer, until the doctor said she would be fine. In Spain he'd been haunted, but what *else* could he have done? Celié's life on Santo Domingo with Raoul and Annalise continued. On his visits, infrequent after that, she'd looked at him longingly, but he had been determined not to be alone with her again.

From Spain he'd migrated to America, to Louisiana and New

Orleans at DeBeau's urging that he was bound to become a resounding success as a master *forgeron*. And that new country was booming.

Not until his last visit to Santo Domingo, three years ago, when he went to beg his mother to come to America and rest from the hard work she still did growing vegetables and melons, did he talk with Celié. She'd been blunt.

"The accident on the road that night, Martin . . ." she'd begun on the porch when they were standing alone near the railing. Celié had his attention, and she waited.

"What *about* the accident?" he asked more sharply than he intended.

"Raoul and I have no children, as you can see."

A streak of unfamiliar cruelty welled in him. "Did you ever really *want* children, Celié? With Raoul? With me?"

"That's unfair," she'd answered quietly. "That accident left me *unable* to bear children. You remember where I struck myself?"

Not answering, Martin had certainly remembered, just as he remembered now. The old doctor who'd tended her was dead; he couldn't talk to him. If it was a lie, then she would have lied to Raoul as well. One thing was true: She had no children. And Martin was sorely afraid then, as now, that Celié might have been telling the truth.

"It could have been *our* child I lost, Martin. You left in late July. I persuaded Raoul to marry me the last of September."

He'd caught her shoulders roughly, unmindful that Annalise or Raoul could return at any time. "Then if the child *could* have been mine, why didn't you write to me? I would have come back, you know. I would have married you."

"You're bruising my shoulders. Let me go." He'd taken his hands away from her. "I have my pride," she'd said. "After you left, I saw no need to tell Raoul that it was not the child of his and my impulsive lovemaking. For all I know, he never knew or cared that you and I were . . . intimate, since he knew you didn't wish to marry me."

"I had to finish my apprenticeship," he'd groaned. "Had I known about the child . . ."

"I thought you should know now what you've *cost* me," she continued softly, yet there was a terrible edge to her voice.

"Celié, I'm so sorry," he'd said. It was all he *could* say.

She'd moved away from him then and refused to talk to him again. He'd stayed four more days after that, at a time when the island was buzzing with new intrigue. Yet another repressive regime with its bullying police force was cracking down on the freed slaves who fought back—his mother, his brother, and DeBeau's oldest son, among them, were leaders of that crowd.

Sunlight played on a black leather-covered violin case resting on the other side of the trunk. In his mind's eye he saw the violin inside that case—a gift from his mother when he was a boy. On the mountain in Santo Domingo that night nine years later, on a visit, he'd played that violin to great merriment, with Annalise, Raoul, Celié, and many friends and acquaintances. They'd celebrated freedom they intended to keep. And they celebrated life. Then the dreaded bully-police had come with their accusations and their guns. And Raoul had quickly said to him that someone had betrayed them.

Martin put his fist to his forehead as if to ward off the horrible memories. He *had* to remember the carnage of that night, and he had to remember it clearly. But three years had not been enough to dim that savagery. Would *any* span of time be long enough?

He picked up the box with the nightgown and the stack of daguerreotypes and went downstairs. He was going to talk with Celié. He was bitterly sorry for any wrong he'd done her, but that had happened a long time ago. Now Katherine had entered his life. He was going to make a clean break in whatever chains of his past bound him. For he keenly felt that his new life with Katherine held a promise of heights and depths and breadth of love and passion that he had only dimly perceived before.

* * *

At Celié's side door, Martin knocked sharply and waited. He dreaded meeting Celié again, yet looked forward to having this long nightmare at least partly over.

"Mr. Dominguez." The small, high voice belonged to Susie, Celié's shop assistant.

"How are you, Susie? Is Mrs. Dominguez in?" A Creole of color, pale-skinned with dirty brown rough hair, the young woman peered at him.

"Why, no, sir, she's gone out for the afternoon. Is there a message, sir?"

Martin frowned. "When do you expect her back?"

"Oh, sir, I couldn't say."

"Please give her this," Martin said, handing her the box.

"Yes, sir," she assured him, "I certainly will."

A man cackled as he came up the walk. A drunken Mims, Celié's handyman who'd summoned him from his shopping trip with Katherine, staggered along, indulging himself in Celié's absence. Sober, he did *her* bidding; drunk, he did his *own*.

"You be lookin' for the missus?" he asked gleefully. "Well, I c'n tell you, *she* be lookin' f' *Dahomey Sinclair,* like half this city be. Magic man. Devil man. Dahomey Sinclair."

"Now you stop that, Mims," Susie said with no heat. Mims looked at Martin, whom he greatly admired.

"Ev'a there be anybody you wants to hurt, help, or put out o' business, jus' you git Dahomey Sinclair," Mims proclaimed as Martin turned and went down the walk.

"Don't you want to leave a message, Mr. Dominguez?" Susie called after him. He turned to say no and found Mims smiling.

"Now you com' back t' see us, y'hear?" he said.

Martin nodded. The old man tried to be as kind as he could, considering his being pulled between Celié and everybody else.

* * *

The governor's mansion did not stand out, but it was impressive. A red-brick structure, English ivy climbed the walls. It seemed richly comfortable rather than opulent. A gray-haired, chocolate-colored butler greeted them with formal warmth.

"Good afternoon, Dr. St. Cyr, ma'am."

It delighted the man to be able to call his own race of women "ma'am" now that slavery had ended. If whites didn't like it, there was little they could do. He smiled as Katherine passed. Surely now, this was a lovely woman. Who was she?

"Thank you, Emil. You'll need to know . . ." he hesitated a moment. ". . . or *she* will need to know you. Mrs. Dominguez, I'd like to introduce you to Emil Campbell, the *royal* butler. There's little he cannot help you with."

Emil's bald head gleamed as brightly as his eyes. He was an attractive man by virtue of intelligence and confidence, as well as a kindly regard for others. Katherine liked him immediately.

The doctor had introduced her by title—*Mrs.* Freedom or not, most whites refused any kind of social recognition to people of color.

The stairway, which was the loveliest Katherine had ever seen, even in pictures, was winding and highly polished, with mahogany and brass banisters. She admired it all the way to the second floor, looking back as they reached the governor's wife's bedroom. The doctor knocked and a maid opened the door to the stuffy room, huge and elegantly decorated, the drapery closed against the light. Only one flickering candelabra burned. Dr. St. Cyr and Katherine walked to the bed.

"Well, Mrs. Montrose, how are you feeling?"

A tall, saffron-skinned maid hovered about, straightening covers, patting pillows under the patient's head.

The woman on the bed kept her eyes closed, and she seemed listless.

"I can't imagine why you bother to ask anymore, Dr. St. Cyr," she remarked languidly, "yet I do thank you for doing so. I am no better."

He sat on the bed beside her and took her hand. "I have brought someone who I feel can work with me to help you. This is the young woman who knows so much about herbs, who preaches with grace the need for fresh air and health-making food and drink—and a healthy spirit. Are you interested?"

Natalie Montrose opened her eyes and merely glanced at Katherine, finding she admired the humor that lurked at the corners of those almond eyes and those full lips.

"You seem to demand a great deal of a sick woman, doctor," she said throatily.

"Perhaps if you will agree to do what Dr. St. Cyr and I suggest," Katherine ventured, "you will gain great benefits in your health, not to mention your baby's."

"Are you saying you'll have me up and running around in no time?" the woman began to tease, but her eyes brimmed with tears as she touched her stomach. "I suppose I'm deranged," she continued sadly. "Certainly Father said so often enough. I have spells—hysterical spells in which I weep and storm and love no one, least of all my miserable self."

"You're a beautiful woman, Mrs. Montrose," Katherine said calmly. She spoke no lie, for twenty-two-year-old Natalie Montrose's beauty was certain, if presently unfashionable. She was boyishly slender in a time of full bosoms and heavy hips, sharply intelligent and levelly outspoken in a time of feminine twittering and curbed tongues. Katherine looked at her even more carefully. She did not think she was mistaken. This seemed a passionate woman in every way. What was wrong here?

As if in answer to her question, Natalie burst out, "I do not think the governor wants to be saddled with a child just now. He has held his appointment less than two years, and he is busy beyond what I can tell you."

"But, my dear, what man spends so much time in the raising of a child, especially one child, as not to be happy to be a father?" Dr. St. Cyr reassured her.

Natalie looked at him, despair in her eyes. "How can I make you understand? I hid my pregnancy even from you. I've longed to talk with someone and I do not make friends easily, so I am alone. The governor needs me by his side . . . needs my help to entertain. It is a difficult time for him. His policies for the people of color are unpopular, and he must persuade people to our side."

"Yes, how well I know this," Dr. St. Cyr acknowledged, sighing. "But you will deliver in three more months. And with a nanny's help, you can fulfill your usual social obligations. You know, Natalie, I've told you I think you *can* feel much better than you do. I know it is hard for you just now, but you do not *let* yourself be nearly as physically healthy as you could be. Why?"

At first they could not hear what she said because tears muffled her voice. They waited until her weeping subsided and the maid handed her another handkerchief. Blotting her eyes and blowing her nose gingerly, Natalie Montrose plainly steeled herself to tell them something.

"Speak up now," Dr. St. Cyr ordered, as if to someone far younger. "I think what you're going to say is important, and I hope it's what you've been holding back. Katherine will be my right hand with this. She is young, but she has the wisdom that God grants us sometimes."

"I think you are . . . nice, Katherine," Natalie said. "I feel at ease with you."

"Thank you."

The governor's wife took a deep breath. "*I* will be my child's nanny as much as I can," she stated. "It is one bone of contention between my husband and me. *I* was left alone by my mother, and I cannot tell you the hunger of the spirit this has brought me. An alienist who was my father's friend said this about me. That has not changed. No, I will nurse *my* child in every way, but I . . ."

She doubled over with sobs then and curled herself into the fetal position.

Katherine went to her, sat on the bed, and stroked her heaving body—slowly, patiently, and with infinite care. This woman was badly frightened, some instinct told her. She murmured soft assurances until Natalie suddenly sat up, gently asking her maid to leave the room.

The governor's wife collected herself, breathed deeply, and began to speak, her voice trembling. "I overheard Jenny, my maid, gossiping about me with another maid. Being Jenny, she simply listened and offered few comments. The other woman is no longer here, but I cannot erase from my mind what she said: 'Miss Natalie is built like a boy. That baby's going to kill her getting born. You mark my words: going to just kill her.' "

A sudden, guarded smile spread across Katherine's face, which she quickly explained. "I don't wonder you were terrified. I know it's widely held, Mrs. Montrose, that women with slender hips have great difficulty in childbirth. In the bayou country, we prepare such a woman long before her time. There are so many considerations. There is so much we can do, with your cooperation. As late in your time as it is, I cannot promise you an easy birth, but I think it will be less painful than you fear. Barring other complications, I don't think it's likely that you'll die."

"Is this true?" Natalie looked to Dr. St. Cyr for corroboration, then back at Katherine, whom she sincerely hoped didn't think she was one of those whites who believed nothing a person of color said unless it was supported by a white.

"Oh, Katherine," she declared, "certainly I do not mean that I don't believe you, and I'm so happy to hear you say this."

Dr. St. Cyr bit his top lip. "I'm fast beginning to think, Mrs. Governor's Wife, that anything this lady tells me is true. Her grandfather is a legend in the bayou country, and a lot of the rest of Louisiana, and he trained her. Did a damned fine job of it, too, if you ask me.

"Now, Natalie, you need more fresh air than you're getting. I know you don't feel well just now, but I want you to go out more, at least as far as the side or back porch. Out there, leave off your corsets—not that you need them—and your bustles and petticoats. And breathe deeply and long and from your *belly.*"

He emphasized the last word and laughed heartily. "I don't mean any disrespect and you know that, but I'm your doctor and I want you to think about what I say . . . *feel* what I'm telling you. You're *not* going to die. You're going to put away your brandy snifter. No need to blush. I know the signs. Now, Katherine, please tell us what you propose."

Fear still clouded Natalie's face, but it had greatly lessened. She took Katherine's hand.

"Thank you," she said. "I'm ready to listen—and cooperate."

Katherine found herself wishing that it were she who was pregnant with Martin's child, and she grew warm with the thought.

So much had happened in three weeks. She had been able to help Guy DeBeau, the cause of her abduction, and she felt hopeful about bringing Natalie's pregnancy to a successful birth. They had been lucky. Martin's eyes had been disapproving when she said that Guy DeBeau had spoken of Barataria, the island home of most of DeBeau's men, just across the Mississippi levee.

As Dr. St. Cyr listened quietly, Katherine explained that she'd like Mrs. Montrose to eat a wide variety of foods: small amounts of red meat and a little pork, as much poultry and seafood as she wished. Vegetables, both raw and cooked, not overdone. Grains. Fresh fruit and fruit juices. Could she give up coffee? So many people swore they could not live without it.

"It would be hard, since I drink it all day and into the night,"

Natalie declared. "But for my baby's health, I will give it up." She sighed deeply.

Katherine asked that she be allowed to instruct the maid, along with Natalie, about occasional salt glows and other baths she recommended.

"But won't you give those to me personally?"

"I will certainly give you some, but I will need help. And there will be other rubs and manipulations. It's later than I'd like it to be, but I want to strengthen the muscles of your back and pelvis. Mrs. Montrose, one of the Indian tribes of the bayou country has prolonged training for women readying themselves for childbirth. My mother found, and now *I* find, their customs useful beyond belief. Later, there are special herbs to prepare the womb for childbirth—slippery elm, for example. . . ."

"But I have heard that those were for women trying to abort." Natalie blushed as she looked at Dr. St. Cyr. She didn't want him to think her too forward. Should she know about things like that?

Dr. St. Cyr laughed. "How often I, fogy old country doctor that I am, Natalie, have used slippery elm in delivering."

"There are others," Katherine stated firmly. "Many others. I ask, too, that you relax and hope and, above all, *pray* for a favorable birth."

Natalie nodded. "I will pray as I prayed as a child," she said, "when I believed in prayer."

"I need you to believe again," Katherine urged. "That will help us more than anything."

Dr. St. Cyr asked Katherine to give the maid her instructions while he talked alone with Mrs. Montrose.

"Already she seems better," the maid remarked sympathetically as Katherine briefed her on what needed to be done.

"I think we can bring her through successfully," Katherine told her, "but I really need your help."

"Oh, ma'am, you have it—I promise. Miss Natalie has been good to me."

"Jenny!" a summary voice spoke from the doorway.

Katherine froze. That was not a voice you easily forgot.

"Miss Celié! I expected you tomorrow!" Jenny responded, clearly intimidated by that high-handed manner.

Even so, Celié came into the room in a more subdued manner than she had swept out of Martin and Katherine's house that first night. Unsmiling, she looked at Katherine disdainfully.

"Jenny, would you excuse us? I would like to have a word with this . . . woman. I have brought the unmentionables that I finished early for Mrs. Montrose. I put them in the closet where I leave her things."

"Oh yes, ma'am," Jenny said, actually seeming to scurry in a way she had not done even for the woman she officially served.

Katherine stood up, a little taller than Celié, fighting for composure. After all, this woman had the power to command Martin's presence when he was on a shopping trip with his wife. They had been lovers, and no diamond ring, no black pearl, could change that.

"Could we be seated?" Celié asked, as if entertaining in her own home. And how beautiful she looked, quietly dressed in heliotrope cotton of her own exquisite design. Katherine, however, liked her own cool sprigged blue cotton voile that quietly flattered her superb figure.

Katherine shook her head. "I do not have time to sit down," she told Celié. "My business here is almost finished."

"And just what *is* your business here?" she asked after a very long moment, smiling narrowly. She had noted Natalie's thicker figure, although she apparently carried her baby high and showed little. She had begun to order looser, fuller garments and unmentionables. And the bustles and the crinolines further obscured her figure, even with the narrow waistlines.

Katherine answered sharply, "It is nothing you need to know about."

"Mrs. Montrose tells me everything."

"I doubt that, but if she chooses to do so, then it is up to her."

"It's about her pregnancy, isn't it? About her not being able to carry her baby to term?"

"I will not discuss it, Celié."

"Then discuss *this,* if you can. I sent for Martin to remind him of our bargain. Men are fickle. You will find that they easily forget."

"What is it that they forget so easily?"

"You will note that Martin came to me, *mam'selle.* I cannot bear children, and at some time I—or Martin—will tell you why. We have always been in love, even when I, in a fit of anger at Martin, married his brother. . . ."

"Why do you tell me this?"

Celié laughed scornfully. "Why indeed, *mam'selle?* Like all Santo Domingan men, Martin wants heirs. He would deny this to you, of course, but we have chosen you to bear his children—one if the first is a boy, two if not—then he will divorce you. *We* will marry then."

She looked triumphant enough to be telling the truth. And, in fact, Dahomey Sinclair had sent word back via Mims that he would immediately begin to weave the spells she wanted.

"I see," Katherine responded slowly, her heart constricting. She wanted to call this woman a liar, but could she? She *had* sent for Martin and he had gone. *Why* had he gone to her? He would tell her when she returned home, but could she believe him?

They had talked about Celié and she believed him, but he had admitted that his love for the other woman had lingered. And in spite of what he believed, did that love linger still?

Katherine found her voice. "I am *Madame* or *Senora* Martin Dominguez, as you prefer. Calling me *mam'selle* changes nothing. Even if, as you say, he doesn't love me, I am his wife."

At a knock on the door, Celié opened to Jenny, who told Katherine, "The governor's come home and the missus wants him to meet you."

Katherine went out of the room with Jenny, leaving an enraged Celié standing there. The governor, Celié thought, liked people of color, treated them with respect. He had been courteous when Natalie introduced her. She clenched her narrow fists. Women carrying babies were vulnerable. Of course, Natalie would like Katherine. An expression of distaste crossed her face. Something was going to have to be *done* about that woman.

"I am more pleased to meet you than I can say, Mrs. Dominguez," the governor declared when Dr. St. Cyr introduced Katherine in his wife's room. "I certainly hope you can work the same miracle with my wife that you did with Guy De-Beau."

His handclasp was firm. Katherine remembered Martin speaking of the governor's youth. At twenty-nine, he was a remarkably handsome man of ruddy complexion and light brown hair. His eyes were a warmly intelligent, piercing bright blue.

"You flatter me, Governor Montrose," Katherine said evenly. "So much will depend on your wife."

The governor smiled as they stood by her bedside. He bent and lightly stroked his wife's hand. "*I* will see that she fully cooperates with you," he promised.

Natalie Montrose smiled at all three, her gaze lingering on her husband.

"If my cooperation is all it takes," she said, "this will be easy."

And she did look happier, but her words masked a strong residue of fearfulness that Katherine had been unable to dispel.

Eight

Returning from the governor's mansion around five that same afternoon, Katherine felt a chill run up her spine. "Goose going over my grave," she told herself quickly, thus rendering harmless any attempt to hex her; it was an old southern superstition.

"Martin," she called, "where are you?"

"In the kitchen, love," Martin answered. He met her at the kitchen door and hugged her tightly, holding her close to him. She felt the slow beat of his heart against hers, then pulled away to look at him, tracing his cheekbone with her index finger.

"You look a bit down, Martin. What's wrong?" There was a tension and strain reflected in his face that hadn't been there when she'd left earlier.

He expelled a harsh breath. "I went to the attic to get that damned nightgown and take it to Celié. . . ."

"That's good. Did you?"

"Yes, I did. She wasn't there. I meant to have it out with her and put this wretched foolishness behind us. . . ."

"Martin . . ." He put a finger against her lips.

"She was away for the afternoon—gone, I was told by Mims, to find Dahomey Sinclair. Have you heard of him?"

"No."

"You will. He's a friend of Celié's, and the city's best-known conjure man. As well regarded, as much feared, as Marie

Laveau, the voodoo queen. New Orleans is *very* fond of voo-doo—people of color *and* whites. Even the aristocrats."

Katherine thought a moment. "Madame did mention Celié's using Dahomey Sinclair to work magic for her. Martin, what does this mean?"

"Nothing special, I suspect," he answered evenly. "Celié was *interested* in voodoo even on Santo Domingo, but she'd never soil her hands with actually *practicing* it herself."

He sounded less than convinced, asking now, "How did you find the governor's wife? Can you help her?"

"Yes," she replied. "She's a lot like Guy DeBeau. Terrified of what she's been told, dispirited by what she's heard. Guy felt trapped by his father. Natalie Montrose feels trapped by her fear and perhaps by being a woman. Martin, the governor's a good man. They're both good people. I'm pretty certain Dr. St. Cyr and I can pull her through to a healthy delivery. He spoke highly of you."

"I'm glad both that you can help her and that the governor thinks well of me," he said. "I made fresh coffee. Worked in the flower beds a bit and . . ." he paused a moment, "I went up to the attic."

"Yes, to get the gown?"

Martin bit his lip sharply. "I looked at photographs of my mother, Raoul, me. My father. Celié. I looked at the case with the violin I've played since I was a boy."

"I didn't know you played the fiddle."

"Yes, but not in the past three years. It was someone else's violin I played that last night on Santo Domingo. Dear God, Katherine, I remembered so much this afternoon that I've not been able to focus on before. But there's still so much I just can't bear to remember."

"Martin . . ." She stroked his back, longing to comfort him but feeling a sense of unease, foreboding even, that bothered her.

"I want to show you the pictures of my family," he an-nounced, taking her hand. They left the kitchen and walked

up the hall to their bedroom. The photographs lay spread on
the bed, as Martin and Katherine sat down.

Martin picked up each one and told her a little about that
person. Annalise. Raoul. His father. Celié.

"Your mother was a beautiful woman," Katherine observed
quietly. "Your brother and your father, handsome. You're more
handsome than either. Celié, of course, is beautiful."

Martin laughed mirthlessly. "I think my mother said it best.
The face and body of a goddess; the heart of a poisonous
serpent."

He told her then about Celié and the accident on Santo
Domingo, with him driving the cabriolet. He spoke with little
emotion, but his eyes were full of pain.

Then he told her what Celié had said to him later, that she
could not bear children because of the accident. His voice was
ragged when he finished.

"But it wasn't your fault," Katherine protested. "Celié must
know that in her heart."

"That much is true," Martin agreed. "But on the road that
afternoon with Celié, I was so hurt, so angry. I thought I'd
gotten over her, but I still cared, although I realized how cruel
and deceitful she could be."

"Do you *still* love her?"

"No. I meant what I said to you that first night here—that
I want *you* for . . ."

". . . your present and your future," she supplied gravely,
"as I want *you*. Martin, I think Celié is *obsessed* with you.
Your love for her was your first love. Then, too, we don't
always know our own hearts."

"I believe I know my own heart," he told her. "I have seen
too much misery in my own life to hurt you by lying. I do
not love Celié, but I *do* feel guilt about the accident. *I love
you*. Not the way I believe I will grow to love later. It is still
so soon. I know people connected to me have hurt you. . . ."

He'd said he loved her, and he'd been clear about it. Cau-
tiously, her heart opened to him.

"I hope one day you'll forgive me for whatever part I play in this. . . ."

"I think I am certainly beginning to forgive you, Martin, as I am beginning to love you too soon. We both must do what we can about Celié. If we talk with her together . . . Martin, Celié was at the governor's mansion this afternoon."

"I'm not surprised. She is a modiste to many of the wealthiest families."

When Katherine told him what Celié had said, he reacted explosively. "That is a lie! But knowing Celié, I'm *not* surprised. No, Katherine, I will talk with Celié alone."

She touched his arm. "For what it's worth to you, I believe you."

Martin's heart quickened with Katherine's words. Perhaps she would forgive him in time. But just now he would woo her, make her know what he felt.

So she was psychic. His own senses told him that together they could know a richness and joy of life that each had only dreamed of before.

Katherine saw the warmth mirrored in his face, yet she saw that he held himself back.

Fans whirred overhead. Katherine suddenly found the gray and rose checked gingham dress uncomfortable, clinging to her stickily. She rose to go behind the screen and pull it off, change into a ruffled rose cotton plissé negligee. Martin's large hand grasped her arm, none too gently, pulling her back to him.

"Where were you going?" he asked.

"To take off my dress."

Smiling, he told her, "Let me." His hands were clumsy in their haste to undo the small buttons of her bodice front from the spaghetti loops.

With a haze of lassitude and ease washing over her, Katherine was suddenly free of her earlier foreboding. She sat still while he finished undoing the bodice, throwing it aside, pulling the camisole over her uplifted arms. In a short time, more deftly now, he stripped her of her light stays and drawers and stockings, until she was naked beneath his gaze.

Katherine sat up. "Now you. I'll take off your . . ."

In an incredibly short time, Martin stacked the photos and put them on a table. He lowered the shades and locked the door, then swiftly removed his garments and flung them aside.

And after all that hurry, he stopped and stood by the bed, looking down at the woman he'd married just over three weeks ago.

"How beautiful you are," he declared, "and how I *want* you."

Katherine was quiet as she waited. Martin fought to slow himself. It was their first time, and he wanted it to be right for her.

He had intended to cut her a bouquet of roses and put them on the table by the bed. He had intended to chill champagne. But he'd gone to the attic and reawakened that past horror.

Now he *needed* Katherine even more than he wanted her.

With infinite care, Martin lay beside her, kissing her heatedly, fervently. Her body was warmly voluptuous to his touch, silken and yielding, luring him on. In this moment, he could forget his past torment and live deep within himself. He entered her welcoming body, gliding smoothly. But his avid thrusts were too swift. Both were overripe with wanting, and it was over too soon.

But to Katherine, Martin's kisses, his presence, and his sinewy body brought a totally satisfying resolution of the desire that had rushed her since her very first dreams of him.

"Feeling your warmth and sweetness is like a blessing to me," he told her, "but your response to me is pure lagniappe."

Katherine smiled, mouthing the word *lan-yap*—an added bonus for her.

Filled with new resolve after his first night of consummated love with Katherine, Martin got up very early and full of energy. With Katherine still sleeping, he stoked the fires in the kitchen stove and made coffee. Zell and Singing Bird slept later on Sundays.

"On this your wedding day," Martin hummed to himself. Katherine had taught him the tune, which he liked. He was a bit sorry he'd let Madame Le Blanc talk him into such a lavish wedding when it meant waiting until September.

He was going to pay Celié a visit early this morning. Have it out with her. God, he had suffered torturous nights and days thinking he *might* have caused the accident that killed his own child with Celié.

DeBeau and a Madrid priest had been a godsend.

"Lad," DeBeau had said on a visit to Madrid and Martin. "I don't want to know what's tormenting you, unless you want to tell me. I've never known a man to look the way you do except over a woman. Your father was my dearest friend, although we'll both need to pray throughout eternity for any small salvation. He cared about you boys, Martin, especially you, whom he thought smart and talented. . . ."

"He sure as hell never said it," Martin blurted out.

"And neither did *my* father, the pirate," DeBeau retorted. "But he left you enough money to help ease your way. Can you talk about what else is wringing you out?"

Martin had tried, but he couldn't talk to this old reprobate about Celié, whom he still loved. DeBeau had sent him to the priest, and somehow he *had* been able to talk to him. But the guilt had never left him.

He walked outside and sat on the backyard steps. His last dog had died, and he wished for another one. He thought about what he would say to Celié, but one thing was certain: He would see that she never humiliated Katherine again.

He went in and poured himself a cup of strong black coffee, sipping it without cream or sugar.

"Good morning," Katherine called shyly from the kitchen door. She came across the room, smiling, dressed in a rose-flowered silk dressing gown, smelling of castile soap and

French lavender. As she passed him on the way to the stove, he reached up and pulled her down onto his lap.

"Good morning," he said.

She put her arms around his neck. He felt solid, looked even more serious than usual, and smelled of mint after-shave.

"Why are you up so early?"

"I can come back to bed—if I'm made certain promises," he responded with a mock leer.

Katherine's skin warmed, but she sensed that he had something on his mind other than her and lovemaking.

"I'm going to visit Celié," he announced shortly. "I expect things to be different after this. I should have done this before you ran into her again, but when I asked her to leave this house not too long after I first brought her here, I thought she understood that whatever had been between us was over."

It was one of those unbidden things she said from time to time. "Martin, be careful, will you?"

He studied her for a moment. "Why did you say that?"

"I'm not sure. I just get a feeling—very mild, but it isn't good. I find something about Celié strange, not like most people. Just as some people are *fey*—what I call death-knowing— Celié is harm—or death-*bringing*. Oh, Martin, I certainly don't mean actual death necessarily. But she *is* cruel, unkind, malicious. And she at least *believes* that she still loves you. And who are you and I to say she doesn't? Did you sleep with her here? That would make a difference, you know."

"I did not sleep with her here or ever again after we broke up. For me, Katherine, remembered pain and lust do not blend well."

Still holding her, Martin drained the last liquid from his cup, leaving a trail of dregs from the percolated coffee and chicory. This time, Katherine kissed *him*.

"Perhaps I can let her know in unmistakable words that what we had is over. I don't believe Celié loves me. She is spoiled. Willful. My mother lived with her, and she used to say that *if* Celié had a conscience, it was one with holes in it an elephant could walk through."

Katherine chuckled at that. "I'll go with you if you've changed your mind."

"No. I think this way is best. Celié couldn't resist histrionics if you were there."

"Very well," she said, beginning to get up from his lap. "Please hurry back. We'll have pancakes with maple syrup and sausages for brunch."

"You never kissed me before as you did last night, my love. Suddenly, you've made me into a greedy man."

"We haven't kissed all that much," she pointed out. "We've done so little with each other."

"We'll make up for that," Martin told her, getting up. "Now, I'm off to the stables to pick up Helio and the buggy."

Katherine watched him from the window as he went across the yard on the way to the stable that sat on the edge of the farm. Helio and Patchette, the horses, also stayed at a shed in one near corner of the large backyard, where they spent time when they'd be needed quickly.

Last night had made her know that her intuition was invaluable to her. They had finally come together from his pain and from her still-present anger at being abducted like any slave. And nothing could have been more beautiful than what they'd experienced. DeBeau had been the villain. True, she had dreaded marrying Louis, and true, too, that Martin had brought a current of joy into her life that hadn't been there in the bayou country. The memory of Albert, her young first husband, had already begun to fade when Martin came. But Martin had also brought Celié into her life.

Katherine had come into the kitchen looking for Martin and a cup of coffee. Now she found she didn't want coffee. She picked up Martin's cup and studied the pattern of coffee dregs on the side and on the bottom.

Lifting the cup, she poured the last few drops of liquid into the saucer and stared at the dregs in the cup. Long, narrow patterns faintly resembling a cross lay on the sides. Gently, she shook the cup and the dregs clung. A cross. Illness. Or death. That cross was faint. Illness then.

Katherine leaned on her elbows on the table. Already she had so much. She would talk to Martin about going to visit Papa Frank. How would he feel about Papa Frank coming here? And would Papa Frank and Miss Ada want to *live* here?

"Good heavens, it's Sunday. Why get up with the chickens on Sunday? . . . Well, doesn't somebody I know look *happy!*"

Zell came in, rubbing the sleep from her eyes.

"Yes, I'm at least fairly happy," Katherine said, smiling. "How did yours and Singing Bird's time go with Jules?"

"Oh, that is some dude, that Jules!" Zell warmed to her subject. "Seriously, he's a really good guy. I wouldn't mind it a bit if he took a fancy to me. If you've got the rest of the day, I'll tell you about our afternoon."

Celié answered the door herself and let Martin in. Surprised to see him, thinking it was Mims come early to help her with Sunday chores and errands, she caught her breath.

"Why, Martin! Come in!"

Groggy from too much brandy and crème de cacao at a party the previous night, she wondered if Dahomey Sinclair's magic was already working. Celié favored pale green and her silk-satin dressing gown was of that color, with wide bands of ruffled cream lace. Her slim hand, with its many jeweled rings, went to her bosom.

"Let me get you coffee. But I warn you, I make it without chicory."

Martin had ridden hatless through the streets. It was one of the few hot days they'd had or would have that summer, and it was early to be so muggy.

"I've had coffee," he said abruptly. "I need to talk with you."

"Well, we're alone as we have been before. Mims, apparently, will be on later. I thought you were Mims. Oh, Martin"—Celié put her arms behind her head as she stood there, narrowing her waist, displaying more of her creamy, well-shaped bosom—"I can't think before I have my first cup of coffee. Please join me. I picked up wonderful cinnamon rolls from the French Market."

"I want to make this quick, Celié. I have to get back."

"Oh, yes, of course, to the ex-slave leaf-woman who has the governor's wife as well as you under her spell."

"Don't say *you* wouldn't like to be able to work such a spell on Mrs. Montrose."

"I'd never deny that," she said quietly. "Natalie Montrose thinks very highly of the garments I make for her—and of me. Martin, *querido mio,* please share my breakfast. Then we can talk of anything you wish. But you must sit down. You seem so *threatening* this way."

Celié started away, but Martin's steely grip on her wrist stopped her. She looked down at his fingers locked around her wrist, smiling.

"I did not want to touch you, Celié," he said coldly, "but I mean business. I see now that *you* have always called the shots where you and I are concerned. But no more. I want no more of your meddling in mine or Katherine's life. I'll have no more damnable lies about my marrying her to produce a child for us, for you and me, then leaving her to marry you. . . ."

He released his grip, and Celié rubbed her wrist and forearm. "Did she tell you that? And you believe her? You must admit you don't know this woman very well. Perhaps *she* is the liar. Had you thought of that?"

"I think we both know who the liar is."

"I wasn't lying about the baby for you that I lost, Martin. I swear to you I wasn't. That accident . . ."

And Martin damned himself because that accident still had the power to shake him. But he knew it wasn't just the accident, but also his guilt over the never-born child. He steeled himself.

"Celié," he began, humble now. "I would go through the fires of hell if that would undo the night you were hurt. But you and I both know it wouldn't. I have asked your forgiveness, but you seem unwilling to face two facts: I would have married you had I known it was my child. . . ."

"But your *forgeron* apprenticeship, Martin. Wasn't that far more important?" Her voice was bitterly mocking.

"Yes," he answered evenly. "At the time it was. You know what a man of color's life is like without training." He didn't intend to let her throw him off balance. "As for the *accident . . .*" He willed himself to stress the word. "You were acting impulsively toward me and taunting me. We had been lovers, and you were Raoul's wife. . . ."

"And you were furious and jealous because you thought Raoul and I loved each other."

"Certainly I was jealous—and furious," he flung back at her. "You said you loved *me,* Celié. Yet even when you said it, you and Raoul were too close. I know that now."

Celié was like a chameleon, changing from mockery and derision to guile. "I remember what we had together and, believe me, I never forgot it with Raoul, *querido mio.*

"Please don't use those words with me," Martin said angrily. "They're like poison on your lips."

"But they were not always poison, were they? There was a time, Martin . . . Please let us sit down. Be friends. This is your home as much as mine." For she saw the memories on his face, saw his guilt. Martin was a man who couldn't help caring, who hated to inflict pain, and she intended to take full advantage of what she saw as a failing. But he didn't have to know that. Guile was her best bet here. He would learn later that there are indeed many ways to skin a cat—said cat, to Celié, being Katherine.

Martin shook his head, feeling calmer now. "I won't toy with you, Celié, and I will not *let* you toy with me or my *wife.*"

"I know she's your wife, Martin. You don't have to keep calling her that to me."

"Then why in hell can't you respect the fact that she *is* my wife?"

"Perhaps I feel that *you* deserve better," she replied, looking at him obliquely.

"*You* deserve someone who loves you," he returned truthfully, "as I certainly don't."

But you *did* love me, Celié thought to herself. And you *will* love me again. Without this leaf-woman, you will love me again.

With careful guile and downcast eyes, Celié declared suddenly, "I am sorry, Martin, that what we had has come to this. If I can't have your love, then please keep on being my friend. I see now that I've been wrong. You brought me here from Santo Domingo. Had it not been for you and DeBeau, I would have been slain, along with Raoul and Annalise and the others."

She wondered if he believed her. She almost believed herself.

But Martin well knew Celié's duplicitous nature. One thing he felt fairly certain of: She was afraid of DeBeau. The last thing Raoul had said to him before he died in that horrible Santo Domingan prison hospital was: "Someone betrayed us, Martin. Someone very close who knew exactly what we planned."

"For your sake," he said now, "I hope it was not you who betrayed the band of people who meant to keep slavery from coming back to them again. I consider my mother and my brother heroes, in that they led the people who stopped that from happening."

"Martin, how could you accuse me of such treachery? You know I loved Raoul—oh, not the way I loved *you*—and he loved me. No, I had nothing to do with that horror, I promise you. Martin, can we—if you don't wish to be friends—at least be civil to each other?"

To her question, Martin nodded. "I see nothing to be gained by not being civil. But hear me well: I may go to my grave feeling some guilt for your childlessness, but I will try not to keep punishing myself. And I will not let you harm Katherine, destroy me, or our marriage."

The fight seemed to have gone out of Celié. He and DeBeau only suspected what had happened on Santo Domingo in the massacre. They could prove nothing.

"I am sorry for loving you, Martin," she told him gently. "I cannot stop that, but I won't bother you again—or Katherine. Will you go now? I have so many thing to do, although it's Sunday."

Martin turned and went out the door and onto her patio. He had fashioned the iron grillwork for her—black iron English ivy—at her request. Now he would have liked to tear it down with his bare hands. Katherine was the one with the psychic gift, he thought, but he had used enough of his own hunches to trust the one that said Celié actually might be seeing the light—or Celié might be incapable of valuing or *heeding* the light when she saw it.

Nine

Hurrying in the late July afternoon, Katherine keenly felt the joy of anticipating her wedding plans.

Martin had wanted to be married in three weeks, and she wanted the same. But Madame Le Blanc had insisted, then begged, that she be allowed to put on the wedding they deserved. She estimated needing at least six weeks to complete the beadwork and order the fine silk tulle from Paris.

That would bring the time up to August. And nothing was undertaken in August in New Orleans. For years, yellow fever epidemics had struck the city, taking its worst toll in one of the two hottest months. Summer had been cool so far this year, but who could say it would remain that way? No, August was a month for rest and escape to the country for those who had the means.

So they settled for what she most wanted, a sunrise ceremony in mid-September, when the weather would begin to cool.

And why hadn't she heard from Papa Frank? Katherine wondered, having posted a letter to him the first week in her new house.

She had gone to the French Market to purchase the brown pralines that were Martin's favorite candy, although he ate few sweets. She had stayed longer than she'd intended, buying long loaves of French bread, goat cheese, and lobster bisque for tonight's dinner.

Now she hurried along the narrow street as sundown neared,

her head down. Martin had warned her to be very careful in her travels about the city to help the sick. Certain areas were quite dangerous. Usually both Zell and Singing Bird accompanied her, and they went by one of the several carriages they owned.

Already faint drumbeats could be heard from Congo Square, warming up for midnight revels and the casting of magic spells. Katherine crossed herself. They had known two blessed weeks of peace from Celié. She had not seen her again at the Montroses. Certainly Martin was more relaxed.

"Katherine, the queen!"

That sharply derisive voice was familiar. Indignantly, she shook off his hand from her shoulder and faced Louis Duplessis, who doffed his hat and bowed from the waist.

"I don't reckon you ever expected to see me again," he said.

"I'm in a hurry," she told him angrily. "What do you want from me?"

There were no fumes of liquor from his breath and he didn't have a "brick in his hat"—a favorite New Orleans term for drunkenness—yet his manner was as rakehell as ever.

Duplessis grinned. "Well now, what I wanted most, the furriner took. I wanted you as *my* woman under *my* control."

"I have no time for this foolishness, Louis," Katherine began.

He grasped her arm and would not let go. "I jus' want you to listen while I tell you you ain't the only one to prosper in this city. Now, I may not be as highfalutin as that furriner's made you, but I got powerful friends . . . *big bugs* . . . a woman that's my friend. You know the vegetables and fruit I grew was the talk of the bayou country. You remember."

He shook her a bit. Katherine thought it best not to fight him—yet.

"Yes, I remember," she said.

"Well, she's helped me link up with a white gen'lman that helps me get the same chance here and help t' sell what I grow, some of it right back there in that famous French Market and in Market Square. Me and this woman have got *plans.*"

"For marriage perhaps?" It was both a thrust and a question.

His breathing got ragged. "No, it ain't that way with us. But she's teaching me how to talk and be in society."

"That's nice, Louis, but I do have to go now," she told him, gentling her voice. "I'm glad you're doing well, and I'm happy you've got . . . someone who cares about you and that you care about, but I have to go."

"Well now," he said slowly, "seems you're a little bit less feisty than you was under that magnolia tree. You remember that magnolia tree and me and you under it that last night I saw you? Is it true they kidnapped you and you liked it well enough to *marry* this clown?"

"Don't speak to me about that!" Katherine shouted, anger rising in her breast. "You would understand nothing about a man like my husband." She would not say Martin's name to him.

Louis grinned widely, licking his lips.

"Well, I reckon I understand enough to know I jus' didn't handle you heavy enough. I reckon I know better now, and I reckon I'll jus' finish that kiss I started back then."

Katherine clenched her teeth as his sinewy, hard hands fastened on her jaws. He didn't have a brick in his hat this time as he'd had in what now seemed eons ago. But Katherine knew he would finish what he'd begun, and she would repeat the actions that had stopped him the first time.

This time she was wearing sturdy walking shoes, and her left foot struck his shins with such savage force, followed by her right foot, that he howled in pain, letting her go. The force of her kicks had caused Katherine to lose her balance, sending the groceries flying.

She stood poised to run but he doubled up with laughter, and she knew then that she had to ask him about Papa Frank.

"You know, woman, you always goin' t'be a hellcat," Louis groaned. "All right. I don't need you no more nohow since I got this woman for a friend. You never was all that hot to my notion."

"How is Papa Frank, Louis?" she asked again, pleading this time. Demanding. "You owe him that much, to tell me how he is. He and Miss Ada. They were both good to you."

She was talking too fast, on the edge of babbling. Louis was silent a very long moment before he answered.

"They both dead," he told her. "My stepma and your grandpa. He had a setback, caught summer flu. They both did. Mind you, I don't *know* this. I *heard* it, since I been here right after the furriner took you."

"Oh, my God." Katherine's cry was strangled. "When?"

"You mean when it happened? Well, the man said right after you got yourself kidnapped, I reckon. I reckon you could say he grieved hisself to death and got the sickness due to that furriner taking you off."

"It wasn't that way," Katherine cried, protecting Martin. "Martin didn't know. Oh, Lord, you'd never understand."

"No, Miss Hincty, you never did think I understood nothing, did you? Well, I guess we both understand this: The old man and my stepma is dead and buried, and I reckon you could say that puts blood on that furriner's hands. That furriner you *married.*"

"No," Katherine sobbed, unable to say anything else. Her eyes felt horribly dry, and a stone seemed to be lodged in her chest. Don't grieve before you *know,* she told herself, and felt better.

Surprisingly, Louis bent and gathered the packages of food, most of which were undamaged, putting them in a bag and handing them to her. The lobster bisque container had broken open and its contents were running into the gutter. Louis shrugged.

"I'll walk with you to your buggy," he offered.

Katherine shook her head vehemently, still dizzy with disbelief.

"Yes," he insisted. "I saw you hitch your horse and I waited.

Now devil I be, but I got lines I draw. There's men in New Orleans don't draw no lines, and you know I don't lie. So you be good to yourself and let me walk you."

At the buggy, he helped her in, unhitched the horse, and said, "Now, I hope I be wrong about Papa Frank and my stepma."

Katherine had learned early that she had a veritable gift for divining another person's intentions, a gift she admitted she sometimes ignored, but she felt now that Louis already seemed different and posed no further danger. Perhaps he *was* in love with this woman he mentioned, although he hadn't said so.

And thinking about Louis kept her from thinking about Papa Frank and Miss Ada, because if she thought about them, she was afraid she would not be able to make it home. Lord, Martin had warned her often enough about being home before the sun went down, and she had heeded his warnings. But now . . .

Home seemed much farther away than the three miles of city blocks that it was. Katherine was happy to see Martin waiting for her on the front porch when she arrived. He approached the buggy and, in the flickering gas streetlight, saw her sorrowful expression as he helped her out and pulled her to him.

"I've been going crazy worrying about you."

Silently, she clung to him, trembling, until against the warmth of his rock-solid body, the acid tears of her heartbreak stung her eyes, as they stung her heart.

In the yard, he held her close. "Katherine, what *is* it?"

And she told him about Papa Frank and Miss Ada, but she had stopped crying; just the anxiety remained.

He took her into the house and into the bedroom, where Zell and Singing Bird came in and joined their anguish with hers.

Martin brewed a valerian infusion for her and brought it back in a large cup.

"It will ease you," he said, "but I don't think it wise for

you to sleep until we've talked about the possibility that you've lost Papa Frank and Miss Ada."

"I dreamed of you meeting him," she said and crossed herself, because dreams of meeting the dead were commonly thought to mean the person dreamed of would die.

"I know; you've mentioned that. The same way I've sorrowed that you could not know my mother and brother. But we have each other, *querida mia.*"

"Yes," Katherine murmured, drawing strength and comfort from him. "Martin, why didn't I *know?* Papa Frank and I were so close. I had no dreams, no premonitions. I wanted him at our wedding, but I know how busy you are."

Martin thought a long moment. "But I *did* think about going back to bring him here to live, Katherine, although I know old people hate moving from their homes. You've said he was close to Miss Ada and you thought they'd be happy. So I delayed until next spring. And now . . ."

"Darling, don't. There is no way either of us could have known. It used to bother me to have these flashes of what's going to happen. It used to scare me so. I wish that gift hadn't deserted me with Papa Frank. There's so much I wanted to tell him."

Martin got up and began to pace. "I will travel to the bayou country," he announced. "DeBeau's ship goes there in a few days."

"I should go with you."

"No. There has been flooding lately near that region, as you know. It could be dangerous, and DeBeau's ship is not fit for a woman, as you well remember."

"I told you when we talked about your family that I'm not so angry anymore."

"It will take time," he said. "It was no good thing to be snatched away from those you love."

"Thank you for saying that," she whispered.

As Martin stopped pacing, sat down, and held her hand,

Zell and Singing Bird sadly watched Katherine. Singing Bird got up and wrote:

I am so hurt! I loved him.

And reading the note, Katherine wept a little. Then Martin asked about her meeting with Louis in the French Market, and Singing Bird's expression perked up as she bit her bottom lip. She then went to the table and stayed there a long time writing. She brought the pages back and showed them to Katherine, who read them and handed them to Martin.

Katherine,
I should have told you. I feel bad. When I went to the French Market with Jules last month, he went back inside the market, and Louis came to the coach and we talked.
He asked about you and said he had no designs against you. I know you hate Louis and did not want to marry him. I never thought he was good enough for you.
But Katherine, I have reason to be grateful to Louis, believe me. I cannot talk of why it is that I am grateful to Louis. Perhaps one day I can tell you, and I know you and Martin will understand.
I love you both so much. As Papa Frank loved us all.
                                                  Singing Bird

Singing Bird went out and Katherine turned to Martin.
"Please hold me," she said.
He caught her hand and brought it to his lips.
When she told him Louis was the man she was to marry, Martin's mouth tightened.
"That scoundrel who accosted you today?"
"He's changed, at least a little, Martin. He says he came here shortly after I did."
"Seeking *you*."

"He didn't say that. He claims to have a big bug friend here."

"I just want to make damned certain that he leaves you alone. While I'm away, please tell Jules if he bothers you again."

"You know I will."

Zell had prepared soup for them, but Katherine couldn't eat. Martin was right, she thought. She shouldn't sleep until she could talk about Papa Frank, but her eyes got heavier and heavier, and with Martin sitting on the edge of the bed, stroking her brow, Katherine slipped into sleep and an instant dream.

Papa Frank lay on the front porch propped up by two large bed pillows, the same way he did each noonday to enjoy the cool shade of the giant oaks nearby. Katherine was a child in the dream and she came to his side. He opened his eyes and smiled at her.

"Papa," she asked him earnestly, "if you go away like Grandma did, will I go away, too?" And she had begun to cry.

In the dream, he hugged her gently.

"I want you to always remember, my little love," he told her, "I am a part of you, Katie, as you are a part of me. You can never lose me—unless you *want* to lose me."

It was a conversation they had actually had when her grandmother had died and her mother was away, and she had missed them both dreadfully in spite of his care. Katherine had grabbed him around his neck and hugged him fiercely. And it had been all right.

Martin caught his breath as she smiled in her sleep. He had waited to go home to Santo Domingo from New Orleans, and it had almost been too late. He made a vow never again to be too late if he could help it.

As Katherine woke from her brief nap, feeling strangely refreshed, he told her.

"I will arrange as soon as I possibly can with DeBeau or

someone else to go to the bayou country to find out about Papa Frank and see that he is properly buried."

"But you need to be here," she told him. "Your business is expanding so rapidly."

"Hush," he said gently, tracing her face with his fingers. "Nothing I can ever own or be is more important to me than *you* are. I will go to your bayou country."

"Oh, Martin, thank you" was all she could say.

Katherine felt it a blessing now that the governor's wife was nearing her term. Her grief seemed suspended and she waited for dreams to sustain her. She was preoccupied with thoughts of the past, mingled with her present life. Even without the bad news, Louis's intrusive presence would have brought it all back. She had time once the first shock was past to wonder about the woman with whom he was so smitten. Of course, many women had found Louis attractive. Singing Bird had always spoken of him with kindness, but she didn't defend him when Katherine and Zell mercilessly flayed him with verbal barbs. She remembered the young girl's note of a few nights back regarding Louis. Apparently, he had saved her from something so terrible that it had robbed her of her speech.

That afternoon at the governor's mansion, Katherine talked with an effusive Emil, who chatted about the city. And about Martin. "That husband of yours, lady," he said, "he's a smart man, but not highfalutin. Not like some who come here to bring things to Miss Natalie."

Was he talking about Celié? Probably so. What he said next made her almost certain.

"I guess by now you've heard plenty about *color* in this city. It's a cryin' shame, if you ask me. Why we've got to divide ourselves up so. Creoles that whites laugh at, sayin' there's no creoles save the *white* ones that's Spanish and French."

"Whites say the same thing in the bayou country," Katherine told him. "It really upsets them."

"Now here in New Orleans, wouldn't you say we mostly fall in the *gens de couleur* class? Fancy words. Seems that's anybody that's not a pure black African—a Negro. And that's most of us. There's the *passe pour blancs,* of course," he added scathingly.

"Which my grandfather is," Katherine acknowledged quietly. She wanted to tell Emil about Papa Frank and Miss Ada, but she knew she'd start crying.

"Well now," Emil said. "We've got a rose garden of a race, all right. Tommy Lafon's as white as they come and a nicer man of color—or *any* color for that matter—you won't find."

"My grandfather was . . . a wonderful man. He cared nothing about color."

Emil smiled. "Lady, the good in you—you had to get it from somewhere."

"Thank you, Emil. You know how highly I think of you."

"I feel I know. Now don't let me keep you too long, or the missus'll be sayin' I take up too much of your time, Miss Katherine."

"Listen," she remonstrated. "I won't stand for you to call me by title when I call you Emil. You know I won't."

Emil sighed. "You're dear to me, lady. Not one single herb you've given me or told me about has failed to work. Now, that's more'n I can say for even Dr. St. Cyr's medicine, as much as I like him. My wife likes you, sight unseen," Emil rambled on, but he caught himself. "What I'm saying is I think the world of you—next to my better half—and I do you honor as a lady of color by calling you Miss Katherine. But, well . . . *everybody* calls me Emil."

"I see," Katherine said. "I appreciate the honor and I'll call you Emil, but I really must insist that you call me Katherine."

With a flourish, Emil bowed, took her hand, and kissed it.

* * *

Katherine found Natalie in an effervescent mood. Her closet was now filled with lacy silk and fine cotton bedjackets and gowns, three new silk robes, and two cotton robes—all pastel.

"I don't suppose silk will be practical for a while," Natalie commented. "I'm not that fond of cotton, but the baby will be drooling all over me."

"You won't mind once the baby gets here."

"I hope you're right. I worry that I won't be a good mother. Do you think I'll be a good mother? Dr. St. Cyr thinks I'm spoiled, flighty."

Katherine honestly pondered this question a few moments before she answered. "I think you *can* be a good mother. And I think the fact that you're worried means you want to be. Don't sell yourself short, Mrs. Montrose."

"You may call me Natalie—if you wish—Katherine. Especially when we're alone, if you're comfortable with that." She paused a moment. "I'm different, you know, in the way I see social things. My father was very different in the way he saw social and racial matters. He felt it was simply what he called 'our time' for whites, and that all other races had had—or would have—their 'time.' What do you think?"

"It's a lovely thought. I certainly *hope* we'll have our 'time.' "

"You know, the governor really *believes* in equality. He's far from the opportunist he's held to be by these damned Orleanian aristocrats. They're giving him a terrible time—most of them. A few friends are courteous to us and even kind. Others tell us these so-called new friends are using us. I'm a southerner—from right here.

"But Lord, Katherine, right now New Orleans is different from any place on earth, I hear. It's Europe and it's not Europe. It's America and it's *not* America. What do the *gens de couleur*—the people of color—think about this? I guess what I want to know is what they think of my husband as *their* governor, and he is as much yours as he is the governor of any white aristocrat."

"Well, I've only been here a few weeks," Katherine declared, warming to her subject. "Martin thinks very highly of him. He seems a good man to me. I've met Lieutenant Governor Drumm, who nearly reveres him, and he says that most folks in every segment of the people of color think highly of Governor Montrose."

Natalie laughed aloud. "Oh, Katherine, if he hasn't done so already, ask Emil to tell you about what he feels is the unnecessary division of people of color here. He has a droll way of putting it. It was a long time before he would talk very much about it. I consider Emil a friend, you know, as I'm sure I'll consider you a friend by the time my baby is . . . born."

She had hesitated before speaking the last word. Now she said thoughtfully, "Remember, Katherine, how *terrified* I was to bear this child? And I'm still frightened a little. How sure I was that my slender hips could never deliver what my womb carries. I'm so glad that you came."

"I think Dr. St. Cyr would have pulled you through."

"Perhaps. But I didn't feel free to talk with him about how terrified I was. Now at least that's in the past, thanks to you and your understanding. I've been meaning to ask you, too, how is it that you speak so well? Were you free in the bayou country?"

"For four years, a little less, we've been free. No, Mrs. Montrose . . ."

"Natalie, at least when you feel like it. But I won't press you."

"Very well. I was born a slave, but I worked at the plantation big house. And I was with the women of the house tending the house, but also taking care of their clothes. They talked to me a lot—about fashions, what little they knew of politics. They were not especially kind—or unkind—but I'd say what my grandfather always said, that they *saw* you when they looked at you. A lot of white people don't."

"Yes, I've heard that from whites and yes, from people of color. Your husband, Martin, is a splendid man. He and his sister-in-law, Celié, who's nearly *passe-pour-blanc,* are both from Santo Domingo. If color prejudice is what I hear it is, does *she* scorn you? Or does she dare?"

Katherine smiled a bit, to her own surprise. "I'm afraid Celié is not an easy woman to know," Katherine said quietly. Then she understood that her smile was based on nervousness.

"Today I gossip," Natalie admitted, "the New Orleanian's favorite pastime. Please forgive me. But one more question. Martin married you, I suspect, because he was entranced by your beauty and even more by your spirit. . . ."

"You're very kind."

"You must know that he is a 'catch' among the women of color in this city. Have they been unkind to you?"

"I have not found them unkind. It's still so soon."

Lying there, relaxed and happy, Natalie plainly saw the tension mount on Katherine's face, and she broke off the conversation. Natalie thought that Katherine *used* the blessings God and fate had bestowed on her, and as with everyone else, there were always some who would seek to make her pay for this. Natalie would bet, though, that Katherine was more adept than most at defending herself.

As Katherine sat in the little room at the other end of the hall, Emil stuck his head in the door.

"The missus wants me to bring up some preserves from the cellar for dinner," he reported. "I'll be coming back to take you home in a little while. Is everything all right, *Katherine?*"

She sighed. Louis had said he'd *heard* that Papa Frank and Miss Ada were dead. Martin had begged her not to borrow trouble, to wait until he could go to find out.

"Yes," she replied, "I hope so. Mrs. Montrose told me to ask you about your view of the world of color in New Orleans. Will you tell me?"

Emil threw back his head, laughing delightedly. "Lord, lady, I'd *love* to give you my view on that."

The deep blue chintz cushions of the white wicker rocker felt good beneath her. Next week Martin would go with De-Beau to find out about Papa Frank. Certainly, she had had no premonitions, no extra-sight, no dreams. But psychic powers often failed. Papa Frank wisely said that man was never meant to know everything. What if he had gone from this earth and she had not *felt* his leaving? She had dreamed of snow again and again in the heat of the bayou country when her mother had died. She had dreamed of raging, muddy water for four nights straight before that death, and there had been no floods there for several years.

Martin was a jewel of a man, Katherine thought now. Deep. Caring. She warmed greatly thinking that he was also an accomplished lover. Already she felt that she could love him more than he loved her. She closed her eyes and waited for Emil to return, opening them against her volition to find Celié standing before her.

"I didn't hear you come in," Katherine remarked, sitting up straighter.

"I was in the linen closet in back of you," Celié told her, "and I was outside Mrs. Montrose's door when she questioned you. I didn't want to interrupt. Color is only *one* strike you have against you," she continued. "You are no more than a healthy wench to bear and nurse a child for Martin and me. The sooner you do this, the sooner you can be out of our lives."

"It is not a matter I'd ever discuss with you." Katherine spoke as evenly as she could, unwilling to quarrel in someone else's house, but determined to take no abuse from this woman.

"Martin is a lover to make a woman dream, isn't he?" Celié asked throatily, causing Katherine to lean forward.

"I know the whole story about you and Martin," Katherine said.

Celié looked surprised. "Be careful. Martin betrayed me. He will do as much to you."

"No, Celié. I think *you* betrayed *him.*"

"What lies has he told you about me?" she demanded. "He had no right to talk about *me* to *you.*"

"He had every right," Katherine reminded her. "I'm his wife."

Celié touched her own flat stomach as she stood there, her eyes unfathomable. "If there had been no accident, if *our* child had lived, he would not have needed to turn to others."

Katherine stood up, angry now. What in hell did this woman want from her? She was not easily threatened, but she had to admit that Celié made her very uneasy. Celié carried a flat package, and she finished undoing the loose wrappings and held up a daguerreotype.

"Please look at this carefully," she said cruelly, "and *remember* well what you see here."

At first it was hard for Katherine to focus, but when she did she saw that the photograph was of Celié in a dark, low-cut gown that exposed her lovely bosom and displayed *the black pearl.* Martin had said the necklace was one of a kind. Had Celié perhaps had another fashioned like it?

Katherine's head spun. Celié's wicked smile said that the black pearl she wore so effectively was the same one Martin had given Katherine, pledging his love. She felt slightly sick, and Celié gloated. After all, even though her intuition said to trust him, did she really *know* this man?

"Why don't you ask *him* about it?" Celié suggested. "Two people who have known what Martin and I have known together cannot be easily torn apart by a country upstart." She closed her eyes, smiling, "New Orleans is a city where *anything* can be bought or sold. Look *carefully* to your wedding vows, *mam'selle.* They may be fake. Why would a man like Martin marry *you* when he has loved someone like me?"

"Yes, you *are* a fashionable, sophisticated woman, Celié,"

Katherine acknowledged. "I could never deny that. And I don't know why you wear the black pearl here. Perhaps you were in Santo Domingo when this photo was taken."

"You *are* an idiot," Celié said sharply. "Look at the imprint. Badon is one of the best-known photographers in this city. No, it certainly was not taken in Santo Domingo."

As Celié was not now in Santo Domingo. Martin had not showed her this photograph of Celié, having possibly considered it cruel to do so. She and Martin had talked and she had soothed his torment. Still, Celié had *commanded* that he come to see her that first night at the house. And he had not gone. But the second time she had sent for him and threatened to come to him, and Katherine had bade him go. But he would have gone even if she had not; she was certain of this. He and Celié had been lovers. A baby unborn, an accident on a country road. And her husband was still sick at heart with guilt. Or was it more than that? In spite of what he said and thought, did some part of him still love Celié?

"If you will excuse me," Katherine said coldly, "I'm finished in here."

"Yes, of course," Celié agreed. "Now that the governor's child is almost born, you will soon not be needed here either. *I* have prepared Mrs. Montrose the many garments she will use for herself and the baby. Like the garments on her bed upstairs. Like Martin and me, Katherine, the governor's lady and I go back a very long way."

Celié's smile was one of a cat anticipating a canary. Martin had come to see her and had refused to recognize what she, Celié, knew was true: that *they* belonged together in spite of her having married Raoul and his marrying Katherine. So, Celié thought, this Katherine had quickly made a name for herself with her herbs and midwifery.

Heavily veiled, she and Dahomey Sinclair had met the night before to bask in the moonlight and firelight in Congo Square, and to invoke magic with potions she was certain were far more potent than any this simple countrywoman could even imagine, let alone concoct.

Riding along with Emil in the governor's buggy, Katherine felt better with the sharp breeze that came in from the river. There were coachmen who could have taken her home, but Emil usually sought the job when he wasn't too busy. And often when he was, he would plead an errand that needed to be run and could only be handled by him, not by the careless young Negro boys hired to do such jobs.

"Now, I couldn't help overhearing Miss Celié talking to you. I wasn't of a mind to *doorpop* on you two, but I figured from the sharp tone of her voice it wasn't all good." Katherine always had to smile at the "doorpop" term, which normally meant a meddling interest in some outside affair, but which some used for listening in with any meddling interest.

"With Celié, I wonder if it ever is good," Katherine answered.

"She's Mr. Dominguez's sister-in-law, I know. When she first came to New Orleans, he used to squire her around and she lived with him. But I don't believe she was there two months. I guess *he* found her that shop in the French Quarter. Few people of color there, lady. But your husband, now, has connections, him being friends with our lieutenant governor and all. He's a damned good *forgeron,* and it seems that for the past two years everybody and his brother is building houses and buildings. People of color getting houses close to or every bit as good as whites."

"I'm just enjoying talking with you, but we get home so quickly when you drive," Katherine pointed out. "Please don't forget to give me your views on color."

Emil slowed the horses as they drove past the French Quarter and headed out Gentilly Way. Katherine noted that he relaxed and a grin spread across his face. He was onstage.

"Color now," he said grandly, "it's part and parcel of the

Crescent City—New Orleans—the way it may not be anywhere else in the world.

"It's changing since we got our freedom, but ma'am, in the old days, when there were slaves here, most of the artisans—the people who *built* this city—were always free. Mind you, not the freest—and the law's never been for *us* the way it was for *them*—but it wasn't slavery.

"Pure-blooded Africans've been called Negroes, but *never* colored. *Gens de couleur* is anybody *blessed* enough to have *one* drop of white blood running in their veins.

"And I hope you know I'm being sarcastic, Katherine, because to me this is the most wretched of all kinds of slavery. Setting a man against his own blood. That takes gall, and we swallow every drop of it.

"The way I've seen it and the way it's been told to me—and my family's been here in New Orleans for three generations—it started with the first slaves coming over. Reckon you know better than most that you mess up a man's mind, and the rest of him comes willingly. You getting tired of listening?"

"You know I'm not."

"Well, I wanted to rest a bit before I get to the rest. It's even more sickening. I'll tell you, lady, as far as most whites are concerned, we're all darkies, if not nigras. They don't give a damn about what color we are—a whole lot, if not most of them. Mostly, they call us mulattoes if we're lighter.

"But us—Lord, *us*—we're the ones who made it a *religion*. If whites are up there with the angels and I got one drop of white blood, then I'm a little closer to heaven. You got two drops and you're even closer to heaven than me. Black man's the devil. White man's God, the way they set it up.

"Like I said, *we* took it a few steps farther. Griffes. Mulattoes. Quadroons. Octoroons. I mixed 'em up, but you can set them like a staircase—from the black of the devil to the white of God—with no more to base it on than God sending us here as one color or another.

"I said it's changing, but not nearly fast enough for me. We got two words in this city that say perfection: *white blood.* We got one word you don't want to be—that is according to the fools: black."

Emil leaned forward, his bald head glistening, his hat on the seat beside him. His merriment had vanished.

"You look suddenly sad," Katherine said gently. "I feel sad about this."

"Yeah. We got a right to feel sad, I reckon. You were a slave, I hear. How many beatings did you suffer?"

"I was never whipped," Katherine replied quietly.

"House slave?"

"Yes."

"I thought so. Elegant, pretty woman like you would have had to be a house slave. Bet the white men gave you plenty of trouble."

"Not the man who we called master," Katherine said. He set great store by being a Christian. . . ."

"That's never stopped them."

"I know. Some of the overseers were vicious." She thought of Singing Bird's mother. "My grandfather is a leaf doctor."

"So I heard. And he taught you what he knew."

"Some. I've got a lot to learn."

"You *know* a lot, too. So they was scared of your grandpapa; thought he was a conjure man, I'll bet."

"Yes, but he wasn't—well, not altogether. Papa practiced . . . he believed in good magic. He *hates* the evil kind."

She noticed having used the past tense when she'd said, *practiced* and *believed,* then changing to the present tense. She was going to wait and see if he was gone. And hope. And *pray.*

"Might as well tell you what little more I tell people. Louisiana in the old days was an armed camp. Whites are *scared* of blacks. On the old Louisiana plantations my great-grand-daddy told me about, and a whole lot later, they had military camps, and white men were trained to be soldiers who knew how to keep a black man under their heels. Treat 'em just bad enough to keep them slaves, and just good enough not to kill them and keep them happy enough to work. You want me to, at some later date I'll tell you about the quadroon balls. You've heard about them?"

"Long before I came here."

"I had a cousin once you couldn't tell from white. Red-headed girl. Lovely. She killed herself when the white man she loved married a white woman who refused to tolerate her in his life. Lots of folk said later *he* had the wife killed with voodoo drums. Your sister-in-law—the modiste, Celié—now would be a natural for that life of quadroon balls. But they like women sweet, and she's pretty stuck-up. But then, I don't reckon she'd be interested in—"

"Why do you say that?"

"I'm getting old, I know for sure," Emil acknowledged, "and my wife has begun to tell me I talk too much." Dang, he'd almost let some comment slip on how much Celié seemed to want Martin for herself.

Martin was home when she got there. He and Emil greeted each other warmly. Katherine invited Emil in for tea but he asked for a rain check, saying he needed to get right back to serve dinner.

Martin followed Katherine into the bedroom, where she'd gone to loosen her stays. After she'd gotten out of her clothes, he loosened them for her, kissing her back.

"Celié was at the governor's again today."

"Oh," Martin responded. "What did she say to you?"

"She showed me a photo of herself wearing the black pearl and the diamond you gave me."

He nodded briefly as she waited for him to speak. Martin thought for only a moment before attempting to explain. "On the escape DeBeau's friend arranged for us on his ship, it was Celié's idea that in case the police came aboard to inspect at

Haiti, we had best pretend to be married. The captain agreed. I saw no real reason to object, and we had both lost so much.

"There was a ship's photographer who was smitten with her. He asked to take her picture. She asked to wear the jewels for the daguerreotype. I agreed. There were three photographs— apparently the one she showed you, one of Celié and me together, and one in the trunk upstairs."

"She is *obsessed* with you."

Martin looked suddenly tired. Katherine had not spent a lifetime trusting her intuition to believe in Martin to deny it now. And yet with Celié this afternoon, she had come close to doing just that.

"If what she feels for me is love, she has a strange way of showing it. Celié's eyes for me are as full of hate as they are of love. She is full of guile."

"She said you were a good lover."

"Do *you* think I am?"

Katherine couldn't help but smiling, and a thrill of warmth coursed through her.

"Yes. Splendid."

But the desire and passion they had for each other in abundance were not necessarily love. And it was *love and* passion *and* desire she wanted with him.

"That makes me happy. Then it doesn't matter what *I* knew with any other woman any more than it matters what *you* knew with . . ." He thought of the bastard Louis, now in New Orleans and probably still in pursuit of her. And he thought of her first husband of whom she spoke well.

"No," he corrected, "I lie here. Lord, I *hate* any man who's touched you. I know that's wrong, but I can't help it. Forgive me."

Katherine simply looked at him. "Celié will cause us more trouble, Martin. . . ."

"I know that now. She is spoiled, vain, selfish."

"Don't see her alone again. It only seems to stoke her fantasies."

"Yes, I think you're right. Celié has too much to lose to play the fool. We'll fight this through together. . . . By the way, I saw DeBeau today. I can leave early next week with him for the bayou country."

"How I'd love to go," Katherine told him. "Martin, I hope Louis is wrong. Even he said he might be. My faith in God is strong. Very strong."

"Yes, my darling, I know. That's why I asked Madame Le Blanc to wrap a special gift for you. My faith is as strong as yours."

He went to the highboy and removed a small package from the top drawer. Wrapped in blue linen, a bunch of fresh-blooming arnica adorned it. He kissed her hand as she took the package, looking at it a long while before she undid the wrapping.

"Exquisite," she said. "Like Madame."

Putting aside the wrappings, Katherine looked at the new and rough-grained black leather Bible with its gold lettering and delicate tissuey pages.

"How beautiful," she stated simply. "I've always wanted one of my own."

Martin got his Bible, and they went out on the front porch and sat in the wide-slatted white bench swing that was suspended from the ceiling by chains. Jules and Zell and Singing Bird chatted over the far fence with neighbors. Like other New Orleans neighborhoods, they had neighbors of mixed races who lived in harmony but mingled little.

"Could we turn to 'The Song of Songs'?" he proposed. "Should I read a verse and you another? Or perhaps a chapter each?"

Katherine thought that idea delightful. There was at least a half hour more of daylight, although the sun's kaleidoscopic rays fanned out low in the pale blue sky.

"Oh, I'd like a verse each, to hear the sound of your voice more often, but don't you think a chapter makes it easier?"

"Then why don't you begin?"

With the cape jasmine massed against the porch wafting

full, rain-drenched fragrance, and a covey of blackbirds lining the branches of a nearby magnolia tree in full bloom, a whippoorwill chirped fitfully and Katherine began to read:

> "The song of songs, which is Solomon's.
> Let him kiss me with the kisses of his mouth—
> For thy love is better than wine."

She paused a moment as Martin listened to the lyrical beauty of her voice, beginning to allow himself the right to be happy. Years had passed when she had not been a wondrous part of his life, and he fervently vowed that now that they were together, he would let no one come between them—ever.

Passage for Martin came through on one of DeBeau's ships, and he left the following week for the bayou country to gather news about Papa Frank—good or bad. If the news was bad, he would give him a proper burial.

Papa Frank had been a simple man, and he had spoken of a simple burial in his passing on. He wanted to lie beside his wife and daughter, to have fragrant herbs planted all around him, and to be remembered with kindness.

Two days before leaving, Martin told her that Lieutenant Governor and Mrs. Drumm had invited them to potluck dinner and had also invited Jules, Zell, and Singing Bird.

"Oh, Martin, and you won't be here."

"I want you to go ahead. We'll have them here when I return."

He had pulled her to him then, saying, "Jules and my next best man, Antoine Smith, can hold down the fort easily. Business slows in July, August, and early September.

"Be careful about Celié, Katherine. She may prove to be more of a problem than we know. Her showing you that photograph after I'd asked her to stay out of our lives bothers me. I told you she is spoiled, selfish, willful."

He looked so worried.

"I'm *always* careful of Celié," she said quietly. "I'm not afraid of her, though."

"I pray you have no *need* to be."

But it had come to her later that she *was* at least somewhat afraid. As smart and as talented as Celié seemed, she was singularly blind to other men save Martin.

Katherine hated being without Martin now. Jules was staying with them. Laughingly, Martin had reminded her, "You have the ship's doctor to look after you. That is, if after work he can tear his eyes from Zell long enough."

It still amused Katherine that the ship's cook was called the ship's doctor. Certainly, she believed that what you took into your body was all-important. But she had even further come to fervently believe that the mind and the emotions dominated life in far deeper ways than most others seemed to currently realize.

After Martin had gone, Katherine thought a great deal about Papa Frank but did not brood. He had been a sage as well as an herbalist, and his fondest advice was that in the loss of a loved one, you dedicated your life to that loved one's memory.

Martin would return in ten days, and Katherine began to count the days as she busied herself in routine tasks with Zell and Singing Bird. Madame Le Blanc visited from time to time, as they visited her. Katherine thought she would invite her to dinner soon, preparing something special. Madame never tired of good food.

It rained the entire third day of Katherine's time apart from Martin. From the moment she had begun to help Martin, Jules, and other teaching volunteers, she actually looked forward to teaching the class of fifteen to thirty adults. Twice weekly they worked on reading, writing, arithmetic, civics, government, and voting registration. They met in the greenhouse but would meet indoors on the few coldest days of winter.

Both Katherine and Martin felt this keen sense of exhilaration at helping others to meet a potential that *they* had been helped to achieve. All were welcomed, helped, and asked to train others. Of course there were severe limitations to what they could hope to accomplish, but their efforts rippled powerfully and pleasantly through the community like tidal waves of empowerment.

The big pot of jambalaya on the iron wood-burning cookstove sent its spicy fragrance throughout the house. Red beans and rice bubbled. Mixed vegetables simmered in the three-legged skillet, and the ubiquitous coffee and chicory were kept warming on the edge in a coffeepot over the hot water well in the stove.

How Papa Frank would have enjoyed this. And how he and Martin would have loved each other. Katherine glanced at the clock on the kitchen wall and frowned. Four o'clock. Singing Bird should have been back by now. They had all met and fallen in love with the Little Sisters, a lone order of black nuns who worked with the homeless and the destitute, as well as with the merely poor. Singing Bird quilted expertly, and the beautiful coverlets she and others made for the sisters were sold to the city's wealthiest people for a goodly sum. The sisters especially loved Singing Bird and she them. Sing seemed so much happier now.

Life was surely strange, Katherine thought. Martin had *insisted* on going to the bayou country to find out about Papa Frank. He looked at her fondly with each passing day. Their desire for each other was pristine, beautiful. If it wasn't love, at least they traveled the sidepath of love's enchanted highway.

Ten

"My dear, you're as lovely as my husband said you were. And so are these two ladies."

Inez, Lieutenant Governor Drumm's wife, met them at her door and greeted Katherine, Zell, and Singing Bird with a little hug for each.

They stepped up and into a wide marble-tiled foyer.

"And as always, Jules, you're looking wonderful. You do yourself proud to escort them. But we all miss Martin, of course."

"Oh, yes," Katherine agreed. "He had to go to see about my grandfather." Mentioning that made her feel sad. Ordinarily reticent, it seemed to her quite natural to tell Inez Drumm this news.

"I hope it's not illness."

"Unfortunately, we won't know until Martin returns," Katherine said. "I certainly hope he's all right."

But the psychic powers that so often had sustained Katherine now seemed to have deserted her. Inez Drumm was compassionate. She placed a slender, well-manicured hand on Katherine's arm.

"And I hope for his good health along with you. Please come into the living room. Wilson will be down in a minute. Make yourselves at home and look around a bit. Then we'll move to the courtyard. Heavens, this is a scorcher of a day."

The invitation to the Drumms' was for three that afternoon. The heat in the city that day had lingered, but the house on

Chartres Street in the French Quarter was cooler than many by virtue of its tall ceilings, ceiling fans, and large oaks outside.

Dressed in beautifully made and heavily bustled pale blue linen, Inez was tall and slim, with dark, straight auburn hair worn in a chignon. Fair-skinned, she radiated middle-aged vitality.

"Ah, what a wonderful couple you and Martin must make," she offered now.

Katherine laughed as they sat down on the Hepplewhite chairs and sofa, admiring the satiny wood and intricately shaped backs and graceful legs of the popular furniture. "You know, Martin greatly admires you both," Katherine said truthfully. "Now that I've met you, I must say I admire you both, too. I think our city is lucky to have Mr. Drumm as lieutenant governor."

"Believe me, we *are* lucky," Jules agreed.

Inez Drumm smiled. "Of course *I* think so," she said. "And I'm Inez to you three ladies, if you're comfortable with that. Jules and I are old friends. We've taught so many reading and writing classes together."

A slight cough from the doorway made them look up to see Wilson Drumm standing there, smiling at them.

"Forgive me for not being down here when you came. I couldn't help overhearing your compliments, and Lord, I'm afraid the *Picayune* editor has a different opinion. Not to mention the *Bee*. They never tire of calling me 'The *Colored* Housepainter Lieutenant Governor.' "

"Well," Inez offered staunchly, rising and going to him, placing her hand on his arm. "Nobody ever accused our New Orleans papers of being fair-minded or of lacking in racial prejudice. But the governor is certainly quoted as thinking highly of you, and he's told you so often enough."

"I've heard him say so myself," Katherine chimed in.

Wilson Drumm looked very pleased.

"And you," he said to Katherine, "are doctoring Mrs. Montrose for a difficult pregnancy."

"Midwifing is more like it," Katherine amended. "So far, she's doing well."

"I'm glad," Wilson said. "She's a gracious lady."

"Yes," Katherine responded, looking around again at the rose and gray needlepoint Hepplewhite furniture, the white sheer curtains, and the heavy rose velvet drapes. Turning to her left, she vividly admired a fan-shaped window.

"Your house is beautiful," she declared. "I don't recall ever seeing a window like that."

Inez laughed. "I'm glad you like it, because such windows go with houses far more expensive than ours. We have a friend who builds for aristocrats and he was kind enough to do this one for us. We have our faults, we Orleanians, but we *do* have a history of helping each other."

"I keep admiring your dresses," Inez told Katherine and the other women. "Am I right that all three are Lillian's designs?"

"Yes. Thank you." Her own dress was ivory silk pongee, lightly bustled, the bodice filled with sheer lace and fastened with tiny buttons, the sleeves long with a single very wide ruffle. Zell wore medium green flowered cotton muslin, Singing Bird white eyelet.

"You're very quiet, my dear," Inez said to Singing Bird. "I want you to be comfortable. May I get you something special to drink? I usually have help, but today *I* wanted to do the honors for my guests. Singing Bird. That's such a beautiful name."

"Sing does not *choose* to talk just now, but she understands," Katherine explained simply, as she had done with Lillian Le Blanc. And Inez Drumm acknowledged and accepted that explanation as graciously as had Lillian.

Quickly, Singing Bird took out her pad and pencil, and wrote that anything cold was welcome.

As Inez thanked her and rose to go to the kitchen, Katherine asked if she could help.

Wilson laughed. "Never ask if you can help Inez; she'll take you up on it. She's dying to talk with you alone."

"Oh, Wilson," Inez giggled shyly. "But he's right, you know. However, this time, just be my guest and be comfortable. Bread is the only hot dish I have. We also have delicious ice cream . . . Wilson's specialty."

Inez's dress moved with its folds in an especially graceful way, and Katherine remarked on it.

Inez looked at her a moment. "It's a new one."

Wilson Drumm stood up and put his hands behind his back, facing Katherine, Zell, and Singing Bird.

"God certainly knew what he was doing when he made beautiful women," he announced gallantly. "From my wife to the youngest one here." His hand went out to note Singing Bird. "What a joy you all are to behold."

Jules laughed. "While these ladies are certainly beautiful, as you say, sir, *all* women are, or can be, works of art. It's simply given to their gender."

Katherine smiled. She had gained more compliments during her time in New Orleans than in the whole of her life in the bayou country, having often felt far plainer than others seemed to think she was.

"You're such a gentleman, Jules," Inez told him, as Zell looked with added admiration at the man she liked more and more each day.

"I'll handle the drinks for you, my dear," Wilson said. After asking each person's preference, he went out to the kitchen with his wife.

By five it was cooler, as they sat on the courtyard flagstones in deeply padded black wrought iron chairs. Trellises adorned with pink and deep red roses climbed the wall. English ivy clung on either side. And near the table stood a big hibiscus bush with its scarlet trumpet-shaped flowers. Inez had covered the large iron table with padded scalloped linen cloths. The table was set with delicate rose-patterned, translucent ivory china. Wilson and Jules pushed a tea wagon laden with dishes of food back and forth. In a shaded corner, the covered hand-cranked ice cream freezer sat deep in a barrel of chopped ice.

As they walked around, enjoying the cooler breezes, and admiring the weeping willow and goldfish pond, the nearby sound of heartbeat drums and raucous trumpets split the air. Katherine looked startled to hear this music on the Sabbath.

"They're probably coming back after a funeral at St. Louis Cemetery," Wilson told her. "Out your way, you won't hear this."

Katherine listened closely to the words:

> *"Oh, didn't he ramble.*
> *Rambled all around . . .*

The hoofbeat of carriage horses drowned out a line or two, but she heard the last lines clearly:

> *He rambled 'til de butcher*
> *Cut him down."*

Dinner began with gazpacho and paper-thin cucumber slices. Iced shrimp with oyster crackers followed, along with cold lobster salad, tomato aspic, a large tossed salad, lemon-flavored wild rice, and delicious buttered hot rolls.

"With you cooking like this, can't you fatten Wilson up?" Jules teased him.

Inez rolled her eyes heavenward. "Lord knows, he eats enough. I suppose it's like my mother used to say in Mississippi: 'He eats so much, it makes him po' to carry it.' "

"At least we've *got* food in plenty these days," Wilson commented. "Thanks to men like Governor Montrose and the generals. The Reconstruction has brought a new day of prosperity to people of color—at least in New Orleans." He stopped, pursing his lips. "But we've paid and we're *still* paying with our blood for it . . . just not as much of it right now."

We've got your authors!

If you seek out the latest historical romances by today's bestselling authors, our new reader's service, KENSINGTON CHOICE, is the club for you.

KENSINGTON CHOICE is the only club where you can find authors like Janelle Taylor, Shannon Drake, Rosanne Bittner, Sylvie Sommerfield, Penelope Neri and Phoebe Conn all in one place...

...and the only service that will deliver their romances direct to your home as soon as they are published—even before they reach the bookstores.

KENSINGTON CHOICE is also the only service that will give you a substantial guaranteed discount off the publisher's prices on every one of those romances.

That's right: Every month, the Editors at Zebra and Pinnacle select four of the newest novels by our bestselling authors and rush them straight to you, usually *before they reach the bookstores*. The publisher's prices for these romances range from $4.99 to $5.99—but they are always yours for the guaranteed low price of just *$4.20!*

That means you'll always save over 20%...often as much as 30%...off the publisher's prices on every shipment you get from KENSINGTON CHOICE!

All books are sent on a 10-day free examination basis, and there is no minimum number of books to buy. (A postage and handling charge of $1.50 is added to each shipment.)

As your introduction to the convenience and value of this new service, we invite you to accept

4 BOOKS FREE

The 4 books, worth up to $23.96, are our welcoming gift. You pay only $1 to help cover postage and handling.

To start your subscription to KENSINGTON CHOICE and receive your introductory package of 4 FREE romances, detach and mail the postpaid card at right *today*.

we have 4 FREE BOOKS for you
as your introduction to
KENSINGTON CHOICE
**To get your FREE BOOKS, worth
up to $23.96, mail the card below.**

FREE BOOK CERTIFICATE

As my introduction to your new KENSINGTON CHOICE reader's service, please send me 4 FREE historical romances (worth up to $23.96), billing me just $1 to help cover postage and handling. As a KENSINGTON CHOICE subscriber, I will then receive 4 brand-new romances to preview each month for 10 days FREE. I can return any shipment within 10 days and owe nothing. The publisher's prices for the KENSINGTON CHOICE romances range from $4.99 to $5.99, but as a subscriber I will be entitled to get them for just $4.20 per book or $16.80 for all four titles. There is no minimum number of books to buy, and I can cancel my subscription at any time. A $1.50 postage and handling charge is added to each shipment.

Name _____

Address _____ Apt. _____

City _____ State _____ Zip _____

Telephone ( ) _____

Signature _____

(If under 18, parent or guardian must sign)

Subscription subject to acceptance. Terms and prices subject to change.

KC0295

"So many of the whites hate Governor Montrose," Jules pointed out.

"Ah yes," Wilson agreed. "Change sits poorly with many people. Men in power will certainly not give it up easily, or at all, if they can help it. As people of color, we must *win* their respect, and we can."

"We've got to respect ourselves more," Jules offered. "And those of us who have a great deal must help others get ahead."

"Oh, I have Creole friends of color who need to heed this advice," Inez said gently. She turned to Zell and Singing Bird. "We don't mean to dampen your spirits with too much political talk. I want us all to enjoy this afternoon."

The main course finished, an ebullient Wilson winked at his wife, pulled a cheroot from his linen vest, and bit off the tip.

"Oh, Wilson," Inez complained, "as much as I like your cigar, the perfume of roses is so much better with dinner."

Shrugging, he laid the unlit cigar aside, saying to his guests, "My wife thinks I smoke too much. And in answer to her earlier remark, I'd say politics is where the fun is these days, my dear. Ever since General Sheridan and General Hancock began calling the shots—and General Rousseau continues—the rabble-rousers have been under control. What a shame that we can't all work together."

Low in the sky, the sun threw rays against the fan-shaped window, changing the clear glass to a kaleidoscope of pearly pastels.

"How truly lovely," Katherine observed, pointing to the window.

"I see you're a lover of beauty," Inez made note. "I'm glad you like our humble place. Katherine, please help me get some dishes to serve the ice cream in. Wilson's ice cream deserves the best. And with my help's help and the Lord's cooler weather yesterday, I made a praline cake with pralines from Market Square. They make brown pralines that I think are far better than those sold in the French Market."

"Pralines are Martin's favorite," Katherine said. "I'm sure he'd love the cake."

"Yes, at the Crescent Balls, I've always made a special one for him. My dear, I'm so glad he found you. I've never seen Martin look so happy the one or two times I've seen him since he married you. Shall we go now?"

Katherine sat by Jules at the table, across from Singing Bird. She and Inez smiled at both. Singing Bird was quiet but seemed happy. Zell obviously was having a very good time.

"I'll be glad to help, too," she offered.

"Thank you," Inez said. "Why don't we all clear the table, then I'd like you two to keep the men company."

Katherine and Inez rose and, with Inez pushing the tea cart, went through the parlor and dining room into the kitchen.

Once the others had brought in food and dishes, they left Inez and Katherine in the dining room. As Inez removed the crystal from one of two china cabinets, Katherine admired it.

Inez smiled. "They tell a story that some of my more snooty new friends think I shouldn't repeat, but I'm proud of it. My mother, you see, was a Virginia slave and was given to one of the family daughters as a wedding present. The daughter was marrying and moving to Pass Christian, Mississippi, with her husband. They thought my mother would be good company and would keep her from getting lonely. Before the woman died of scarlet fever, she asked her husband to give my mother this crystal, because she'd admired it so and had taken such good care of her."

Katherine stood there thinking how wonderful it was to have a family that loved their daughter so much they didn't want her to be lonely. But what about the *other* young girl, Inez's mother?

"It's a sad story, isn't it?" she asked. "In so many ways. My mother was a mulatto. I never knew my father, but I was told by an old woman that he was white. Color is for some like a disease here, Katherine. I didn't notice it as much in

Pass Christian. We were all just Negroes. How is color looked upon in the bayou country?"

"Well," Katherine answered, "in the short time I've been here, color certainly is talked about more."

"I suppose Martin's told you that *gens de couleur* is any person not of absolute African origin."

"He mentioned it—with distaste. Martin's mother is deep brown. No, it was Emil, the governor's butler, who told me recently about color in New Orleans. He has a very funny speech about it."

Inez laughed aloud. "Then you've been perfectly indoctrinated. Oh, yes, I know Emil very well, Katherine. He was once a housepainter, as was my husband. Martin, Jules, my husband and I, Emil, others of differing colors and levels of wealth, are all trying to form a group of people who passionately believe in the future of our race, whatever the class or the color. As long as we believe in ourselves and our lives, we belong. Does that make sense to you?"

"All the sense in the world."

"I find you easy to be around, easy to talk to," Inez said now, suddenly somber. "If there's anything you need to know about the city that I can help you with, please don't hesitate to ask me. Lillian is an old friend. She does most of my clothes." Inez chuckled now. "We go back to the days, too, when her late husband, as well as Wilson and Emil, were housepainters. Wars can certainly change lives."

"We were surely happy to be freed by the war."

"Yes. My dear, forgive me for asking, but how does such a cultivated woman like yourself become that way if you were so recently a slave? Just four years of freedom. So many Orleanians—people of color who've always been free—don't begin to have your class and bearing."

Inez thought of her sometimes-modiste Celié, Martin's sister-in-law. She, too, was cultivated, but cold and haughty. Men—including Wilson—thought her beautiful. Inez was glad Martin hadn't married her.

"Oh," Katherine answered, "the man who was master on that plantation insisted that we all learn to read and write. He simply said he hated ignorance and didn't want it around him. He said he felt *safer* with a man who was treated like a human, even if he was not as *good* a human being as a white person."

Inez nodded, and Katherine continued.

"I used their library whenever I could to read about medicines and herbs." She laughed a little. "I liked romantic novels, and I looked at fashions. I helped the mistress and her two daughters with their wardrobes, and the Keyes women loved fashion. Then, too, the Keyes *saw* you when they looked at you, even people of color. They were a little different—not very—but a little. Inez, *you're* a very cultivated lady."

Inez blushed. "As a girl, I was a house slave, too. I listened and learned. Wilson courted me when he came to paint the master's houses. He has always been free. The man who owned my mother and me had friends here, and that friend hired Wilson to paint his mansion and liked his work. He recommended him.

"My mother begged for my freedom, and with Wilson willing to pay, the man who owned us freed me. My mother didn't live a long time after I left." Inez paused a long time before continuing. "Here I met women like Lillian and others. I already spoke decent English, and I found New Orleans women had . . . a natural grace and class. I try to be a lady—but not hincty, not highfalutin."

"And you succeed very well."

"And so do you, my dear. You're sweet," Inez told her.

Katherine laughed. "I can be sweet at times, I suppose. But I will fight fiercely for what I believe in and for what is mine."

Inez smiled to herself and wondered if Katherine were speaking of Celié, whom she had long admired but did not *like*. The arrogance. The haughtiness. But the garments the woman designed and had made up had no equals in the city. Only in Paris could one find better.

"Lillian has been especially helpful," Inez said. "She's been my friend for all these years. I suppose, too, the fact that we're both childless has drawn us closer. She's been like the mother I lost."

"Yes," Katherine agreed, "she's been particularly helpful to me, too. She's planning Martin's and my wedding, and her plans threaten to go on until Christmas. She thinks now it'll be in mid-September."

Inez smiled broadly now. "I'm so glad you told me. I wanted to ask, but I didn't want to be nosy."

Katherine thought a moment before she spoke again. "Martin and I were married in such a simple ceremony at first. Bless his heart, he feels I deserve something special." She added, in a soft voice, "As if I need anything special other than him."

Inez searched Katherine's face, feeling that this woman cared deeply for Martin, and she was glad because in the ten years that she'd known him, he had often seemed sad to her. And especially so since he had lost his mother and his brother in that uprising in Santo Domingo three years ago. She'd felt, too, that his relationship with Celié made him uncomfortable sometimes.

"If there's anything I can do to help with the wedding," Inez offered, "promise you'll ask me."

"I will, and I'm sure I'll need help with everything."

Inez lifted the big silver domed cake cover. *"Voilà!* This is the praline cake I mentioned earlier."

Katherine looked at the caramel-colored cake with its nut-filled frosting of whipped fudge and crumbled pralines.

"Oh my, this looks inviting."

"Why, thank you. And I have the recipe for you—if you want it."

"You know I do."

Back in the courtyard, Wilson uncovered and scooped out his peach ice cream with a flourish, heaping the crystal bowls. Inez cut the praline cake in generous portions, as Jules complimented her, adding, "You've outdone yourself. When I marry, my wife must come to you for cooking lessons."

Zell felt a small pang of jealousy but smiled past it. Did he have someone in mind? Jules caught her eye and winked. Singing Bird watched the byplay between them silently.

"Bonjour, my friends," a man's voice called from the shadowed entrance of the courtyard. Wilson got up and went to the wide gate, unbolting it to let someone in. Enjoying the ice cream, Katherine noticed the man who entered seemed white, and she felt a bit uncomfortable.

"Let me introduce you to our esteemed guests, Maurice," Wilson said smoothly.

"I, of course, know the gentleman," Jules chimed in, his face suddenly cool. "Hello, Maurice."

Wilson brought the man to Katherine first. "Mrs. Dominguez, may I present Mr. Delacroix—Maurice to his friends, as I am Wilson to mine."

"I am honored beyond words. . . ." The squat, middle-aged man with the waxen pale skin and straight, sparse black hair spoke smoothly. As Katherine offered her hand, he lifted it to his lips. Jules looked as if he would choke.

Inez watched with a bit of annoyance as Maurice Delacroix came to her. "Since I have admired your beauty for so long, I felt you'd find it boring if I greeted you first."

"Oh, no doubt," Inez said noncommittally. She was surprised at this show of gallantry from Maurice to the wife of Martin, whom he detested.

"Ah, those desserts seem fit for the gods. I gratefully accept a large portion, even before it is offered."

Maurice sat at the table by Inez, who could smell the liquor on his breath, too strong for mint to cover. He knew that they were well aware of his friendship that only began with Wilson's political plum of lieutenant governor. Hell, let them call him an opportunist. Who else got rich? Didn't they say the same thing about the governor?

Wilson looked thoughtful. "Perhaps I should tell you ladies

that Maurice is the richest man of color in New Orleans. Also, that he is being sought as auditor for the city by Governor Montrose."

"Yes, this is so," Maurice acknowledged. Katherine murmured that he must be very pleased. She didn't like this man; there was something cold and slippery about him.

As for Maurice, he narrowed his eyes and let them rove over the four women. Inez, of course, was a bit too old now to be truly attractive, but ah, the young ones. Martin's wife was certainly a good-looking woman, surprisingly adept at the social graces and beautifully groomed.

"How is the *forgeron* business, Jules?" Maurice asked.

"We're doing quite well, thank you," Jules answered dryly.

"Fantastic what Dominguez has achieved since he came here ten years ago," Maurice remarked. "Sometimes it seems now that it's more advantageous to be foreign than to be native—especially if you're a man of color."

"Well, I'd certainly say *you* haven't done badly for a native, Maurice," Wilson shot back. "You have no room for complaints of any kind, I don't think."

"Yes, Maurice," Inez interrupted. "Before you came, we were talking about people of color pulling together for all our benefits. Wouldn't you say the gifts of a foreign-born person of color are at least as much needed as those of a native-born one? Just think, we've had freedom only *four* years. And we don't know if it'll last."

"I've always been free," Maurice announced grandly. "And so has Wilson."

"Well, *I* haven't," Katherine cut in hotly. "And neither has any of my three friends here. I was a slave and I'm not ashamed of it. I don't feel any less a person for having been a slave. Mr. Delacroix, surely you've heard the saying 'There but for the grace of God go I'?"

"Apologize, Maurice," Inez said. "Remember, I also was a slave for many years."

"But so long ago," Maurice pointed out. "Good Lord, I *do*

apologize to all of you. But mine is a sentiment going around the city, that there are far too many foreigners here among the people of color. It is simply my nature to *speak* of it."

"I'd say it's a part of your nature you ought to change," Inez sniffed. "There are many, many immigrants coming into the city now from the West Indies, from Santo Domingo, and from Haiti. Surely, even you can't argue with the fact that men like Martin and Jules do high honor to this city."

Maurice raised his hands in mock defeat. "I offer my most humble apologies for a second time, and my lips are sealed. Heap my dish with more of this ambrosia for the gods, which you say is Wilson's concoction, and I will be silent. The cake is delectable as well."

Wilson rose, took Maurice's bowl, and went to the ice cream freezer. Inez cut him more cake, looking displeased. She had so wanted this visit to be perfect, and they had been enjoying themselves so much. Then this fop of a rich man, said to have so many women that he refused to choose one as a wife, and who made millions and was stingy, had come in. Their friend, indeed!

Jules sat up straighter. "The dinner has been better than I can tell you," he declared, "but we're going to have to get back out Gentilly Way before dark. These days the night, as you know, is for thieves and pickpockets and those others who must be about their business."

Inez went inside and got their parasols and summer burnooses. She handed Katherine the praline cake recipe, wrapped a very large section of cake in a linen napkin, and gave it to her. "For Martin." She kissed each woman's cheek, patting Jules's shoulder.

"Now, you drive carefully, and whatever you do, don't forget to tell Martin how much we missed him. Oh, I do hope your grandfather is all right."

"So do I," Katherine said fervently. "Inez, we've had a wonderful time, and we look forward to having you come to our house."

Maurice Delacroix watched the leave-taking, thinking sourly that he was, as always, the outsider in spite of his money. Well, thank God, he was a *rich* outsider. And Dominguez wasn't in his class—yet. It had never occurred to him that he *chose* to be an outsider.

Celié and Dahomey Sinclair sat among the revelers in Congo Square. Each night was a special kind of carnival there. Voodoo drums. Heartbeat drums. Chicken feathers and bones. Smeared chickens' blood for power. For wealth. For a rival's poverty and weakness. For love. For hate. For long life. For long and merciless death. Congo Square was a microcosm of the world.

Tonight was especially bright with moonlight as Celié leaned toward Dahomey Sinclair, lifted her veil a bit, and asked, "How long will it take you to teach me?"

He looked at her and breathed deeply, wondering if she really believed the thick black veil hid her identity. She was his kind, with a mind like his. No, he amended, with a far quicker mind, but one that was rockier, more unsettled. He was as steady as an oak and knew his own mind. She was a strong sapling, swaying in any wind.

"You are an impatient woman," he told her. "Do you think I became Dahomey Sinclair, the conjure man I know myself to be, overnight? No, it came with me from Africa's veldt, where I lived for so long before I was sold by my own brother and brought here.

"I have tasted gall, woman, and others have tasted it, too, with my revenge." He laughed harshly. "I thought I was a bitter man, until I met you. We are two of a kind, Celié, but you would not consider me as a husband, would you?"

Celié's recoil was swift. A husband? No, there was no husband for her but Martin. Dahomey Sinclair was *unthinkable*.

"Dahomey Sinclair," she said, "you are a dear man, and I like you very much. But it is Martin I have always loved. . . ."

"Yet you married his brother, as you yourself told me. And

I would have known, even if you had not said so. Did you love him when you married his brother?"

"Yes, but there were reasons."

"You carried this man's child?"

"Yes," she lied. He heard the quickening of her breath, the unsteadiness of her hands, and *knew* she lied, but he said nothing.

"Please, I cannot talk about it," she said.

"I understand." A lie did not tell itself easily; with friends, the tongue rebelled on a lie.

Dahomey Sinclair chuckled. "Once you would not have dirtied your hands with voodoo; you left it to me. Why do you now wish to know how to work the strong magic yourself? Your man is gone . . . *if* he was ever yours to begin with. To know another's body is not necessarily to know *them,* and surely not to possess them. Possession is a thing of the heart—and the soul. Our river gods and the gods of our forests are the strongest in the world. Time is what you'll need, Celié. . . ."

"And time is what I don't have anymore. Didn't you know, and if you did, why didn't you tell me that he would meet another woman on the bayou country trip? That he would marry this ex-slave?"

"You have an unfortunate tongue, woman. *You* yourself might have been a slave. *I* was brought here a slave, and I lived here as one. I tell you no lie, Celié, when I say that you have the tongue of a viper. It is your worst enemy."

Chastened, suddenly frightened, Celié told him, "I know what you say is true and I'm sorry. I don't look down on you for being a slave, and yes, I know I could have been one had not the slaves been freed the year after I was born. My mother was a mountain woman and they were free in Santo Domingo; there were so few. Dahomey Sinclair, I *am* sorry, but my heart is sick. I must have Martin for my own."

"You wish to kill the wife, of course."

"Is that so terrible? I don't give a damn what happens to her. It is Martin I care about."

"But you hate him, too."

"No, I love him."

"You have heard the old saying, and I know it to be true: Both are sides of the same coin. You feel hurt by Martin Dominguez, I know, but you may very well have hurt yourself and blame him. I have given up weaving spells of death. I am too old. If it is a very long life I seek—and it is—why should I study death except to overcome it with life?" He paused. "So, I will help you drive a wedge between them. Did you put the circle of feathers in her path while he is away?"

"Yes, tonight I went there and put it just under the gate."

"Good. It will encircle her heart . . . keep her away from him."

"And if it doesn't?"

"Without unquestioning belief," he said coldly, "not even the river god's magic is possible."

Celié bowed her head. For the life of her, she couldn't completely believe. Like many Santo Domingans, she believed at least some in the mixture of Christianity and African magic that was voodoo. But she believed far more in Christianity. Or did she anymore?

She touched his arm again. "Please teach me what you know, what you do. I will pay you well. I have done you favors."

"I acknowledge that you have. I like money, but not more than my soul. I tell you I have given up death magic, Celié."

"But you said yourself that one must know death to stay alive."

He fell silent, reflecting on her questions, on her aura.

Celié dreamed a bit in his silence, remembering the mountains of Santo Domingo where she'd lived with her crippled mother. She never known her father, and she and her mother had nothing except Celié's wit and beauty. Her mother had been an excellent seamstress and she'd taught her how to sew, even how to piece leather and furs. At twelve, her mother had apprenticed her to a Santo Domingo modiste; she'd learned her trade later.

To placate her wrath over yet another one of his extramarital affairs, Raoul had taken her to Paris to study with a designer for almost a year. Celié knew she was good, that her garments were among the best fashioned anywhere. She knew, too, that her life was empty. With Martin hers again, she would be able to fill this gnawing emptiness inside her. With the dimness of hindsight, she felt she'd known a perfect sense of fullness when they had been lovers.

He was tired now, and he was easily swayed by pretty women. And this one was beautiful. She was cruel, but then nature was cruel. He smiled a bit to himself. She cried pitiful tears about Dominguez's rejection, but *she* rejected *him,* Dahomey Sinclair, who might have loved her as much as she thought she loved Martin Dominguez. She would never be a conjure woman. She was not wise enough.

As the drums beat, Dahomey Sinclair felt old. Why did he bother with this lovely, evil woman by his side?

At their gate, Jules helped the three women down, then went to put the carriage in the shed and the horses in the temporary stable, because he needed them very early the next morning.

Inside the gate on the flagstone walk lay a circle of something white. It was the size of a goblet bottom. From several feet away, it looked like feathers—a circle of white feathers.

"Katherine, what *is* that?" Zell asked behind her.

Katherine began to go toward it as a wave of pure fear struck her, immobilizing her where she stood. Celié. And voodoo. Those words were a kind of chant in her mind. She quickly crossed herself. Quietly, she said the incantation that Papa Frank had taught her to use against injurious magic:

"I believe that the magic of God and his
Heaven is more powerful than *any* magic the
devil could ever dream of."

Eleven

Katherine had anxiously counted the days until Martin would return with news of Papa Frank. They should reach port tomorrow at the earliest. The ring of feathers still left her with an erie feeling several days later. Martin had said Celié would not dirty her hands with conjuring. But she depended on Dahomey Sinclair, a voodoo master.

Jules was off to a house site where they were placing grillwork. Singing Bird worked that day with The Little Sisters, and Zell made desserts and wanted no help. Katherine decided it would be a very good time to wash her hair. Surveying her lineup of excellent herbal rinses, she decided to use henna for its strengthening agents.

"I can tell you're still worried," Zell remarked, appearing in the open doorway, wiping her floured hands on her apron. "It's enough we don't know yet about Papa Frank, although I'm hoping, but that Celié . . ."

"I keep thinking she surely wouldn't act so desperate if she really was certain of Martin's love," Katherine said.

"And I think that's smart," Zell agreed. "I'd like Papa Frank's advice on Jules and me."

"Did Jules ask you to marry him?" Katherine inquired excitedly.

Zell grinned widely. "Is there anything wrong with *me* asking *him?*"

Katherine crossed the room and hugged her tightly. "Oh, I'm so happy for you!"

"How do you know he didn't turn me down?"

Katherine stepped back and looked at Zell. "Because Jules is far too wise to pass up a woman like you. Did you set a date?"

Zell shook her head. "Not yet. And thanks for the vote of confidence. Me, I just want to be courted, maybe for a long time. Men notice a sweetheart much more than they do a wife." She smiled impishly. "Martin excepted, of course. Jules is no slouch in the romance department, but you might push Martin to make a courtship master of his best friend." Zell rolled her eyes heavenward. "Your coming wedding. The black pearl necklace and the rings. Do you realize, Katie, just how lucky you are?"

"I know," Katherine replied. "And I know, too, that the house and the jewels and the wedding—as magnificent as all that is or will be—well, I treasure them, yes. But more and more I'm coming to love Martin deeply, and it *scares* me. There was an early bond between him and Celié. And he very well may be over their love. But *she* certainly clings to the past . . . a woman who has carried a child for a man for even a little while. Oh, Zell, no matter how I despise Celié, I can understand what she feels."

"Perhaps she's lying," Zell offered. Katherine had told Zell, but not Sing, a little about Martin and Celié's affair. "What if it were her husband's baby? Probably, it was."

"Yes, of course that's true," Katherine said. "But what if she's telling the truth?"

"I happen to believe in Martin," Zell admitted. "I don't think he'd be in the bayou country to find out about Papa Frank if he didn't care about you a lot."

Katherine hugged her. "You're the best friend a woman could have. I'm happy for you. Listen, make Jules court you as long as *you* want him to."

Zell smiled. "Katie, you don't think Sing really cares about Louis in any special way, do you?"

Katherine looked grim for a moment. "Well, I certainly hope she doesn't. She's grateful to him."

Zell nodded.

Katherine's hair with its kinky curls fanned out around her head, unbound, earth-brown, beautiful. She held a large comb in her hand.

"You're going to wash your hair?" Zell asked. "Mine needs it."

"Yes. I'm using rosemary and sage teas."

"My favorites," Zell told her. "Those two make my hair so soft. Listen, love, you're going to have to start thinking about getting in the family way. . . ."

"Don't rush things," Katherine said, laughing. "Speak for yourself, because I'll bet you and Jules get married soon."

Zell sighed. "I hope so, but I guess I can wait for babies. You're an only child, love. I'm the oldest, and it wasn't easy helping Mama with all those little crumb crushers. With the other children, it sometimes seemed I lost Mama altogether." She sounded wistful.

"I know how it was when my mama passed on and with Grandmama," Katherine reflected. "But somehow Papa Frank tried to make everything right—and he did."

"The way you—even if we *were* the same age—made it all right for me."

"How did you happen to think about my getting pregnant when we were talking about rosemary and sage being good for our hair?" Katherine asked.

"But you *know* pregnant women shouldn't use rosemary tea," Zell said. "Folks say it can make you miscarry."

"Oh, I'm watching that closely," Katherine told her. "I haven't missed one of my usual heavy monthlies yet."

"Don't look to *that* for guidance," Zell scoffed. "My mother got tripped up on that twice."

"Thanks for reminding me. Next shampoo, I'll begin using nettle or sage."

The two women looked at each other with deep affection

before Katherine began to gather shampoo paraphernalia, and Zell returned to the kitchen and her dessert making.

Castile soap shampoo. Two beaten egg yolks. Lemon juice rinse. Then the strong rosemary and sage tea rinse, left on to dry. Katherine felt a sense of luxury washing her hair in the wide white facebowl, then rinsing it as she bent forward and down. How nice and convenient to have running water.

The tea, prepared with the other hair-washing potions earlier and cooled, felt good on Katherine's buttery-soft scalp. Except in the dead of winter, she always washed her hair in cold water; it seemed to prevent snarling.

The clock struck eleven. Lord, where had the morning gone? She would go out to the backyard by the greenhouse and bask in the summer sunlight, let it dry her hair. In the afternoon, she would begin to bake the meats and stuff the sausages. Jules, with his expertise in meat cookery, would give her a hand when he came home. Fortunately, they had no one to tutor that night.

Suddenly, there was a commotion outside as a carriage pulled into the side yard. Katherine heard his voice and went tearing out the side porch and down the flagstone steps, her hair dripping. And she was in first Martin's, then a remarkably fit-looking Papa Frank's arms, hugging one, then the other fiercely.

"Lord, is it really my grand girl?" Papa Frank asked hoarsely. "Baby, you don't know what we went through when those bastards took you away." His old hands trembled and his eyes watered. "I didn't know if you was alive or dead until I got your letter."

"I know," she said. "But Martin told you what happened."

Martin laughed nervously. "He had his shotgun ready for me when I told him who I was. He thought *I'd* kidnapped you. I had to beg him to listen, with my heart in my mouth that I was dead meat any minute. Finally, he relented."

"Well, how else was I likely to come to know how you

was?" Papa Frank asked. "If I killed him, who'd tell me? I met that bastard of a pirate anyway," he growled.

"DeBeau," Katherine offered. "His father was a pirate, and so was he as a young man. But that all ended forty years ago. They're respectable citizens now, Papa, all wrapped up in politics and civic affairs—the ones who aren't dead."

"Nothing respectable about kidnapping," Papa Frank said. "Had me worried to death."

"I can't tell you how sorry I am, sir," Martin expressed humbly.

"How's the son he brought you here to heal?" Papa Frank questioned. "Martin told me what a fine job you did. Delivering babies for poor folks, too. Working on the governor's wife. The pirate told me about it, too."

He paused, looking at her, then hugged her again.

"I guess it's a pretty good man you got here. He married you. Reckon he was smart enough to know what he had. He told me about glimpsing you in the woods back in February. Said he liked you then. . . . I remember *you* got pretty restless about that time."

The old man was smiling a bit now, his eyes closed. "It's a real nice place you got here, Martin."

Zell came out, whooping joy, flouring the men's clothes in her rush to hug them.

"But where is Miss Ada?" Zell asked.

Papa Frank laughed. "She left me for another man," he said.

"Oh, Papa Frank," Zell commiserated with him. Katherine saw then that while he missed his close friend and may have hated losing her, his heart was far from broken.

A wagon pulled up and came into the yard at Martin's beckoning.

"Things Papa Frank wanted to bring," he announced, as the driver unloaded parcels and crates. Prying open one large, slatted crate, he unmuzzled Muffin and Ruff, who couldn't wait to fall on Papa Frank and begin yelping and licking his hands.

"Oh," Katherine exclaimed, scratching each of them affec-

tionately as they sniffed her and whined. "I have something
you'll love." And Ruff put his head to one side, as if he just
knew she was talking about big hunks of yellow cornbread
filled with crisp porkskin cracklings.

"Welcome to our house, Papa Frank," Katherine told her
grandfather, hugging him tightly again. "May you be as happy
here with us as I was in your house."

"It was always as much your house as mine, but it's a mighty
fine place you got here," he acknowledged.

Going close to Martin, Katherine said, *"Querido mio,* thank
you."

Dinner that night was lavish, country-style. When Singing
Bird came in, dropped off by two of the Little Sisters, she
hugged Papa Frank again and again.

Later, Jules arrived, and with him Madame Le Blanc, magnificent in lavender silk and lemon verbena essence. Papa
Frank lit up when she came into the room. A fine specimen
of a woman, he thought. Her husband was a lucky man. As
she sat at the table, vividly enjoying herself, Katherine mused
on how the usually effervescent Lillian Le Blanc was subdued,
and the usually quiet Papa Frank entertained them all with
tales of his life as a young man.

Madame Le Blanc hung on his every word.

If there were no Celié, Katherine thought wistfully, her life
would be nearly perfect.

That night Katherine and Martin went to their bedroom
early. Her hair had dried and she'd brushed it thoroughly, then
lightly oiled her skin with almond oil. Her happiness at Martin's return and Papa Frank's presence made her radiant as she
faced him. As soon as they were in the room, he lifted her
and held her in his arms, thinking how much he was coming
to love her.

Good memories of Martin and bitter ones of the *Robber Baron* crew assailed her senses. Martin was the silver lining behind that cloud, Katherine thought now.

As he put her down and sat beside her on the bed, she asked, "Did you have trouble on the way? Or coming back? I keep pinching myself, thinking it's a dream."

Martin grinned. "I'm afraid all the trouble began when I got to Papa Frank's house. He was furious when I identified myself and told him about your kidnapping. It was gossip there that DeBeau had done it. Nothing done in the dark but comes to the light. He was still too grieved to do anything. Miss Ada hadn't been gone two weeks. He was a doubly wounded man. No, love, it was an easy trip travel-wise. The flooding had stopped a few days by the time we got there.

"After he got a bit calmed down, Papa Frank asked me to stay and talk. I did, and I talked him into coming back with me pretty easily. He grumbled that he'd nothing to stay there for. When I told him about our wedding, wild horses couldn't have stopped him, and he said he sure wouldn't miss it. But he was still one angry man, I tell you. Katherine, he was even angrier when he met DeBeau."

Martin looked bemused. "I've never seen DeBeau act humble before, but he did then. And I think your grandfather saw it. DeBeau even told him, 'Think, man, how you love Katherine. Can you say you wouldn't do the same if she were dying? It was you I was going to *ask* to come, offer you a king's ransom if I had to.' "

Martin took her hand and squeezed it, glad to be home. "They'll never be friends, those two," he said, "but I guess they came to some kind of understanding. Or maybe one day your grandfather will forgive him."

"Papa Frank likes you," she stated. "I'm glad. Thank you again."

"He seems like a wonderful man, Kate. You know I had little of a relationship with my own father."

He had called her Kate for the first time. Somehow that seemed even more intimate.

"It seems that there are many things we can give each other," she said quietly.

"We've already been able to give each other a lot," he acknowledged. The eyes he focused on her were full of desire when he asked, "Nothing . . . bad happened while I was away?"

Katherine mentioned the visit to the Drumms and what a good time she'd had.

"I thought you'd like Inez. Wilson and Inez and Lillian have gone out of their way to help me since shortly after I came to the city. Wilson wasn't lieutenant governor then."

She mentioned meeting Maurice Delacroix. "He's a very unpleasant man," she pointed out.

"Yes," he agreed, *"rich* and unpleasant—and unhappy. How did he treat you?"

"Actually, he tried to be charming," she said flatly, "but I don't like him. Is he any danger to you?"

Martin thought for a moment. "I don't think so. Although he dislikes me intensely, Delacroix attacks only the weak and the defenseless. That's his style. But he's being talked about for state auditor. It seems Governor Montrose is impressed with his business acumen. If that happens, who knows what mischief he'll be able to put over then." He looked at her narrowly. "Celié gave you no trouble?"

Katherine hesitated a long moment, breathing shallowly.

"Katherine, what is it?"

"I wanted to give you one night's peace," she said.

When she told him about the ring of feathers, Martin was full of anger. "Damn it!" he uttered sharply.

"I've never cared for conjuring, black magic. I asked no one what it means, although I should have and I will. Martin, do you know what a ring of feathers means?"

He nodded. "Like you, I don't care for black magic or conjuring, but my mother was superstitious and often sought out a conjure woman. Can you guess what kind of feathers?"

"Chicken, I'd say." Katherine shuddered, remembering. "I burned it . . . sprinkled incense and poured kerosene over it and burned it. I knew that much from the bayou country—just about objects intended to do evil."

"That's good, although in Santo Domingo, we buried them. A circle of feathers is said to envelop a heart—to crush it if it's the heart of an enemy, to capture it if it is the heart of someone you wish to love you. *Damn* that woman!"

"Calm down, love. I'll talk with Papa Frank about it. Then what do you say we let it go for a little while longer, if she does nothing terrible? I think she's just trying to frighten us both."

Martin nodded. "Her closeness to Dahomey Sinclair bothers me. He's revered in the city as a voodoo priest, even among some of the aristocratic Creoles."

"Very well," she declared. "But for now we will do nothing."

"But if she continues with this madness," he told her, "we'd best present a solid front. What is to be said to her we'll say together, only . . ." He paused, frowning.

"Yes, my darling?"

"Katherine, I cannot help the guilt that tortures me to know that *I* caused the accident that made her barren. That it may have been my own child. Oh, I've prayed long years over this and a priest absolved me, but I *was* drinking, and I still feel it in my heart."

"And in your *soul,* Martin," she said, "because you're that kind of man."

Somber now, Katherine was nevertheless filled with a happy plan that had grown as they enjoyed dinner and each other's company tonight. And with the joy of seeing Papa Frank again.

"Martin, I asked you this once before and it had a bitter ending. Now I ask it again, for a happier time. Please leave me for fifteen minutes or so, as I asked you to do my first night here."

"Fifteen minutes," he groaned, "is about as long as I can stay away now that I'm back with you."

When he was gone, with one fond look back over his shoulder, Katherine languorously set to work. She looked down at the gleaming gold band on her finger, with plans to seduce her husband filling her. Going to the bureau drawer, she removed a rose-pink silk-satin gown, with wide lace inserts and a tucked and fitted bodice, which bared the top of her breasts.

Katherine undressed and slipped into the lovely gown, smoothing the silk satin over her hips. She was ready. It seemed a long time, but the clock on the mantel said a bit under fifteen minutes when he knocked.

Softly, he closed the door behind him and approached her. "Katherine, how beautiful you are." For the lamplight caught the soft nimbus of her earth-brown hair and shadowed her lovely nutmeg-colored skin in a way that set him on fire. Undressing as swiftly as he could, Martin came to her.

Katherine thought she'd never seen a more enthralling vision than Martin's body, deeply bronzed from his trip to the bayou country.

"Wife," he whispered as he pushed her gently back to the bed and onto it. She lay silent and relaxed. With a deep moan, he began the tender ravishing they had first known too long ago.

Twelve

Jules would be by around six to take Martin to the ironyard, so Katherine and Martin were both up by five the next morning. They wanted a big country breakfast to continue the celebration of Papa Frank's coming.

As Martin stoked the stove and made fresh coffee, Katherine rummaged around for the makings of buckwheat cakes.

"Here's the praline cake I wrapped so carefully that Inez Drumm sent you. It's really good, Martin. She gave me the recipe. Are you coming home for lunch?" He frequently did when he worked within several miles of their home.

Martin shook his head. "We're too far away over in the Garden District, but I plan to be home early. Inez knows how much I like her praline cakes, so she always saves me an extra big helping. Cut a piece for Papa Frank. Did she tell you about her madeline cakes?"

"She mentioned them. Martin, I have so much to learn."

"I'll tell you," he said, "I question that. You already know so much."

Martin sipped the strong chicory and coffee brew and watched his wife's rounded figure as she made the buckwheat batter, beat eggs to scramble with large hunks of cheese, and panfried pork sausage. Her summer-fresh cotton pelisse robe was ruffled and flowered. She looked pretty, and he never tired of watching her graceful movements.

The dogs yelped outside. Martin rose, found some biscuits and old fried bacon in the cupboard, opened the kitchen doors, and threw them food in the yard, where Ruff and Muffin gobbled it greedily. Wagging their bobbed tails, their quizzical looks thanked him and asked for Papa Frank. They were lonely. He stopped and stroked the hair on their backs. If they hadn't come with Papa Frank, he'd been about to talk with Katherine about getting a dog. Martin's eight-year-old dog had died that past winter.

"Madame is coming over today," Katherine announced, "to do a next-to-final fitting on my wedding gown. She's through with Zell's and Sing's bridesmaid dresses. Martin, they're so beautiful, but you can't see them. It's bad luck if you do."

"She's certainly taken long enough." He laughed. "Remember *I* wanted a wedding in three weeks, and so did you. Madame wanted to pull out all the stops, and even with her promise of six weeks couldn't do it. So, now it's August when *no* one does anything he can help doing in this city. The memories of the yellow fever rages are too strong. So, love, in early September, at sunrise, we'll be more formally wed. I wanted something beautiful for you. . . ."

Katherine looked at her ring, speaking mischievously. "I have something better than beautiful—a wonderful man . . . *you.* I'm happy now, Martin. Oh, I know it won't last. Other things will happen, but I'm just going to be happy with you and Papa Frank being here. Zell. Sing. Lord, Ruff and Muffin as well."

They both thought about Celié but said nothing.

"Coffee can wake me from the dead," Papa Frank declared, his tall frame in the doorway. "I heard my dogs raising hell out there. I reckon you fed them or they'd still be at it. It's a wonderful thing, that running water you've got here."

"Sit down anywhere, Papa Frank," Martin told him as Katherine hugged her grandfather, noting the heavy stubble on his face.

"I suspect you're going to have to shave," she said. "Oh, not for us, but Lillian's coming by today to fit my wedding dress."

He nodded, smiling. That had certainly been one fine figure of a woman. And his ego smarted from Miss Ada's desertion.

Papa Frank leaned forward as he sat down, looking at Martin, demanding, "But I thought you told me you married her on that ship. Had too much on my mind. I should've asked about that before."

Martin laughed. "I *did* marry her shipboard, Papa Frank, and believe me, it's legal. But I want to give her something special, like *she* is. I love your granddaughter."

Katherine's heart danced with joy.

"Yes, I reckon you do, when you come all the way back to the bayou country with floods nearby to find out if I was dead or alive. Well, if anybody *deserves* love, it's Katie."

"No. If anybody deserves love, it's you, Martin, and you, Papa Frank."

"Miss Ada sure as hell didn't think so," he grumbled.

Martin looked at him, smiling. "There are women here in this city who can make you forget Miss Ada." He had Miss Lillian in mind.

Thoughtful for a moment, Papa Frank spoke. "Yet, I notice you're from Santo Domingo, and you've been here ten years. How do you reckon it is you got a hankering for Katie out there in the bayou country, and none of the women here or in Santo Domingo struck your fancy hard enough?" His eyes were mischievous, warm.

"Touché," Martin said after a moment. "You're a smart man, Papa Frank."

"Folks've always said I was," Papa Frank offered sadly. "I don't reckon, though, Miss Ada thought so."

"Give it time, man," Martin told him.

"Don't have a whole world of *time* left, I don't reckon," the old man said. "But I surely do intend to *live* right up until that last second."

Zell and Sing came in with hugs all around, and Zell teased Papa Frank. "You look twenty years younger," she told him.

"And I haven't seen you and Sing that gussied up and good looking since I've known you. You're city women already."

After Martin asked the blessing, he and Papa Frank praised the buckwheat cakes with maple syrup, the scrambled eggs, and the fried-in-egg-batter green tomatoes that the women served. Katherine and Sing sat down to eat while Zell packed lunches in dinner pails for Martin and Jules.

"When you're rested, I'll take you with me to see my iron-yard," Martin said proudly.

"I'd like that," Papa Frank responded.

Martin leaned back, enjoying this moment, enjoying the sparkle of Katherine's laughter. That circle of feathers Katherine said she'd found just inside their gate bothered him greatly, yet he told himself he wasn't superstitious; surely, didn't believe in voodoo. But it had been all around him in Santo Domingo, permeating his youth with its spells and charms and chants. New Orleans took it to new heights with its recently arrived African slaves and emigrés from the islands of the world, many of whom were of African birth. It might, he conceded to himself, be like saying he didn't believe in the stars, the moon, and the heavens.

"You're so quiet," Katherine commented.

"I was just thinking about a project DeBeau has asked me to do for a friend of his in the Garden District. Another *big bug*. He has a huge estate over there, and his wife of twenty-five years died last year. He had a crypt built on the grounds and he wants a special fence built around it. He asked me to design it the early part of this year. I sent him three designs and he's finally chosen one.

"He picked the most difficult one, of course," Martin said ruefully.

"What is that design like?" Katherine asked.

Martin thought a moment. "It's an iron fence, for strength— slender iron posts, that is." He paused a moment. "Then I thought fine wires and iron teardrops. Time-consuming and expensive, so I submitted other designs. He chose the teardrops design, and we decided on a starting date in early October."

"It sounds odd—and lovely," Katherine added. "Will you need to stay over there?"

"No. Which means we'll truly be getting up early."

He saw a shadow of worry cross her face and wondered about it. Standing up, he picked up the two lunch buckets, kissed Katherine, and said goodbye to Papa Frank and the others, as Jules blew the buggy horn for him.

"Tell Jules I said hello," Zell called after him.

"Why don't you come out and tell him yourself?" Martin suggested, as she rushed to do just that.

Papa Frank watched the group, and he was happy and full of wonder that after all the pain and anguish of Katherine's abduction, there could be this joy.

They'd all settled down to a second cup of coffee and to talk about the bayou country and Papa Frank's trip. Ruff and Muffin hunkered down on the spotless kitchen floor, full of good food and doggy dreams.

At a brisk knock on the outer back porch screen door, Katherine got up and went out to find her closest neighbors, the Byerlys, standing there.

"We just thought we'd walk over to chat a bit," Ellen Byerly said.

"Won't you come in?" Katherine offered, going outside with them.

"Well, we don't have a lot of time," big Tom Byerly replied gruffly, "but I thought I'd warn you-all that there's a band of white thugs roaming around that the police haven't caught up with—*if* they've tried. Never seen a sorrier bunch of police than we got now. Oughta be ashamed to call themselves *white* men.

"You have any trouble now, you send somebody to get me.

I know Martin can look after you well enough, but it's gonna take *all* of us."

"Why, I certainly thank you," Katherine said as she and Ellen Byerly exchanged pleasant glances.

"I'm bringing over—when I get a chance—a jar of persimmon jelly I made. I'll give you the recipe. Now please, you be careful and you tell Martin."

"Oh, I will," Katherine promised.

"Good-looking hounds you got there," Tom Byerly remarked. "New, aren't they?"

"They're my grandfather's dogs. He came yesterday." Ellen Byerly noted the joy on her face. She wondered now what had become of the striking woman who'd lived in this house with Martin for less than two months. She'd always wondered. His sister-in-law, he'd said. She'd left, and nearly two and a half years later, he'd married this woman, Katherine, who seemed smart enough. Pretty. Still, she wondered.

"Yeah," Tom said, "I remember the old bulldog Martin had for years . . . ugly rascal. Gentle as a lamb, until he thought you were after Martin; then he'd have a piece of your hide."

He paused a moment. "Until they catch these rascals, maybe you need still another dog, but Martin'll decide that. Tell him to talk to me soon. And you take care and send word to us if anything happens, or if you see anybody strange that don't look right. Now, Curtis, in the place over to your left, don't talk much and it's said he don't care much for colored, but he's no fool. He knows damned well we have to protect each other out here—white and colored."

The Byerlys left then. Katherine raised her eyebrows as she went back in to where the others sat at the round oak table.

"You look a bit bothered," Papa Frank remarked.

When she told him what the Byerlys had said, he shook his head. "I'm old, but I can still shoot. So can you. And coming from a place like Santo Domingo with all the uprisings there . . . well, Martin told me a bit about his family on the way here."

"Let's hope trouble doesn't happen," Zell said.

"Best hope in the world," Papa Frank stated, "is to be prepared for it if it does."

There'd been trouble, too, with whites in the bayou country, during slavery as well as after. Mr. Keyes, the master, had gotten rid of those overseers who were outrageous, and he'd warned the other white overseers, as well as the black ones. The man who'd raped Singing Bird's mother and killed her father had been fired.

Katherine shivered a bit as she remembered the white man called Fitch, the meanest of her kidnappers. There'd been more than a hint of madness in his eyes as he'd both ogled and glared at her as the other kidnapper, the big one, held her too closely in his arms to taunt Martin, a man of color. Why did she think of Fitch now? She hadn't remembered the names of the other two men. Sadly, she thought she simply had not been able to forget that threat or those moments of terror.

A look passed between Katherine and Papa Frank. It was an old look of understanding that had begun in her childhood. She had known something good would happen before Martin came, but had not divined the bad part of that journey before it happened. Now she knew, as did Papa Frank, that there was an aura of danger in the air. She'd known it even with her happiness over his arrival. She had thought it had only to do with Celié, but it could be other trouble as well. Katherine needed no patterned coffee grounds or tea leaves to tell her this.

In her bedroom a few minutes later, she opened the safe to look at the black pearl pendant and the diamond ring, and to show them to Papa Frank. She removed the jewels from the boxes and sat on the bed holding each in the palm of her hand, then setting it aside to look at the other. She could never think of the jewels without thinking of the heartbreak connected with them. "It was not a happy time," Martin had said, "but they had something together. My mother said she'd been happier with my father than she could have been with anyone else."

Katherine walked to the kitchen where Papa Frank sat, still sipping coffee. He drained his cup and took the jewels into his hands, admiring them. Very briefly, she told him their history.

"Well, now," he sighed, "I'd say that Martin cares a lot about you, Katie, to give you something as fine as this. I reckon many women would give their eyeteeth for gifts not a quarter as good. You've been happy with him, haven't you? That he was with the likes of DeBeau tells me a little about him, but the fact that he protected you as best he could from his own friend is what matters to me."

"I have been pretty happy here with Martin," she said. "I forget a little more each day how I got here. I don't fault him, but he *is* part of the pain. There was a woman in his life, Papa, who he loved as a young man. She married his brother. Her name is Celié, and she wants to rekindle what she knew with Martin. . . ."

"Giving you trouble, is she?"

Katherine nodded and told him about the ring of feathers they'd found on the sidewalk. "Did I do the right thing?" she asked.

"You did right to chant the way you said you did to break that spell, the way I taught you. Now, Katie, you know I stopped having anything to do with evil magic a long time ago. Any damned fool can hurt and kill. All I ever wanted for you or anybody I love is for them to be able to protect themselves from somebody's evil magic. And I've been good at that.

"Katie, being a leaf doctor is why I figure God put me here. And it brings me joy. Now, for evil magic, I always say how can anybody spend time hating when they could be spending that same time loving?"

He paused on a deep sigh. "I ramble, and when I do, I'm bothered, as you well know. How does Martin feel about this woman?"

"He is honest, I think," Katherine replied. "He once loved

her, even after the affair. And he feels so guilty. She was in the family way—after they broke up and she married his brother. She says the child was his, but she lies. It may not have been."

He listened carefully, hearing the stress in her voice, hearing how she cared about this man.

"There was an accident that he caused, and later—not right then—she lost the baby. She blames him."

"Wouldn't matter if he didn't blame himself, but of course he does. He's a tender man, Katie. Now, from what I see of Martin, he can be a tough man to deal with, but he's got a soft spot for women, and it's plain.

"Like I said, he *cares* about you. *Help* him to deal with this woman. Make her back away from you; don't give an inch to her! You be sure to tell Martin—and me—if you find any more bad conjure mess she puts around. We'll all three deal with her."

Katherine told him about Dahomey Sinclair then, and he nodded.

"I believe I may have heard about him in the bayou country," he commented. "It don't matter. I reckon he's heard about me. I believe, girl, that what we've got inside, when we work for good, is stronger than anything outside of us."

Katie hugged him as Zell answered the door knocker, and brought Miss Lillian, Pierre, and Monique into the kitchen. Miss Lillian flung her arms around Katherine. "Ma chère," she exclaimed, "the necklace, the ring . . . oh, how magnificent!" To Papa Frank, she said, "Mr. Keyes, I am so happy to see you again."

Papa Frank stood up, dressed in blue denim overalls and a blue chambray workshirt, his garments in sharp contrast to those of this fine city woman, with her lavender and cream lace dress that made her look so fetching.

"No happier than I am to see you," he replied. It beat all how he could talk so handily around her, when he'd had trouble at times with other women. It had taken Miss Ada and him a long time to get comfortable with each other.

"Pierre. Monique," she said now to the children, who quietly stood back but were looking livelier today, "please say hello to Mr. Keyes, won't you?"

"Papa Frank," the old man insisted, "and that's for you, too, Miss Lillian." He bent to pat Monique's cheek, then to shake Pierre's hand, putting both children at ease.

"Well," Papa Frank announced, "I've got two old hounds I think you'd both like to see, and there's a big backyard with a swing made to order for young'uns. What d'you say we go outside?"

Pierre made a beeline for the door, but Monique stayed behind a moment to look back at the jewels and Katherine.

"They're so beautiful, Mrs. Dominguez," she said in her young-old voice. The girl sounded wistful.

Katherine put her arms around Monique. "Thank you, my darling. Would you rather stay here with us?"

Monique shook her head. "Oh, no, I want to go and swing and talk to Papa Frank. Miss Zell will help Madame with your fitting."

"Don't forget I'm training you," Miss Lillian reminded her. "But, of course, run along if you wish."

Monique fairly skipped out the door. Miss Lillian turned to Katherine. "I have orders coming in, or I would spend the day with you, if you agree. *Mon Dieu,* your grandfather is a handsome man."

"He thinks you're special too," Katherine told the older woman, winking.

Miss Lillian's hand went to her throat. "Oh, my," she said. She and her late husband had been very fond of each other. He had been gone seven years and she still missed him, but he had begun to fade in her mind.

"We have plenty of coffee, and would you—and perhaps the children—like pancakes and sausage?"

"No, no," Miss Lillian replied. "You wouldn't believe the

breakfast Monique insisted on fixing this morning. A shrimp-and-cheese omelette, buttermilk biscuits, and strawberry jam." She touched her stomach. "But the coffee and chicory I get here seems a bit better than mine, so if you'll insist, I'll have another cup. Then, my dear, we must get started."

Katherine got the coffeepot from the stove and poured Miss Lillian a big cup of coffee. She found it charming the way New Orleanian people of color accepted an offering by saying "if you'll insist." She excused herself to put the jewels back in the safe.

"You look both happy and sad," Miss Lillian remarked when Katherine returned. "I can understand the happiness."

"I saw the box with my wedding dress on the dining room table. I'm afraid to peek in—afraid to be so happy—and yes, I'm also sad."

"Celié, of course."

"Yes." She told her about the circle of feathers and about the Byerlys' warning of possible thugs in the neighborhood.

Miss Lillian pondered both bits of news. "With the riffraff coming to plunder if they can, forewarned really is forearmed. Once they know you're on guard, they may leave you alone." Here she laughed abruptly. "As for Celié, I never thought she would stoop to this. Dahomey Sinclair probably had one of his many henchmen do it for her. I've heard he has a crush on her, so perhaps she was able to inveigle him into doing it himself, in which case it would be far more powerful as a charm. . . . Celié collects men's hearts. Several men are ensnared by her. It's said there's a new one she's taken over, a man from the bayou country. Oh, Lord, let me not become a *grande* gossip, and forgive me my *petit* news."

Katherine's mind had lingered on Miss Lillian's assessment of Celié and Dahomey Sinclair and magic spells.

"Do you believe in conjuring, in magic, in black magic?" she asked.

Miss Lillian thought a moment. "This is a city where it seems nearly everybody believes in magic, black and otherwise. I don't approve of it. I'm a Christian and it's forbidden. And I don't practice it. I've never needed to. But *mon Dieu,* in this city, one does not believe or disbelieve in conjuration. It's a fact of our life here."

It was eight o'clock when Martin answered the door, to find Louis standing there, hat in hand. They'd been laughing and talking, so they hadn't heard the buggy approach.

"Come in, Louis," Martin said.

"I came to see Papa Frank," Louis announced a bit defensively.

Papa Frank was on his feet and started toward the door.

"Louis!"

"Papa Frank!"

The two men hugged each other.

"You sure are a sight for sore eyes," Louis said fondly. "Didn't my stepma come?"

"She got married, son, to a root doctor."

"Well, if that don't beat all," Louis commented.

"Come in, boy, come in. I can tell you all about the bayou country at the same time."

They sat or comfortably sprawled about the living room, Louis as close to Sing as possible. Papa Frank was the raconteur, with African, Indian, and American roots as they talked far into the night.

Later that same night, Martin listened to Katherine as she told him about the Byerlys' visit.

"I'll stop by on my way to the ironyard tomorrow morning," he said. "Katherine, I want you to be very careful. I brought you out here because there's so much space, so much less danger of yellow fever spreading. . . ."

"And because it's so beautiful," Katherine added.

"It can also be dangerous—but less so if we're prepared for

it. We've got ten families in this area with small farms or big estates. Three or four poor families who own and link with us. We're one of five people of color; there's one Indian family. This land's becoming valuable. Our ten acres are worth six times what I paid for them seven years ago.

"I imagine now with this new threat of roaming thugs, we'll start back to having weekly, or at least monthly, meetings and target practice. Everything had gotten pretty quiet. I don't want to frighten you, but tell me anything you see that's at all suspicious. And like Byerly told you, go to them or send for them. Even send for Curtis if you have to. Like Byerly said, he's not a fool. Papa Frank said you handle a gun well. We've got two rifles and two shotguns here. And a derringer I keep loaded." He took her in his arms. "Honey, I don't want to scare you to death, but we—"

"Martin, is that horrible man called Fitch still on DeBeau's ship?"

Martin shook his head. "No. DeBeau got rid of him that same trip. I understand he was pretty hot about it. Why do you ask?"

"I don't know," she said slowly. "I'm not a terribly fearful person, but I was terrified of him."

Thirteen

The mid-September morning of Katherine and Martin's sunrise wedding was splendid by any standards. The pale coral and yellow of dawn fanned out over distant Lake Pontchartrain. Mist and dewdrops glistened on the grove of dark green, waxleafed, blossomless magnolia trees behind the wedding party. The ceremonies were held on the far side of their ten-acre spread out Gentilly Way.

"Dearly beloved, we are gathered here today . . ."

The minister spoke in the mellifluous voice that made his wedding ceremonies so sought after.

Katherine could hardly contain her joy in the man by her side or the life she had come to know with him. How wonderful he looked in his black broadcloth frock coat with the snowy piqué vest, his equally white shirt, and his black cravat. His face, as he glanced nervously and proudly at her, was so earnest, almost like the little boy he must have been. But the looks he sent her way were those of a man with a man's desires.

There was, of course, Celié, but Katherine was determined not to let her spoil her wedding day. Katherine and Martin had not spoken again of the ring of feathers.

Martin's joy was no less than hers, but it was tinged with sadness. He thought Katherine beyond mere beauty today. Her nutmeg-colored satin skin was luminescent, unpowdered, and her golden brown almond-shaped eyes sparkled. She had the added grace of a shapely body that was elegantly molded by the wedding gown.

Madame Le Blanc had outdone herself, as he had known she would, creating a gown of off-white gossamer satin outlined in seed pearls, appliquéd onto heavy off-white satin throughout the bodice and onto the full skirt in peaks and valleys. Fashionable leg-o'-mutton sleeves and a high neckline banded in gossamer satin and seed pearls completed the excellent design.

Her veil was towering off-white tulle gathered under a garland of fresh, creamy white cape jasmine, fastened over her earth-brown thick hair, which was drawn back smoothly from her brow and fastened into a topknot. Alternate rinses of nettle leaf, lemon balm, and rosemary leaves had brought lifelong luster to that hair.

Looking with such pride at the granddaughter he'd raised, Papa Frank felt his heart close to bursting. And Madame Le Blanc certainly looked lovely, too, he thought.

Watching Katherine, Martin's heart hurt with wanting his mother to have known her. They would have loved each other, because they were so much alike. And yes, his brother Raoul would have loved her, too.

Katherine looked at Martin anxiously because she knew something was bothering him. He saw her concern and began to give her a reassuring glance, but it didn't work. In such a short while, she had taught him a new openness of spirit—at least with her. He took her hand and squeezed it, as the minister smiled at the gesture.

"Do you take this woman to be your lawfully wedded wife? . . ."

Jules, resplendent, too, in his black garments, looked across at Zell and both smiled. He thought she was really pretty in aqua taffeta. A pleased Singing Bird saw the look that passed between them and smoothed the skirt of her deep rose taffeta dress. Having not been able to dream since bad events had caused words to dam up in her throat so she couldn't speak, now she often dreamed of getting married. She sighed deeply, as she had just seen Martin do.

"Do you take this man to be your lawfully wedded husband?"

"I do," Katherine answered.

The ring bearer was Pierre, the little boy Madame had saved, along with his sister Monique, from the wretched streets of New Orleans. Like a little statue of polished ebony, he solemnly brought the ring forward on the white velvet pillow. Martin took the ring and placed it on Katherine's finger, this time in *public* proclamation of their intent to share a life. As much as she thrilled at this, Katherine thought it paled beside the first time he had given her this ring and told her, *"You* are my present and my future."

Martin kissed his bride's ring-adorned hand and looked into her tear-speckled eyes, even as his own eyes glimmered with tears.

"I now pronounce you man and wife!"

The minister looked at this couple before him, who had been such a joy to join together. Warmth and good feelings enveloped the crowd of several hundred people on the multi-acre house and magnolia forest site. Even nature had been kind, the minister thought, for September had been cool, where it had carried unbearable heat in other years. And there had been no yellow fever epidemic this year.

"You may kiss the bride."

Papa Frank smiled at them both, remembering Katherine's brief marriage to Albert, remembering his *own* broomstick wedding to her grandma.

Martin looked at Katherine long and ardently at first, but did not touch her. I would like to take my bride, he thought, to some far-off place, where there is no trouble of the kind I fear may be coming here. And if nothing else could be done, perhaps he would consider that. He was not a coward for himself, but for Katherine he would ask the blessings of heaven and battle the fires of hell to keep her safe. When he finally kissed her, it was with a fervor she wondered about as she responded.

So that frightening journey from the bayou country, she thought now, had come to this: a life she could not have valued more with a man she was coming to love more and more.

The minister congratulated the couple and left their side in search of the sumptuous feast set out on long, white damask-covered tables.

Jules, Zell, Singing Bird, and Madame Le Blanc, with Pierre and Monique in tow, hugged Katherine and Martin in a circle. All four women cried. Both children looked subdued, well behaved, and old beyond their years.

Dr. St. Cyr was just getting over the flu. In helping to tend him, Katherine had listened to him grumble. "I don't want to miss your wedding to Martin, Katherine, but you can see the shape I'm in. Otherwise, I'd be there with bells on, waltzing and eating and enjoying myself." Slyly, he'd glanced at his wife. "I'd even make Blanche go."

Katherine had smiled a bit. Mrs. St. Cyr was never less than pleasant to her, but her segregationist views were well known by her intimates. Now the doctor's wife smiled tightly as she said, "But I'm the one who has already selected one of the nicest gifts you can imagine."

She'd sent a truly beautiful teakwood chest of fine silverware. The Byerlys had given them a lovely large ecru lace tablecloth. Natalie and the governor had been away, but had sent translucent gold-rimmed china, service for twelve.

As they drew a little apart, Madame surveyed the couple. *"Ma chère,"* she began softly, "I have made many wedding gowns in my time, but none have I fashioned to give me joy like this one."

Katherine and Martin nodded. "It is so beautiful," Katherine said quietly. "More beautiful than any I have seen, and I suspect, more beautiful than anybody else has, either. Thank you so much, Madame."

"No," Madame murmured, "thank *you* for bringing into my

friend Martin's life what I have long wished for him—a healing love." Her eyes twinkled. "And for bringing warmth into my own life for even a moment on meeting your grandfather."

Papa Frank mingled with the crowd, some of whom had heard of his powers with herbs and his less heralded skills as a man of *good* magic.

Madame put her arms around Pierre and Monique. "Tell her, Pierre," she directed the boy.

The child's eyes lit up. He'd liked this sweet and pretty woman from the time he'd first met her at Madame's.

"My leg I cut on barbed wire is almost well," he announced proudly. "I did all the things you told me to. Madame helped me make the coneflower poultices. Then we put vinegar and paddings of soda. Look, it's . . ."

He bent to unfasten his long white socks, but a laughing Madame stopped him.

"Pierre, my darling," she said gently. "Shall we wait until later to show Madame Dominguez?"

Slightly abashed, the boy agreed, "Very well, but you *must* see it. You would be so proud. I think I will be a leaf doctor."

Katherine bent and hugged him, this child who Madame had told her had found it difficult to get from one day to the next when he'd first come to her.

What they could see of Lake Pontchartrain now sparkled like cut diamonds in the early sunlight. Others came to them now, people Martin had joined with in home-building bees. Lodge brothers. People Jules and he and others met with to discuss how best to take advantage of the people of color enfranchisement the new governor seemed determined to make a reality instead of a farce.

"Ah," Madame said, to no one in particular. "This wedding is a mixture of so many good things—even as we, as a race, are a mixture of so many good things."

When Katherine threw the wedding bouquet it was Zell who caught it, glowing with happiness.

Madame whispered to Katherine, "Oh, you are so beautiful.

Had I been fortunate enough to have children, it is a daughter such as you or a son like Martin I would have wanted."

Preparations for this wedding had begun at two in the morning. Martin had spent the night at Jules's house, since it was considered bad luck for the groom to see the bride before the wedding. No matter that it was their second wedding. Madame, Zell, and Singing Bird, as well as Ellen Byerly, Martin's white neighbor, had come in and helped Katherine dress, loading the items that would go from their house to the magnolia forest into coaches, buggies, and wagons of other friends. Katherine had been so nervous she was slightly ill with anxiety, yet she felt a keen happiness that positively lifted her. There had been no sleep for her that night.

Katherine and Papa Frank stood a moment as he surveyed the wedding crowd.

"I like this wedding, grandgirl," he told her. "It's got a *mix* of us, the way we need to be. There's me in the fanciest clothes I'll ever wear until you put me under," he grinned, admiring his black broadcloth frock coat and trousers, his white piqué vest like Martin's and Jules's, and his black cravat. He'd shined his shoes until they gleamed.

"Seems to me there's the rich and the poor. Martin said maybe DeBeau, the old bastard, will be here. Do you reckon he will? Seems like it's the least he could do. Yet, I don't know as I want to see him again. Did you have nightmares about that kidnapping, Katie? I raised you as gentle as I could. Maybe I was wrong."

"You weren't wrong, Papa," she said, hugging him quickly. "No," she answered then, "I had no nightmares. I guess nightmares might come when you try to forget. I want to put it past me, but I won't be forgetting any time soon."

Martin had slept fitfully at Jules's house, because he was too tired *not* to sleep. Because he was considered the best *forgeron* in New Orleans, his business was very successful, especially with many newly rich Yankees moving to the Crescent City and natives growing wealthy beyond their fondest dreams. He had dreamed the night before of a wedding in which he could not see the couple's faces. Everything was going smoothly. Then a green snake, coiled to strike, spoke, protesting the wedding. Martin woke up, furious. Celié had worn an emerald-green dress the day she had summoned him from Madame's shop.

Many good friends had organized the wedding feast. One of the big tents they had erected was partitioned so that the bride and groom could change into something more comfortable, and they and their guests could nap—those who did not choose to sleep on quilts and blankets under the magnolias and giant oaks. For this was to be an all-day affair.

"I have married many people," the minister greeted them again. "I have not seen the likes of this magnificence. May I congratulate you both?"

"I'm afraid you must congratulate Madame Le Blanc," Katherine told him. "Her hand is the touch of Venus that brought us this."

The minister clasped his hands behind his back and spoke to Madame, whom he had known since they were both children.

"Ah, Lillian," he said, "such a lovely woman to be left a widow at such a tender age." He had been a friend of her husband.

Madame Le Blanc flirted a bit. "But Percy, I was forty-eight when Ernest passed on."

"Not all that long ago," he recalled, admiring his friend. Madame was fifty-five; she adored a compliment.

The pianist who had played the wedding march now launched into something sassier. Fiddlers followed along, patting their feet, and harmonicas warmed under ardently cupped hands.

By eight-thirty that Monday morning, a holiday for Martin and Jules, the wedding festival was fully under way. Weekday weddings were common, because ministers were busy on weekends saving souls.

Inside the tent, Katherine approached her husband. "My darling, what's wrong?" she asked.

Martin thought a moment. "Perhaps I'm being foolish," he said. "I love you and I want the best for us." He paused. "Katherine, growing up in Santo Domingo, I used to hear people say that we mustn't make the gods angry by being too happy. We must hide our happiness, at least a little bit. Ah, Lord, please let what we have last."

Katherine touched his face. "I only ask that He let *us* last, sweetheart, and any children we may have. With you, I need nothing else to be happy."

Martin's face brightened as he kissed her lightly. "You like the magnolia forest, don't you?"

"I love it. It's one of the most beautiful places I can imagine there being."

"Long ago a man is said to have planted it for his wife. They had little money, but each year he planted magnolia trees—in honor of their love. They had many children, and it's also said that they lived to be very old."

"I'm glad you told me that," she said softly. "Martin, I wonder what happened to Inez and Wilson. They said they'd be here early."

Martin frowned. "I've wondered, too. But a lieutenant governor can't always control his own schedule."

Zell and Singing Bird came in, blushing. "Madame Le Blanc says that we are to begin helping you to change. She'll be along in a minute. Oh, Katherine, Martin, the food and the music are so good." They joined hands and began to circle the couple, clapping hands and singing:

> "*Ma chère,* on this your wedding day,
> I wish you love!
> *Mon cher,* on this your wedding day,
> I wish you joy!

For him, the first nine months,
a dimpled baby girl!
For her, the second year,
a bouncing baby boy!"

Madame came in and joined them, singing along until she stopped, hands on her hips, addressing Katherine.

"And now," she announced, "for my second superb creation. I kept it a secret because I wanted to surprise you." She turned to Martin. "I think you will find it is one of a very few possible dresses that does the black pearl justice."

Once Katherine was dressed and outside among the wedding guests, a ripple of admiring comments rang out among the nearby guests.

"Why, ma'am," a young gallant came up to say, "I'd fight a duel for you and figure it was worth losing. Your husband is the luckiest man alive."

"You're very kind, sir." Katherine accepted the compliment gracefully.

The dress Katherine wore to display the black pearl was of pearl-gray sheer silk lace. The plainly fashioned bodice had a deeply scooped neckline and long, fitted sleeves. The lightly bustled skirt was softly draped over starched cotton petticoats. It was, indeed, a perfect setting for the black pearl, which caught and complemented the luster of her skin. Katherine wondered if the black pearl were not too grand for a daytime affair, but Martin wanted her to wear it. New Orleans was fast becoming a city of pomp and fashion, and people expected men like Martin to flaunt their wealth—but gracefully, while helping others to gain their share.

Papa Frank and Miss Lillian had gotten together again. She began to teach him how to waltz.

"An old country man like me will never master this stuff,"

he teased her. "How've the New Orleans men let you get away?"

"My husband died quite a while back," she answered, flattered.

"I'm sorry," Papa Frank said, "but a woman like you shouldn't be alone." Then, to get away from being so drawn to her, he surveyed the table.

"Food here's enough to last a family five or six years in the bayou country. Lord, will you look at that liquor and soft drink table."

They danced over and stood eyeing the table with the kegs of apple cider. There was also hot coffee and tea, as well as iced coffee and tea, and barrels of ice water.

"Is that dandelion wine I see there?" Papa Frank asked. "Looks like it."

"Umm-hmm," Miss Lillian told him. "There's plain old root beer if you want it, as well as some fine bourbon and brandies. But if you've a mind to take my advice, I wish you'd try the champagne."

"Well," he began hesitantly, "you're offering a mighty fancy drink to a mighty plain man."

"Someone's just opening a bottle," Miss Lillian informed him. "One sip, and if you don't like it, switch to bourbon or brandy. And if you don't mind my saying so, you're worth all the fancy men I've ever seen."

Lord, Papa Frank thought, pleased. What folks there were in New Orleans! Hell, not just *folks,* but Miss Lillian had a honeyed tongue and looked far prettier than he'd ever before seen a woman of that age look.

Katherine watched Papa Frank and Miss Lillian as they talked quietly, sipping champagne, then moving to the white damask-covered tables that labored under silver and china tureens of crab and shrimp gumbo and bisque. Oysters—ubiquitous in a city that celebrated them—fried or in ice, to be eaten raw, stuffed with crabmeat or shrimp, or both.

"Katherine, Martin," a familiar woman's voice called. "Oh,

my dear, how ravishing you look." She gazed at the black pearl pendant, exclaiming, "Magnificent! Today, my dear, you and the rings do each other honor. How beautiful you are, and how happy you must be."

Inez Drumm's own ice-blue silk voile dress was simple and charming. She wore several strands of pearls. "The dress is Lillian's design," she explained.

"And like you, it's lovely," Martin said, with Katherine seconding.

Inez kissed Katherine's cheek and patted Martin's arm. She had to catch her breath. "Wilson will be on as soon as he hitches our carriage. My dear, I've failed you and I'm sorry."

"I'm so glad you're here, and don't be sorry. You're out of breath," Katherine noted. "That's what I'm concerned about. What on earth happened?" She wiped a small smudge from Inez's cheek.

"We had carriage trouble. One of the spokes broke. We had to go back and borrow a friend's carriage. We intended to be among the first guests. Now I've missed seeing you in your wedding gown. How handsome you look, Martin."

"Thank you," Martin responded, turning to Inez, "but you've rushed yourself. We knew something must have happened. Let Katherine take you inside the tent to sit down for a while. I'll look out for Wilson."

Inez laughed. "Soothe his nerves if you can. He's a wreck. I'll go in in a minute, but I want to talk to you a bit. I must be worse off than he is, because *he* offered to bring in the cake I baked."

Katherine stepped aside a moment to let the old friends talk.

"Praline, I hope," Martin said. "The big piece you sent home with Katherine was one of the best you've ever made."

"Wait till you taste this one. Martin, we missed you at that dinner, but I trust Katherine and the other two ladies—and, of course, Jules—had a good time."

"They're still chewing it over. Yes, they did. We'll be inviting you for dinner very soon, and please don't let state business interfere."

"Martin, let me talk to you about two things. I hear Katherine's grandfather is here, living with you."

"Yes, as you know, that's why I missed your dinner."

She wet her lips. "It would have been a perfect dinner if Maurice Delacroix hadn't showed up."

"Katherine said he was civil, which is more than he is most of the time."

"Oh, I detest that man. He's the closest thing to evil I've ever been associated with."

"You said there were *two* things. . . ."

"Oh, Maurice is the second thing I wanted to mention. I'm just so annoyed with him."

"I gather he talked about foreigners in New Orleans again."

"Yes, his usual conversation if you're around. Martin, he's so envious of you. You're young, handsome, successful. Now you've got Katherine, who's not only beautiful, but a talented herbalist as well."

"Well, he brags that his riches keep him all the company he needs. He complains that women pursue him only for his money."

"He's a sad, pathetic, and, somehow I feel, sick man."

"He's also a very rich, successful man, Inez, who could be your next state auditor. Quite a plum," Martin said as Katherine returned.

Inez laughed. "Lord, I'm a bit faint. Katherine, I'd surely appreciate it if you showed me where to sit or lie down a minute or so."

As he stood at the table that contained the racks of lamb, beef, and pork, Martin caught sight of Wilson rushing along. He went to meet him, and the men clapped each other's backs heartily.

"Inez told you what happened?" Wilson asked. "Damn the luck . . . of all days."

"You got here," Martin said. "So I consider us lucky. You

don't make your own time anymore. I was afraid the governor needed you."

"Not today, but he's a demanding fellow, as I've told you. I don't mind, Martin. I've found him to be a fair-minded man who demands no less of me because I'm a man of color. He does us the honor of having high expectations. You haven't by chance seen today's *Chronicle?*"

"On my wedding day? I wouldn't dare."

"I think you can take it. It's no worse than usual."

Wilson drew a clipping from his inner coat pocket and showed it to Martin. An editorial about the newly passed revenue bill of that year. Martin scanned it quickly, then read it slowly.

It was the work of the lowest and most corrupt body of men ever assembled in the South. It was the work of ignorant Negroes cooperating with a gang of white adventurers, strangers to our interests and our sentiments. It was originated by carpetbaggers and was carried through by such arguments as are printed on green-backed paper. It was one of the long catalogs of schemes of corruption that makes up the whole history of that iniquitous Radical Conclave.

"Governor Montrose is determined to ignore this editor, but I don't know how much longer he can keep his famous temper."

Wilson's face had looked more and more strained as Martin watched him, and he understood well the pressure that rode his friend as lieutenant governor—with the derisive title the New Orleans papers had bestowed upon him: The Colored Housepainter Lieutenant Governor.

Now Wilson spoke ruefully. "Good thing nothing ruins my appetite or my passion for a beautiful wedding—although I missed the ceremonies. Martin, I'm going to sample the turkey, the fried chicken right out of the washpot's sizzling fat, and some of that paella. A helping of green peas and carrots. Wild rice. One big baked, buttered yam. And a couple of rolls. That ought to do it for me."

"You'll never make it without your favorite garden salad," Martin told him, directing him also to the potato and macaroni salads.

"My dear wife, I gather, is with Katherine."

"Yes, I think she's a bit tired."

"Funny thing how I don't tire easily," Wilson pointed out. "I don't lose my temper easily either, but . . ."

Martin waited a while before he asked, "But that article today got under your skin?"

"Didn't it get under yours?"

"Of course, but they're printed every week by three news-papers, all seemingly of one mind against us. Why is this one so much worse?"

"Because I did work on that bill I've never really discussed with you or anybody else because the governor asked me not to. I guess I feel that *I'm* the chief ignorant, corrupt, green-back-minded nigra they're referring to. It's an open secret that the governor used me to carry the message to the congress-men."

"Wilson," Martin began, choosing his words carefully to comfort his friend. "We've known each other a long time. Those of us who know you know you're a man of integrity and honor. I'd say *damn* the clowns who've given up a smidgen of power they consider fit only for them."

Wilson was still smiling and eating ravenously when Papa Frank and Miss Lillian approached. They both stood as Martin introduced Wilson to Papa Frank.

"You do honor to our city, sir," Wilson said, meaning it. "I've heard of your wondrous cures, and I've been fortunate— my wife and I—to know your granddaughter."

"And I, sir," Papa Frank replied, "am more than honored to meet a lieutenant governor who's also a man of color. I'm glad I've lived to see this day."

Later, with Inez feeling rested, Katherine mingled with the guests, smiling at the ample array of desserts. Hand-cranked ice cream made from vanilla beans, chocolate, coconut, and pineapple, and fruits of the season. Cakes piled high with coconut and chocolate, with butter cream frosting. Pies of every description. Tea cakes and delicate lace cookies. Pralines. Martin sampled one after his dinner, which had consisted of small portions of a variety of foods. There was ambrosia, too.

And the wedding cake! With Martin's hand on Katherine's, both pressing down into the delectable confection prepared by Madame with the help of a prominent male baker friend, the newlyweds made the first cut. The cake was of rich batter with small chunks of candied cherries, pineapple, apricots, golden currants, dates, figs, and shredded coconut, all laced with brandy and sherry, then frosted with white butter cream piled high and intricately decorated.

Bride and groom joyfully fed each other.

"Martin," Katherine questioned, "how could anything be so beautiful?"

"*You* make it beautiful," he answered.

Madame Le Blanc, Zell, and Singing Bird cut and began to serve the rest of the cake.

Tears had misted Katherine's eyes since she stepped out of the tent and into the wedding crowd. As they cleared, she looked around her at the magnolia forest behind them. On the fencerows around the magnolias were blackberry bushes and wild plum trees. On a table and among the food were cuttings from the magnolia branches, bouquets of late roses, cape jasmine, and honeysuckle, at her request. The glistening large, clear pond rippled with the winds.

Guests had been lavish with food and bouquets. Wine and gifts by the hundreds were stacked on the table and in the tent. Handmade as well as store-bought, there were exquisite things.

"Congratulations, you two. I like what I see here."

Captain Paul DeBeau's gruff voice cut through the conversation just behind Katherine. Martin faced him.

"Yes, but I would have expected nothing less," DeBeau continued.

Martin, dressed comfortably now in black broadcloth pants, a plain white shirt, and a black jerkin, accepted the compliments, along with Katherine. DeBeau, he thought, was one of a kind. A rough, old, now-venerable ex-pirate in his youth, he honored the rules of etiquette with less than the usual distinction of color.

The band of fiddlers, harmonica players, banjo and guitar strummers, and the pianist, who had had his instrument moved farther down, had tuned up and swept into the bayou country music.

"You'll want to dance with your bride now," DeBeau said, "but I need to talk with you before I leave."

Martin nodded and swept Katherine out onto the freshly mowed carpet of grass. She was light in his arms, firmly soft, and the tiara of cape jasmine she had worn earlier had left its perfume in her hair. He had wanted his own place in this world, and Martin had long ago begun to find it, but other than the few months of overheated happiness with Celié in his youth, an emptiness had persisted and deepened until he'd found this woman. Now he felt his life beginning to fill.

He drew in a sharp breath—except for the threat that Celié posed. What *could* they do about Celié?

"How beautiful you are," he told her again.

The black pearl glowed under the slender gold fingerlike bands and the sparkling diamonds above it, fulfilling his mother's legacy and her wish that he be happy.

DeBeau walked around, sampling the food, limiting himself to cider as his son Guy, who had accompanied him, clapped to the music.

A waltz began and others joined the dancers. A radiant Singing Bird loved waltzes. It was plain that Madame Le Blanc, her two small helpers, and Papa Frank were enjoying themselves immensely.

DeBeau and his son walked over to them, the older man

bowing to Madame Le Blanc, whom he didn't know, but had seen in the French Quarter going back and forth to her shop. Lillian recognized him and nodded pleasantly.

"I came to wish Martin and Katherine well," DeBeau said to Papa Frank. The two youngsters moved off.

"I see," Papa Frank responded noncommittally. They had talked on the ship, he and Martin *and DeBeau.* It was as Martin said: DeBeau had literally begged for Papa Frank's forgiveness.

"This," he declared now, presenting his son Guy, "is my reason for incurring your wrath and your hatred. He was a far cry from what he is now the day I did that dastardly deed."

Ruefully, Guy DeBeau spoke. "I'm afraid my father thinks largely of his own welfare," he began.

"No, of your living to be a decent age," DeBeau retorted. "I'm proud to meet you, sir. Your granddaughter saved my life, as my father has told you."

Hesitating a moment, Papa Frank shook the young man's hand with a firm clasp.

"Well, he damned near took *my* life when I heard what had happened from some people a long way up the beach, who were too scared to go near. You took off like a thief, I reckon," he said to the older DeBeau.

"I was wrong, man," DeBeau acknowledged, "and I've never been one who couldn't admit to being wrong. But *I've* forgiven things another man'd kill for. . . ."

"Leave it be, man," Papa Frank told him. "What's done is done. You won't die from my being mad at you." He drew a half circle in the air with his gnarled hands. "A lot of good has come of your dastardly deed. I tell you, *leave* it. Who knows what'll come to pass?"

Guy grinned. The old pirate-cum-businessman had met his match.

So many people who had known Martin and Jules, who had been helped by them, and so many whom Katherine had helped to heal, came to congratulate them.

This was the day when they both officially learned that Jules and Zell were courting.

The dance finished, Katherine saw Martin dance off with Madame. Zell came up and hugged her tightly.

"My prayers on the ship were answered," she announced happily. "Today, Jules said he loves me. He asked me to marry him."

Katherine hugged her friend as she saw Martin and DeBeau talking on the sidelines, their expressions earnest and absorbed.

Now with food-sated stomachs and warm with the wine, some of the crowd, with great merriment, launched into a quadrille, led by Jules and Madame.

Singing Bird handed Katherine a note.

I have never been so happy.

When she read the note, Katherine hugged the young girl to her for a long moment and talked to her about the wedding, deciding that she would ask Martin to join the quadrille after she had taken off the black pearl and given it to him for safekeeping. When she saw him again, he was walking with the DeBeaus to their coach.

Hungry, Katherine sat in a chair someone had brought her and feasted on paella, turkey, potato and garden salad, and macaroni and cheese. She had chosen the plain food and it had never tasted so good.

"I saved you some of the wedding cake to enjoy now and a little later," Zell said happily. "I want Madame to make one for *my* wedding."

As Martin came to sit at her side, a large group encircled them, singing again the wedding day song, serenading them with fervor. They sang briefly, before they rejoined the quadrille.

"DeBeau and I talked about the fence we will build for his

friend in the Garden District, whom I told you about. But he also wants yours and Papa Frank's forgiveness."

"I may always be angry with him, but I lean toward forgiving him—in time."

"And even so," Martin said, "I suspect you will forgive him a long time before Papa Frank does."

Later that afternoon, as they sat in the front porch swing, Katherine kicked off her gray satin button shoes and massaged her feet. Then Martin massaged them for her.

"Let me massage yours," she offered.

"Later." He smiled. "Let's concentrate on you just now. Are you happy? Have I made you happy?"

"Yes," she answered simply. "Oh, Martin, *yes.*"

A moment later, Martin excused himself, got up, and went into the house, climbing up the attic stairs. Inside the large, dusty room, he quickly found his violin case, opened it, and removed his instrument and bow. Taking it up, he played a bit and listened. It needed tuning after two years of not being played, but the tone was reasonably good.

He played a few bars of a Santo Domingan love song, then went back downstairs and onto the porch, where Katherine sat swinging and relaxing.

He stood before her as he announced, "I will play a Santo Domingan love song for you that I have not played since that last night I was with Annalise and Raoul there."

He played and Katherine listened. It didn't surprise her that Martin played so well, with such feeling. As he played, she closed her eyes and imagined, from what he had told her, his life as a boy and as a young man on Santo Domingo. His life in Spain. His unconventional Spanish father and his rakehell brother, Raoul. His mother, Annalise. Strong, proud, and beautiful—indomitable to all save a love that enslaved her. And Celié, enslaved by her own pain and malice and unwillingness to ever forgive.

Martin finished and sat down.

"That was beautiful," Katherine told him. "You play so well."

Martin squeezed her knee. "Kate, you cannot know how much it means to me to be able to play again. I couldn't, you know. I played that last night on the mountainside that Annalise, Raoul, and I were together. Perhaps the whole nightmare is ending."

"I believe, my daring, that we can *make* it end," she declared.

They were silent in the late afternoon with pink clouds and the setting sun, thinking about their splendid wedding day. Soft breezes blew across their faces, as the smells of summer flowers, fresh cut grass, and the overflowing baskets of food left from the wedding drifted up the hall. She would take that food into town the next day to be distributed among some of the street children and The Little Sisters whom Sing adored and worked with.

That night, Katherine dressed in the thin, white silk nightgown and the satin-beribboned peignoir Madame had fashioned for her. She put Egyptian jasmine on her wrists, behind her ears, and in the hollows of her throat. When Martin knocked and entered a few moments later, his eyes roved over the lush and silken nutmeg body and finely molded face of his bride. Her flesh and perfume were heady, alluring.

Katherine put her arms around his neck, her desire-swollen breasts pressing hard against him.

"I love you," she whispered.

Martin pressed her back against the bed and bent over her soft, yielding, inviting body. Her eyes were limpid, dewy pools in which he could have drowned, yet they would resurrect him, he knew.

She unbuttoned his pajama top and slid the fabric from him, tossing it aside. He rolled off her and sat up, undoing his pajama bottoms. When he did this, she stood up, lowered her nightgown from her shoulders, and let it slip past her hips and onto the floor, exposing her slender, voluptuous body to his loving gaze.

Martin groaned deep in his throat, then stood and lifted her, holding her, before he laid her on the bed, arching his lithe, hard-muscled body over her. This, then, was the way it had to be, he thought. He kissed her open mouth, his tongue probing hers, his mouth pressing hers with eager need. And Katherine returned his ardor, breath for breath.

His lips sought her breasts and found them, moved over them, then nestled before he found the desire-hardened nipples, sucking them gently at first, then harder. He found her flesh firm and sweet, like newly ripened fruit. He found her spirited coming to him like an emotional ambrosia. Martin began to roam her body with loving hands.

And Katherine opened up to him like a night-blooming cereus. Excitement as she had never known coursed through her veins like liquid wildfire that heats but cannot burn. How could she love him, want him, with a passion that barred all else? But she did, and that was all that mattered.

"Please hurry, my darling," she whispered as he arched again above her, his manhood thrusting gently and smoothly into the oven-warm satin sheath of her yielding body, then becoming still for a moment to slow himself. But she began the movement of her hips in measured rhythm beneath him, which drove him into ecstasy beyond the telling.

With the joy of the day and love and champagne bubbling in their blood, they swam together in a sea that eddied wildly and spun them into a maelstrom of passion, leaving them spent on the softer shores of their deep-feathered bridal bed.

When it ended, Katherine begged him not to leave her—which he had no mind to *ever* do.

"Katherine, my wife," he murmured, "how I love you."

"And I love you," she told him, then whispered, biting his ear, "and love you and love you."

Martin nonetheless shuddered for a moment at the memory of the coach that had sat on the road during their wedding, apart from the others. When DeBeau's carriage had pulled away and Martin had begun to walk back to the celebration, someone in a black veil had drawn back a curtain from the windows and peered out directly at him. He was too far away to see clearly, but Martin was certain it was Celié, and he was even more certain that she *meant* for him to see her—and wonder. He and Celié had once loved each other. Was he to spend the rest of his life paying for the love he no longer felt? He would tell Katherine about it tomorrow. He'd be damned if he would disturb this perfect night.

Katherine sat bolt upright at the sound of the din outside. How long had she slept and what time was it? There were loud, mocking voices, metal pounding on metal. Yet, there was fiddle music, too. There had been disturbances throughout the city over the governor's less-than-popular proclamations concerning more rights for citizens of color. But the fiddle music hardly fit in with that.

She got up and pulled her peignoir around her, irritated more than frightened. Where were Zell and Singing Bird? They had always come to her at any sign of trouble. And where was Martin? Padding hurriedly across the floor in her bare feet, Katherine opened the door to find the three miscreants standing in the hall near her door, their faces wreathed in merriment. Before she could ask him, Martin spoke up.

"It's a charivari, love."

"A charivari? But in the bayou country, only when someone very old marries someone very young, or there are other differences people find amusing, do they have charivaris. I thought of that for a moment, but we're both young, not *too* different in any way that matters. . . ."

Now Jules's voice and other voices Katherine recognized as belonging to neighborhood men began serenading with the wedding song and livelier comical songs. "A shivaree," Jules called out.

"It is the way of our city," Martin explained. "Appropriating and adapting every custom to itself, making them its own. Do you find it unpleasant?"

"You know I don't, sweetheart," she answered. "But at home, charivaris mostly last until dawn. And I'm so tired. You need rest, too, to work tomorrow."

They looked at each other and, in drawing together, neither felt tired anymore. It was a fitting end, Martin thought, to the happiest day of his life.

Fourteen

The weeks just after Katherine and Martin's September wedding were quiet and uneventful. By the first week in October, the Drumms had been to their house for dinner and had complimented Katherine as an excellent cook. Inez had brought many Creole recipes. Wilson had brought along a clipping from the *Chronicle,* and it seemed to Katherine now as she sat in the little room down the hall from Natalie's bedroom, that she could remember one entire section of the governor's annual message.

The issues of the conflict have been settled, we hope, forever. Slavery has been swept away, and along with it all the train of evils growing out of its wickedness, and has left us—master and slave, white and black—with the same rights under the law, the same chance to succeed in life, and with equally unrestricted aspirations and hopes.

Remembering those words made her feel proud to help care for the wife of this man and to help to deliver his child.

"Are we really to come fully into our own the way people of color never have before in this country?" she murmured to herself. "We helped to build this country, to sustain it and protect it. We deserve this chance to be citizens."

At a light tap on the door and Katherine's response, Natalie's maid, Jenny, came in.

"We're waiting for Dr. St. Cyr, ma'am, but the missus wants

you to come up. You told her to sleep a bit, I know, but I suspect she's full of nerves. She has slept off and on."

But when they got upstairs, nerves or not, Natalie was dozing from the valerian tea—which was a good sign. Katherine sat in the tapestry rocker not far from Natalie's bed and watched the swollen body. She suspected Natalie wanted her close by just in case.

How much she had been able to change things! The room was opened daily now for a couple of hours to let autumn breezes sweep through, and it had lost the staleness that bothered Katherine when she'd first begun attending Natalie. Even with her own wedding under way, she'd come for a short while every day for the past month to oversee food preparation, to prepare infusions and decoctions herself, and to supervise the lemon balm and lavender baths that relaxed the mother-to-be and helped her circulation.

Jenny scurried about the room, as nervous as she'd said her mistress was.

"Ah, tum-te-tum and a fiddle-de-dee. The governor's wife, how do you be?"

Dr. St. Cyr came into the room, singing in his gruff, bass voice, mocking the poor country boy he'd been before being adopted by a wealthy relative, educated, and sent to medical school. Natalie smiled but didn't open her eyes. The doctor gazed at both women thoughtfully.

"Well, ma'am, I'd suppose you can say you wrought a small miracle here with the governor's wife and her baby-to-be-born. She was a bundle of nerves, a screeching harridan, before you came."

"You're being really mean, Dr. St. Cyr. I was never any of those things you call me. I was ever sweet, gentle, relaxed, and never threw things across the room in conniption fits. Be honest now."

The doctor laughed, rubbing his small paunch. "I'm an old man, Natalie, and I've known you since you were a girl. As a woman, your beauty has always dazzled me. You and Katherine here are both unusual women. Out of season. Both be-yoo-ti-ful . . ."

He looked at Katherine more closely but said nothing else.

"I've gotten the angelica ready, doctor," Katherine told him. "Would you prefer black or blue cohosh to help speed delivery?"

He looked up sharply. "Which would *you* prefer?"

"Either is fine," she answered, "but somehow I like the blue cohosh."

Dr. St. Cyr rubbed his hands together, studying Natalie keenly. Her breath was shorter and she kept biting her lips against the beginning pains, until finally she cried out with the evenly spaced contractions.

Katherine, the doctor, and Jenny rushed into action, with the young maid bringing up the slippery elm and squaw vine decoction for Natalie to drink again to shorten her labor.

But the baby wasn't ready yet, and in the lull, Katherine reported, "I've had her drink red raspberry tea and fresh orange juice—three cups daily—for a month now."

To their surprise, Natalie chuckled. "I expected to feel the devil's own pain," she said, "but, you know, I've made myself relax. Yes, it *hurts,* but it's easier than I'd ever dreamed. This time, I think I'm right."

The rubber sheet was white and glistening on the bed, and the slender-hipped woman, entranced now by giving birth, was no longer afraid as Jenny and Dr. St. Cyr each gripped one of her hands.

In the dimly lit room, Katherine's voice was hypnotic with her gentle commands. "Breathe deeply now. Press hard! Press down! It is up to *you* to deliver this gift from God." When she'd said this a few times, Katherine hummed a lullaby:

> "Into this world comes a baby
> Into this world comes a child
> Mama will let nothing hurt you."

After ten to fifteen minutes of encouragement for resting and pushing, the doctor and Jenny looked up as a cooperative Natalie gave one mighty, unbidden push and the baby's head appeared. Dr. St. Cyr gently pulled the infant clear of Natalie and the afterbirth, lifting the babe and slapping its red bottom. The old doctor whooped with joy at the piercing howl of anger.

After a while they cut the umbilical cord and, using angelica, removed the afterbirth. Dr. St. Cyr teased them all. "Now this is where Katherine's and my magic comes in. You didn't know this, did you, Natalie? Angelica drives witches and evil spirits away."

So soon delivered of her baby girl, Natalie was beaming. She couldn't compliment enough the three people who'd helped her.

She turned to Katherine. "Is this true? If it is, I'm delighted. With what the governor's going through these days, I'll ask him about serving angelica tea in his office."

Dr. St. Cyr shook his head. "Not a chance, my dear . . . unless it's at least half bourbon and a quarter branch water. Bully for you and this young'un. You both did a wonderful job. Katherine, you were magnificent! You have to teach me your prayers." He slid, as he often did, from country usage to more formal language. Strange, Katherine thought. Zell had said those same words to her about Martin, and Zell had found Jules.

Back in the small sitting room she used while at the mansion, Katherine sat alone, grateful that Natalie had delivered in daylight so she could be home with her own family by night. She felt a keen sense of accomplishment; midwifery was one of the things she most enjoyed. Sitting in the deep tan wicker chair, she placed her hands on her own stomach. Celié's taunt that Martin had married her because Celié could not bear children continued to haunt her, even if it was a lie. What if, without realizing it, he really *had* married her to beget a child on her healthy body? She, too, wanted his child, but she also wanted his love. So many things said he *did* love her. His trip to the bayou country to get Papa Frank, his anger at her hurt by Celié, the splendid wedding he'd arranged. His deftly tender touch on her body that thrilled her very soul . . .

"Well, ma'am, congratulate yourself again, as I do, on one hell of a delivery."

Dr. St. Cyr strode into the room through the door left slightly ajar. Still grinning as he paced, he said, "I don't mind admitting it now, Katherine. I felt she could indeed bear this child, but I thought it would be difficult, and Natalie's got a child's pain threshold. Let me tell you, you've taught an old dog new tricks."

"I'm pleased, too," Katherine told him. "I thought we could bring her through without too much suffering, but I wasn't certain. All of us have really worked for this birth, nobody harder than Natalie."

The old doctor stood in front of Katherine, bending a little from the waist. "You're blooming lately. Excuse an old man's inquisitiveness, but are you in the family way?"

Katherine's skin warmed quickly. "I don't know yet," she answered softly, "but I *hope* I am."

He nodded. "Then don't be like me, one of your teachers. You know it's said the shoemaker's children have no shoes, while he sees that the rest of the community is well shod. Take the best possible care of yourself, beginning now. With what seems to lie between you and Martin, you should get pregnant and have wonderful children."

"Thank you. I hope we'll have many."

"Now Natalie's so fond of you, she'll use any excuse to keep you here. I want you to get home early and get plenty of rest and sleep. I know how dedicated you are, but don't get so busy you don't have time for yourself."

"I won't," Katherine promised quietly.

"I'd like to pin a medal on you for what you've done for Natalie and the baby. I tell you, the governor would do anything you ask, he's that grateful. Katherine, you've given an old duffer like me an education."

Katherine was pleased and she thanked him. "But I'm the one who's learned the most from *you.*"

Gruffly, he said, "That well may be, but I doubt it. Now do me one more favor. I haven't seen Martin lately, or I'd have asked him. I have heard that your legendary grandfather, Papa Frank, is living with you."

"Why, yes, he is," she answered.

"I would very much like to meet that gentleman. Is it possible for me to do so?" the doctor asked.

"My grandfather would be delighted to meet you," she told him.

Dr. St. Cyr looked pleased. "Then I will check with you in a few days to set a time convenient to your family. And I thank you in advance."

He left then to return to Natalie, and Katherine sat there, rocking. Tiredness she hadn't realized before seeped through her flesh; her bones even ached a bit. She'd missed one monthly cycle, and she had always been quite regular. Katherine often used the same angelica that helped remove the afterbirth and heal the womb to make herself fine teas and relaxing baths. But with the chance of pregnancy, she would stop using it until she needed them to assist in her own childbirth. It relaxed the womb too much. She'd stop even the rosemary leaves mixed with thyme, which made such an excellent hair rinse, because the tea wasn't recommended for pregnant women. A rinse probably wouldn't hurt, but she intended to take no chances if there were a baby between Martin and her.

Fifteen

"You certainly look like a courting man to me!"

Papa Frank blushed as he came into the kitchen, where Katherine was drying and putting away the dinner dishes. Dressed in his Sunday-go-to-meeting garments of black gabardine and a black cravat, he looked a dandy. His salt-and-pepper hair was slicked back, his white mustache neatly trimmed.

"Ah, grandgirl, you think you young'uns have the whole lover band playing all the time. Well, I've not hung up my fiddle yet."

"You didn't eat my cooking tonight. Does that mean dinner with Madame?"

He grinned broadly. "The old girl's quite a cook . . . Miss Lillian's a lovely woman, Katie. Like I keep saying, she's the only woman since your grandma died sets my heart a'beating that way. Miss Ada and I got close, but your grandma and me had a wonderful life. It's a shame you hardly got to know her." He sounded a bit sad, remembering.

"I knew my *mama* for a few years. She always said you and grandma had something special. I don't have to wonder whom I inherited my romantic ways from. . . ."

"Now I'll just bet ol' Martin's a happy man you got your loving ways from somebody."

It was Katherine's turn to smile. With each passing week, it seemed she and Martin grew closer.

"I checked on Singing Bird," he said. "That lemon balm tea's got her a mite sleepy, but her cold's a whole lot better."

"She tries to do too much. She's such a good kid."

"All three of you are fine young women—you, Zell, and Sing. You'll never know how I worried when they kidnapped you."

"It's all right, Papa. Martin came to my rescue. DeBeau was looking for you to cure his son, and thank God that on that trip Martin was with him. I hated him and I was even mad at Martin at first."

"Fate's often been kind to you, Katie, as well as cruel, and to me, too."

"You've been kind to me. You taught me to be kind and it's worked—up until now."

Unbidden, thoughts of Celié crowded her mind.

"It will always work, kindness will," he declared staunchly, patting her shoulder. "And when it doesn't, there are other, harsher remedies. You think I'm good enough for a woman like Miss Lillian?"

Genuinely taken aback, Katherine thought at first he might be teasing, but he was dead serious. Quite truthfully, she reassured him.

"I could never imagine a woman you weren't good enough for," she told him. "Oh, I'll bet you Miss Lillian is smart enough to know that. Are you two getting serious? First Jules and Zell, and now . . ."

"Well, it's not like we have a lifetime," he said, "although I think now that would be nice. You and Martin surely got set up in a hurry." He was teasing again in the gentle way he had always teased her.

"He's been a wonderful husband," she reflected.

Papa Frank saw in his granddaughter's eyes the vivid love and the deep determination to keep what was hers. He felt that Katie was his best contribution to his life.

Getting his hat from the rack, he turned back to her. "Guess

I'll be hitching up Helio and going on over to Miss Lillian's," he announced as he went up the hall.

After he left, Katherine sat at the dining room table with a large three-sectioned basket of dried herbs—lemon balm, lavender, and lemon verbena—inhaling the perfume that permeated the room. She filled small bags made of fine cheesecloth with the herbs, then sewed them shut. These were for her baths and sachet, for herself and for Singing Bird. The men mostly used epsom salts and occasionally soda, to ease aching joints and soothe jangled nerves, but they used herbal baths, too. And they all used powdered ginger baths and infusions to warm and soothe themselves.

She got up and looked in on Singing Bird, who slept peacefully, snoring a little from the still-harsh cold that rattled in her chest. The room smelled of lemon balm and peppermint. Katherine saw that Sing had drank the cup of echinacea infusion she'd left. She closed the door quietly so as not to disturb her sleep.

Martin would be late. He had begun constructing an estate fence. She'd made wild rabbit stew and dumplings with red wine, with carrots and little green peas. Martin really enjoyed food. He was not a finicky eater, and his face lit up when she fixed a favorite dish.

Katherine went to the window and pulled back the drapes. The night was overcast and bleak, but no rain had been forecast. It was not quite seven, and as she watched the full moon, a cloud began to pass over it and lingered. She let the drapery fall back into place and returned to making the bath bags.

"Hallo-o-o!"

The voice was accompanied by loud knocking at the front door. She glanced around the curtains that covered the glass panels, then opened the door.

"Louis! What on earth?" She had not been in his presence since the night he had come to see Papa Frank.

He laced his hands together, a supplicant. "Katherine, please come with me. I know you got no real reason to trust me. But

I loved my mama, and I'll swear on her grave if you want. I'll see I don't do you no harm, and nobody else will . . ."

In the lamplight, she could see that his face was ashen, and that he trembled with fear and anxiety.

"What is it you need, Louis?" she asked coolly. "Sing is sick and there's no one here to care for her except me. . . ." It was an excuse, for in reality Katherine thought Sing well on her way to recovery.

"Lorda'mighty!" he said, half babbling. "It's Celié! A rattle-snake's bit her and she's gonna die if she don't get help quick! Lord, I hate snakes! Please, Katherine!"

Katherine's mind moved in slow but crystal-clear motion. She would need the decoctions that came from the root of the common ash bark tree. She brewed this decoction from time to time and kept it on hand. Snakebites were infrequent, but they happened throughout the area. Something safe to quiet the nerves. Echinacea. Black cohosh. Oils of pennyroyal. For the healer in her did not question that she would treat anyone in danger, even Celié. But still she hesitated.

"I may well ask you to place your hand on *my* Bible, Louis," she announced grimly.

"Just show me where it is," Louis said. "Only please hurry!"

Katherine didn't think this was any trick. Louis often played the fool, but he was not an actor.

"You'll have to come in and sit down while I get a few things together to treat the snakebite." Looking at Louis as he half fell into the chair, she felt he was changing for the better, and Katherine found that, surprisingly, she didn't loathe him anymore.

"How in the world did she get a rattlesnake bite?" Katherine asked him as he got up and followed her to the kitchen.

"Katherine, don't ask me. That woman's into things I don't want to know about. Voodoo. Hoodoo. Black magic. I'm find-ing out some things. . . ." He would go no further.

Suddenly, Sing entered the room, notepad thrust before her.

Make him get someone else to help Celié. You don't go with him!

Katherine and Louis turned to look at Singing Bird, who had hurriedly gotten into her robe but was barefoot.

Katherine spoke first. "Sing, go and get back into bed. You know better than to be up with no slippers on your feet."

Louis got up, his hands outstretched. "Singing Bird," he said, "we're friends. You know I helped you. How can I not help Celié?"

Singing Bird scribbled furiously and handed Louis her note.

You're in love with this witch. She's teaching you how to dress, how to talk—everything!

Louis read it and chuckled dryly. "That'll be the day," he said. "*You're* my friend, if you want it that way, but Celié's helped me to make connections a man of color needs here. She's got her eye on just one prize. . . ." He glanced at Katherine, his mouth grim. "Now, I couldn't find Dahomey Sinclair, whom she wants to treat her, but I just figured if you do her this favor, even *she* can't be evil enough to keep on chasing Martin. *If* you can save her, that is. She may have done it this time."

Sing marched up to Katherine and wrote:

Don't go to Celié. Please don't.
Why should you help her?

"Go back to bed, Sing," Katherine instructed gently. "Even those who perform the worst deeds deserve life, and if I *can* do that, I must. I'll write a note for Martin. Go back to bed, sweetheart, and don't worry. I won't tarry for even an extra moment."

Moving swiftly then, Katherine put the decoctions and dry

herbs she'd need in a black "doctor's" bag, got boots from the closet, and put them on. Donning her gray cloak and bonnet, she told a terribly worried Louis, "Now we really have to get a move on."

"You must hurry!"

Katherine put down her bag after opening it, and spread out the packets and bottles. She removed her bonnet and cloak and placed them on a chair, then sent Louis to the kitchen to heat the ash tea and begin brewing more of the ash tree decoction, the echinacea, and the black cohosh used to treat poisonous snakebites.

Lying there in a robe of the black silk she seemed to favor, Celié's wavy black hair spread out around her shoulders. Both sleeves of her robe had been pushed up.

"Good," Katherine approved when she saw Louis had already fashioned a tourniquet.

Staring down at her rival as she lay propped up on a number of snow-white linen-covered pillows, Katherine couldn't help a rush of anger.

"Why send for me?" she asked Celié. "There are doctors you know."

"Don't flatter yourself," Celié said through clenched teeth. "I would never compromise myself with the doctors I know trying to explain this." She stopped and licked her lips as she flinched with pain. "I wanted Dahomey Sinclair. But *truthfully,* Louis thinks you can work miracles. Well, I am waiting."

Coldly, Katherine told her, "Truth is a circumstance you are not even *acquainted* with. So let us not speak of truth."

Again Celié clenched her teeth with pain, but she smiled.

"Well, *mam'selle,* work me a small miracle, and do hurry!"

Taken aback that Celié would resort to calling her the insulting "mam'selle," Katherine suddenly saw the woman who lay there in malevolent bruised colors—bilious green, choleric yellow, rusty purplish blue. Her very aura was negative, where she had not seemed to Katherine to radiate this before.

What had changed in her life?

Examining the snakebite, Katherine saw that Louis had done a good job making a clean and useful incision to drain the poison. She checked Celié's heart and pulse, alarmed now at her waxen, clammy, pale skin and slow heartbeat. Bending down and raising Celié from the pillows to a sitting position, she was relieved when Louis brought the warm ash tree tea.

"She looks bad," Louis complained. "Celié?"

Celié didn't answer as Katherine shushed him. Somehow they got the decoction into the semiconscious woman, spilling some onto robe and bed, and Katherine held her, watching her closely. Celié moaned faintly, but she breathed easier.

"Help me lower her robe from around the top and put some towels down, will you?"

Louis nodded and went for the towels. So it was Katherine who first saw the pale green silk nightgown exquisitely appliquéd with darker satin-shaded green flames that swept around the bodice and the skirt.

It was the gown Celié had left in the chest of drawers Katherine's first night at the house she shared with Martin.

Stiffening with remembered pain, she talked to herself.

A woman may be dying, Katherine told herself sharply now. I must move. Forget about the gown for the moment. Forget who she is.

With Louis's help, she moved Celié to her chaise lounge and removed her robe and gown. Katherine dipped her hands in the ash tree tea and lavished the liquid onto Celié's entire body. She seemed for a while to rally, and they made her drink more tea.

Tiredly, Katherine reflected that it well may *not* have been a lethal amount of venom, no matter how poisonous the snake. She decided that if Celié did not rally sufficiently in the next five minutes, she'd send Louis to fetch Dr. St. Cyr.

"Celié!" Louis kept calling her. Katherine didn't shush him again. Perhaps it would help.

For a brief moment, the woman seemed lifeless in their arms as they took turns holding her.

"Bring me the rest of the ash tea. I want her to drink it," Katherine ordered sharply.

A little color had returned to Celié's face but her breathing was still labored. In repose, the woman's features were sharply perfect, her skin silken, but the ugly aura was still there. Katherine jumped a little as she saw for the first time the rattlesnake lying in the shadows by Celié's bureau drawers.

"Don't worry," Louis said, chuckling a bit as he came in with the tea. "I killed it for sure. Celié didn't want me to. Said she hadn't handled it right. Said it was her fault she got bitten."

How interesting, Katherine thought sourly. Pity she saves all her compassion for poisonous snakes and has none for humans. She forced herself to look at the woman and not think of the nightgown.

"You want me to get that snake out of here? You scared of it? Most women . . ." He stopped with a shrug.

"Leave it and help me get her to drink the rest of this. I'm not afraid of snakes—not the dead, God-made ones, anyway."

Celié murmured unintelligible phrases now, what seemed part of a song or a poem.

"She was singing some kind of hoodoo song when it bit her," Louis said. "I ain't—I"m not sure I care for this kind of mess."

Celié's words were plain to them. "Don't kill him, Louis. I'll need him again. Save him. . . ."

Once all the tea was down, a little more color returned to Celié's face and her breathing eased again. She was coming around. Her eyes fluttered open.

"I'm afraid it's too late," Katherine told her. "Your snake is dead. Louis thought it best to kill it."

Of course she wanted to ask her questions about what had

happened, Katherine thought to herself, but she didn't want to hear Celié's answers. What she meant to do was return home as soon as possible. A grandfather clock, not unlike the one in their house, chimed the hour.

Celié breathed deeply now. Her eyes on Katherine were again amused. "Thank you for not letting me die," she said. "God, I hate pain!"

Getting up, Katherine responded, with no particular malice, "But you're pleased to inflict it on others."

Celié ignored her remark. "You know, even *I* am becoming persuaded that you well may be the black pearl they call you. *I* would not have come to *you.*" Her eyes clouded as she murmured, "It's really too bad, you know. . . ."

"What is too bad?" Katherine asked, as Louis watched them, frowning.

Celié shook her head.

Not usually given to inquisitiveness, Katherine now noticed more fully a large framed photograph turned halfway to the wall. The daguerreotype was like the one Celié had showed her at the governor's mansion. But it was also different. This was a photograph of Martin and Celié *together,* looking into each other's eyes. Again Celié wore the black pearl against a high-necked black dress, and the hand that Martin held was graced by both the diamond *and* the wedding ring that Katherine still wore. The photo was inscribed, "With love forever. Martin." The daguerreotype Celié had shown Katherine, however, had borne no inscription.

Katherine felt nauseous. They *had* been lovers, of course, and Martin had said Celié wore the jewels to help them escape, on pretense of being his wife. Even knowing that, she wanted to curse and hit this woman with powerful, punishing blows, this woman who looked at her with gloating, satisfied eyes.

Oddly, Celié quieted now, and looking into Katherine's furious eyes, her voice held an edge of sadness.

"I thank you for coming here, but Martin will *always* belong to me, as I will always belong to him. Louis, please take mam'selle home. And please hurry back."

"Listen to me, Celié," Katherine began coldly. "Don't call me 'mam'selle' ever again! I married the man you wanted long after you'd been fool enough to throw him over to marry his brother. *You* put the circle of feathers inside our gate, didn't you? Or had them put there.

"I want you to leave Martin and me alone. . . . Stop this madness!"

Katherine paused, aware of Celié's eyes on her belly, sick with envy. Even loathing her, she felt sympathy for a fellow human being who wanted with such desperation something she could no longer have.

Katherine left the jars that had held the ash tree tea, where she usually carried them back with her. She wanted *nothing* that had been in this witch's house. She left packets of echinacea and black cohosh to be brewed into infusions. She left plenty of the ash bark tree root powder. She would have left her valuable medicine bag behind, too, if she could have. Gathering her belongings, Katherine left the room in a hurry and stood in the short hallway, putting on her cloak and bonnet.

She felt Louis's hand on her shoulder. "I'm sorry, Katherine," he said humbly. He had his coat slung over his arm. "Let's get out of here now.

"He's *your* man, lady, or her nose wouldn't be so out of joint. If he ever *was* hers, he's yours now. And that ought to make you feel a little better."

By now they rode along near the French Market, past the night crowd and the tourists, and Louis rushed the horse a bit.

"Now, Celié didn't say to me to get *you* right away. She wanted me to get her hoodoo buddy, Dahomey Sinclair. Well, you won't find that clown early in the night like this. He's got *business* to tend to. Monkey business, if you ask me.

"No, *I* told her I was going to get you if I couldn't find Dahomey Sinclair, and I sure didn't try very hard to find him.

She didn't say I *couldn't* get you, so I did. She could've died, couldn't she, Katherine?"

Katherine answered truthfully, "I think she could very well have died from that snakebite. I don't pretend to know. But you started the saving work when you made that cut and did the tourniquet."

"Papa Frank taught me to do that," Louis announced humbly. "I'm glad he's here."

"Katherine! Stop the buggy, Louis!"

The passing buggy pulled up abreast of them, the driver sharply reining in Helio just ahead. Louis reined in his horse also. By this time, Martin was already at her side of the buggy, reaching up to help her down.

In his arms, she could feel his heart pounding, could virtually feel the anxiety, the fury in his voice. And yes, there was fear there, too.

"What is the meaning of this, Duplessis?" he asked.

"Celié got herself snakebit . . . rattlesnake," Louis explained quickly. He wanted no quarrel with this man. "I got the best help I knew how to get."

"Martin, darling, it was early, or I wouldn't have gone. She's all right now."

"And what about you, Kate? Are *you* all right? My God, I was insane with worry!"

"I'm going to go back now," Louis called from the buggy. "I thank you more than I can tell you, Katherine. Blame *me*, Martin. I'm the one who begged her to come."

"Goodnight," Katherine called out. "Thank you for starting to take me home."

When Louis had ridden off, Martin pulled Katherine to him and kissed her so hard that her mouth hurt.

"My God, Kate, I was so worried," he reiterated.

* * *

It was early, so Papa Frank was still out courting Miss Lillian. Singing Bird met them at the door, hugged Katherine fiercely, and handed a note to Martin:

> I begged her not to go.

"She's beautiful, sweet . . . and hardheaded," Martin said.

"Celié might well have died if I hadn't gone to her," Katherine began to explain. "Louis tried to get someone else. He came here as a last resort."

"It will sound cruel," Martin told her, "but even if she had died, I don't want you ever again to risk your life for her . . . for anyone. Katherine, please, my darling."

Katherine kissed him. "I won't, love," she promised.

She turned to Sing, who watched them. "To bed with you, young lady. Would you like me to make you some hot chocolate . . . or a very mild hot toddy?"

Sing shook her head no and returned to her room.

"She has taught him how to dress, how to talk," she whispered to herself. "Is he in love with her? He says he is my friend. He looks so handsome now."

Her whispers sounded strange to her own ears.

Sixteen

Martin was home early. As he came in from the brisk late November air, Katherine went close to him, hugged him, and kissed him full on the mouth.

"Hey!" he reacted, surprised. "I'm much too dirty and sweaty for you to be near. Lord, honey, you do look good!" He took her hand and twirled her around, admiring the periwinkle calico print with its frilly bodice and bustled skirt.

"No, you're not too *anything*," she said, going close to him again.

"Sweetheart, you're trembling," he noted. "Has anything happened?"

"Martin, last night another house was approached by the robbers. Ellen Byerly came by to tell us. Three men were there, where they'd expected only one, and they drove the robbers off. She said they went back toward downtown. Papa Frank, Sing, and I have been guarding the house all day. . . . It happened so suddenly they never got a chance to send for help."

Martin looked around at the shotgun and the rifle in different parts of the living room, at the boxes of shells on a table.

"We've been doing more target practice, too," she informed him.

Martin took her in his arms. "Kate, you've missed your second cycle, so we can be pretty sure you're pregnant. You've got to be careful, and *I've* got to take care of you."

Martin had never been a man to be particularly frightened for himself. Raoul and he had been hassled for being the bastard sons of a wealthy landowner and they'd sometimes been attacked in their childhood days on Santo Domingo. But he was afraid now for his woman, whom he was beginning to love more deeply with each passing day.

"Yes," she said, "I'm pretty sure now that I'm in the family way, but don't worry about me. I can take care of myself."

The words came unbidden from Martin, and they were bitter. "The way you took care of yourself the night we abducted you?"

"*You* didn't do it, love. You married me to keep me safe from danger."

"I think something in me loved you, even then."

"Thank heavens! Martin, we've got Celié to contend with, although we've heard nothing lately from her. Now this. If anything should happen to me, please know that you've given me some of the happiest days and weeks of my life."

"Now look here, lady," Martin said sternly, "I know we all can't help being edgy, but what's this about?"

"Oh," she sighed, as he pressed her closer, "you know what you always say about not tempting the spirits to cut us down for being too happy? I guess I've simply been too happy since I've known I was in the family way. I want your baby, Martin."

Martin brought her fingers to his lips and kissed them.

"I'll draw your bath," Katherine told him. "I made a praline cake that turned out rather well."

Martin laughed. "A cake for which I think you needed to use no sugar."

Katherine smiled. "Speaking of sugar, I wonder what the two sweeties, Jules and Zell, are up to. Taking off to go to a country fair in Slidell. It's the people of color's night there tonight."

"Wouldn't you have liked to go, Kate?" he asked. More and more he called her Kate, and she liked the sound of that name on his tongue.

"I'd much rather be alone with you . . . once dinner is over and Papa Frank and Singing Bird are out playing checkers in the greenhouse."

They had eaten very early and now sat in the kitchen enjoying praline cake—Martin, Katherine, and Papa Frank.

"It's a great cake, *wife*," Martin told her. He was always so pleased when she baked something special for him.

"I'll say," Papa Frank commented enthusiastically.

"Where's Sing gone off to?" Martin asked.

"She went to her room," Katherine answered. "Sing's a bit uptight lately. Something's bothering her."

Katherine sat pensively, comfortable in the presence of the two men, thinking of Natalie's baby, Athena. Assisting in a birth never failed to excite and satisfy her, no matter how many times she did it. She folded her hands over her stomach, enjoying the anticipation of giving birth to her own child.

Natalie's baby was doing well, gaining and thriving. And to the new mother's delight, she had plenty of milk.

Martin smiled as if he could read her mind. Standing, he picked up the bowl of scraps from the table.

"Why don't I give this to Ruff and Muffin," he proposed. "I'm so glad to have dogs around again."

When Martin left, Papa Frank spoke up. "Katie, I don't want to meddle, but Martin's got a lot on his mind and he's looking a mite run-down."

"I know," she replied quietly. "I've been wondering how best to help him."

"Well, for one thing . . . what do you say I suggest he start on some saw palmetto decoctions, with a bit of damiana and echinacea? I'll be glad to grind the berries for you and make it. It's sure pulled me through a number of hurting times."

When they heard the dogs' shrill barking and the clop of hooves, Katherine's heart jumped. She and Papa Frank got up and went to the window. Martin was already at the side of the house. There was a loaded gun on the back porch, and he stepped back a bit to retrieve it before he recognized DeBeau's carriage and coachman as they pulled up in front of the house. He breathed a sigh of relief.

Martin went to the front, where he spoke to the coachman, opened the carriage gate, and invited the men in.

"We'll have to get back before dark," DeBeau announced. "And Doc, here, asked to ride along to meet Katherine's grandfather. I'd like Katherine and Mr. Keyes to hear this, too, Martin."

He sounded grim. Martin went to the side door and asked Katherine and Papa Frank to come out. Once they were there, neither DeBeau nor Martin introduced Papa Frank to Dr. St. Cyr, because it was plain something else was more pressing.

"Well, sir, I've come with good news for all of you and me, but damned bad news for some thugs we've all heard about doing the robbing and worse."

Katherine's heart leapt, as did Martin's and Papa Frank's.

"Seems we caught the bastards who were doing all that damage out this way and in the French Quarter. I brought my own men over from Barataria, and they did what the police couldn't do alone but sure as hell helped with. They stopped them in their filthy tracks. *Caught* them red-handed. They won't be doing any more damage."

"That's wonderful," Katherine breathed.

"Yessir, they're *under* the jailhouse now. They tried to rob a place a mile or so from here, as you probably know, and more men than they thought were there chased them back toward the French Quarter. Before they realized there were other men, they bragged about what they'd do to one of the daughters of that house. By that time, my men had followed them, captured them. One was fool enough to fight back. Well, he won't be boasting about that—or anything else."

"They were probably headed here then," Martin ventured, "this time or the next. In September, it was the place adjoining that one. They seem to have been smart enough to wait until things cooled before coming out again."

"They were indeed headed here," DeBeau said, "according to one of my men. November's not too early to begin collecting Christmas loot."

Here DeBeau's eyes shifted from Martin to Katherine, then to Papa Frank. "I'd save myself a lot of trouble by not mentioning this, but you'll remember, Katherine, one of the varmints on my ship, and Martin, you surely do. He was Fitch by name, and he was the ringleader of this gang. I fired him right after that trip and he hated my guts, swore he'd kill me. But I got him . . . or my men did."

"I'm damned glad for that," Martin stated, clenching and unclenching his fists. "We've been a kind of armed camp around here."

"Oh, thank God," Katherine said. The men looked at her, as if to protect her. She could still recall vividly that slimy toad of a man Fitch when his eyes had raked her in the full moonlight the night they'd kidnapped her. The things he'd said before the blond man had pressed his fingers into her throat and she'd lost consciousness. The night they'd kidnapped her in order to save Guy DeBeau. Even now, Katherine shuddered. Martin saw that shudder and was as angry now as he had been back then.

DeBeau began now, deferential as he'd been at the wedding. "Well, Mr. Keyes—*Doc* Keyes—I reckon since you're the great leaf doctor I was after from the beginning . . ."

He was asking absolution for one of a long string of transgressions, and Papa Frank felt he didn't have the power to grant it. And would he if he could? He honestly didn't know. Now he said what he felt.

"Best I can say to you is a man pays his debts in many ways, but if and when he pays them, consideration has got to be given to that paying."

DeBeau made a slight movement as if he might shake hands, before he saw that the old leaf doctor didn't wish to go that far. It was done and over, but it could never be forgotten by any of them.

Papa Frank saw the gesture and admired the man for not

pushing. "I thank you," he said, "for saving us the trouble of having to kill last night, or being harmed or killed. I reckon we and the whole damned neighborhood out here's been an armed camp."

"Doc St. Cyr, I guess we'd best be getting back before dark," DeBeau advised. "Plenty of other varmints out here to take the place of those."

After they'd gone, Katherine, Martin, and Papa Frank hugged each other.

"Oh, thank God," Katherine said again.

Inside the house, Singing Bird had heard the conversation from her open window and she rejoiced. She had not gone out, because she was again remembering that night so long ago when the man had accosted her in the woods, just as the overseer had accosted and raped her mother, Gray Eagle, so many years ago. She had been determined to fight him until the death of him and her, but Louis had materialized like a warrior from heaven. The man and Louis had fought, and Louis had been by far the stronger.

For the man who had sought to rape her was slightly built, but his eyes were those of a madman. Louis had pummeled him, beat him senseless, but had left him alive.

She had watched Louis bloody the man's face, and she had wanted to say, *No, you'll kill him! Don't!* But she had also wanted him to suffer the torment on his body that he'd inflicted on her body and her spirit. Singing Bird had not spoken then; she had not spoken since that day.

Now she whispered again, as she had done only recently, to herself, "Why when you saved me, Louis, did you try to *force* Katherine to at least kiss you, even if she was to marry you? I hate that kind of force. You were my friend back then when I needed you. Are you the man I think you can be? Or are you the man who gave Katherine every reason to detest him?

She put the fingers of her right hand to her lips. Singing Bird was sixteen now, having had a birthday in July, and for eight years she had written everything she had to communicate. But the memories were still too strong, the hurt and fear too deep. She still didn't wish to speak to others, but she knew she would speak again to herself in the safety of her own company.

Papa Frank turned in early. Sitting with Martin at the dining room table, as he worked further on the sketches of the teardrop fence he was erecting for the man in the Garden District, Katherine knit pale yellow baby booties. He felt more sprightly and virile than usual, but her presence always gave him a lift.

So this nightmare was at least over, Martin thought, as he toyed with ways to finish the strong, yet delicate memorial fence.

"Martin," Katherine said gingerly, "the saw palmetto seems to be working well."

"I'd say it is," he agreed, smiling.

Looking at him, her heart filled with love and tenderness. "Oh, I'd say it's helping you do a very good job of keeping up with *all* your responsibilities," she smiled, touching her stomach. Just now, there was so much on his mind. His *forgeron* business was surging from the riches the Reconstruction had brought to New Orleans for people of color as well as whites.

Martin laughed, then reached over and tapped her stomach. "How are we doing in there?" he inquired. Over three months along carrying his child, he thought, and she was more radiant than she had ever been.

"How would you like café brûlot to go with your cake?" Katherine asked.

Looking up, Martin said, "I'd love it, honey, but it's far too much trouble this late."

"No. I've put all the utensils out. I just have to bring them in."

"Then, by all means do. We deserve a celebration. I'll bring the utensils in for you."

Before she could answer, he got up and brought in two trays containing ingredients for the café brûlot, two china cups, and saucers. He stopped to watch her put the brandy, sugar, cloves, cinnamon, and orange and lemon slices into the bottom of a silver bowl held in silver arms. Very slowly, she lit the mixture and even more slowly poured the brewed coffee and chicory in as flames burned in blue and yellow.

After he finished his cake, they held hands at the table in the room illuminated only by six rose-pink tapers. In the shadows that the candles cast, their glances met and clung, then danced away, only to return with increasing ardor. It was a beginning. . . .

The opening side door brought a gust of wind that flickered the candles but did not blow them out, as a jubilant Jules swept in, carrying Zell.

"Where have you? . . ." Katherine began.

"Getting *hitched*," Zell declared, then, "Oh, I wish you could see your face, Katie. Surprise!"

"But I had made plans," Katherine wailed. "You like weddings, Zell, and I was going to see that you got a beautiful one. But I must admit, I've had a feeling something was going to happen with you two."

Zell stood as close to Jules as she could get, one hand on her hip, laughing merrily. "That's exactly why we ran away, Katie," she declared. "You and Martin have enough on your backs now, what with him running a big business and you midwifing and doctoring half the city. . . ."

"No excuses," Martin laughed as he got up and hugged the beaming couple, clapping Jules on the back and kissing Zell on her brow. "We would have *made* time for your wedding. I know my friend Jules. He gets in a real hurry sometimes."

Katherine rose, hugged and kissed both Jules and Zell, but she was disappointed. Zell and Sing had worked so hard on *her* wedding; she had wanted to return the favor.

"Well," Katherine said now, as Martin went to the door and called Papa Frank and Singing Bird. "At least I made this great praline cake. As you can see, we've got café brûlot here and I'll make more."

"Oh, no, you don't," Zell demurred. "I'll cut us a lot of cake and take it along, but we're *both* in a hurry like Martin accused Jules of being. We're guilty of that. We wouldn't have even stopped by, except we knew you'd be worried."

"But I'll bet you haven't eaten all day," Katherine protested.

Martin and Jules looked at each other, smiling raffishly. "Now there are times, lad," Jules conceded, "when just the sight of my beloved pushes food right out of my mind."

Zell did look lovely in a bustled, apple-green lace-trimmed silk dress, over a subdued crinoline. An apple-green velvet shell hat dipped over her brow and tied with wide ribbons under her chin. Jules wore a well-tailored black flannel frock coat with matching trousers and a snow-white shirt.

Martin shook his head. "I hope you know, lady," he told Zell, "he's a wild horse to harness."

"But, I *like* wild horses," Zell replied, laughing.

Papa Frank and Singing Bird rushed in and hugged the happy couple. Then Sing stopped to scribble.

I'm happy for Katie and Zell but I think I want something else. Maybe.

"Well, I've got two of my girls off my hands," Papa Frank declared. "I guess Sing's got a little while left, but don't take too long, ma'am."

"Oh, I *am* cross," Katherine said now, her attention returning to the newlyweds. "I would have liked to have at least prepared your wedding bed. I'd have put in lavender and lemon balm and dried honeysuckle. . . ."

Zell arched her brows. "And what makes you think I didn't take care of that before I left? Or for that matter, that we *need* it?"

It was Katherine's turn now to laugh merrily.

A moment later, with fresh hugs and kisses all around, Zell and Jules were gone. After chatting a few moments, Papa Frank and Sing went back to bed.

Martin and Katherine sat at the table again, side by side in the candlelight, and resumed their game of passionate glances. They drank the last of the café brûlot from the delicate floral china cups, and Katherine finished the last few crumbs of her piece of praline cake. She reached for Martin's cup and drained the remaining bit of coffee into his saucer.

For a long moment she lightly shook the tracings of coffee grounds left in the cup, looking for patterns that could foretell the future. She held the long fingers of his left hand in hers, pressing them harder than she realized.

After a while, he asked her, "Does what you see alarm you, Kate?"

She nodded. "Yes, a little. No, more than that. This pattern of hills and valleys tells me that there will be both happiness and sharp pain ahead. But perhaps that is life. At least there is *both* happiness and pain. This tracing is in shadows, love, and not plain at all. Martin, I'll snuff the candles and lock up. Then will you carry *me* over the threshold?"

Jules carrying Zell over the threshold had reminded her of her own wedding night.

Martin's eyes filled with desire. He spoke not a word, but swiftly set about doing as she had requested.

Lying on their large canopied bed, Martin glanced around him at their bedroom, redone by Katherine in cream wainscoting and dark rose upper walls and ceiling. The quilted rose satin counterpane and pillow shams had been a gift from Madame. The sheets were crisp white linen, covered in the colder months with cream French cotton flannel. He marveled that he had slept in this room, in this bed, for years before she had come here, and had hardly noticed his surroundings. Now, it was an extension of her, and lying naked on the bed Martin waited impatiently for his wife.

She came from the bathroom wrapped in a rose fleece robe.

"You cannot look at me yet," Katherine said, opening the door gently and coming into the room.

"Not even one innocent peek?" he asked meekly, pretending to close his eyes.

Katherine gave a mock sigh. "Somehow it seems to me your eyes on me at times like this are far from innocent." She came to him, still in the robe, leaned over the bed, and kissed him on his forehead. When he reached for her to pull her down, she deftly moved away, taking off her robe as she did so. The room was filled with the fragrance of her sandalwood perfume.

"Am I to *blame* for wanting you the way I do?" he asked as she let the robe drop to the floor. He had expected a gown but she was as naked as he, only slightly showing, as flirtatiously she began to gracefully turn. His breath caught in his throat as he sprang from the bed and went to her. God, she was beautiful!

"No blame for you on *my* part," she told him as he caught her soft, silken body to his, but gently, groaning that he could not crush her to him as he wished. "Only *appreciation*," she whispered. "More appreciation for everything you do to and for me than you will ever know."

He kissed her then, as they pressed against each other, his tongue probing her mouth that she had rinsed with myrrh, her glistening white teeth opening beneath his onslaught. It seemed that he would search out all the hidden softnesses of her body, to share in the recesses of her soul that waited the way souls do until they can trust and safely open.

Lifting his mouth from hers, he spoke, his voice hoarse with passion. "You could never appreciate what I do to and for you half as much as I admire and appreciate and love what you *give me*—and yes, what you do to and for me as well. From the first, Kate, I was wild with desire so deep I could hardly believe or stand it," he said. "And it thrilled me that you wanted me, too, but I could see it frightened you. Kate, I *desired* you then, but I truly *love* you now."

Katherine's heart was so full she couldn't speak, nor did she try to for a moment. Then she found her voice. "I love you just as much, Martin, or more. I'm just as wild for you."

Her eyes were full of tears as he lifted her and took her to the bed. We need music, she thought, but already there seemed to be music. The wind thrummed through the trees and around the corners, whistling gently, but the music was also inside them as they feverishly kissed each other. Against his deepest urges to enter her, he kept stroking her, caressing her to fully prepare her, until he thought he'd go mad with desire. She thought she understood then the rhythm of their spirits no less than of their bodies, the rhythm that spun into lingering melodies. They whirled in a maelstrom of passion that shattered every barrier between them, leaving them fertile for new love, new hope, and ever-deepening desire.

His hotly seeking mouth explored her body, sucking her breasts gently, then harder. Yes, she thought, *that* was the music. Drumbeats. Heartbeats. Lovebeats. *Life*beats.

Feeling his maleness inside her was only part of the fragile, yet powerful surge of music . . . music that swirled and eddied around them. The intense softness of her body seemed to meld with the sinewy hardness of Martin's. But the real melding was of their hearts and their souls.

"What *is* it you do to me?" she asked in a whisper. "My darling, do you know at all how you make me feel?"

As volcanic eruptions of passion surged through them, she felt it first, shaking her as if she were a rag doll, until Katherine was limp and totally relaxed. Seconds later, the tremors surged through him, arcing through every fiber until he was spent. Together, they surrendered to this wonder without a murmur of dissent.

A very satiated Martin turned to his wife and held her. He kissed her belly, his hand flat on her, listening for heartbeats. None yet. "Better let you rest," he told her, "so you can make more honey for this bee. And, sweetheart, I'll tell you what it is I do to you if you'll tell me what it is you do to *me*."

Seventeen

In early December, Katherine and Martin spoke about plans for their own Christmas, and for a party they wanted to give Christmas week—a Christmas Gift Party—for the street children. They both had approached the Little Sisters, who enthusiastically supported the idea. Sing had been ecstatic. It had been all she could do to keep from talking, but she couldn't bring herself to break her eight-year silence—not yet, anyway.

As they talked in the kitchen, Martin said, "I vote for that party one hundred percent. I'm working on the teardrop fence, and this is one of the busiest times in the *forgeron* business. Everybody wants his fence finished for the holidays. You must promise me you won't overstress yourself. . . ."

"In my condition?" Katherine gently mocked him.

"Well, I worry about you, Kate."

"You're forgetting I have Papa Frank and Madame to help me, as well as Zell and Sing. Sing tells me that Louis offers a hand when he isn't busy helping Celié."

"That's a friendship I wonder about," Martin said. "Louis wanted to marry you, and if his head's screwed on right, he feels cheated at not getting you. And Celié . . . well, I surely don't know about her. . . ."

Katherine sighed. "At least she hasn't done anything recently."

"That we know of. Except for the ring of feathers, we've met her bluff each time. It makes a difference when you come from a position of strength."

Papa Frank came into the kitchen then. "Couldn't help overhearing what you said about coming from a position of strength," he said, "and I couldn't agree more. Strength with a mite of compassion thrown in."

"She's obsessed, you know," Katherine stated. "When I treated her for the snakebite, it was as if I had come by for no more than an unwelcome visit. Oh, she thanked me, but she said *she* wouldn't have saved *me*."

"One truth in a lifetime of lies," Martin commented.

"Martin, I think the circle of feathers was a warning, no more, no less, that she *does* intend to harm us if she can."

"I think we'd be wise to look at it that way. Don't you agree, Papa Frank?"

Papa Frank pondered for a moment. "I pray for you both all the time," he said. "Sing writes me that she has enlisted the prayers of the Little Sisters. She and Zell and Jules pray. And I know you both pray. I believe with all my heart that the power of love and good can overcome the power of evil. I *know* it can. I've had it happen in my life too often. I will step your whole place over all this coming week with holy water and oil. And I will chant the ancient magic that drives demons and evil away.

"Our good magic will overcome the bad magic that Celié casts. I have talked with people about this Dahomey Sinclair, whom she consorts with. He's a powerful man, but he is a *man*, with a man's weaknesses. All conjurers, men or women, are mere humans when all is said and done."

Martin and Katherine both felt so much better after Papa Frank had spoken that they began to talk again of the Christmas Gift Party for the homeless children.

"You go on with your *forgeron* business," Katherine told him. "I also have Inez, if not Wilson, to help. The Little Sisters love the idea and have so many friends to help them. Martin, the children themselves would love to help, and they'd be so proud."

Jules came into the kitchen quietly. He had been in the dining room looking at some of Martin's drawings.

"I couldn't help listening to your conversation," he said. "I like the idea, and don't get me wrong, but a great many of these children are rough, Katherine; some are mentally unbalanced. By all means, let us give the party, but have special people on guard. You've got to be careful, you know. Petty thievery is one of the traits these kids must learn in order to survive. . . ."

Singing Bird let herself in, coughing a bit from the cold. She put her cloak in the closet and Katherine told her about the party. Eagerly, she sat down, took out her pad, and wrote:

Oh, I've talked to the Little Sisters about this party, and we're all so happy. Bless you all. The Little Sisters will open the hall behind the convent. They will even arrange for chaperones from the people who will help us. There'll be no trouble. This is wonderful!

Katherine found the party preparations far easier than she had feared. The air had turned to the crispness that made it seem more like Christmas, which was one week away. They had collected numerous gifts, a great deal of money, large volumes of food, and an incredible amount of goodwill.

With the Little Sisters included, there were at least fifty people who helped them. Several marveled that not one of them had thought of this before.

The afternoon of the party, the large hall was filled with more than one hundred twenty-five mostly ragged, shivering children. Each child selected a cloak, shoes, and other articles of their choice; there were barrels of clothes donated by stores and wealthy people, enough to start a small shop.

Inez Drumm came in before the party was fully under way, dressed in a severe but bustled dark beige frock that complemented her auburn hair and fair skin. She hugged Papa Frank, Katherine, Miss Lillian, Zell, and Sing.

"I've got a carriage load outside," she told them, "and I've been cooking all week. Beginning with praline cake and madeleine cakes." She looked sad as she reflected. "My heart both lifts and sags when I see these children. There's so much hope there, so much potential and promise, but they so often come to disappointment."

Katherine liked the concern in her voice, the tenderness on her face. "With Wilson as lieutenant governor, and a man like Governor Montrose, seven black senators, and half the legislature being people of color, we should be able to do a lot," Katherine commented.

"I hope you're right," Inez said rather wistfully. "Oh, my dear, it's just that Lillian and I have seen so many new starts, so many new promises. . . ."

Miss Lillian nodded. *"Mon Dieu,* it is true, Inez, but we survive on hope."

Papa Frank nodded, pleased at Miss Lillian's graciousness and pleased at her appearance in the plain gray silk twill outfit. Pleased, too, at his own white linen shirt, black flannel trousers, and black frock coat, which he had thrown over a chair to free him to help with the children. Quietly, Katherine had turned the coat over to one of the nuns for safekeeping. A part of Papa Frank would never leave the freedom of the bayou country.

Games of ring-around-the-rosy were in full swing and the party was nearing a close when Martin and Jules entered, loaded with additional gifts.

"The man I built the teardrop fence for," he explained, "insisted on contributing. The women in his family sent a lot of gifts."

So there was yet another gift for each of the children. But more than anything else, there was the gift of love.

The long tables were covered with good cloths, borrowed from various households. And the food was carefully prepared and beautifully served—delicious hams, roasts, turkeys, every type of seafood, salads, fresh rolls, and other breads. Cakes and pies and cookies had been donated by bakeries and baked by loving hands.

There were toys of every description. Katherine had insisted on books for those who wanted or would accept them.

Small Santa Claus figures and gingerbread houses and gingerbread men were placed on the table. A huge, well-decorated Christmas tree stood by the windows. And a big, jolly, red-faced Santa Claus held—one at a time—one hundred twenty-five happy children on his lap before the afternoon was over.

There were games and dances and caroling outside and around the block.

As they left the hall that afternoon, surrounded by happy children, Martin told her, "Kate, the Mardi Gras season is around the corner, early this year. Pregnant as you are, I'd hate to see you miss it. There's a *loges grillées,* you know, that you can sit behind and enjoy the ball without being seen. Remember Antoine Smith, one of my overseers whom you met?"

"Yes," she recalled. "Antoine Smith, from the bayou country."

"His wife's pregnant, too, and she's been to several balls, but she and other women will be there for company. So far, you're not showing very much. But I'll leave it up to you. I'd love you to go if you'd like to."

Katherine glanced down at her wedding ring. She wanted to go to this ball. Madame and she had talked about the *loges grillées.* Madame has suggested a certain gown she could create of heavy silk crepe in periwinkle, one of Katherine's favorite colors. The sketches had promised a fetching gown.

"I think," she said, "I would like nothing better than to go to the Crescent Ball with you."

At first dark two hurrying figures—a man and a woman—sprinkled the mixed blood of two chickens, toad venom, fingernail scrapings from a three-to four-months pregnant woman, and graveyard dust in a large circle in front of the rose and thornbush fence surrounding Martin and Katherine's house.

"We must hurry," the man cautioned. "They could be home soon."

"I know. I'm glad we have your carriage," the woman said, "in case we pass them going back."

They both stomped the blood, toad venom, and graveyard dust well into the grass. They had made two circles, but only one circle was stomped. The grass was dry here; no one would notice until perhaps the next day when the spell would have taken.

They threw more graveyard dust onto the stomped circle, and they chanted as they left.

"This is the last time that I do this, woman," Dahomey Sinclair declared. "Papa Frank is not a man to be trifled with."

"But, my dear," Celié purred sweetly, "I only want to cripple Katherine or make her ugly so he won't love her. . . ."

Dahomey Sinclair looked at her evenly in the early moonlight. "You cannot cripple her spirit, Celié, or make it ugly. No wonder you have little success with magic. You do not truly believe. I have given you my most powerful gris-gris charms. They have seldom failed to work for others. Also, your bitterness is eating into your soul. In your blindness to get what I suspect you never will, you are willing to do anything but you *understand* nothing. Ah, Celié, we two could be such a couple, you know. We could learn perhaps even to love each other. . . ."

Celié could not help recoiling. True, she sometimes reached for him in passing affection, but she could not bear it when he reached for her. And he saw now something he had not let himself see clearly before: Celié did not consider him her equal. He might be a voodoo priest to the thousands who would feel themselves privileged to kiss the hem of his black frock coat or the African robes he wore to call up the spirits. But to her, he was a powerful voodoo priest that she used heavily and paid very well. As a *man,* he was of little consequence to her.

Knowing this angered him greatly. He hated being angry, for such anger as he felt now signaled a deep bruising of the spirit. He thought he knew what he would do.

"We must go now," he told her.

In the buggy, he hit his horse harder than he intended, and it made him even angrier. Dahomey relaxed as a brisk breeze fanned his face. He had never before set up a spell and wished for its failure, but he did so now.

When their carriage pulled up at the house just after dark, Katherine felt a finger of chill trace along her spine, felt her skin prickle.

"Another goose going over my grave," she said.

Papa Frank could not see her clearly, but he heard the tremor in her voice. Martin had gotten down to help them out, but Sing sensed anxiety in both Papa Frank and Katherine as they listened intently. But there was only the barking of the welcoming dogs and the sound of a lone whippoorwill. Papa Frank bade them go inside while he stayed out front, sensing evil. For a long time he chanted and prayed as he walked in circles across the grass, where Helio and Patchette and a few sheep grazed. And after a while he was finished and his spirit was at peace.

Their own Christmas Day was a promise fulfilled. They had decorated the house with silver and gold and plain pinecones. They'd cut and potted poinsettias from the huge bushes that grew in their backyard and down by the pond.

At sunrise they'd gotten up to open the presents under the seven-foot-tall green cedar loaded with ornaments, candy canes, and gingerbread men.

As they stood admiring the tree, Martin murmured, "Next

year our baby will be nearly seven months old, if everything goes according to schedule."

"With a first baby, *nothing* goes according to schedule." Katherine laughed as he nuzzled her neck.

Sing came in then and handed Katherine a note:

Merry Christmas to you, Katherine, Martin, and Papa Frank. Mistletoe! Maybe by next Christmas, I will need mistletoe, but I wonder if I ever will.

Sing was unhappy that Louis hadn't come to the party, although he'd helped with preparations the day before—moving and setting up tables, picking up food from donors. As they had entered the house, she had muttered to herself, "Why weren't you there, Louis?"

The others had been a porch length away.

Katherine had turned, asking, "Sing, did you *speak?*"

Sing had shaken her head no. Perhaps she would never again speak, except to herself.

Now Katherine read Sing's note, then passed it to Martin, who read it, too. She took Sing's chin in her hand and turned her face to her.

"My darling, of *course* you will need mistletoe—whenever you wish. You never paid any attention to boys, but they've always been attracted to you." She stopped a moment. "What you went through as an eight-year-old makes it hard, but if we all pray that God helps you to get over this, sweetheart, I can't help but believe it'll make a difference and there *will* be someone for you."

"I second that in every way," Martin agreed.

Sing sat, silent. When, she wondered, in the days of seeing Louis from time to time at the Little Sisters convent had she come to care so much? She realized that she'd liked him since the time he'd stopped the plunder of her womanhood as a child, preserving it so that *she* could decide when and with whom.

Celié, whom Sing detested, with reason, had helped a willing Louis with his diction, had taught him the essentials of male grooming, and had given him hope. Now what chance did Sing have with the glamorous Celié as a rival? She felt certain that Louis had given up on Katherine and that had made her happy, but she could never divine how Louis really felt about his benefactress, Celié. Nor could she get up the nerve to ask him.

Martin and Katherine watched Sing in her silence, until Katherine spoke. "We've got a glorious Christmas this year. Crisp and sunny. Just cold enough. Let's call Papa Frank and open the presents, then we can all make the café brûlot and the biggest breakfast of the year. After that comes the best dinner of the year."

"No need to call me," Papa Frank blurted out. "I just fed Ruff and Muffin and wished them Merry Christmas. Lord, they've been with me many a happy year. Merry Christmas, everybody!"

Katherine went to him and kissed his old, parchmentlike cheek. "Merry Christmas, Papa Frank! You've made us a family by being here."

"No," Papa Frank said, "the first of summer will make your family." He glanced at her stomach, smiling.

Katherine and Martin's hearts were so full of thoughts of their coming baby, which was a little more than five months away.

Sing scribbled a note to them.

I think this baby's going to be just wonderful.

"Amen to that," Martin agreed when they'd read it. "Let's get coffee and open the presents."

And a few minutes later, with their steaming cups of coffee in hand, they sat down to open the gifts.

When Katherine opened her present from Martin, she was delighted. "Oh, Martin," she cried, "I simply cannot believe this. Madame and I were talking about a certain periwinkle silk crepe gown she wanted to make me to wear to the Crescent Ball. True, I'll be behind the *loges grillées* and not many people will see me, but I want to be beautiful for you."

Martin grinned crookedly. "Ah, yes, Miss Lillian also mentioned a periwinkle silk gown to me."

The large stone in the pendant was an amethyst of the deepest purple, surrounded by clear, brilliant diamonds. And there were matching earrings. It was a beautifully crafted, exquisite set.

"You really like it?" Martin asked.

"Oh, my darling, *yes.*"

"Then why not fall on my neck and kiss me in appreciation?"

Katherine warmed greatly, laughing.

"I will later, sweetheart, I promise. Already, the baby makes it a little difficult for me to move about easily. But I'll save you my sweetest kiss."

Watching them, Sing wished for such a marriage. And for Papa Frank, memories came flooding back of his time with Katherine's grandmother and their Christmases together. Much simpler times, but the love and the caring had been there. And he knew very well that those were the wellsprings of life itself.

There were more presents for Katherine, including a knitted soft yellow scarf from Sing and a rich periwinkle silk-satin nightgown from Madame. And for both Katherine and Martin, Papa Frank had carved wooden figures of animals and birds, along with an owl for Sing.

Katherine had gotten Martin knitted vests, silk cravats, and a note that he could take to his tailor for a new broadcloth suit. She'd saved from her household money, having taken lessons from both Inez and Lillian in managing her finances.

Papa Frank and Sing had presents of clothes and sundries— Sing a fancy, beautiful porcelain fashion doll and Papa Frank a silver harmonica on which he played a few bars of "Jimmy Crack Corn."

Katherine went out and returned with Martin's violin. "I

had it tuned for you," she told him. "Later, perhaps we can persuade you to play for us. . . . Martin, that pendant must have been frightfully expensive."

Martin shrugged. "We're getting to be pretty well off, Katie, Papa Frank, Sing. And what's a life without sharing with those we love?"

"What's for breakfast?" Papa Frank asked. "A country man's got to be fed early, even on Christmas."

"There's café brûlot, for one thing," Katherine began, "which we ordinarily brew for dinner but which I've come to like in the morning as well. Cheese rolls and pastry, apple strudel. Pancakes for whoever wants them . . ."

"Fried oysters, oysters on the half shell," Martin cut in. "Thick-sliced bacon, sausage, eggs and cheese, grits . . ."

Sing wrote on her notepad:

And nobody's talking about sweets. Maple syrup, scuppernong jelly, plum preserves, and persimmon marmalade.

"Lord, what a spread," Papa Frank remarked, laughing. "Think we'll have room for Christmas dinner? Turkeys, ham, and pork roast all baking. Cakes and pies all made. Will we have room, even after waiting all day?"

"Well, we've sure got enough company to eat it if we can't," Katherine told him. "Zell and Jules; Miss Lillian; Inez and Wilson; your overseer next to Jules, Martin; Antoine Smith and his wife, Carolyn; and Pierre and Monique. Thirteen people. Oh, I think we're going to need *plenty* of dinner.

"Now, you three, on to make Christmas breakfast, 1869!"

Looking at his granddaughter, Papa Frank thought she looked radiantly happy. He prayed with all his wisdom, experience, and faith that God would keep her that way.

Eighteen

By the time of the Crescent Club Ball in early February, Katherine was nearly five months pregnant. She still carried her baby high and showed little.

"Ah, but soon you'll be massively *en ciente*," Madame often giggled, identifying closely with the younger woman. She had once added wistfully, "It is the only thing I devoutly wished for that God did not see fit to grant me."

"Then will you be our baby's godmother?" Katherine had asked.

Madame had flung her arms around Katherine's neck and hugged her with enthusiastic care.

"*Ma chère,* I've wondered how long I should have to hint!"

With the help of Governor Montrose, Martin and Wilson had gotten a ballroom in an elegant building on Royal Street. Katherine sat now with Carolyn, the wife of Antoine, Zell, and Sing behind the *loges grillées,* a fairly large open compartment covered by intricate fretwork that let those behind it see out but others not clearly see in. These *loges grillées* were also fashionable at opera houses, allowing pregnant women and others who wanted it privacy. After all, this was New Orleans, the city that care had forgotten. The city's inhabitants pursued joy for as many hours of their life as they possibly could.

It was lost on few, however, that the city's male population of all colors pursued such joy far more avidly than did its womenfolk.

Carolyn, dressed in intricately draped sky-blue silk, which

flattered her dark coffee flawless skin, and Katherine exchanged comfortable glances. Carolyn had carried her child for about the same length of time as had Katherine but showed her pregnancy more.

Martin was the ball committee chairman this year, and he had been busy in his spare time for much of the past three months trying to make this fête the best of the season. Now he entered the *loges grillées*.

"Ladies, you are both stunning tonight," he complimented them. Katherine flushed warmly. She *felt* beautiful in the periwinkle silk crepe that Madame had lovingly designed for her. The gown was an empire style, out of fashion but perfect for her softly swelling body. No bustles. No high-fashion crinolines that would have better camouflaged her pregnancy. Her only jewelry was the marvelous amethyst pendant and matching earrings that Martin had given her for Christmas.

"I'll be back as often as I can," Martin said. "Are you feeling well?"

"I don't see how I could feel much better," she replied.

Martin closed his eyes for a minute, drinking in her radiance, a private moment in a place of public merriment.

As Martin left, Katherine mused at the power of this man to stir every facet of her being. If life granted nothing more than she had now—and indeed she would happily settle for a lot less—she would say that God had been good to her.

Madame came to them, and Zell moved aside to give her room to sit down. But Miss Lillian stood, surveying her handiwork for both women.

"Ma cherès," Madame said. "You both do my gowns honor. You have never looked lovelier, either of you. And you, Katherine, *create* fashion rather than follow it. You were born, I think, to be gloriously out of season. Thank heavens you have that courage."

Both women thanked her, with Katherine musing that Dr. St. Cyr had referred to both Natalie and her as "out-of-season."

"You and Papa Frank make a handsome couple," Katherine told Madame.

Madame was not one to blush. "Oh, my dear, he makes me realize how much I've missed the company of a man. He is a wonderful man, your grandfather."

"And he thinks you're a wonderful woman."

Zell and Singing Bird looked at each other over their fans. Zell had chosen pale yellow silk crepe that flattered her greatly, and Singing Bird looked sweetly innocent in ivory satin and a matching beaded fan.

Breathlessly, Zell turned to Katherine and Madame. "I think this is the most gorgeous moment of my life. True, your wedding was superb, but this . . ."

"It helps, I'm certain, that a handsome prince husband brought you to the ball," Katherine teased her.

Again and again Zell had looked anxiously at Jules. Each woman here tonight was a lovelier princess than the next. How could she compete with them? It did not occur to her that these women had been at balls with Jules before she, Zell, had come. And he had not married one of them.

Singing Bird wrote on the pad she carried in her evening bag:

Surely this is heaven before heaven.

Carolyn Smith found she was already enjoying herself immensely, although she often had so little to say that others forgot her presence.

The Crescent Club Ball deliberately set out to include *all* people of color who wished to join and embrace their rules of integrity, community service, and political awareness. So, unlike more narrowly favored balls, there were Negroes, then, as only those brought from Africa as slaves were called. And there were the Creoles, who called themselves that name to the haughty denial of the French and Spanish mixture of whites, who held themselves to be the only *true* Creoles.

No matter. The people of color who were *passe pour blanc*—who could pass for white if they wished—went on calling themselves Creoles with a capital C. And then there was the *gens de couleur*—of every hue save black or white. This was the group to which Martin and Katherine, and most of their guests belonged. Carolyn thought the city was changing for the better. She and her husband had a really good life, with more wealth from Antoine being one of Martin's overseers than they'd ever dreamed of as slaves.

Color had been a vicious problem in the city in the days of slavery, with lighter-skinned people of color acting disdainful toward their darker brethren, and darker-skinned people of color being bitterly derisive of their dying-to-be-but-ain't-got-a-chance-to-be-white lighter brethren.

Why do we put ourselves in this bind? Carolyn wondered. If God made us all, how could any race be better or worse than another? Carolyn smiled. Tonight she felt beautiful and loved. She patted her belly. She had a cake in her oven, and she was happy. Let the fools of this world wallow in color-misery if they wished.

"Isn't it marvelous that we can be here in *our* condition," Carolyn declared, smiling wryly.

"I find myself thinking the same thing," Katherine said. "We can see and hear almost everything, but we're seen by few."

The stage was a short distance from them to their left. Katherine watched Martin now as he faced the merrymakers and asked for silence. At that moment, little liquor had been consumed and they cooperated as he began.

"In this time of merriment before the season of Mardi Gras, we welcome you to the Crescent Club's Seventh Annual Ball. In recent years, we have withstood political pressures, a pestilence, and a flood, but we have persevered. We are fully dedicated to a life of fulfillment, excellence, challenge, and contribution. As this year's chairman of the Seventh Annual Crescent Ball, in this beautiful ballroom with the even more beautiful women, each a queen, we salute you, for you are the jewels in our crown! My fellow club members, families and guests, I salute you! And our fair city of New Orleans, so lately torn apart with strife, and perhaps now at last on a road to peace and equality, I salute you!

"The evening is young, as this land is young. The Crescent Club has but one command tonight: It is the carnival season! On this night you must know all possible joy! And now our lieutenant governor par excellence, Wilson Drumm!"

There was a soft roll of drums for a long moment as Martin was vividly cheered. The drums quieted and Wilson came onstage. As he did, Inez entered the *loges grillées* and sat down with Katherine and the others, saying "We were a little late getting here. I'll talk when Wilson's finished. We did get here in time to hear Martin's wonderful speech, though."

Wilson Drumm's voice was not as strong as Martin's but it was resonant. He was known and liked all over the city.

"Welcome!" he declared mildly. "I want to thank my friend, and well-known businessman, Martin Dominguez, for his excellent introduction. I will not take much of your time from revelry, but I know you rejoice as I do in seven senators being appointed to our state legislature by The Louisiana Assembly. This year we will see to it—with our *blood,* if necessary, as in the past—that they are *elected!*"

Here a deafening roar arose from the merrymakers. Cries of "Yes!" and *"Oui"* and a loud, deep bass "You're damned right about that!" went up.

"And I want you to know," Wilson continued, "that every one of the seven senators is at our ball tonight."

Again cheers and whistles as Wilson waited patiently.

"Quite a few of our state representatives are with us, and I say about them what I said about the senators: We *will elect them again!* This city will be better for our men of color helping to steer this ship of state. We will need the help of *all* in the uncertain times ahead. But for tonight, let us put aside care, as my friend, Martin, has commanded, and in the spirit of Mardi Gras, *Let There Be Joy!*"

It was like a fairyland, Katherine thought, yet so very real. The music was formal, with a band of expert musicians playing violins, bass fiddles, a harpsichord, and a piano. There would be waltzes and two-steps. Quadrilles. But there was also a relief band of fiddles and harmonicas, as there had been at their wedding, and there would be a hoedown later on—a dance most Creoles of color considered far too rowdy for their cultivated taste.

Through the fretwork, Katherine saw an effervescent Madame, a little high on champagne, begin to teach Papa Frank to waltz. As the music began and they moved out onto the highly polished dance floor, Katherine and Carolyn saw the couple move toward the *loges grillées,* as Antoine entered the enclosure.

He sat on the arm of the divan by Carolyn. "You two ladies look wonderful," he said. "Mrs. Dominguez. . . ."

Katherine held up her hand. "Please call me Katherine," she insisted.

He smiled a bit sheepishly. "Martin is my boss. . . ."

"But you call him Martin."

"He calls my wife Mrs. Smith."

"Don't you think that we should stop the formality?" Katherine suggested. "We are becoming friends. You and Martin and Jules have *long* been friends. What do you think, Carolyn?"

Carolyn nodded. *"I* certainly like informality. But, Katherine, don't be surprised if it takes a while for my husband to call you by your given name. He would fight his weight in elephants, but he is bashful."

Antoine laughed. "My wife betrays my secrets."

Antoine and Carolyn smiled at each other companionably.

At that moment, Martin, Papa Frank and Madame came in.

Inez had been quiet throughout the interchange, observing, enjoying the extended friendship. Now she spoke to Carolyn and Antoine. "I hope Wilson and I can include you in our circle of friends. You see, I know how valuable you are to Martin's business."

"Yes," Katherine offered, "Martin's often said he could hardly run the business without Jules and you, Antoine."

"Now, is my jewel of a wife praising other men when I'm not around?" Martin asked as he entered.

"If she did that," Antoine said, "I'd feel honor-bound to stop her. You're the giant behind that business, Martin. Jules, perhaps, is indispensable, but certainly I'm not."

Katherine could see Jules and Zell waltzing on the dance floor. Sing danced with a slender brown youth. How resplendent the men all looked in their tuxedos and stiff white shirts, she thought.

"Papa Frank, you're dancing like you've gone to balls all your life," Katherine teased when he and Madame came in.

"Ah, he is a natural, this man," Madame told them. "There is the rhythm of dance in his very bones. I shall have to fight off the women, even the young ones." She smiled mischievously.

Papa Frank rose to the occasion. "But I like my good-looking present companion," he informed her.

As the older couple danced away, Katherine said to Martin, "It's early, so I think I could have one glass of champagne."

Martin looked at her fondly. "Don't I remember you cautioning women for whom you're going to deliver babies to drink as little as possible, and stick to milk, fruit juices, and herbal teas?"

"But one little glass is surely allowed me," she retorted. "Martin, Carolyn, Antoine, next year we'll all be waltzing, two-stepping."

A little while later a waiter wheeled in a table laden with light liquors and liqueurs, brandy, rum, hard liquors, wines, a magnum of champagne in an ice bucket, and a silver pitcher of water. There was also root beer, sarsaparilla, and draft beer.

Two men brought in a long table and covered it with a snowy damask tablecloth. On long tea carts two other men brought in silver and copper tureens filled with shrimp and crab gumbo and oyster bisque, and pots of crayfish bisque. They set up a buffet of cheeses, crackers, and hot breads.

As Katherine, Inez, Wilson, and Antoine and Carolyn Smith exclaimed over the delectable food, richly served, the two waiters went out and returned with an assortment that made those present groan—a dessert festival that included strawberry shortcakes and praline cakes. "Not my praline cakes this time," Inez said. She went to the end of the table and pointed out a dozen madeleine cakes, golden with butter crusts.

"Now these, my dear, are the madeleine cakes *I* made that I boasted about when you and Martin were over for dinner the first time. No doubt you've tasted them by now . . ."

"I haven't," Katherine replied. "But I've certainly heard enough about them."

"They're sinfully rich," Inez said. "I make mine with a butter batter laced with black walnuts and brandy. And they're browned in the oven in a heavily buttered special pan. Let me cut one of these for you."

Inez cut a madeleine cake in half and served a half cake each to Katherine and to Carolyn.

Katherine tasted it and exclaimed, "Inez, this is so good I think I'll just eat it a few crumbs at a time." Carolyn agreed.

"I'll save you both one each to take home," Inez promised. "I made ten dozen in all. Wilson can eat one in little more than a gulp."

As she sparingly ate the madeleine cake, Katherine thought how much she had come to like Inez. Fond of *petit* gossip about the city and its people, what Inez didn't know she found out from her husband in his new position as lieutenant governor. To Katherine, it seemed she knew everything about the city.

Martin returned again for a moment. "You look radiant," he told his wife. "I'll bore you with so many compliments."

"You know you won't," she assured him.

Carolyn had gone to the nearby bathroom, its passage from

the *loges grillées* shielded by potted palms and rushes. Martin, Inez, and Katherine were alone.

Katherine was having such a good time as the evening raced along. Martin took her hand. "Next year," he promised.

"Oh, Martin, you're impatient," Katherine said, laughing. "I love *this* year, and so little of it has passed. In the bayou country, we always said we'd savor every moment. Here, in New Orleans, you seem to always look to tomorrow."

"Today *and* tomorrow. Next year," Martin told her, "we'll have a child old enough to show daguerreotypes of the ball."

"I don't think he or she will be very interested," Katherine responded.

They were all merry from the music and the food and the glitter of the people. Inez watched Katherine and Martin a long while, with little envy and much affection. "You two have such a vibrant life-force," she observed. "The currents between you are rare, and they're beautiful. You create quite a special climate."

A voice from the doorway could be heard. "I don't know where to feast my eyes first—the beautiful womenfolk or the tantalizing food. Ladies, you rejuvenate my tired old eyes. Antoine, did you know what a lucky man you are to be surrounded by this female garden of Eden?"

"Yes, I do know, Emil," Antoine replied, smiling.

"And Mrs. Dominguez—Katherine," he began, kissing her hand as a small, vivacious dark brown-skinned woman came in.

"I knew I'd find my beloved husband paying court to some beautiful woman somewhere," she said. "And here he is with not one, but several."

Emil went to the woman, introduced her as his wife Marian, and kissed her hand. "Ah, what harm does it do you?" he asked. "You and I know that I long ago picked the most beautiful one of all."

"Now you all know why he's the governor's butler," she

grinned. "It's wonderful skills that got him the job, but it's his silver tongue that keeps it."

The people in the room laughed as people often did around Emil.

"I'm happy at last to be able to thank you for all that delectable food you sent me from your wedding, Mrs. Dominguez. I was ill at the time, but I've heard about how fabulous it was from Emil and others."

As Marian talked, Katherine remembered her beautiful wedding gown and the gray lace that had set off the black pearl. Her delicate condition meant she could not wear the black pearl tonight, at what would have been a perfect setting. A *loges grillées* was no place to display all that splendor.

"You're welcome," Katherine said. "Your husband is a love, and I can see that you're a well-matched pair."

She smiled, thinking that she, too, was becoming as adept as any New Orleanian at the honeyed phrase that eased a basically hard life along.

By midnight, although the ball would last until three or four in the morning, Martin knew that this celebration had been the club's most successful one of all. He looked around him at the decorations that carried out the "Wonder of Winter" theme. They were lucky this year to have had colder than average weather since November.

Evergreens from the nearby tree nurseries and the forests were placed about the room in silver-colored pots. Simulated snow—cotton spread with shiny crystal and silver and gold dust—glittered on the trees and gold- and silver-dipped pinecones from the neighboring Mississippi forests formed wreaths with natural pine and cedar branches.

Poinsettias were everywhere and they gave the final elegant touch, providing a background for gowns as rich in fabrics and creativity as any New Orleanians would ever see. Beaded gowns, sequined gowns. Chiffon and lace. Velvets. Gossamer satin, moiré, and plain taffeta. Lush velvets. Silk was almost universal. Gowns that had been fashioned by modistes. Gowns that had been beautifully fashioned at home by women gifted in making life beautiful with little money to spend. Katherine felt her very toes tingle with the joy of it all. Stunning coiffures and headdresses, carefully powdered faces. And what a display of valuable and beautiful jewelry.

As Martin left again, Carolyn returned, and just behind her was Maurice Delacroix, the man Katherine had met at Inez and Wilson's house.

"Ah, Inez, here you are!" he exclaimed. "I've been looking all over for you."

"Why, yes, indeed, Maurice, here I am," Inez said. She always dreaded what Maurice might or might not say next. He had never been their friend when Wilson was a housepainter. She'd have been happy if he'd continued to consider them beneath him.

He nodded to Katherine and Carolyn in turn. Then he came to Katherine and stood before her, looking down at her.

"I am much older than you," he told her, "so permit me this observation. Had I a creature of such beauty as yours, I'd certainly not flaunt such wealth before others. In my time, women of delicate condition were not allowed . . ."

"Oh, Maurice, *hush!*" Inez sputtered. "The world and this city are fast changing from your time or even mine." She spread her manicured hands. "It is *their* time now. The young people. And in times to come, I certainly hope that pregnant women will be on the dance floor, dancing merrily if they care to and have the energy."

Giving Inez a dim smile, Maurice seemed not to have heard her as he addressed Katherine. "May I sit down, my dear?"

"If you wish," Katherine answered coolly.

Maurice found Katherine's presence bothered him. She had bothered him when he'd met her at the Wilsons' house. She attracted him in a way he couldn't deny, in spite of a forty-year age difference. He had been rich most of his life; she'd been a slave most of hers. He detested her arrogant, talented husband Dominguez—a *foreigner*.

Inez cringed inside, hoping Maurice didn't start his favorite conversation regarding how foreigners had ruined a lovely city. But she needn't have worried. He had another line of interest tonight.

"It always amazes me," he said now, "when I look about the city that once abounded in masters and slaves and a *few* free people of color. . . ."

"Maurice," Inez responded tiredly, "there've always been a great many free people of color in New Orleans. People have come from Santo Domingo, from Haiti, from the West Indies, for forty years or more—good people . . . perhaps better people than the natives."

"I hardly think so," he returned, dismissing her and turning to Katherine.

"It is difficult for me to imagine you as a slave. My family had quite a few slaves, as you've probably heard. We dealt in cotton and later in India silks. It's the way we gained our wealth. Negroes may find freedom not too enjoyable as it's touted, eh, Inez?"

"Oh, I don't know why you always deliberately choose to ignore that I certainly was a slave as a girl," Inez flung back at him.

"Perhaps, my dear, because you're simply too fair a lady to have been one. Ridiculous. You should have been freed at birth."

Katherine was taken aback by the effrontery of this supposedly cultivated and certainly articulate man. But she'd always felt some degree of equanimity in the face of what often enraged others.

"And are Carolyn and I to be slaves all our lives because we're darker than Inez?" Katherine asked him. "Mr. Delacroix, I think you're an insufferable, bigoted man."

Maurice **Delacroix** stood up. "Then I'm sorry, because I think you are one of the most beautiful women I've even known. Inez, I will see you later, and please save me a dance or two. Get out and help your husband make this ball a success. You and Wilson have an invitation to our ball, you know."

Maurice Delacroix looked back over his shoulder as he left the *loges grillées*. A man in deep pain in spite of his wealth, he hated happy people and made his tongue the pin that punctured their balloons.

"Oh, Lord, he's such an idiot," Inez stated.

"Yes," Katherine agreed. "A rich, unhappy, and quite *powerful* idiot."

Inez's eyes on her were warm and supportive. Carolyn seemed a bit amused and untouched, the way pregnant women sometimes are.

That ball he had mentioned, Katherine thought now, was far and away the most fabled of the people of color balls. They called themselves the Mountain Club, and the members were all *passe pour blanc*. Theirs was the most elegant of balls, rivaling the "real" Creole balls, thought by many to be long on stuffiness and short on enjoyment. In the past few years, there were darker-skinned people of color invited. One could hardly *not* invite a state senator or state representative, nor fail to invite a man whose wealth and power next month could be as great or far greater than your own.

Suddenly, there was a lull and a ripple of excitement among the revelers. *The governor was here!*

Martin had told her that Governor Montrose might attend the ball, but that his hectic schedule probably wouldn't allow it. Now the governor and his entourage were welcomed at the door by Lieutenant Governor Drumm.

The governor and his people sampled the lavish display of food, ate the madeleine cakes, and sipped both muscadine wine and vintage champagne. They mingled with the revelers. After all, these were to be the voters in the coming fall election.

They stayed twenty minutes at the most, but the excitement they left behind them lasted. For certain, no other governor had ever attended a ball for people of color.

The revelers settled now for serious merrymaking as the relief band started up.

Sing had come in as Inez left to be at Wilson's side. A sparkling Sing began to write notes to Katherine.

Feeling compelled to turn, Katherine did so in slow motion—and froze.

Escorted by a fashionably attired Louis, and dressed in black silk gossamer, satin bustled, and draped over crinoline as wide as could be carried, a regally sylphlike Celié stood in splendor. On her left hand she displayed the flashing diamond and on her haughty, pale bosom was the glorious black pearl that Martin—in love and in passion—had given to Katherine. *Mon Dieu!* thought many of the revelers who knew Martin's family and others who craved gossip tidbits. *What is behind all this?*

Katherine watched as an obviously enraged Martin faced Celié, who held out her arms.

"Martin, please dance with me. I will explain the jewelry I wear. Please don't be angry."

For one moment Martin felt a nearly uncontrollable urge to grab those thin, pale shoulders and shake Celié breathless.

In that same instant, he saw what went on even as she explained.

"I had the black pearl and the diamond ring made up from the daguerreotype, Martin. As Raoul's—the firstborn's—wife, *I* should have inherited them, but Annalise hated me. . . ."

"Not without reason," Martin said acidly. "You wore them here tonight to embarrass me and to hurt Katherine."

"Damn Katherine," Celié taunted. "I wanted to hurt *you* as I have been hurt *by* you. She carries your child. Because of you, I have no child. I will *never* have a child."

"Celié, for God's sake," Martin grated. "How many times have I said I was sorry, asked your forgiveness? I would have married you had you not chosen my brother. It was an *accident,* and I will not keep saying that. Don't ever do this to us again!"

To her dismay, Celié saw that he looked at her with new

loathing mixed in with the old anger. And it hurt her badly as he walked away.

Martin felt a growing fury at Celié's unfairness as Louis came up and surveyed the situation, trying to decide what to do next.

With contained anger, Katherine watched the tableaux. At least she and Martin were together against Celié. Or were they? Those two had shared a past that inextricably connected them. How had Celié gotten the jewels? She must have gotten the key somehow and gone there tonight while they were here at the ball. Celié knew the combination to the safe.

Her heart heavy, Katherine wondered if they would ever be free of Celié.

Sing watched the three on the dance floor with fury as hot as Katherine's. Louis had certainly changed, she thought. Celié had changed him. Louis had brought Celié here. Why had she, Sing, ever bothered to care about him?

Singing Bird scribbled furiously.

Katherine, don't let her get to you.

Katherine nodded. She wouldn't.

Celié turned to Louis, speaking huskily. "I would love to have this dance with you."

Louis had just approached, having lost himself among the revelers because he had no desire to face Katherine's and Martin's wrath. Not to mention Papa Frank's. Handsomely attired in a tuxedo by Celié, he had been pleased beyond words to attend a high society ball. Now he wasn't sure, but he took Celié's hand and led her onto the dance floor.

Dancing with a flirtatious, sparkling Celié, who covered her pain with gaiety, Louis felt confused. This was the fabulous side of New Orleans he wanted to be part of and Celié had promised to help him make his entrée. But first, there were things she said he must do for her. And damn it, where, he wondered, was Sing?

"Well, Katie," Papa Frank said as he came into the room with Martin and a hornet-mad Madame.

"Shameless Jezebel!" Madame hissed.

"You saw what happened?" Martin asked Katherine. "It's *not* what it seems. Those are not your jewels Celié wears, but similar ones she says she had made from the daguerreotype. You or I would know that immediately up close."

"But *why?*" Katherine cried.

"An aberration, *querida mia,* as this whole affair is an aberration."

Jules and Zell came in, too, and sat quietly near Katherine. The Drumms came to their side. Wilson Drumm bowed to Katherine and spoke gently. "My dear, it *happens.* It is of *no consequence!* It is not necessary for me to say that next to my beautiful wife, you are the most ravishing woman here. And my wife shares my views." He bent and kissed Katherine's hand.

She was not a woman who withered without the approbation of others, but in the midst of Celié's savage machinations, it did feel good to be surrounded by friends.

Katherine tried not to watch as Celié moved about the ballroom, pleased with herself, triumphant at what she imagined to be the hurt plainly mirrored on her hated rival's face.

"Am I beautiful?" Celié demanded of Louis.

"Lord, lady, there never was a queen more beautiful." Louis rose to the occasion willingly, if unhappily.

"My dear Louis," Celié said coquettishly, "I do believe I could fashion you into a proper suitor if you will help me do the things I ask of you."

"Celié," Louis implored, "why can't you just relax and be happy?"

Celié looked at him from beneath her long eyelashes, moving her black lace fan as she flaunted her crinolines in dancing.

"Do I look well, Louis? Do you like this dress? It's another color, but the top is a bit like the one Katherine wore after her wedding. You didn't go to that wedding."

"No," Louis grumped. "You've sure told me about it often enough, though."

Celié seemed to go into a trance. "We were lovers, Louis, but I married his brother. Martin brought me here, so he must still love me a little. I can make him love me again, as *I* love him."

"Uh, Celié, hadn't you better stop? Every time you talk about it, you start crying and you need a drink."

Like some kind of bad magic, his words seemed to make her think of the liquor she so often needed to steady herself.

"A crème de menthe," she announced too gaily. "That's what I want. Would you be a prince and get me a cup?"

"No," Louis said firmly, surprising himself. "We'll finish this dance, and I'll take you home. They hate us here, Celié. This ain't—it's not—our territory, and I'd like to be able to come back to some other dance here sometime and not feel I'll be cut down at the door. True, you might like liquor, but it doesn't like you."

His fingers bit into her arm. This woman had helped him to change his speech, his clothes, his manners. But he'd felt himself changing inside, too. It seemed to Louis that Sing's guarded interest in him as they worked with the Little Sisters had done that.

Once he had saved Sing from a brute who would plunder her body. Now, it seemed *she* had saved him from his selfishness and his ignorance.

"I think I like you, my handsome friend," Celié whispered.

Louis shook his head. The dance was ending. "I'll get your cloak," he told her, "and take you home. Celié, let Martin and Katherine alone for now, you hear! You've proved your point. Hang up your fiddle just for a minute, will you?"

To his surprise, she listened, continuing to stare at the *loges grillées,* where Katherine would be.

With rising eagerness, Louis wondered where Sing was.

"I might have needed a *loges grillées* once," Celié muttered,

pointing out the private enclosure to Louis. "But Katherine is up there with him now."

Louis's antennae went up. "Is that what you call it?" he mumbled as it hit him. If Katherine was there, Sing was there, too—if she had come.

"Celié, you stay right here, and excuse me one minute," he said, as he rushed toward the *loges grillées*.

Standing in the doorway, he spoke to Katherine, Martin, and the others. "God, I'm sorrier than I can say. Celié . . . well, I don't think she always *knows* what she's doing. I had *nothing* to do with this, and if I'd known, I certainly wouldn't have brought her."

Katherine and Martin couldn't answer, but Papa Frank said sadly, "I certainly *hope* you're telling the truth."

"Sing, please talk with me a minute," Louis pleaded.

Sing wrote angrily on her notepad:

No, Louis I have nothing to say to you.

"Martin! Katherine! I want you to know that I will not bother you again!"

Celié stood in the doorway, her hand with its flashing diamond to her bosom, on which glowed a black pearl. Neither jewel was as magnificent as the ones Martin had given Katherine, but they were close enough. Others would certainly *think* they were one and the same.

For Celié it was a moment of triumph. Louis, on the other hand, felt hollow as they left the *loges grillées*.

As Martin sat beside her, his hand gripping hers, the sandalwood fragrance from Katherine's skin and hair soothed him, affecting him more than usual. He felt his heart stripped raw from what she endured for him, and it infuriated him.

"Sweetheart," Katherine said, interpreting that look, "she's leaving, at Louis's insistence. You say you love me, and beside that love, the copy of the jewels pale. It is herself she has made a fool of."

"I'm proud of you both," Papa Frank declared. "It really is a little thing, this is."

"That *woman* . . . that *creature*" was all Madame could sputter.

Sing continued to write angrily:

And I won't forget that Louis brought her.

"It simply does not matter, you know, my friends," Jules told them. "Celié will one day prove her own undoing." Tears of anger stood in the usually ebullient Zell's eyes as she squeezed Katherine's arm.

New Orleans, for all its frivolity, was a man's town. Celié's malevolence would possibly hurt Martin's reputation among a few men not of his race and looking for a *reason* to reject him. Most others would never let it matter. But Celié's appearance wearing the black pearl would stoke a month's gossip furnace.

And Katherine thought that yes, Jules was right, Celié might very well one day prove her own undoing. But how much suffering and humiliation would she manage to inflict on them before she did?

At Celié's house, Dahomey Sinclair was waiting when they returned. He dismissed Louis and faced Celié.

"So you went to that ball when I had advised against it. It is *never* wise to play the fool, which is what you did, Celié."

"Dahomey Sinclair, you have never understood. . . ." Celié began.

"No, it is *you* who has never understood," Dahomey Sinclair thundered. "I have suggested that you visit Santo Domingo when you can, but as soon as you can. Sometimes going back to the site of a painful incident can help to heal you. It is certainly worth a try. Unless you go—and I would say by fall—

I will not even *try* to help you. In the summer, I myself will go to Haiti for several months. We could arrange it so that I will come to Santo Domingo when I leave Haiti, and we can return together. I could also help you cleanse yourself of this old love and prepare yourself for a new one."

Celié nodded yes. Perhaps she would do as he asked and perhaps not. She did not want Dahomey Sinclair as a lover. Why couldn't he accept that? And there was one thing she had to make him understand: She would *never* give Martin up.

At three o'clock that morning, Martin and Katherine stood in the backyard by the greenhouse, cloaked against the February cold. Standing there, the ball was a memory, both delightful and scalding. In the night air, her face was cool and wonderfully soft against his as he held her against his own hard body.

"Katherine," he said simply. "Kate." Then, "You must be exhausted."

"No," she replied. "In spite of . . . everything, I enjoyed the ball."

He pulled her to him and kissed her long and hard, his tongue probing her mouth and crushing her full, soft lips beneath his own until it hurt a little. But this was the depth of his need, of his anguish, that he could press against her so fervently it seemed they would meld.

"I want to give you everything," he said, as he lifted his face from hers. Instead, I cannot even protect you from the malevolence of my own past."

His words alarmed her more than anything Celié could possibly do. She brought his lips back hard against hers and this time her tongue sought his, trying to soothe him with her passion, seeking to heal with love as deep as any he would ever know.

Martin took her in his arms, as a sharp wind came whistling

around the corner, and carried her to the side door. Even here, he folded her against his body and pushed open the door the others had left unlocked for them.

Part Three
Danger, Resolution, and Love—1870

Nineteen

During the months of March, April, and May, the cool weather continued for the second year in a row. The city held its collective breath, praying to avoid a yellow fever epidemic for another year.

The Creoles and other whites had taken their political case to the courts, and elections were to be held in November. People of color were banding everywhere to hold on to their gains bought with the bloody riots of 1866.

For days now in mid-June, they had awaited the birth of Katherine and Martin's baby with great anticipation. It was pleasantly warm and growing warmer each day. The house was greatly cooled by ceiling fans, and the large oaks afforded good shade. Cape jasmine and azalea bushes grew in front, and in the back Singing Bird had planted honeysuckle.

Since learning she was pregnant, Katherine had made sure she consumed an abundance of vegetables and fruits. She drank echinacea infusions from time to time to build up her general health. Daily she had done the exercises that bayou country Cherokee Indian women had done for centuries to insure an easy birth and a healthy child. Her mother, Delpha, had seen to it that Katherine trained with these women as *she* had done, and for the month before her delivery she had drunk several cups of red raspberry leaf tea with fresh orange juice squeezed into it.

"Relax, *ma chère*, and I will sing you a song," Madame told her.

"Just now, I could use some music," Dr. St. Cyr grumped. "I never wanted a birth to go well so much in all my days."

Zell took Katherine's hand and held it. "How do you feel, Katie?"

Katherine laughed. "Wonderful is the only way I can describe it. But with all your anxiety and peering at me as if I'm some exotic bird, you'd surely think no woman had ever gone through this."

"*You* haven't gone through it, *ma chère,*" Madame pointed out. "And don't mock our concern. We know you'll give us this baby in your own great style, but we want to make it easy for you."

Lying on the white rubber-sheeted bed in their bedroom, Katherine was uneasy, but she hid it from those in the room. She wanted Martin at her side, wanted his steadying hand and presence, but fathers weren't permitted in birth rooms. The windows were draped to darken the room, a few candles dimly burned under glass, and ceiling fans whirred. The room smelled of lavender oil and lemon balm. Cardinals sang lustily in the great oaks as Ruff and Muffin chased some small animal outside, barking wildly.

Grinning impishly, Singing Bird came to the bed and handed Katherine a note. She had expected it to be from Sing, but as she read it, her heart quickened.

My darling,

I am with you every minute of this very special time for us. Surely you know how much I long to be by your side.

Kate, if ever there was a time when no expression of love suffices, then it is now, when I feel desperately lacking in any way to make you know what you and this coming baby mean to me.

This all began in desire and passion and grew into love. For me, it will end only when my life will end.

With so much devotion,
Martin

"Bring me a pen and some paper," Katherine requested, beginning to get up to sit on the edge of the bed.

"Oh no, you don't, young lady," Dr. St. Cyr growled at her. "You lie right there, and you . . ."

As Madame took the pages from her hand, a sudden pain knifed through her belly and she cried out. But the pain stopped as abruptly as it had begun. How strange, she thought, as Sing gave her more of the blue cohosh tea that relaxed her so. This pain she felt was deep and thrummed across her nerve fibers, biting her to the core. Yet it was *good* pain, which went straight to her heart and lingered there.

Zell brought Katherine the springy dry moss small pillow, covered in an embroidered silk jersey with a forest and river design, to clutch. Carolyn had sent this over. Antoine's and her baby had come the week before. Martin and Katherine had sent a very large bone toy with which the baby could safely play.

"This pillow carries the spell of blessing and good luck of the river and the forest gods of my native Africa," Carolyn had explained to Katherine at the ball. "Clutch it when the pains of birth come to you, and remember the child that comes of this pain."

Carolyn had been sold into slavery by a friend jealous of her father's prosperity.

Zell and Madame hummed as they soothed her through the contractions that hurt and yet felt good, stroking her while Madame held her right hand tightly. As she had counseled Natalie to do, Katherine had drunk squaw vine, slippery elm, and blue cohosh to prepare her womb for early delivery.

"Bear down—*hard,*" Dr. St. Cyr commanded. And she did as he ordered.

Madame softly hummed an old lullaby.

> "Into my arms this child now comes,
> Love and my newborn ba-by.
> Into our life she brings her charms
> Love and my newborn ba-by."

Again and again Katherine bore down as the doctor instructed. But again the oddly satisfying pains stopped, as did the contractions.

Dr. St. Cyr stood up, expelling a harsh breath. "I want you to open the door," he told Singing Bird, who rushed to do as he bade. "Open it just a bit. . . . In spite of the fans, it's a mite warm."

He glanced at the mantel clock. 11:45. This young'un was sure taking its time. Well, who in the hell would be in a hurry to come into this crazy world? Still, he'd bet that Katherine and Martin Dominguez's child would see a better time than most. He spoke to the women.

"Hold up for just a minute," he told them as he walked to the door, opened it, and called Martin in. "Oh, I know nobody wants a *man* in a delivery room, let alone the *father*," he said gruffly. "Now, I happen to think Katherine needs you and you can help her a lot. Mind you, I've never done this before, and if I'm wrong . . ." He shrugged his bony shoulders.

"Pass out on me, Martin, and I'll never let you live it down. We need help with this little baby, not hindrance. Do you understand?"

Martin nodded, smiling nervously, so excited he could hardly breathe, as he went to Katherine's side and knelt by the bed, taking her hand from Zell, who stepped aside a bit.

"Well, I was going to tell you to do just what you did," Dr. St. Cyr said. "I guess you bear out that I've got good judgment."

Katherine realized the contractions that had resumed even before Martin had come in had gotten more purposefully violent, and the gorgeous, creative pain that struck her soul and filled her took over. She cried out once, and her short nails bit into Martin's hand as she grasped it tightly.

Over and over the women softly sang the lullaby, and Katherine felt like laughing a bit hysterically. The child hadn't come into the world yet, but already Madame had referred to it as a *she*. What if it were a boy? If so, they had chosen the name Martin Frank Raoul.

If it were a girl—as Madame and Zell and Papa Frank insisted it was because of the gentle movements—then Delpha Annalise, her mother and grandmother's name and Martin's mother's name, was the only one they had considered.

Her mind was a bit foggy. It seemed to her now that she could remember her own birth. The contractions kept their hard and demanding rhythm, and the soft voices of Zell and Madame were soothing:

"Into my arms this child now comes."

Martin's eyes on her were love itself. Drops of perspiration from his anxious face fell on her body. He shouldn't be here, she thought, no matter how much she wanted him there. Men, for all their bravado and genuine strength, were dandelion puffs at times like this, emotionally blown away. But Martin was not a dandelion. He was with her and she was glad.

"Kate, I would never willingly put you through this. You know that, don't you?" Had his mother suffered like this with Raoul and with him? Martin wondered. Kate looked so vulnerable, so uncharacteristically frail, in the movements of childbirth.

"Easy, lad," the doctor soothed him, all but reading his mind. "It *is* hard, I tell you no lie, but she'll tell you what my wife has always told me: Nothing on this earth is more satisfying."

Martin couldn't wait for this to be over so he could ask Katherine about that.

More anxious minutes passed before what they'd waited for finally arrived.

"Eureka! We're getting us a baby!" Dr. St. Cyr's rasp of a shout sounded when the baby's head popped out. The rest of the boneless little bundle followed effortlessly as if to say,

Well, enough of playing hide-and-seek and giving you a rough time. I'm all little Miss Cooperation now.

"Delpha Annalise," Katherine whispered, and Martin was so choked with tears he couldn't speak. The doctor held the baby up as if she were his personal victory and sharply slapped her tiny bottom. Her cry was a long, lusty wail of outrage. What strong lungs! The doctor grinned to himself. Delpha Annalise, eh? Sounded musical enough. Born to lullabies. In a softly lighted room. With a mother who cried out no more than she could help. And with adoring parents from the beginning. Loved and wanted and healthy.

After a while, Dr. St. Cyr cut and tied the cord, placing the baby's face down on Katherine's breast as he thought, Well, little one, you could do a whole lot worse. He held out his hand to Martin. who took it.

"I have to congratulate you," he said, "on the help you gave us. I'll be doing this more often now—letting the fathers in. In a minute, we'll get that afterbirth and use the angelica."

Tears ran down Katherine's face as they took the baby, oiled her thoroughly, then placed her back on her mother's breast, where grasping, delicate fingers fumbled to find and feed.

"Delpha Annalise," Martin pronounced with awe, and the middle name didn't seem to catch in his throat the way it had for too long.

Katherine glanced at her wedding band as Martin lifted her hand from Delpha's back and kissed it.

Madame and Zell were singing softly now, and Katherine found it soothing. Singing Bird came into the room with a large cup of fresh squaw vine tea. The same tea that had prepared her so well for childbirth would now help her body to quickly and completely recover. And that pain she had felt; Katherine thought she would have to tell Martin about that wondrous pain that had surged through her as Delpha Annalise demanded birth.

Shaking her head in wonder, she told Martin, "Remind me to talk with you about something strange—and beautiful."

Martin promised he would, then pondered what it was that lit her face so movingly at that moment.

"What is the tea you bring her?" the doctor asked Sing.

"Squaw vine."

"Let it stay and she can drink it later. I'd give her valerian just now. She could use a bit of rest."

Singing Bird nodded and looked at Zell. Katherine heard and was pleased. Dr. St. Cyr had taken to herbs with a vengeance.

"Where is Papa Frank?" the doctor asked.

"Outside whittling," Madame volunteered. "They've all told me that Papa Frank's the kind of man you should never let into your birth room."

"I thought you'd like these," Papa Frank said now to Katherine as he entered into the room, carrying an armful of deep purple, pink, and white dahlias and gladioli. "Your neighbors brought these."

Bursting with pride, he gave the long-stemmed blossoms to Miss Lillian, who took them and went to find a vase. Tired as she was, Katherine smiled and thought that these two always looked as if they were up to something these days.

"Well, lovebirds . . ." Papa Frank walked to the bed and bent down to peer at the baby. "Looks like you two've made a prime contribution. And I'm finally a *great*-grandpa."

Sitting up, Katherine sipped some of the valerian tea with honey and lemon that Sing brought, then set it aside. She couldn't stop looking at Delpha Annalise. The baby seemed perfect, but she would have loved her no matter what. She was Martin's gift to her and hers to him. How wonderful she felt!

Madame returned with the dahlias in one large crystal vase and the gladioli in another, both perfectly arranged. Putting the vases on a table, she came to the bed and looked down at the sleeping baby nestled in the crook of Katherine's arm.

"I, too, finally have the baby I have long dreamed of," Madame said quietly.

"And here, I thought all the time it was *me* you wanted," Papa Frank teased.

Quite seriously, Madame replied, "Believe me, *mon cher,* it *is* you I want. But you know I am to be Delpha Annalise's godmother."

"And I remember that, my dear, but it won't do," Papa Frank declared as they all looked at him in surprise; even Dr. St. Cyr glanced up as he finished gathering up his tools.

Madame looked a bit perplexed.

"What do you mean, Frank?" she asked him.

"Well, what I mean is, why be a godmother when you can be the baby's *great-grandmother?*" He walked over to where she stood and took her hand. "Come outside with me, Miss Lillian. It seems to me that we've got a good bit of talking to do."

Katherine was up and about again just three days later. Zell had moved back in for a few days to help, and Madame came by each day as well. But as much as Katherine enjoyed Delpha Annalise, the plump, sparkling infant was Martin's special joy from the beginning.

That night he came home with a stuffed toy he bought in Market Square.

Katherine had held back as long as she could.

"You love her so much," she told Martin. "Celié once said you and she wanted a son."

Martin's glance swept her with love and exasperation. "Forget my sister-in-law's rubbish," he snorted.

"Yet all men do want sons, don't they?"

"Do you think Papa Frank would trade you for anyone? Think about it, Kate. Yes, I want sons, and I won't deny it. But if God should decree that you bear no more children, then we'll quadruple our love for Delpha Annalise. And I'll have no regrets, believe me."

His words soothed her heart. Standing close to him, she hugged him and he nuzzled his face in the softness of her throat.

"Do I make you happy?" she asked.

Martin thought a long moment before he answered, and his voice was quiet, somber. "So much so that it scares me—that the envy of others could ruin both our lives.

"Kate, I asked it when I first knew you, and I'll plead again: *Please keep trusting me.* I know you *feel* my love for you. And if you find at any time that you can't trust me, then trust your own heart. Your body knows how I love you and how you love me. How else could we know the passion of the spirit and the body that we do?"

Twenty

"Mam'selle! Mam'selle! Mam'selle! When will you face what you know in your heart—that Martin loves me? Ask him about the beautiful pale green nightgown that I wear. Ask him about the diamond and the black pearl that was mine by right of my husband being the firstborn son. We were once lovers on Santo Domingo. We *will* be lovers again. This is the truth, *mam'selle,* you interloper into our lives!"

Under a black silk cloak that covered the pale green nightgown—the gown that had made Martin cry out in anger, Celié stared at Katherine as they stood on the edge of a bluff. A maelstrom of muddy water swirled just below them. The river had risen rapidly and was still rising.

"We must go back!" Katherine cried to her.

"No! I alone will return!"

Celié's eyes were as wild as the black, coarse silk hair that whipped around her face. She made no move toward Katherine but she gloated, and her laughter was harsh and shrill. Fierce winds arose to match the wild river and the woman before Katherine, in her tangle of black hair, deathly pale face, black cloak, and pale green gown she wore beneath it.

She had to say it again, no matter that Celié refused to listen. But why on earth was she trying to warn Celié when it was she, Katherine, who was in so much danger?

Katherine came awake from the nightmare, gasping for breath, her skim clammy and dotted with goose bumps, her body tense.

Quickly, she looked around for Martin and sat up. He had had to leave very early, she remembered, to pick up one of his men whose buggy had broken down yesterday.

Katherine would have welcomed his arms around her just now as she hugged herself, trying to steady her trembling body. The dream had seemed so *real*. What did it mean? Celié had seemed calmer the night Katherine had treated her snakebite. Calm, and yes, confident. Confident enough to taunt her as *mam'selle* when she could very well have died without Katherine's help. Yet, she had carried the aura of evil incarnate. At the Crescent Ball she had seemed defeated, had said she'd leave them alone.

Katherine sat up. Delpha Annalise, now three months old, lay in her crib, cooing as she waved her chubby tan legs. She couldn't help smiling at the baby, but the dream unsettled her because Celié *had* kept her word. She'd stayed out of their lives since the night of the Crescent Ball.

Katherine glanced at the clock on the mantel. Seven-thirty. She was usually up and about by or before five. Why had she slept so late? Placing a hand on her brow, she felt no sign of fever. A light knock sounded. When she responded, a pleased Papa Frank entered.

"You feeling all right, granddaughter?" he asked, frowning. "You look a little peaked."

"I had a nightmare, Papa Frank, but I won't talk about it until the sun's well into the sky—to keep it from coming true."

"All right," he agreed. "Maybe a good idea. I've got some good news, Katie. Miss Lillian and I have been working on setting a wedding date. We finally decided on the last of next month, October. Weather's much cooler then. Only thing is it's been raining more than usual for September.

"We're going to have the broomstick wedding like you and Albert and your grandmama and me had. Lord, Miss Lillian's a card. I think she just likes the idea of outraging her persnickety New Orleans friends, some of them."

"You two really have something going," Katherine said softly. "I'm so happy for you."

A loud wail from Delpha Annalise meant she was hungry. Katherine got up and went to the crib, picked up her daughter, and sat on the bed, nursing her.

Watching them, Papa Frank felt his heart fill with happiness. "Katie," he chuckled, "I've just got to find a shorter name for that young'un. Delpha Annalise is real pretty, but it's a mouthful."

Katherine laughed. "You call her Delpha most of the time," she said. "Then you change and say Annalise. That's fine. This is one happy kid. She doesn't care what you call her."

As Katherine went into the kitchen, the smell of fresh-brewed coffee further lifted her spirits. Carrying Delpha Annalise in her arms, she looked with dismay at a downcast Sing, who sat at the table.

"What's wrong, love?" Katherine asked.

Sing wrote on her pad:

Am I being a fool, Katie? I haven't told you, but I see Louis at the Little Sisters more and more. I think I'm beginning to care for him. He saved me and he has changed, and you know what you said about redemption being possible. But don't make him a bishop the first day.

As Katherine read the note, Sing felt frustrated. She still talked to herself in whispers, but she could not bring herself to speak aloud to others. It was as if to speak would bring back all the breathless horror of her screams of protest before Louis had come along and stopped that nightmare.

Remembering Louis and his dismay and sympathy at Celié's behavior the night of the Crescent Ball, Katherine felt he certainly *had* changed, but she couldn't say how much.

Katherine spoke what was in her heart. "You're wise for

your years, Sing, and you're not meeting a stranger. You know
Louis. You're young so I'd say go slow, but *talk* with him.
Invite him over. I don't think Martin will mind too much.

Sing nodded, then wrote:

> He will have to leave Celié alone.
> I loathe that woman.

"So do I, Sing," Katherine agreed. Delpha Annalise squirmed
as Sing took her. "It may well be that Louis will have no problem
doing that."

With Sing holding the baby, Katherine went into the bathroom. Staring at herself in the mirror, she saw that her face
still looked haunted. Running the water she could never quite
get used to having inside the house into the white porcelain
facebowl, she uncovered a small bowl that contained powdered
myrrh and pulverized charcoal. She dipped a twig brush into
the mixture, added a bit of honey, and brushed her flawless,
large white teeth, finishing with mint rinse. Her mouth felt
wonderful.

The night before, she had separated an egg and beat the
yolk with a fork, putting it into a small covered jar. Now she
opened the jar and poured part of the yolk into her palms,
spreading it over the almond oil already on her face. This done,
she sat at the vanity and buffed her nails, then combed and
styled her luxuriant, lustrous hair into bouffant rolls around
her head. Good health and love and alternate rinses of henna,
nettle, and rosemary teas had done wonders in the years she'd
used them.

People of color spoke of "good" hair and "bad" hair. Katherine saw only healthy hair, which she called "loved hair," and
unhealthy, or "unloved" hair. Her own hair, like the child and
then the woman herself, had always been loved. Martin went
into its smooth, mercerized cottony depths often, sliding his
fingertips along the buttery-soft scalp and burying his face in
the fragrance.

He had said to her last night, for the first time in a while,
"Behold, you are black *and* beautiful, my love." And they had
read to each other from "The Song of Songs."

In her French Quarter apartment, Celié paced in agitation.
Where was Dahomey Sinclair? She turned to Louis.

"Did you tell him I wanted him to come by early?"

"Sure did," Louis said, frowning. He intended to go and see
Sing tonight, tell her how he felt. The thought soothed him.
Even if she turned him down flat, he wanted her to know his
feelings.

Looking at Celié pace, Louis reflected on how she was becoming bossier, which he hated in a woman. Hadn't being
bitten by that damned rattlesnake done *anything* to slow her
down? And what did she need Dahomey Sinclair for, since
she'd promised, at that grand ball back in February, to leave
Katherine and Martin alone. And she did seem to have kept
her word. Was she changing now?

As if she could read his thoughts, Celié stopped in front of
him as he sat on the divan in her living room.

"Don't worry," she declared coldly. "I won't bother your
precious friends again. God, don't I wish I could get this kind
of loyalty from *my* friends and those I help."

"And I'm grateful for your help," Louis told her heatedly.
"But to me, *loyal* doesn't mean the same as *lap dog.*"

"My business is off in these days of plenty," Celié said.
"Magic can do many things. Perhaps it can put me on top
again. I'm going away, Louis . . . a week from today. I may
be gone two weeks or a month. Susie is well trained and can
take care of everything. I'll return when others come back into
the city, late September or early October."

When the knock sounded, Louis admitted Dahomey Sinclair.

Immediately, Celié demanded, "Did you bring the strongest
potions and your magic books so that I might study them carefully?"

Dahomey Sinclair set his worn black leather bag on a chair, frowning deeply as he watched her come toward him. An aura of dissonance surrounded Celié. Her usual superb gracefulness was changing into a decidedly unattractive stridency. Putting a finger alongside his nose, his voice was cold.

"I am not a fool that you can control, Madame Dominguez. Yes, you *have* helped me greatly, but I have never *needed* you. And I have helped *you* even more. Martin Dominguez, the brother-in-law you eat your heart out for, might have been yours, but *you* must rule; *you* must conquer. That is not his wish. I told you this, but you did not listen."

Very slyly, he went a little closer to her. "The woman he married proves me right. It seems she is a woman in every way you deliberately choose not to be. Wearing jewels that were an exact copy of hers to that ball was despicable. Ours is a city of *intrigue,* Celié. We have never been especially fond of viciousness."

With seeming carelessness, although she seethed inside, Celié told him, "So you, too, worship at the shrine of this *black pearl,* this unsophisticated bayou woman who is not *fit* to be his wife."

Afterwards, Dahomey Sinclair could never explain why he crowded and bruised her so with his words. "And *you* are fit for that position in his life, madame? Three years you were here before she came. Why blame *her* that you could not make him love you?"

His arrow reached its mark. Celié cringed as her eyes flashed fire.

As a root doctor, he worked the best magic he knew. In his youth, he had flamed with power that was naked and uncaring. As an old man, he found himself full of regrets. Her rejection of him had begun to sting. How had he linked up with this Jezebel?

It was Celié's turn to be cold now. "Very well, I cannot argue with you about your precious books, since they are yours, but I had hoped . . . There was a time, Dahomey Sinclair, when you needed someone, because not even your own potent magic could save you, and *I* knew a politician who helped. . . ."

Dahomey Sinclair held up his hand. "Say no more, Celié. I never forget a favor, and I pay you a special favor in suggesting that you visit Santo Domingo. Will you?"

"Yes," she said without hesitation. "I will go the first weeks of September."

Dahomey Sinclair flashed her his warmest smile.

Perhaps she was growing wiser.

When Dahomey Sinclair had left, Celié picked up a priceless vase and threw it against the wall, smashing it. She walked over to Louis and looked down at him. He had begun to snore a little when she had smashed the vase.

"Louis!" She shook him awake.

His eyes were red and he looked so vacant that Celié believed that he was too intoxicated to have heard the noise, although in actuality he had drunk little and had absorbed more than she dreamed.

"Whatzit?" he mumbled, sitting up.

"Oh, never mind," she snapped. "Isn't it about time you went home?"

"Sure. If you want me to. Dahomey Sinclair gone?"

"Yes," she said curtly. "I cannot imagine why he came."

"You sent for him."

When Louis left, Celié went out in her courtyard. She did not even notice that it was raining lightly, and her black silk robe and gown were soon damp. But she was *keenly* aware of the ivy leaves of iron that Martin had molded.

Perhaps Dahomey Sinclair was right. Going to Santo Domingo could heal her heartache. Surely, it was worth a try.

* * *

Out in the backyard swing, Louis talked and Sing wrote back by lantern glow.

"Just give me a chance to show you what you mean to me. I'm falling in love with you, Sing. . . .

"You know I've changed," he continued. "The city's changed me. I'm on the way to making a good living with land rented about twenty miles from here for truck farming. Two years ago I couldn't have said 'I love you' pretty like women like you want to hear it. Now I can. Please, Sing, what do you say?"

With the ball in *her* court, Sing became coy. She wrote:

> We will see, Louis.
> I want to think about this.

But she knew she wouldn't need to think too long. Her heart kept racing. Louis had said he loved her and he'd said it "pretty-like."

Twenty-one

"It's hard to believe that Celié really decided to go back to Santo Domingo," Martin commented as he and Katherine rode along in the buggy to the far side of the farm.

"I certainly feel relieved," Katherine replied. "Although for six months she seems to have done nothing."

"That we know of," Martin said grimly. "She's been obsessed. In this city of excesses, it's quite common. Look at the duels between the young, white hotbloods over Creoles of color women they cannot marry. A kind of madness too often thrives in this city, Kate."

It was late afternoon on a Sunday in September. Louis had come courting, but Sing had offered and insisted on keeping Delpha Annalise, and Louis had agreed to pitch in. It was Louis who'd told them that Celié was away for perhaps a month.

Lately, Papa Frank was with Miss Lillian more often than he was at home. Today they were at a church recital.

As the buggy thumped along the gravel road that ran the length of the ten-acre farm, Katherine said, "We could have walked."

"It's a bit hot for walking at this time of the day."

"Why did you want to come out this afternoon? And isn't that your violin case?"

"You're a sweet woman, but you're far too inquisitive right now. I have a surprise for you." Looking at her sideways, he spoke softly. "It's been far too long."

"Oh, Martin!" Katherine blushed furiously, her brown skin reddening beneath his gaze. "You're such a romantic."

"With you, *querida mia*, it's almost impossible not to be. You don't know how much I've missed making love to you."

Thrills played up and down her spine when he said it.

The back section of the farm was the most beautiful, with the magnolia forest where they'd held the wedding; the expanse of meadow where sheep grazed; the good-sized clear pond with its ducks and lily pads, and its two weeping willows on either side. Martin drove to the section where thornbushes grew into a thickset fence and wax-leaved magnolias grew close together, making a large, secret cove.

Shading her eyes and looking up, Katherine remarked, "Those pink clouds are beautiful," as Martin stopped the buggy and she gave a cry of pure joy. "Those peacocks, love, and the two black swans . . . When on earth did you get them?"

For there on the pond, on one side of the magnolia forest, the swans preened themselves and the two peacocks ambled along the edges. This view had been partially obscured by trees along the way, and in truth, she had been aware mostly of Martin.

"Perfect timing," he chortled, as he got off the driver's seat, came around to her side, and lifted her down. He held her close to him before he gently lowered her, then took a quilt from under the seat.

"I hope there're no wild animals around here," she said. Martin looked amused.

"Only one," he responded, "and you can tame me if you wish."

In the late afternoon sunlight, suddenly exhilarated to be free of Celié, if only for a while, Katherine began to run, crying over her shoulder to Martin, "Catch me if you can!"

As swiftly as she ran, hampered by the strapped and buttoned shoes she wore and the long indigo blue muslin garments, she was no match for Martin, who caught her in a few minutes and lifted her, holding on to her.

"That's not fair," she panted, laughing. "You're supposed to give me a good start."

"I'll give you a good start on anything except running away from me," he replied. Setting her down, he caught her by the shoulders, turned her to face him, then spoke softly. "Kate, please don't ever leave me."

"Only if you promise that you'll never leave me."

He studied her face in the late sunlight, tracing the planes and angles of her sturdy beauty, inhaling the lavender and lemon balm fragrance she wore today. Then he kissed her gently, fighting a fierce desire to take her at that moment.

He let her go and they moved to the cove, spread out the quilt, and sat down.

"Will the male peacock spread that gorgeous fan?"

"Oh, I'll see that he does, if you wish," he told her as he drew her close again. Her dress was soft under his stroking hands. He had asked that she leave off her stays, and she had known then what he was about.

"You know," she smiled, "I would've been terribly disappointed had you not brought me somewhere like this. I want you to know, Mr. Dominguez, my darling, that I knew just what you had in mind. . . ."

"And?"

She took his face in her slender hands and kissed him slowly, ardently, running her tongue lightly over his face and into the corners of his mouth. "We are," she said, laughing, "as always, of *one* mind."

His mouth came down hard on hers, seeking honey, seeking love. Seeking that part of life itself that he needed from her.

They were well hidden here in this part of the forest. Bramble bushes formed a long fence in the large area around them. Honeysuckle vines grew on top of massive blackberry bushes. It was September, green and lush, just before the changing colors. There was a quietness broken only by robins and whippoorwills. Nature certainly does her part, Katherine thought, to keep the race going.

She had seldom seen Martin so aroused, she realized, and it awakened in her a flowering that quieted her as she unbuttoned his shirt. She was still, hardly breathing, as he unfastened her blouse and camisole, then began to remove her other clothes.

"It's really warm, and it feels good to be naked," she murmured.

Martin patted the wedding-ring quilt that lay beneath them.

"Believe me when I tell you that making love to someone who is love itself to you is the healthiest activity in this world. You've always brought 'The Song of Songs' to mind. My own version. 'I am black *and* beautiful' and *'Thy navel is like a goblet that wanteth not liquor. The rose of Sharon.'* Bending forward, he gently kissed her navel, then his tongue began patterning delicious swirls across her stomach.

He was intent now, covering her face, then her breasts with hot kisses, before he took each soft, tender mound of silken brown flesh into his mouth and sucked them gently at first, then with growing hunger. Her nipples hardened under his ardor and she moved against him, moaning in the back of her throat.

Yet with all the thrills along her spine, she was compelled to look toward the pond where the peacock had spread his fan against the lowering sun. At this moment of passion, this scene was indescribably and painfully beautiful to Katherine.

"Look, sweetheart," she whispered against his ear. "The peacock is spreading. You don't want to miss that."

Martin had seen the peacock several times, and just now, his attention was riveted on this woman. His bloodstream churned, rich and heavy, fueling his loins to white-hot heat that dimmed his vision. He kissed her long and deep and even harder as he murmured, "Don't ask me to look at anything, Kate, except *you.*"

He placed a hand on each side of her face, blocking her

vision, bringing her even closer to him so that the world was cut off, and there was only the two of them. Just as there was only this very special moment in time.

His mouth moved over her breasts, *seeking* pleasure but no less intent on *giving* pleasure. She cried out beneath him in rapture and delight. No alcoholic spirits lifted them; love and desire spun them higher than any vintage champagne, any old, sparkling wine. He kept pressing and stroking her, as she did him, kneading his back, feeling the rippling muscles of his arms, hard from the iron he molded.

"Oh, my darling," she whispered again and again. "How can you know exactly how to please me?"

Martin stopped for the briefest of moments. "You *tell* me, Kate, what it is you want. And whatever it is, I'll do it for you."

Kate began to say she would do the same for him, but he had arched above her, his engorged maleness throbbing like a heartbeat, his face like a god's knowing glory.

When he entered the moist, satin sheath of her body, Katherine cried out the way she had always wanted to cry out at home. But there had always been others around.

Now, they both were free to cry out each other's names, letting the moans of growing ecstasy well up from their very souls and travel out into the late summer afternoon. Radiance was all around them as the sun continued its blazing descent.

As the sun set, pleasure was *rising* in Katherine. Inside her body, this man she loved with all her being throbbed richly as they moved in rhythm, he thrusting, she responding in nearly perfect unison.

Paradoxically, each could let go of self for that moment in time, secure that they were separate enough, mature enough, to fuse and be one gently explosive whole, then return to his or her own space.

"Oh, my darling," Martin whispered to her as they spun out in time, lifting, lifting upward. "How can anyone be so beautiful?" This time, the passion in his loins was like an erupting volcano, bringing no destruction, but only joy.

To Katherine, beneath him, waves of passion had begun in small, gentle ripples, before they broadened and surged, so that she was totally unmindful of anything save this man, this achingly satisfying moment, and the transcendent love they shared.

For a long time they lay, naked, in each other's arms. "You missed the peacock's show," she murmured deeply relaxed.

"You're far more beautiful to me," he responded.

"You always flatter me."

"No. You *are* as I compliment you."

They slept for a short while, exhausted from that wild siege of ecstasy and enchantment. Martin was without dreams, while Katherine dreamt of the church of her childhood that was filled with lush, green, growing plants.

Once awake and clothed again, Katherine and Martin walked to the pond, where three brown ducks floated in straight formation. The black swans lazed along. Back in the magnolia forest, robins had joined in a full-throated, round-robin songfest.

"Martin," Katherine said suddenly, "the swans and the peacocks are new. When did you get them?"

He grinned. "Early this morning," he told her. "A man slipped in and put them here. All the better to seduce you with, my love." He paused to kiss her throat. "With Jules's help, I found the pair of swans and the two peacocks. I like to make things perfect for you. You *respond* to beauty"—He kissed the tip of her nose—"as I respond to *you.*"

Oh, he looked handsome, this husband of hers, Katherine mused. Dressed now in black trousers, a white broadcloth shirt, and a black linen jerkin, he was bareheaded. His virility was not a narrow definition of that word; his power grew from deep within a caring self.

Yellow and rose water lilies lined the edge of the pond. Standing by a rowboat on shore, Martin pulled it closer and held out his hands to her. He helped her into the boat as he pushed it off, got in, and began to row to the other side. It was a fairly large, clear pond, with catfish jumping and turtles still sunning themselves.

Katherine picked up a set of oars to help him row.

"No," he protested, grinning wickedly. "Put them aside. Save your energy."

"Hm-m-m," Katherine said, laughing. "Well, I *do* plan to wash dishes when I get back."

"I had something far more elemental and way more interesting in mind."

"Honey, I don't know where you get all this energy," she remarked, complaining not at all. "I'd think that with your running a *forgeron* business and all . . . well, it takes a lot out of you."

He looked at her as a yellow butterfly alighted on her dress, stayed a moment, then flew away. The swans coursed nearby and again the peacock spread his fan, as Katherine thought that no matter how often she bore witness to that magnificence, she would never tire of it. She told Martin as much, adding, "That's the way I feel about *you,* love."

"And the way I feel about you," he responded. "*You* are the source of my energy with you. Here comes a jealous honeybee who thinks you're a flower. . . ." He teased her as he fanned the bee away, telling it, "Touch this nectar, buddy, and you go to bee heaven right now! I share this nectar with no rival!"

Katherine burst out laughing. "You're a clown, you know." Lemon balm repelled other insects but attracted bees, she had discovered at an early age.

"I'm whatever you want me to be."

Katherine shook her head. "No, you already are what I want."

As they sat again on the quilt, Martin removed his fiddle from the case.

"The painful memories of Santo Domingo are fading, Kate," he reflected. "Thank God."

"I'm glad," Katherine said simply.

Wordlessly, Martin tucked the fiddle into the curve of his neck and shoulders, took up the bow, and began to play a soft and tender melody she did not recognize. His face was beatific as he played. The birds competed, with no loss of melody on either side, and the swans and the ducks looked over that way. Helio, the horse, came near and stood there, munching grass.

Changing positions slightly, Martin smiled at her vividly and swept into the "Bayou Country Wedding Song."

> "*Ma chère,* on this your wedding day,
>   I wish you love!
> *Mon cher,* on this your wedding day,
>   I wish you joy!"

The melody and his heartfelt playing brought back a thousand old and recent memories, back from the beginning. Her rage at DeBeau and his ruffians—the rage that spilled over to Martin and mingled with desire. After all the heartache, it had come to this spot in the Garden of Eden. But she simply didn't *feel* that Celié had hung up her fiddle. Santo Domingo might simply help her to fine-tune her hellish fiddle.

As they walked back to where Helio stood sleepily at ease, Katherine took a couple of cubes of sugar and fed him.

"Well, you do add sweetness to his life as well," Martin

said, turning to look at her. "But you know, I personally like the sugar from your lips better."

Katherine laughed aloud. "This evening, you're a romantic nut. But oh, don't stop. I love it!"

Going to the buggy, Katherine took a small flat covered basket from under the seat, then lifted a slender bottle of cool, red wine.

As Martin took the wine bottle from her, she uncovered a small platter, saying, "Voila!" Madeleine cakes, her favorite, and slices of his, praline cake.

"I've never been sure I deserve you," he said, eyeing the food, "but I'm glad *you* think so."

Slowly they made their way to the cove a short distance away and sat again on the wedding quilt, eating slowly.

"We probably should go in, sweetheart. It's getting dark. Martin, why are you courting me so today? True, you're usually a silver-tongued lover, but this evening. . . ."

"You make me happy," he told her. "I do what I can to return the favor and I owe you."

She raised her eyebrows. "Consider your debt paid."

After eating half of one madeleine cake, Katherine got up and in the twilight walked over to a treelike bush of greenish-yellow blossoms and sniffed them. Sassafras. The citrus odor was light, fresh, deliciously pleasant.

Going back to Martin, she said, "Please lend me your knife."

He began to get it from his pocket. "Why do you need it? I don't want you to cut your hand. My knife's sharp. *I'll* cut whatever it is you want cut."

Katherine put her hands on her hips. "You're talking to the woman who prepares your meals. Than a meat cleaver, there is nothing sharper. But if you feel you must protect me from all harm today, then please cut me a piece of sassafras root."

Martin groaned as he got up, complaining, "Never come between me and your praline cake." He took the cake with him, eating the last bite on the short distance to the tree.

He cut a piece of the sassafras tree root and smelled it, then passed it to Katherine who inhaled deeply, savoring the odor of root beer from the root.

She rubbed a bit of the root against her wrists, then behind her ears. Martin sighed.

"Kate," he said, smiling. "That's kind of like rubbing a rose with honeysuckle blossoms. Your natural fragrance is already giving me trouble—the desirable kind of trouble."

"Still?" she questioned him slyly.

"Still."

She put the platter and the folded napkins back into the basket, setting it near the end of the quilt.

"I'll put it back into the buggy," Martin said.

While he was gone, she poured the wine he had uncorked into two wine glasses, shaped to let the drinker savor the bouquet of the muscadine wine.

He came back, sat down, and raised his glass to her saying, "Just now I can think of no toast that could begin to do justice to how I feel about you. See, my darling, the moon wants us to stay out. It's only three-quarters and see how bright it is."

Katherine sat beside him, silent, her feelings too deep for words. This moonlit early evening was perfect. It was warm for September. A time to drift, she thought, to let life push them along in its varying streams.

Martin drew her to him. "When I think of the sadness in my life and the torment," he said. Then urgently he asked, as he had asked her before, "Do I make you happy?"

In exasperation, Katherine threw herself across him. "How can I make you know how happy you make me?"

Before he could answer she softly pressed her lips against his, her breasts against his hard, muscular chest. He drew her down onto him, the complete length of her body over his, and he pressed her against him so swiftly and so hard she gasped.

"I can," he said, "think of one way you could make time itself stop for me. If you really mean it, make me know how much I matter to you."

This time they were slower, more aware, and they moved further back into the cove, taking the blue wedding-ring quilt with them. As she lay naked by his side again, she teased him, "Why did we bother to dress? We should have run around the grounds naked. Adam and Eve."

"How could I want you so much that each time we make love, it's a renewal of some deep pleasure that just never ends? Why?" he asked her.

"I don't know, my darling," she answered, "but I do know this. I treasure being with you—your body, your mind, your spirit—the way I could treasure no jewel on this earth."

Watching her tender face, he knew she meant it, and it turned him on vividly that she cared so much about him, valued him and his love so highly that he could not wait for foreplay or more hugs and kisses. He was a man driven by a sudden mission, and he was not certain just what that mission was. But he had a dim view of it mixed in with the passionate impulse to meld with this beloved woman above him now.

As he embraced her tightly and began to roll over so that she was on her back, he entered her body with nearly the same fevered passion as at first, the moist oven-warm sheath of her body surrounding his vividly pulsing maleness.

"How greedy we are for each other," she murmured as she kissed him along the side of his face.

He slowed a moment, willing himself to hold back. "No, love, I don't think we're greedy, just hungry. I know *I* am. Honest, healthy hunger to experience every joy we can with each other. It seems to me this is one of the very best ways I can give you love that holds back nothing of myself." And he added a little anxiously, "Do you feel that now?"

"I feel it, love. I can't tell you how much I feel it."

She was fully open to him now, in the throes of an even deeper passion than at first. This time they moved like the surging waters in springtime of Lake Pontchartrain that lay beyond them, and the Gulf of Mexico that lay beyond that. Surging waters. Volcanoes that erupted to create, and not to destroy. Martin felt a wave of heat like molten lava flood his loins, and he was rejuvenated to his bone marrow—then he was spent as well.

Katherine merely stroked his sinewy back hard at first, then cried out as her fingers dug into his back; she didn't want to scratch him, to hurt him at all. But when she felt the wonder of his body as he connected with her more deeply than before, she cried out and clung to him, unknowing if she did or did not cause him pain. What she clearly knew was the singular rapture that she felt that seemed to go on forever. The seas they swam in now were dangerous and deep, fulfilling with joy, nourishing their bodies and spirits, and promising more to come.

And they both felt the end of this passion that shook them wildly, hurling them into space before gently lowering them on a cloud-soft windswept beach. The end of all this glory carried a beginning in its depths.

Twenty-two

The next week the September rains began in a time of expected drought. Katherine used that time to make herbal packets, lavender oils, and herbal extracts. She also put in and pruned new herbs.

In addition to his *forgeron* business, Martin helped Wilson Drumm set up new agendas and register voters for their party to use in the November elections. Wilson would run to be *elected,* whereas before he had served as the Louisiana Assembly's appointee. Enemies of Governor Montrose were growing bolder and more outspoken in their efforts to limit or even stop political power for people of color.

Dinner cooked and put aside to be eaten later when Martin got home, Katherine set the table, then sat in her needlepoint-covered rocking chair. Papa Frank was off courting Miss Lillian, and Sing was working in the greenhouse.

"On this your wedding day, I wish you love," Katherine sang softly to herself, blushing as she remembered the recent Sunday afternoon she and Martin had spent in the magnolia forest.

"You're awfully quiet, you little usually gurgling bundle of activity," she said to Delpha Annalise, who lay in her crib nearby. Katherine bent forward and tickled her chin, causing her to smile. How dear her daughter was.

Katherine picked her up and held her close. Delpha Annalise responded by cuddling and laughing, then cooing with delight.

The back door slammed as Sing came in and went down

the hall. A loud knocking sounded on the front door several moments later, and when Sing answered it, Katherine heard a man's voice asking for Mrs. Dominguez. She put Delpha Annalise back into her crib and went into the hall.

A wizened old pecan-brown man stood in the doorway with his battered hat in hand, smiling ingratiatingly.

"Good evening, sir," Katherine greeted him. "What can I do to help you?"

"Well, ma'am," he began warmly, "you don't know me, but Mr. Martin does. I'm Will Moody, and your husband's been helping us to register to vote, for which I'm mighty grateful. I've met you a couple of times, but I bet you don't remember."

Katherine looked at the old man a long time, but she could not remember having met him. As deferential as he was, there was something about him to which she didn't cotton. Still, since coming to this city, she had learned to work with different kinds of people she hadn't before known, and no alarm bells went off. She saw that he was greatly agitated.

"It's my daughter, ma'am," he went on. "She's in labor and in a bad way. Just a young'un, just thirteen. *Too* young, and her ma's having conniption fits. We couldn't get a doctor on account of we live in a new section and the roads ain't too good. . . ."

There was severe tension in his voice as he pleaded with her. "They call you the Black Pearl now and say how good you are helping women having a hard time delivering. I can pay you whatever you ask. I'm a carpenter and I work regular. If I could speak with Mr. Martin, I'm sure he'll vouch for me."

"Well," Katherine said, "he'll be along any minute, but right now . . ."

She was not surprised to see tears in the old man's eyes, and his hands were unsteady as he removed a handkerchief from his pocket and blew his nose.

"Excuse me, ma'am. I and my missus been down with flu, and the girl, too. That ain't helping the delivery none."

"Come in, Mr. Moody," Katherine told him finally, "and have a seat. I'm trying to work something out."

Sing stood looking at the two of them as they spoke. Taking her pad and pencil, she wrote:

I will go with you. We can leave Delpha Annalise with Miss Lillian or Zell.

Katherine read it and shook her head. She hated the thought of leaving her three-month-old.

She held her left elbow in the palm of her right hand with her fingers on her face as she mused, planning as swiftly as she could.

"No," she said to Sing. "It's best you stay here with Delpha Annalise until Martin comes." Turning to the man, she asked him, "Where do you live, Mr. Moody?"

"Across the river in Algiers," he told her. "It's a little ways back, but not too far. I'll see you get home safe and soon as possible, ma'am. You don't worry. I'm not a begging man, but I'd get down on my knees like a dog for my girl. She's so puny and having such a hard time. . . . Me and my missus is just about going out of our minds, yes."

The anxiety on the man's face certainly seemed real enough. Difficult births were hard to help. Too many midwives hadn't studied enough, didn't know enough, so Katherine had a responsibility to go. Still, it had rained off and on for several days, and certain parts of his area were flooding.

"You know I want to help you and I will if I can," Katherine told him. "Is the water high out your way?"

"No, ma'am, a bit, but not really. Not out our way. Not so far. And no rain's been falling for five to six hours. I won't hold it against you if you say no to me. You got your little baby there to think of, but Miz Dominguez. . . ."

That final plea as he looked into the living room at Delpha Annalise tore at Katherine's heart.

What if *she* had needed someone to bring her baby into this world? What if she needed someone in the future? Papa Frank had told her stories of her own difficult birth.

"Let me get my bag," she said.

The old man looked so relieved, it was as if the weight of the world had been lifted from his shoulders. But he still looked sad, beaten down.

In the kitchen, she gathered together everything she could possibly need and put the items into her black midwife bag. There had to be trouble ahead. The young girl about to give birth would almost certainly be a stranger to proper food and care, and positively would not have been prepared for childbirth by exercise and herbal infusions and decoctions. And at thirteen, her emotions would likely be shame, not welcome, for her child. Nothing had been said about a husband for the girl. Grimly snapping her bag closed, Katherine knew she was walking into trouble.

Katherine and the man took the Algiers ferry. Driving the buggy off the ramp when they got to the other side, Katherine looked around her, dismayed to find that it had begun to rain again. It was quite cool for September. She drew her lightweight navy cloak tighter around her.

"Won't take us no time," he said, not commenting on the roads that were covered with water in some places.

Mr. Moody did handle his buggy well enough, she noted.

"Was the water this high when you left?" Katherine asked. "You said it hadn't risen much."

"No, ma'am, it surely wasn't," he replied. "Sometimes it rains over here and not in the city. I'm sorrier about this than I can tell you." He reined in the horse sharply. "Up ahead there, something's happened. Seems like a bridge has been washed out since I came along. We go back a bit, there's a boathouse back there."

Katherine was so annoyed that she didn't answer him. They found the boathouse, and the man rented a boat from the owner he apparently knew. He hitched the buggy at the boathouse, and they set out rowing through the rain and the water, which was rising at a fairly rapid pace.

She reflected that she had had misgivings since they set out, but hadn't fully drawn on the psychic power that was her ally. Now, perhaps too late, she knew that she was in danger.

"We *must* turn back!" Katherine commanded him.

"No, ma'am," he said, rowing and looking at her now with indecipherable, shuttered eyes. "She'll die if you don' help her. You got to help my chil'."

Perhaps she was wrong, Katherine thought, but the psychic gift so long denied kept pressing her. No, she was *not* wrong.

The old man continued rowing with a strength that belied his frail body. "There be no words to tell you how grateful I and my missus and my daughter be to you for your kindness, ma'am," he told her as he rowed swiftly toward a lone house on tall pilings up ahead of them.

"What else could I have done?" Katherine asked herself and him against the winds that were beginning to churn the waters. "We have to help each other when we can."

He didn't answer, and she sat thinking as he rowed harder against the dangerous waters that were now forming undercurrents. Papa Frank was fond of recalling when there had been floodwaters on the bayou and a physically troubled Delpha was bearing Katherine. They thought a midwife friend could not possibly get through, but she had. And thus Katherine had come to feel bound, through Papa Frank and her mother's repeating of this story, to help any woman in trouble.

She picked up a pair of oars and, ignoring his protests, insisted on helping him. The rowing grew smoother then, and soon he pulled up in front of the very nice white frame house on tall pilings. With grave care, he helped her out of the rowboat and onto the stone steps.

"I'll just tie her up around here on one a' these pilings and be right there," he said. "No need for you to knock. Just go right in. The missus is expecting you."

More steps that seemed to her to take a long time to climb, then across the wide porch and to the heavy, ornate oak front door. The house seemed far above the circumstances of the man who'd brought her here, but these were times when many poorer New Orleanians were growing unexpectedly wealthy.

The door opened easily, and drawing a deep breath, Katherine closed it behind her and leaned against it for a moment to steady herself, shaking herself to shed the water. Her cloak was drenched.

It was eerily quiet and Katherine wondered if the young girl had lost consciousness or, worse, had died, as all too often happened.

Quickly looking around her at the shawl-draped piano, Renaissance furniture, and the African artifacts, all fairly visible in the hall lamplight, she thought it best to call out "Hello!" before she went on back. Clutching her midwife's bag, she had braced herself to deal with whatever difficult birth situation she might encounter, when the door was flung open.

"Do come in, beloved, miraculous midwife," Celié cackled, her face drained of color, a hag's mask of hatred.

The room spun around her as Katherine fought to steady herself. Then, as soon as she could breathe, she stared, frozen, at this woman whose face now fully mirrored the evil of her soul. Was she mad or simply evil? Or a bit of both?

"You are *not* the Black Pearl fools call you," Celié spat. "Nor will I let you keep it, the diamond ring, or the man. All three are *mine!*" Then she added slyly, "I will also have the wedding band Martin bought you!"

With mounting terror she could barely control, Katherine's vision oddly cleared. In the bedroom lamplight, Celié stood in bold relief, the nightmare come true, and beyond. For she wore the black silk robe she had worn on the night Katherine had treated her for snakebite. Her usually beautiful, wavy black hair had somehow taken on coillike Medusa twinings. Katherine's mind raced to absorb it all, retching inwardly from the evil standing before her.

For Celié wore the black robe open at the ruffled high neckline, revealing the copy of the black pearl she had had made, glowing on her breasts, above the pale green silk with appliqués-of-flame nightgown she had left in the bureau drawer her first night at Martin and Katherine's house. Slowly, she spread the fingers of her left hand and waved it about, letting her copy of Katherine's diamond flash across her rival's face, laughing as she moved it back and forth.

Celié laughed a witch's laugh. "Oh, how I planned and schemed for this day," she said. "Hiding, turning my shop over to Susie, with Louis to 'protect' her. I've taken him away from you."

"Yes, you have." Katherine intended to agree whenever she could, to avoid agitating her.

Celié gloated. "How long I've waited for this and how I've schemed. Had it not rained unexpectedly so that the floods came, I would have needed to change my plans. But no matter, I have many plans.

"Months ago, I spread the word that I would be going away. Someone given my name, disguised as me, boarded that ship— a poor woman I found it easy to pay off to go. She has not seen her family in Santo Domingo for years. And then *I* came here. I have a key to Dahomey Sinclair's house to check on it while he's in Haiti."

Celié paused, her eyes glistening.

"Dahomey Sinclair thinks I am in Santo Domingo. He will meet me there hoping that we will return together."

She threw her head back, laughing as if at some outrageous joke.

"I have had Will Moody watch Martin's comings and goings. He needed to be away when I lured you here. I have tried so many times and the magic never worked for me—until tonight!"

"What if I had refused to come with this man?"

"There is other magic," Celié said almost calmly. "I know a great deal about magic now."

Katherine willed her pounding heart to be still. Some dim hope that the man who brought her here might change his mind and help her faded as soon as it began. She did not think he had ever come in; his mission was probably finished.

Sensing Katherine's panic, Celié moved to destroy her. Even so, she could not help deliciously toying with her first. Let her see how it felt to lose!

"For Martin's love," Celié began, "I betrayed my husband and caused his death. I wanted to marry and Martin wasn't ready, so I persuaded Raoul to marry me. I was such a fool. But Martin rescued me from Santo Domingo after Raoul died. He has always loved me. He had this gown made for me. Oh, Raoul, my husband, paid for it, but it was Martin who chose the silk and supervised the making."

"No," Katherine said, trying to bring Celié to her senses, to force her to think. "Raoul asked Martin to have the gown made up for your because he had betrayed you with yet another woman. . . ."

Instead, her words had the opposite effect; Celié's eyes began to lose what semblance of reality they had held.

"Martin and I were in love from the beginning," Celié began in a hypnotic, singsong voice. "He left me to go back to study in Spain, as his mother wished him to. I turned to Raoul because I wanted to punish Martin for leaving me. I *married* Raoul.

"Annalise, their mother, hated me because both her sons loved me, and I was far more beautiful than she. Martin brought me from Santo Domingo after Raoul and Annalise were killed, by *my* decree."

Too sick at heart to want to know the details of the story Celié told, Katherine still pressed her on, because as long as she talked, there was time and there was hope.

"What do you mean when you say Raoul died by *your* decree?"

"Just this, *mam'selle* midwife. My husband and DeBeau's oldest son, Jean—and yes, the mother, Annalise—fancied themselves revolutionaries. Stupidly, they believed that Santo Domingo was coming under the yoke of tyrants again and they worked against them. The men they hated had long paid me well to watch them, to tell their secrets. Oh, I did not decide that they *were* to die, just *when.* And I used that money to become a modiste, a woman Martin could be proud of. The way he was so proud of his fool of a mother."

"Was it Martin's baby that you lost, Celié?"

"No. It was Raoul's child. Raoul who broke my heart with his other women and his wildness.

"I could have had other children. The accident did not make me barren. I lied to Martin to punish him. . . ."

"But *why?*" Katherine cried. "Why do you wish to torment him?"

Celié's eyes went sad. "Because I love Martin and I mean for us to be together—once *you* no longer walk this earth. The daguerreotype you saw on my bedside table was the one *I* signed, but it's the way he really feels, too. But he is angry at me for marrying Raoul, so I must keep him feeling guilty."

"No, Celié . . ."

When Katherine would have asked yet another question, Celié raised her hand like the tyrants of whom she had spoken.

"No more! Listen!" she directed. "For Martin's love, I betrayed my husband and caused his death, even as my husband had killed me with *his* betrayals. Do you imagine I will let you continue to rob me of that love? No! I will not permit it. Hear me well, *mam'selle,* when I say it."

Coming forward now, Celié sought to grasp her rival's arm, but Katherine moved away from her. They stood too near the open French windows with the swiftly eddying waters below. Icy fingers of fear played along Katherine's spine. Even her eyes felt cold.

But the fear cleared her brain somewhat and she began again to speak.

Celié's voice was deadly, her face grotesque. "Say nothing else! The muddy waters rising outside cry out for you. They will be a womb for you that brings you not birth, but death. Martin will love me even more because he will believe I tried to save you. And I will sleep each night with the man I've always loved and raise the child you bore for Martin and *me*. Together we can find another healthy fool like yourself to bear us sons."

A curious calm had begun to settle over Katherine now. "You're evil," she declared evenly. "I've done nothing to you. I've never hurt you. I saved your life when you would have died from the snakebite."

"You were a fool! You should have let me die. Come, Katherine, I have Arkansas toothpicks—the *longest* of knives—in this house, and loaded guns. My spells were never strong enough for the likes of you. Well, let me see you withstand what I have prepared for you now!"

Celié drew a deep, harsh breath and her voice became hypnotic again, like the night singers in Congo Square weaving their spells. "I want you to step out of this window—into the muddy waters below us. . . . Come, midwife, when Martin gets here, there must be only one of us."

Katherine kept Celié in her peripheral vision as they stood not three feet apart. The waters were rising more slowly now, but they still churned and eddied, raging in some spots. And she knew from past experience how they could suck a person under like a whirlpool, so that she might not be found for days.

The double windows were low to the floor. Icy with fear, Katherine saw that Celié's face was a vision of hell. But a strength she had not known she possessed sustained her. Looking directly into her opponent's face, Katherine spoke. "No, Celié! I will not step down into those waters!"

Her words were calm, even though an edge of hysteria had begun to rise in her because a high wind had suddenly come up like the one in her dreams. Celié's fingers fastened the ornamental frog at her throat, closing the black silk robe. But the wind raised the cloak and blew it open, revealing the pale green nightgown molded against her body by the wind and the rain that swept in.

Enraged, Celié came at her in a rush to push her forward, but Katherine's strength held fast. She was going to fight Celié. And she was going to win! She had too much to live for to let this madwoman kill her.

Blind with fury, Celié's hand struck the side of Katherine's face, her nails drawing blood, as she overstepped and hurtled out the window into the raging muddy waters below.

Celié made little sound as she fell, and there was only the harsh gurgle of rushing waters and the howling wind.

Afterwards, Katherine would feel she must have passed out, because she came to and, feeling curiously safe, slept.

Upon awakening, she groggily got to her knees in the dimly lit room. Her fingers explored her scalp, guided by inner knowledge of bodily injury, and felt the lump on the left side of her head the size of a goose egg. She must have hit her head when she fell.

As she stood up, the memory of what had just happened washed over her with new horror. What if the old man who'd tricked her into coming here had returned and was waiting for her? She stood up, willing her legs to be sturdy, then catching sight of herself in a bureau mirror, Katherine nearly fainted again.

Dried blood from the scratches on her face ran down the front of her cloak, and she looked truly terrible. But that didn't matter. What if Celié had been rescued by the old man and both had come back to finish her? Yes, she had seen the black silk robe and the pale green silk nightgown Celié wore, rushed along by the muddy water, had seen the long black hair and Celié's body tossed by those waves. But Celié knew magic. Celié *was* magic.

Katherine put her face in her hands and wept. Then she forced herself to move on unsteady legs into the living room, where it seemed a little safer. At least there were no open windows. Suddenly, she didn't trust the chairs or the sofas; only the floor seemed solid. She'd wait here until she felt steadier on her feet, then if Celié *were* truly gone and the old man didn't return . . .

Katherine froze again because there were loud sounds of movement outside, men's voices. Panic struck to her bone marrow as she tried to stand, to hide. . . .

"Kate!" And again *"Kate!"*

Oh God, was she hallucinating? That was Martin's voice! And Jules called with him, "Katherine!"

She staggered to the door, opened it, and saw them through blurred vision, in the boat in the water by the steps.

"Don't move, love!" Martin called. "We're coming to get you!"

She clung to the doorjamb, uncertain still that this was not an illusion. But no, Martin was bounding up the stairs, and Singing Bird was scrambling out of the boat behind him. When he reached her, Martin hugged her so tightly that her ribs hurt.

"Oh, my God, Kate, what did she do to you? But thank God you're safe."

His tears fell on her hair, her damaged face, blending with the wetness of her rain-soaked clothes.

"Don't you want to know about Celié?" she asked him.

"I certainly hope she's not still here," he said grimly. "I could *kill* her. I know it's like her to strike and run, or pay someone else to do her evil."

"She tried to push me from the bedroom window, Martin. I fought her, and she fell. She was swept away by the waters."

She put her hands to her face and suddenly became aware that Singing Bird was crying and crying as she hugged her, along with Martin. Jules had anchored the boat to a piling, and he came into the house and into the room. The four of them stood there hugging and crying. Katherine thought her

heart would leap from her breast with joy when she realized
that Singing Bird was *saying*, "Katherine! Oh, Katherine!"
again and again.

The house was ablaze with lamplight and candlelight when
a rain-soaked Katherine, Martin, Jules, and Singing Bird arrived. As they drew inside the gates, even the horses Patchette
and Helio seemed to know they had completed a rescue mission.

Papa Frank, Zell, and Madame ran down the steps and into
the yard, where they helped Katherine from the buggy, hugging
and kissing her as they cried. Zell had braved the night in her
buggy to alert Papa Frank and Madame, and they'd gone to
Katherine and Martin's house to impatiently wait for news.

"This is one of God's miracles," Papa Frank announced now,
patting Sing's shoulder. Zell and Madame hugged Sing tightly,
then turned again to Katherine.

"What on earth happened, Katie?" Papa Frank demanded.

"Ma chère," Madame added, "you cannot know how thrilled
we are they found you. You don't have to tell me that this was
the doing of that witch, Celié."

Furious and sick at the very mention of that name, Katherine
said only, "I want to see my baby. I'm going to her. Martin,
sweetheart, please tell them what happened as best you can."

She had started up the steps when Martin caught up with
her. "I think you should get out of those wet clothes first,
Kate. We all should."

He told the others he would talk to them as soon as he
could.

Katherine turned to Sing. "Please come and undress and
get into bed. You're just getting over a cold." Obediently, Singing Bird followed them.

Going into their bedroom and to the baby's crib, Katherine
looked at the sleeping Delpha Annalise for a very long time.
"I won't wake her," she said. "But oh, Martin, when I think

how close I came to never seeing you or Delpha Annalise or anyone else again . . ."

The tears came for the first time since they'd found her tonight—tears of release coupled with raw anger at the terror she had known.

Martin felt a mixture of joy at finding Kate and anger at how close he'd come to losing her. What could he have done differently? he kept asking himself. It was hard to believe that the nightmare that Celié had set in motion had finally ended.

"Sweetheart, I want you to take off those wet clothes now. I'll draw your bath. Then I'll fix you a cup of our special nectar and heat crayfish bisque for your supper. Just taste it if you don't want to eat. How do you feel, Kate?"

"This moment I'm happy," Katherine said, hugging him. "I'm almost afraid to be happy again, but I swear I'm not going to let that happen. Martin, do you know how much I love you? Do you really know? Because you may very well have a too-passionate woman on your hands for the rest of your life."

"I'll settle for that," he told her, "if you'll stand for my wanting to be too close to you, watch you too much, kiss you too often. . . . We've got to get those wet clothes off you."

Delpha whimpered a bit in her sleep and Katherine wished that she would wake up, but the baby put her chubby fist near her mouth, cooed, and slept on.

After Martin had helped her bathe in lemon balm and lavender oil, he brought valerian tea to the tub to help soothe her nerves. Helping her out of the water, he wrapped a large white towel around her and held her close. She didn't want to think about it, but the gurgling water going down the drain brought it all back in microcosm and suddenly she clung to him, wordless, shaking with remembered terror.

Martin knew from his own anguish that it would take a long time for Katherine to get over what had happened. He wasn't sure *he* ever would. Sitting on the bed beside her, he bent and kissed her gently on the lips. She didn't waken, but stirred and seemed far calmer.

He checked again on Delpha, then went to bed, tossing for a long while before he finally drifted off to dream of the mountains of Santo Domingo, Annalise, Raoul, and for the first time in years, his father.

Their nightmare had ended. The long ordeal was over. Katherine shuddered in her sleep and cried out, and when he drew her to him and held her close, she clung to him without awakening, as if she were certain that she was in arms she trusted, in a place where she loved and was loved.

Epilogue

"Come and walk with me in the moonlight?" Martin asked Katherine early on Christmas night of that same year. "Delpha Annalise is fast asleep. Lord, it's been a blessed year. I know you're tired from all the company we had for dinner, but I still wish you'd come out with me. . . ."

"You know I will, sweetheart," she answered quietly. "I look for times to be alone with you. We had more than enough help to handle the dinner. Martin, I'm not sure I've ever enjoyed a Christmas more than this one. And I'm a woman who loves Christmas."

Martin helped her with her cloak, then donned his own.

Walking along the wide wagon pathway in the cool December air, which was warmer than usual for that time of year, a full moon hung over them. She wondered if that was why he wanted to go walking, but she didn't ask him.

To their right stood the large greenhouse that housed the vast array of herbs she grew and packaged, and from which she extracted lavender and other oils.

"Are we going all the way to the pond and magnolia forest?"

"Are you too tired? It's a long walk."

"No. The fresh air rejuvenates me. It makes me feel like dancing."

Martin held out his hand to her and bowed. "Señora Wife, may I have the pleasure of this dance?"

"Oh, Martin, you are . . ."

She stopped abruptly, realizing she had started to say *mad*, and since Celié's horrific attack, Katherine could not bear to use that word.

Perhaps he knew what she would have said, but if so, he didn't acknowledge it. Instead, he proclaimed, "What I am is wonderful. Admit it, *querida mia*. We both know it's true." Then sobering, he said, "I feel at peace for the first time since Celié's accident. I felt so *guilty*." He would never be able to forget that he had once loved Celié.

"And it was all a lie," Katherine said, "a terrible lie. Martin, I'm sorry."

"Kate, I wanted us out here under this full moon. There was a full moon our first night on the ship. Do you remember?"

"I could never forget any part of that night. And I forgave you long ago—and now I even forgive DeBeau."

"Thank you. This moon is like you, you know, bringing a soft, dazzling light into every corner of my life."

They danced then in the meadow beside the wagon path. He held her close to him, and each felt the other's steady heartbeat. He hummed the Santo Domingan love song he often played for her on the fiddle. On his birthday that past July, she had given him a fine new fiddle handcrafted in Italy of exquisite material. His eyes had been moist as he had thanked her and held her tightly.

It seemed to her that they danced for a long while before Martin stopped singing, kissed her, and they continued their walk, holding hands.

"We're growing very wealthy now in the world's material goods," he said suddenly. "I'd like us to spend a large share of that money helping others to prosper," he continued. "We're living in a time of plenty that will end, Kate, just as it ended on my island. We may well have hard times ahead in the near future, but as long as we have each other . . ."

He stopped and turned to her, tipping her chin, breathing in the fragrances of the night woods and the blended lavender oil and lemon balm freshness of her hair and skin.

"Kate, we've been good *for* each other, and *to* each other. I've thought a lot about my mother and my brother, and yes, my father. I'm at peace now about them all, and I think *they're* at peace. The black pearl that my mother loved so much was a symbol to her, I believe.

"I think now that *she* was a very vulnerable oyster, and that a large grain of sand that was my father and us and her life on that island all got in with her in her shell. The nacre that was her spirit and her courage pearled her and us over and over until we all became what I hope is a valuable addition to this world."

"That's beautiful, Martin," she told him.

"With you," he continued, "your mother's and your grandmother's death and missing them were *your* grain of sand. God knows, you've become a pearl a king could not find in any marketplace. A Black Pearl."

She could not see it but his eyes narrowed, filled with a vision. He had thought it from the first moment he saw her, and he said it softly now, as he had said it many times before: "I am black *and* beautiful."

They walked hand in hand for a long time, both in silence and in conversation. The moon seemed to follow them, in blessing. They were all so happy. Papa Frank and Miss Lillian, who had married and moved into her house, along with Monique and Pierre. Zell and Jules, who were growing wealthy along with their friends. Paul DeBeau and the now-married Guy. Natalie Montrose, the governor, and their only child, Athena. These people were an inextricable part of her and Martin's life now. Katherine smiled as she thought about the more than sixty babies she had delivered since she'd been here and the very few she had lost, grieving them deeply as was her nature.

Singing Bird *talked* now, although it had taken her a long time to say more than a few words. She still wrote when she was tired or bothered, and she and Delpha Annalise were devoted to each other. She continued to work with The Little Sisters, who loved her as dearly as she loved them. Louis worshipped her, and she admitted she was very fond of him but wanted to wait to marry. Though miserable, Louis humbly agreed. Just now, he was learning Spanish.

And what of Celié? For weeks Katherine and Martin talked of her with pain and horror, facing and trying to deal with the torment she had brought into their lives. Two days after that fateful night, her body in the black silk robe and the pale green silk nightgown was found washed ashore a distance down the Mississippi River. Talk now was that Congo Square, where Celié had surreptitiously gone to perfect the magic that would bring her Martin's love, was to be renamed Beauregard Square. To Katherine, it certainly seemed less threatening that way.

After so long a time, they reached the clear pond, patinated in the moonlight, and gazed at their reflections in the water. This time the peacocks were roosting, silent, but there was no absence of beauty or sound. The swans nested. An owl hooted, and some forlorn nightbird sang a mellow, fleeting song.

When Martin and Katherine had come here that glorious late Sunday afternoon in September, he had played the fiddle for her. This time there was no fiddle, but she had found that there was music wherever they were. In their love. In their passion for life. For those they loved. And for each other.

Bushes of red poinsettias massed now by the magnolia forest, as they also massed in their backyard. Walking over to a bush, Martin plucked just one blossom and brought it back, handing it to her.

Did that full moon cheer them on? And did it remember how it had thrown moonbeams onto her as she'd lain on the pallet that hot summer night . . . that night when she first *saw* him, having glimpsed him once and dreamt of him for so long?

"Merry Christmas, Kate," he told her. He brought her hands to his lips and kissed first one, then the other, turning them over so that his warm breath and his kisses caressed her palms like some wondrous magic potion.

"Merry Christmas, *corazon dulce,*" she replied.

"This is only the beginning, love. I want us to go to the mountaintop of joy and run through the woods there. . . ."

"Naked?" she murmured.

"And here," he said, laughing, "I had wondered how come I love you so."

The laughter caught in her throat when he looked at her. He was warmly reliving, under that star-spangled, midnight-blue sky, the first time he had glimpsed her in the bayou country, then the first time he had held her. Softly, he sang the bayou country wedding song to her.

> *"Ma chére,* on this your wedding day,
>   I wish you love!
> *Mon cher,* on this your wedding day,
>   I wish you joy!
> For him, the first nine months,
>   a dimpled baby girl!
> For her, the second year,
>   a bouncing baby boy!"

"We're running late, according to that song," he teased. "We've got Delpha Annalise, who is for me *my* 'dimpled baby girl.' Sweetheart, we need to begin working on *your* 'bouncing baby boy,' don't you think? Why don't we just pretend that this was another wedding day for us?" He paused for a second and went on, "And don't *honeymoons* always follow wedding days?"

Katherine began to laugh with joy that pealed through the Christmas night, and before she could answer, he drew her close and began to kiss her.

Dear Reader:

I certainly hope you enjoyed reading Katherine and Martin's story. These people and those Reconstruction times were fascinating, especially since we now know what a meaningful role African-Americans played in it. New Orleans has always been one of America's most fun-filled, special cities.

Nothing would please me more than getting your comments regarding *The Black Pearl*. Praise *and* criticism are helpful in any endeavor.

I will write a brief newsletter from time to time with tidbits from the romance field and the writing I will be doing. I'll be happy to mail you a copy if you'll send me a business size, self-addressed, stamped envelope when you write. My address is as follows:

> Francine Craft
> c/o C. Kanno
> 2217 Mohegan Drive
> Falls Church, VA 22043

Author's Note to Readers

If you are interested in and plan to use herbs, please consider consulting a reputable herbalist. Herbs are medicine, and strong medicine at that. They're wonderful, but they must be handled with care.

For story reasons, I have slightly altered the time sequence of Louisiana State Legislature meetings during the Reconstruction years.

About the Author

A Mississippi native, Francine Craft has lived in both New Orleans and Washington, D.C. Francine has pursued a lifelong interest in writing, including magazine and newspaper articles and song lyrics. She also composes music and is keenly interested in photography. A retired government legal secretary, Francine has been an elementary school teacher, a business school instructor, a labor union secretary, and a research assistant for a large nonprofit organization.